Praise for
A Boy and His Dog at the End of the World

"Fletcher's suspenseful, atmospheric tale imagines a near future in which our world is in ruins.... An adventure saga punctured by a gut-punch twist."

—*Entertainment Weekly*

"Heart- and gut-wrenching.... *A Boy and His Dog at the End of the World* takes a memorable journey of loyalty and love and transforms it into an unraveling mystery of self-discovery and exploration.... This is the story of trust and loyalty within a family, and finding your own pack—even if they're different from the pack you were born into." —*BookPage*

"The title kind of says it all, doesn't it? We live in anxious times, and apocalyptic visions are a dime a dozen. C. A. Fletcher's stands apart for its singular focus on the title characters: a young boy journeying a blasted landscape with his canine friend, in desperate pursuit of the man who stole away with his other pup. You just don't separate a boy from his dog, apocalypse be damned." —*B&N Sci-Fi & Fantasy Blog*

"An excellent adventure and coming-of-age tale."

—*Los Angeles Beat*

"Has a propulsive and engaging rhythm and should please fans of postapocalyptic dystopias, young adult and adult alike."

—*Booklist*

A Boy and His Dog at the End of the World

C. A. FLETCHER

www.orbitbooks.net

This book is a work of fiction. Names, characters, places, and incidents are the product of the author's imagination or are used fictitiously. Any resemblance to actual events, locales, or persons, living or dead, is coincidental.

Cover design by Lauren Panepinto
Cover photos by Getty Images & Shutterstock

Author photograph by Nazia Khatun

Orbit
Hachette Book Group
1290 Avenue of the Americas
New York, NY 10104
orbitbooks.net

First Paperback Edition: January 2020
Originally published in hardcover and ebook by Orbit in April 2019

Orbit is an imprint of Hachette Book Group.
The Orbit name and logo are trademarks of Little, Brown Book Group Limited.

Library of Congress Control Number: 2018962798

ISBNs: 978-0-316-44943-4 (trade paperback), 978-0-316-44947-2 (ebook)

LSC-C

10 9 8 7 6 5 4 3 2 1

For the midnight swimmers—and all past
and present members of the Two O'clock Tea Club.

Especially Jack, Ari, Molly and Hannah.

May your beaches always have fires, dogs and
laughter on them, whatever the weather.

A note on spoilers

It'd be a kindness to other readers—not to say this author—if the discoveries made as you follow Griz's journey into the ruins of our world remained a bit of a secret between us...

C.A.F.

A Boy and His Dog at the End of the World

A man stole my dog.
I went after him.
Bad things happened.
I can never go home.

Chapter 1

The end

Dogs were with us from the very beginning.

When we were hunters and gatherers and walked out of Africa and began to spread across the world, they came with us. They guarded our fires as we slept and they helped us bring down prey in the long dawn when we chased our meals instead of growing them. And later, when we did become farmers, they guarded our fields and watched over our herds. They looked after us, and we looked after them. Later still, they shared our homes and our families when we built towns and cities and suburbs. Of all the animals that travelled the long road through the ages with us, dogs always walked closest.

And those that remain are still with us now, here at the end of the world. And there may be no law left except what you make it, but if you steal my dog, you can at least expect me to come after you. If we're not loyal to the things we love, what's the point? That's like not having a memory. That's when we stop being human.

That's a kind of death, even if you keep breathing.

*

So. About that. Turns out the world didn't end with a bang. Or much of a whimper. Don't get me wrong: there were bangs, some big, some little, but that was early on, before people got the drift of what was happening.

But bangs are not really how it ended. They were symptoms, not cause.

How it ended was the Gelding, though what caused that never got sorted out, or if it did it was when it was too late to do anything about it. There were as many theories as there were suddenly childless people—a burst of cosmic rays, a chemical weapon gone astray, bio-terror, pollution (you lot did make a mess of your world), some kind of genetic mutation passed by a space virus or even angry gods in pick-your-own-flavour for those who had a religion. The "how" and the "why" slowly became less important as people got used to the "what", and realised the big final "when" was heading towards them like a storm front that not even the fastest, the richest, the cleverest or the most powerful were going to be able to outrun.

The world—the human part of it—had been gelded or maybe turned barren—perhaps both—and people just stopped having kids. That's all it took. The Lastborn generation—the Baby Bust as they called themselves, proving that irony was one of the last things to perish—they just carried on getting older and older until they died like people always had done.

And when they were all gone, that was it. No bang, no whimper even. More of a tired sigh.

It was a soft apocalypse. And though it probably felt pretty hard for those it happened to, it did happen. And now we few—we vanishingly few—are all alone, stuck here on the other side of it.

*

How can I tell you this and not be dead? I'm one of the exceptions that proves the rule. They estimated maybe 0.0001 per cent of the world population somehow escaped the Gelding. They were known as outliers. That means if there were 7,000,000,000 people before the Gelding, less than 7000 of them could have kids. One in a million. Give or take, though since it takes two to make a baby, more like one in two million.

You want to know how much of an outlier I am? You, in the old picture I have of you, are wearing a shirt with the name of an even older football club on it. You look really happy. In my whole life, I haven't met enough people to make up two teams for a game of football. The world is that empty.

Maybe if this were a proper story it would start calm and lead up to a cataclysm, and then maybe a hero or a bunch of heroes would deal with it. I've read plenty of stories like that. I like them. Especially the ones where a big group of people get together, since the idea of a big group of people is an interesting thing for me all by itself, because though I've seen a lot, I've never seen that.

But this isn't that kind of story. It's not made up. This is just me writing down the real, telling what I know, saying what actually took place. And everything that I know, even my being born, happened long, long after that apocalypse had already softly wheezed its way out.

I should start with who I am. I'm Griz. Not my real name. I have a fancier one, but it's the one I've been called for ever. They said I used to whine and grizzle when I was a baby. So I became the Little Grizzler and then as I got taller my name got shorter, and now I'm just Griz. I don't whine any more. Dad says I'm stoical, and he says it like that's a good thing. Stoical means doesn't complain much. He says I seemed to get all my complaining out of the way before I could talk and now, though I do ask too many questions, mostly I just get on with things. Says that like it's good too. Which it is. Complaining doesn't get anything done.

And we always have plenty to do, here at the end of the world.

Here is home, and home is an island, and we are my family. My parents, my brother and sister, Ferg and Bar. And the dogs of course. My two are Jip and Jess. Jip's a long-legged terrier, brown and black, with a rough coat and eyes that miss nothing. Jess is as tall as he is but smooth-coated, narrower in the shoulders and she has a splash of white on her chest. Mongrels they are, brother and sister, same but different. Jess is a rarity, because dog litters seem to be all male nowadays. Maybe that's to do with the Gelding too. Perhaps whatever hit us, hit them too, but in a lesser way. Very few bitches are born now. Maybe that's a downside for the dogs, punishment for their loyalty, some cosmically unfair collateral damage for walking alongside us all those centuries.

We're the only people on the island, which is fine, because it's a small island and it fits the five of us, though sometimes I think it fit us better and was less claustrophobic when there were six. It's called Mingulay. That's what its name was when you were alive. It's off the Atlantic coast of what used to be Scotland. There's nothing to the west of it but ocean and then America and we're pretty sure that's gone.

To the north there's Pabbay and Sandray, low islands where we graze our sheep and pasture the horses. North of them is the larger island called Barra but we don't land there, which is a shame as it has lots of large houses and things, but we never set foot on it because something happened and it's bad land. It's a strangeness to sail past a place so big that it even has a small castle in the middle of its harbour for your whole life, and yet never walk on it. Like an itch you can't quite reach round and scratch. But Dad says if you set foot on Barra now you get something much worse than an itch, and because it's what killed his parents, we don't go. It's an unlucky island and the only things living there these days are rabbits. Even birds don't seem to like it, not even the gulls who we never see landing above the wet sand below the tideline.

North-east of us are a long low string of islands called the Uists, and Eriskay, which are luckier places, and we go there a lot, and though there are no people on them now, there's plenty of wildlife and lazy-beds for wild potatoes. Once a year we go and camp on them for a week or so while we gather the barley and the oats from the old fields on the sea lawn. And then sometimes we go there to do some viking. "Going a-viking" is what Dad calls it when we sail more than a day and sleep over on a trip, going pillaging like the really ancient seafarers in the books, with the longships and the heroic deeds. We're no heroes though; we're just scavenging to survive, looking for useful things from the old world, spares or materials we can strip out from the derelict houses. And books of course. Books turn out to be pretty durable if they're kept away from damp and rats. They can last hundreds of years, easy. Reading is another way we survive. It helps to know where we came from, how we got here. And most of all, for me, even though these low and empty islands are all I have ever known, when I open the front cover of a new book, it's like a door, and I can travel far away in place and time.

Even the wide sea and the open sky can be claustrophobic if you never get away from them.

So that's who I am, which just leaves you. In some way you know who you are, or at least, you knew who you were.

Because you're dead of course, like almost every single human who ever walked the planet, and long dead too.

And why am I talking to a dead person? We'll get back to that. But first we should get on with the story. I've read enough to know that I should do the explaining as we go.

Chapter 2

The traveller

If he hadn't had red sails, I think we'd have trusted him less.

The boat was visible from a long way off, much further than white sails would have been against the pale haze to the north-west. Those red sails were a jolt of colour that caught the eye and grabbed your attention like a sudden shout breaks a long silence. They weren't the sails of someone trying to sneak up on you. They had the honest brightness of a poppy. Maybe that was why we trusted him. That and his smile, and his stories.

Never trust someone who tells good stories, not until you know why they're doing it.

I was high up on Sandray when I saw the sails. I was tired and more than a little angry. I'd spent the morning rescuing an anchor that had parted from Ferg's boat the previous week, hard work that I felt he should have done for himself, though he claimed his ears wouldn't let him dive as deep as I could, and that anchors didn't grow on trees. Having done that, I was now busy trying to rescue a ram that had fallen and wedged itself in a narrow crack in the rocks above the grazing. It wasn't badly injured but it was stubborn and ungrateful in the way of most sheep, and it wasn't letting me get a rope round it. It had butted me twice, the first time catching me under the chin sharply enough that I had chipped a tooth halfway back on the lower right-hand side. I had sworn at it and then tried again. My knuckles were badly grazed from where it had then butted my hand against the scrape of the stone, and I was standing back licking my fist and swearing at it in earnest when I saw the boat.

The suddenness of the colour stopped me in my tracks.

I was too shocked to link the taste of blood in my mouth with the redness of the sails, but then I have little of that kind of foresight, none at all really compared with my other sister Joy, who always seemed to know when people were about to return home just before they did, or be able to smell an incoming storm on a bright day. I don't much believe in that kind of thing now, though I did when I was smaller and thought less, when I ran free with her across the island, happy and without a care beyond when it would be supper time. In those days I took her seeming foresight as something as everyday and real as cold water from the spring behind the house. Later, as I grew and began to think more, I decided it was mostly just luck, and since she disappeared for ever over the black cliff at the top of the island, not reliable luck at all.

If she'd really had foresight, she would never have tried to rescue her kite and fallen out of life in that one sharp and lonely moment. If she'd had foresight, she'd have waited until we returned to the island to help her. I saw the kite where it was pinned in a cleft afterwards, and know we could have reached it with the long hoe and no harm need have come to anyone. As it was, she must have tried to reach it by herself and slipped into the gulf of air more than seven hundred feet above the place where waves that have had two thousand sea miles to build up momentum slam into the first immoveable object they've ever met: the dark cliff wall that guards the back of our home. She wouldn't have waited for us to help though. She was always impatient, a tough little thing always in a hurry to catch up with Ferg and Bar and do what they did even though she was much younger. Bar later said it was almost like she was in such a hurry because she sensed she had had less time ahead of her than the rest of us.

We never found her body. And with her gone, so was my childhood, though I was eight at the time and she only a year more. Two birthdays later, by then a year older than she would ever be, I was in my mind what I now am: fully grown. Although even now, many years after that, Bar and Ferg still call me a kid. But they are six and seven years older than us. So Joy and I were always the babies. Our mother called us that to distinguish us from the other two.

Though after Joy fell, Mum never called any of us anything ever again. Never spoke at all. We found her halfway down the hill from the cliff edge, and we nearly lost her too. Far as we could make out she must have been careering down the slope, running helter-skelter, maybe mad with grief, maybe sprinting for the dory with some desperate doomed hope that she could get it launched and all the way round the island against the tide to rescue a child who in truth could not have survived such a fall. She never spoke because she all but dashed her brains out when she stumbled forward, smacking her head into a rock as she fell, temple gashed and watery blood coming from her ears.

That was the worst day ever, though the ones that followed were barely lighter. She didn't die but she wasn't there any more, her brain too wounded or too scarred for her to get out of herself again. In the Before she'd have been taken to a hospital and they would have operated on her brain to relieve the pressure, Dad said. But this is the After, so he decided to do it himself with a hand drill: he would have done it too, if he had been able to find the drill, but it wasn't where it should have been, and then the bleeding stopped and she just slept for a long, long time and no more fluid leaked out of her ears, so maybe it was best that he didn't try and drill a hole into her skull to save her.

I hope so, because I know Ferg hid the drill. He saw me see him, but we've never, ever spoken of it. If we did, I'd tell him I admire him for doing it, because Dad would have killed Mum and then would have had to live with the horror of that on top of everything else. And, even though she's locked away inside her head, you can sit and hold her hand and sometimes she squeezes it and almost smiles, and it's a comforting thing, the tiny ghost bit of her that remains, the warmth of her hand, the skin on skin. Dad said that day was the darkest thing that ever happened to us, and that we're past it, and that now we have to get on and live, just like in a bigger way the worst thing happened to the world and it just goes on.

He holds her hand sometimes, in the dark by the fire, when he thinks none of us notice him doing it. He does it privately because he thinks we would see it as a sign of weakness, a grown man needing that moment of warmth. Maybe it is. Or maybe the weakness is hiding the need, which is something Bar said to Ferg one evening when she was upset and no one knew I was listening.

I'd had enough time to leave the ram, whistle in my dogs from their rabbit hunting and sail the narrow sea mile back home to warn the others long before the traveller came ashore. I could have taken my time, because sharp-eyed Bar had seen the red sails too and they were ready and waiting, which meant that she and Dad were at the shoreline and Ferg was nowhere to be seen. Bar was not sure it was necessary for him to be hiding and watching over us with the long gun because she thought the boat under the red sails looked like the boat the Lewismen used, and that maybe they had just found new sails. The Lewismen were a six-person family who lived five islands north, the closest people we knew, and we knew them well. Bar wore her hair in a long plait that now reached down her back and she would, in time, pair up with one of the boys. This was what she had decided, though being Bar and thus contrary in all things, said she did not see why she should be in any hurry making a choice as to which of the four it was to be. It was not as if they were going anywhere, or as if there were four other girls they might pair up with instead. They were a practical family, and we sometimes joined together to do things that needed more than four pairs of hands, but we never took up their suggestion that we move to be closer to them, and they never thought of moving south. Or if they did think of it, they did not think well of the idea. But they were our neighbours and the only other people within a hundred miles. They were just the Lewismen to us, though they had a family name which was Little. And when the red sails got closer we all saw Bar had been wrong, that it was a different boat beneath them altogether. It was bigger and the man at the tiller had hair that streamed behind him like a banner in the wind. All the Lewismen cropped their hair close to the skull for cleanliness, even Mary the mother did so, though she was in fact more mannish than woman, for all that she'd borne four boys.

The long-haired traveller proved to be the only person on the boat, though at first sight it seemed too big for one person alone to sail. He neatly drew into the shallower water in the lee of the small headland that topped our beach, showing a good eye for a sound anchorage, and hailed us as he dropped anchor. His voice was hoarse but strong, and he said he was alone and wished to come ashore if we would have him. He had things to trade and indeed had been told of our whereabouts by the Lewismen, who he had left two days before. He bore a letter from them, which he waved in the air, the paper white against the darkening sea behind him.

Dad beckoned him in, and he dropped a small dinghy over the side and rowed in to the beach. I helped him ashore, and we pulled the boat above the tideline together.

I felt Dad's hand like a warning on my shoulder, as if I'd been too enthusiastic and unguarded, but then he ruffled the short hairs on the back of my head which he only does when he's feeling kind.

I'm Abraham, said Dad, nodding at the stranger. Call me Abe. And this is my boy, Griz.

Hello, Griz, he said with an answering grin that I liked the moment it split his thick red beard in a flash of white.

And then the dogs barrelled down to surround him before I could ask his name. They barked and snarled and arrived in a great tangle of teeth and tails and then, as he knelt to greet them, the tails started thumping and the snarling turned to whines as each dog seemed to want to be patted and petted by this stranger from the sea. He had the way of dogs, and he told us he had lost his own one only weeks ago, over the side in a storm around the North Cape and he missed him like an arm. She was a half Husky crossbreed called Saga, clever like a man he said, white, black and brown with a brown eye to match her ears and a blue one to match the sky. He'd had her safely kept below in the small cabin, but when he fell and hurt himself as the boat slammed into the trough of an unusually big wave, Saga heard him cry out in pain and—being a clever dog—pawed the latch and came to help him. The next wave took her over the side and he never saw her again, not even a head bobbing on the face of the mountainous seas piling up behind the stern as the wind blew him beyond any chance of finding her. He showed us the scar on his head, and we could see in the gentle way he ruffled the fur of our dogs as he spoke that the hurt was deeper than the healed skin.

Like I said, it was a good story. And—as I found out later—some of it was even true. The dog with one brown eye and one blue being clever as a man, that was true as death itself.

Looking at a new person is not something you would have found as interesting as we do, I expect. You lived in a world full of new people all the time. If you lived in a city, they must have flowed round you like a great mackerel shoal and you'd be just one of thousands or millions, still yourself alone in your own head no doubt, but part of something much bigger too. Here, every fresh face is an event, almost a shock, every new person rare enough to seem like an entirely new species. The traveller looked like no one I had ever met. His long hair, for a start, was thick and wavy and the colour of flames. A redhead. Something I'd read about and seen in faded pictures but never met in real life. The hair was a startling colour, as alien and abrupt as the explosions of orange flowers we found on the other islands, always close to old gardens, flowers my mother called crocoz, when she still spoke. She knew all the flowers and plants. Bar told me she said crocoz weren't native to the islands, but were tough survivors, like us. And he was not just a redhead, but a redbeard too, a slab of a thing that jutted as far down in front of his face as his hair hung behind it. His skin was pale but weather-beaten and his eyes, which peered out at the world from beneath the high cliff of his forehead, were dangerous blue. I don't know why I thought the blue was dangerous, but that was the word that jumped into my head as I saw them. Maybe it was because they turned on me in the same instant and just for a moment, as he caught me looking at him, I saw them without the smile that followed, and I do know I thought it then and that this is not something I added later, after things happened: I definitely thought dangerous blue, but then I thought better and discounted it.

Maybe you, swimming in a world full of difference and choice, were better tuned to believing your gut when it came to people. I had—still have—little to compare people with. So I dismissed the dangerous blue in his eyes when he smiled at me an instant later, and decided it was just different, the blueness, only having seen brown or green eyes before. And when he smiled it was hard to think of those eyes as cold, but maybe that was part of why he was hard to keep a hold of in the mind, juggling the two things at once, the fire in his hair and the shiver of ice in his eyes. The face that was hard as a hammer when it was not smiling and the smile that seemed to warm the world when it found you.

You look like a Viking, were the first words I said to him. And he did. I had seen him, or faces like him, in history books and old pictures, men in horned hats carrying axes and plunder.

And the second words he said to me, this man who had sailed out of the north, were:

What's a Viking?

Which shows that even a question can be a lie if asked in the right way.

Chapter 3

Who are you?

It was one summer while we were a-viking ourselves that I found you. When Ferg began to tease me for wanting to write things down because who in the whole empty world was going to read it, Dad said that it was a natural result of reading so much. He said if you read a lot you start to think like a writer, the same way as if you grow up with a fiddle player in the house you start whistling and learning the tunes without thinking, like Ferg had. I read a lot. I'll get to that. Dad plays the fiddle. I told him Ferg maybe had a bit of a point, since I didn't know who I would be writing for as everyone I knew already knew my story because they're a part of it. But I wanted to maybe keep a diary sort of thing, and so he said then just write like you talk, don't be fancy, and I said but when you talk you do talk to someone, at least most of the time, and he said then just use your imagination: he said imagine a someone and keep them in mind as you write and I thought of you, the boy with my face.

So. You.

You're in a photograph I found in a house up in North Uist one summer. This time we were looking for parts to scavenge for the windmill that gives us electricity, and Dad knew there were windmills of the same type up near where North Uist is joined to Berneray by the old causeway. We'd sailed the lugger up there and he and Ferg were gutting the turbine off an old fallen mill while I went on the scrounge through the big house on the skyline. We'd decided to camp in the house overnight. It was somewhere we had visited before, solid, stone-built with a roof that still held out most of the weather. Better than that, it had a lot of full bookshelves in it, and a thing called a snooker table.

It was one of the old buildings, a large farmhouse that had been added to over the years, so it sprawled expansively when compared with the other island houses. The walls had once been whitewashed but now little of that remained, so it was a grey house with a dark slate roof and intact glass windows that seemed to watch me approach up the old drive. A car had rotted to the axles and stood amid the long grass by the back door as if waiting to pounce. The door was not as easy to open as it had been when we visited three years before, but I was bigger now and managed to kick it open carefully enough that it would sort of close after us when we left. I left it open as I waited for the dogs to scramble ahead of me and put any waiting rats to flight.

Jip and Jess tore into the house, feet scrabbling on cracked plastic flooring as they went, whining and barking as they always did when excited, but there was no sound of rat murder close or distant, and they soon stopped their noise and trotted back to meet me, looking disappointed and a little bit hurt as is their way, as if I had promised them fun which had not quite materialised.

Something had changed in the house since we had last been there. I couldn't say what it was, and I couldn't see or smell anything that put me on edge, but there was a difference. Before, it had been like many of the houses we went into, damp and mouldering, full of things you could see as poignant or pointless according to your way of viewing the world. Dad, for example, would turn photographs of people to the wall as he passed through derelict houses. I don't know why he did that. He said it was to give the spirits rest, but then he doesn't really believe in spirits, or he says he doesn't. Bar, my sister, has the habit too, and she says it's to stop all the dead eyes watching us.

I don't think she believes that.

I think it's just to try and scare me, because she does like jokes and teasing when she's in a good mood. Apart from the books, it's little collections of things that people used to put on shelves that fascinate me in the empty houses. It's not just the photographs, a lot of which are faded so badly they just look like water-damaged paper now, unless the rooms are dark, but the little china people and the mugs and jugs and bits of glass and wood and stuff. Ornaments. Trophies. Mementoes. Things that meant something to people once, meant enough that they'd make a space for them and display them, something to see every day. We don't really have ornaments, or the time for mementoes. Everything we do is about surviving, moving forward, keeping going. No time for relics or souvenirs, Dad says when we go a-viking, only take the useful stuff. Maybe that's why I decided to write this. A souvenir I can carry in a pocket. Anyway.

The picture of you.

The picture of you was definitely a memento. You meant something to someone, even if it was just yourself. I found you under the snooker table. And the way I found you was strange and secret, and because a photo is a small thing, I took you and no one knew and now you live between the pages of the notebook I write all this in, and until someone reads this, I suppose you're still a secret.

I'd been in the snooker room before, the last time we were in the house. The room was almost filled by the table, which was covered by a dustsheet that had begun to deteriorate into rags at the corners, where maybe a hundred years of just carrying its own weight had worn holes. We'd taken the cover off and rolled the bright balls around the pale green playing surface, trying to bounce them into the pockets. Once there had been poles to hit the balls with, but now the racks that had held them were empty. I had liked the smooth motion of the balls and the healthy smack and clack as they bounced off each other. Not much runs so true in our day-to-day world, patched together as things are. There was a big wall of books to the left side, and a shuttered window at right angles to it. I'd already been through them, but now I was older I went back to see if the grown me would find books I might not have liked the look of last time.

The shutters were stuck shut, and though I could have wrenched them ajar I didn't. Light not getting into the room was helping keep the books safe, and I knew I'd break the shutters opening them which would make closing them harder. Hinges rust, and where they don't screws do, rotting out of old wood that no longer holds them. So I got out my fire steel and lit my oil lantern and used that instead. Then I dropped the fire steel and it rolled under the skirts of the snooker table.

We hadn't found you the other times we were in the house because of the boxes. Someone had stacked boxes of cork tiles under the table, filling the space. They were the same cork tiles peeling off the floor in the kitchen down the hall. What we'd missed was the fact that the boxes were arranged around the edge of the table, and that the centre of the space beneath was empty, like a square cavern, a room hidden within a room. My fire steel had rolled into the narrow crack between two boxes, and I only discovered the secret when I moved one to get at it.

Fish oil lanterns throw more smell than light, but even by the soft glow mine gave off I could see someone had once used the space as a concealed den. It was the reflection of my flame in the glass jars on the opposite side that caught my eye, jars with candle stubs in them. Old candles burn better than the ones Bar makes, so my first thought was to scavenge the stubs, and see if there were any unburned ones left too. So I crawled in, and that's how I found the chamber of secrets.

Someone had slept here, what must have been long, long ago. There was an unrolled sleeping bag and blankets and pillows, and there were books and tins and medicine packs lining the inner wall made by the boxes. A string of tiny little lights was taped all round the edge underneath the table-

top, the kind of things you used to put on Christmas trees in old pictures I've seen. But of course they weren't lit and never would be again. It made me think what the hidden space must have looked like when they had been—cosy, cheerful, maybe a bit magical even. On the bottom of the table, which was slate, someone had glued a few of the cork tiles to make a decorated roof to the den, a roof and a pinboard. The board was covered in photographs and drawings.

Maybe it was because of the string of lights that would never be lit again, but I found I wanted to see what the space looked like when it was illuminated by more than my smoky fish oil lamp, which is why I lit some of the candle stubs, and why I lay back on the crinkly sleeping bag. I felt the synthetic filling crumble to dust under my weight, and that's when I saw you. You were the picture right above the pillows. You must have been the last thing whoever slept here saw before they put out the lights, and you would have been the first thing they saw when they woke in the morning. Or maybe that sleeper was you. Maybe this was your den. Either way, you were important to someone. Loved. Mourned maybe. Or celebrated. Or both.

In the picture, you're doing a star jump on the beach, and next to you is a girl who must be your sister. It's a bright sunny day. You look very alike. She's smaller. The picture has caught you both at the top of your jumps, frozen for ever between sand and sky, your arms and legs wide, laughing, eyes flashing with glee. You're looking right into the lens. She's looking at you with a wild and happy look that's so fierce it hurts me to see it. And beside you on the other side is a short-legged terrier also jumping and looking at your face, mouth wide in a smile or a bark. And just as I sometimes think you look a lot like me, the girl looks familiar too. If I squint and imagine, then she looks like Joy might have been. Maybe that's why I took the picture. Because of course I have no picture of my once bigger—but now forever little—sister. Maybe I thought it would help me remember when I get older and more memories jostle in and fill the space that used to be just the two of us. Or maybe the slight likeness is just the reason why I'm writing this to you. All I know for sure is that I've never seen a picture that made me so happy and so sad at the same time. And even without the girl—which is what the picture looks like when it's folded to fit in my notebook, it's you and your dog—like the last happy people at the end of the world, before the afterwards began.

Or maybe I'm writing my life to you because the people I could talk to about things are gone, or can't talk back to me any more. Dad says I think too much. Says I ask too many questions. Says he thinks the lack of answers always makes me unhappy. Don't know if that's true. Do know he hates the asking. As if it takes something away from him, not knowing how to reply. It's just information I'm after, not responsibility for something that is far too big to be down to him anyway. And why does he spend all the time when he's not working or playing the fiddle with his head in a book of facts if he's not looking for answers too?

And that was the other thing I took from the chamber of secrets. The books. Whoever had made the den had a line of books all along one side, and after I'd lain on my back looking at the photographs, I turned sideways and looked at them. I scanned up and down the row of spines several times, and then began picking them out at random, reading the descriptions on the covers. They weren't practical books, the histories or technical things Dad insisted we read so that important knowledge wasn't lost, something I later began to call Leibowitzing: they were fiction, made-up things. It took me a couple of minutes to work out what these ones all had in common, but when I did so it gave me another jolt, a kind of shock that was close to excitement, though I don't know why it should have thrilled me as it did. All the books were about imaginary futures in which your world, the Before, had broken down. They were all stories about my now, the After, written by people with no real knowledge of what it would be like.

I stuffed my rucksack with the book hoard and found another bag in the attic which I filled with the rest. Dad and Ferg tried to make me leave them behind, but they were in a good mood having found two working spare parts from the old windmills, and they also liked the three and a half boxes of old candles that I found under the table. I didn't tell them about the hidden chamber though, and I slid the box back in place after I came out, so if it was your secret place, it's secret still. As far as I know.

That autumn I read all those books, some of them twice (that's when I started calling Dad's obsession with technical manuals and science books "Leibowitzing", after one called *A Canticle for Leibowitz* about monks in a devastated far future trying to reconstruct your whole world from an electrical manual found in the desert). I read the books hoping to find some good ideas, but what I got was nightmares and a kind of sadness that stained my mind for weeks.

I know you can't be nostalgic for something you never actually knew, but it was that kind of longing the books often woke in me. Dad hated me reading them. Thought they were the most pointless things there could ever be, out-of-date prophecies that had turned out wrong anyway. I liked them. Still do. They may not be accurate about life after the end, but if you sort of look sideways with your mind while you read them, you find they say lots about what things were like before. They're like answers to questions you didn't know enough to ask. Though saying something like that to Dad would only make him even angrier. The past's gone. We only have the now he says, and the only answers that are useful are the ones that will help us survive into the future.

Chapter 4

Traveller's tales

The red-sailed stranger told us his name was Brand.

He had a bag with him. It was heavy enough to pull down a shoulder as he walked up the slope past the drying racks that were thick with fish. There was rain in the air, but it had not yet started to fall, and we paused and took the last of the evening sun on the bench outside the main house. He put the bag carefully at his feet as he gratefully accepted a mug of water from the burn.

Good water, he said. Clean and cold.

He looked at the cod and mackerel on the drying racks.

If you've fish to spare, I've something to trade with you, he said.

We have everything we need, said Dad.

You don't have a voltage converter for the windmill, grinned the traveller. But we'll get to that tomorrow maybe. Your friends in Lewis told me you have been having problems.

Dad looked as if the traveller had already got the better of him in a trade he hadn't even said he was interested in. But it was true enough. The windmill was eccentric in its performance, and Dad felt it was the converter and had been grumbling for a year or so about making a voyage to try and find another one.

Hmm, he said. Eat with us tonight. Trade tomorrow. We have time.

There are two questions that Dad, in my limited experience, always asks the few travellers who we meet: is there anyone else? And: are they coming? I never know if the questions are about hope or fear, though the fact we never go looking for ourselves makes me think that it might be the latter.

Before I was born, Mum and Dad did go to the mainland, way down the chain of islands and into the river called the Clyde. They went in one boat and came back in four, each piloting their own craft and towing a smaller one, all loaded with many of the things I have grown up with. My own boat in fact was the one my mum had towed. I always thought she had chosen it from the other ones because of the name, the *Sweethope*. Dad told me later it was because of all the yachts they had cannibalised in the tilted mess of the long abandoned marina it had smelled the least bad when they opened the hatch.

They had made two scavenging trips into the empty city that was once Glasgow, and then never went back. Ferg asked why, once, and Dad just said there was something there that neither could quite explain, but it sapped them and made them very low, so much so that neither could face a third trip, no matter how rich the pickings still were. One of my memories of Mum when she still spoke was her telling me about the huge library she had found there, miles of shelves and doors wide open. They'd slept there for several nights, camped out safely in a fortress of books. She closed the doors to keep the cats and foxes out when they left, and said if there was one thing that might tempt her back it was that. She loved books when she could read, especially stories, and I expect she gave that to me too.

So Dad asked his first questions, and Brand said yes but not many and seemingly less every year, and no, they weren't coming.

And then, without much prompting from us, he began to tell his story. He was a good talker. His deep voice and easy smile drew you in slowly and gently, so smoothly that you didn't know you'd been hooked until his sharp eyes caught yours, and even then it felt like he was sharing something merry with you, like a joke. It never felt like bait.

What did feel like a lure were the temptations he freely unloaded from his bag and laid out on the grass at our feet as he talked, seemingly without any other intention than getting them out of the way until he found what he was searching for at the bottom of the thing. Soon he was surrounded by a fan of interesting stuff, like knives and binoculars and first aid kits—military-looking—and a pair of hand cranked walkie-talkies as well as various tins and bottles whose contents would doubtless be revealed if we should choose to ask.

I know it's in here somewhere, he said, as he carelessly laid another treasure on the ground and rummaged his hand deeper inside the bottomless bag.

We all exchanged glances over his bowed head, but none of them betrayed anything other than interest. Dad's look contained no hint of a warning and the closest to a reservation about our new guest was the wrinkled nose Bar pantomimed at me.

I knew what she meant. He smelled different. Not bad, just not us.

When the world was full, did everyone smell the same? Or were you all distinct from one another? I can see from the old pictures what a crowd looked like, but I don't know what it smelled like. Or sounded like even. That's something I often wonder about. Did all the voices become one big sound, the way the individual clink of pebbles on a stony beach adds up to a roar and a thump in the waves? That's what I imagine it was like, otherwise all those millions of voices being heard and distinct from one another at the same time would have run you mad. Maybe they did. Anyway. Brand eventually found what he was looking for and pulled it from the depths of the bag with a satisfied grunt. It was a long, clear glass bottle, and he handed it to Dad with a grin.

A guest-gift, he said.

But it came with a warning. We should be careful. It was strong stuff and it would make you woozy if you drank too much of it. Dad laughed and explained we knew all about alcohol since we made both heather ale and mead. But this bottle was from the Before and it was still sealed. It was clear-ish, like peaty water, and though the paper label was long gone there were embossed letters standing proud around the neck of the bottle that read "AKVAVIT".

An unopened bottle from the deep past is a rare thing. The Baby Bust had a lot of sorrows to drown, after all. But Brand made little of the gift. He had more, he said. He had found a military ship grounded and tilting on a tidal flat in the far north, maybe Norwegian. It had unopened crates full of tinned food—all age tainted—and medical supplies. And the Akvavit. Lots of Akvavit. It was good, he said, but tasted of a herb. Dill maybe. Unexpected but not bad once you were used to it.

We moved inside as the sky began to spit, helping him bring in the contents of his bag and laying them anew across the hearth mat. Then Dad opened the bottle as Bar and I got the supper together, making a stew from salt cod and potatoes. We all had a drink, except for Mum who just sat by the chimney as she always did. Her eyes never left the redhead's face. Understandable, because he was a new thing and she saw few enough of those, though she looked less interested than horrified. Dad explained she had injured herself a long time ago, and Brand bowed his head at her and smiled, raising his glass.

To the lady of the house, he said. *Skol.*

The alcohol made me choke. It felt like flames going down and my first thought was that Brand had poisoned us, but then he drank his glass in one gulp and grinned at me.

Firewater, he said.

That's what it felt like, warming me from the inside. I coughed and nodded.

Better than that, Dad said, looking round at us all. It's time travel.

There was a long pause. I didn't know what he meant.

We're tasting the past, said Bar.

Exactly, said Brand. That's what I always think when I drink it. This is what they liked to drink. This is what the Before tasted like.

Bitter. Harsh. And not a bit sweet, I thought, not like the honey mead we make.

But time travel was not the only magic gift he gave us the night of that uneven trade. He had another trick, which was sweeter and being so was of course the one that snared us. And as with everything Brand did, it came so well wrapped in a story that you couldn't quite see where the danger was.

He came from a family down south on the other side of the mainland, he said. But his family had taken ill and died, two sisters and a father, a long time ago. He had been on the move ever since. This was a surprise to us as we took it as a fact that the mainland was empty. He said that it was now, as far as he knew, but that he and his kin had grown up in a forgotten wildness of reeds and water on the south-east coast called the Broad or the Broads, a place so empty and unvisited that everything had seemed safe until it wasn't. They'd lived in a big house on a flat island in an estuary, a place that was close enough to dry land on both sides that you could swim back and forth, not live like us perched on the wave-torn edge of things.

His father had been what he called a tinkerer, a man who understood the old machines, and who knew how to make and mend the mechanical ones. He was good at Frankensteining, said Brand, who then explained that a Frankenstein was a monster in the ancient stories made from bits and pieces of human beings. I didn't tell him he was wrong, or that I'd read the book and knew that Frankenstein was the mad doctor who created the monster. He just meant his dad was good at cobbling together old machines that were meant to do one thing and joining them to other ones so that they did something new, like rigging a waterwheel scavenged from the mainland to make a tide-driven pump to bring clean water from a deep borehole on the island. I saw Dad's eyes light up when he told us about that. We're all Frankensteins now that nothing new is getting made and we have to stitch together our tech from the old, unrotted bits of what's left behind. Brand learned from his dad, but he didn't stay once everyone died. He left the Broads and took to the sea, looking, he said, for others.

He was, he explained, a mapper of people, a wanderer and a trader, though since his meetings with others were so rare, he did not live by trade but by fishing and gleaning. But it was trade he wanted with us, and though he talked of salted cod and vegetables and whatever food we could spare, I saw his eyes were on the dogs. And especially my dogs. He was very taken by Jip and Jess, I could see that from the first, though in truth he was open and made no secret of it. He crouched down and stroked them while pulling back their lips to see their mouths. They look small enough at first sight, but they've got long jaws and fierce teeth under that fur. He nodded in approval.

Good hunters your dogs, I'll bet, he said, looking at Dad. Dad nodded at me.

Griz's dogs, he said. And you're right. They're the very death of rabbits, those two.

Indeed if Jip and Jess had a fault it was that they took rabbits as a special challenge and would hunt them all day, given half a chance. There were none on the home island, nor had there ever been in my lifetime but there were some warrens on Sandray, and the Uists—now that people had gone—were heaving with them. It was an obsession they must have inherited from their parents: their mother Freya went rabbiting in the dunes one day and never came back, though we searched and searched. Their father Wode is so old that he now moves even less than Mum, at whose feet he sleeps most of the day, but once he too was a gleeful rabbit-slayer. Jip and Jess would start whining half a mile out whenever we went to the big islands, and were always first over the gunwales when we landed, tearing across the dunes and onto the machair where the rabbits sunned themselves. The only things they hunted more obsessively than rabbits were rats, and there were plenty of them in the abandoned houses. Rabbits they seemed to hunt for a game, chasing and doubling back and forth across the sand and grass in a kind of murderously happy abandon, but rats they took personally, as a kind of grim affront, and their assault on them was definitely war, not sport at all. Whenever we entered an abandoned house, we'd send them in first to clear any rats.

As he stroked the dogs, Brand told us he had spent thirteen years on his travels, looking for people and seeing the world. He had sailed the Baltic and up into the fjords of Scandinavia, and he had then hugged the deserted coast of Europe all the long way down to Gibraltar and then the Atlantic coast of Africa. He had not entered the Mediterranean, though he had gone quite far up some of the navigable rivers that penetrated the mainland. We all leaned forward as he spoke of what he had seen and what he had not, like the three families living together in a big ancient house in the Stockholm Archipelago, a scrabble of tiny islands around the old capital of Sweden.

When I first spotted them I thought they were ghosts, he said. They were like copies of each other—pale-eyed and pale-skinned with flyaway white-blond hair like bog cotton.

He said the women were very beautiful, but he had found them unnerving, and not just because of the strong physical resemblance that now spread across three families. He said they smiled just a little too much and left it at that. He had not minded leaving them, or that all he had taken from them were strange memories and their habit of saying *skol* when they toasted.

He told us of an eerie sailing ship suddenly seen on a windless, murky day on the North Sea that had sheered away as soon as he hailed it and then disappeared into a fog bank and never been seen again, something that had happened so fast he almost put it down to hallucination until minutes later when his becalmed boat had been rocked by the bow wave of the mysterious craft which seemed—even more mysteriously—to have been moving silently under its own power since there was no wind for the sails to catch.

He had sailed down into the Channel and then gone down the Seine where he found not only burnt Paris but before that, on the estuary, the nearest thing to a village he had ever seen, five or six families living like us, fishermen and farmers.

I liked them a lot, he said. I thought one day, when I'd

travelled enough, I would go back and learn their language and live with them.

Only when he sailed back two years later, coming north from his great voyage to Spain and then Africa, they were gone.

Not a sign of them, he said. And their fields were so overgrown they might never have been there at all. They might as well have been something I dreamed.

And for a moment, as he spoke, his eyes seemed to be seeing something a great deal further away than the fire he was looking at.

Africa, said Bar. Was it hot?

All the time, he said.

I'd love to travel, said Bar, ignoring the look Dad threw her. Just to know what somewhere else was like.

And then Brand stood and said he must go outside for a piss, and I stumbled over the things laid on the floor as I hurried to show him the shed where the earth closet was. In truth I was just trying to stop him exiting first, in case he surprised Ferg who I knew had been leaning close to the open door so he could hear what was being said.

I saw him slip out of sight as I paused in the door and pretended to sneeze to buy him time, and then I stepped into the fading light of the evening and pointed to the outside toilet. The squall had passed and the rain had stopped spitting.

There, I said.

Brand looked at the tall upright shack. Of course it stood out like a sore thumb when compared with the other low-built stone outbuildings.

Well, he grinned. Good job you came to show me. I'd never have found it on my own.

I wondered if I'd made him suspicious, but his smile took

the edge off his words. I watched him walk over the low heather to the toilet, and noticed how his eyes never stopped scanning the island as he went. At the time I thought he knew he was being watched.

After what happened, the way it happened, I'm not so sure. But the end result was just as bad.

Chapter 5

Marmalade

The stew smelled good and the talking around the table was better, and the excitement of having someone new to talk to gave the whole meal a holiday air. We still have holidays, because Dad says you need to mark the passing of time and the seasons, so we have birthdays and Midsummer and Christmas Feast, though we don't have a religion to go with it. I felt bad for Ferg, outside, hidden and on guard. I kept looking at Dad, expecting him to relent and announce his other son was due back any minute, which would be the signal for Ferg to wait a while and then come in, all innocence, and join the five of us round the fire. But he didn't.

I saw Bar also looking the question at Dad and saw him give the smallest shake of his head. A few minutes later, she got up and went behind Brand to get the pot, saying she hadn't got enough cod in her helping, only potato. I was deep in conversation with him, but I saw her open the small window in the wall beside the fire and slip a bowl out into the darkness.

Sorry, she said as Brand turned, feeling the cool draught on his neck. It gets a little fuggy in here.

Nothing wrong with clean air and a breeze at your back, he

said. I've been at sea so long I get a fit of the get-me-outs if I'm stuck inside a house too long. I can't sleep ashore at all now. I need the sea to rock me until I drop off.

Dad sat next to Mum and fed her alternate spoonfuls, one for her then one for him, as he always did. Bar sat on the other side and wiped Mum's chin whenever she dribbled. It was a routine so normal to me that I hadn't until then thought others might find it strange or uncomfortable to watch. Though I had of course spent very little of my life wondering what strangers might think of us and our way of living, there being so few of them.

Brand, though, seemed uncomfortable with the sight of a grown woman being fed like a child. He looked away and saw a pile of books against the wall. He caught me watching him and asked what they were for, and then we began talking about them as a way to allow him to give Mum a kind of privacy he clearly felt she needed. When I told him they were my books and just stories, not anything anyone else thought was useful, he began to quiz me about what I liked and why. It was a new sensation to have someone ask me about myself, and I suppose that was why I opened up and told him.

I said I especially like the ones about apocalypses and dystopias because it's always interesting to see what the Before thought the After would be like. He said he didn't know what the word dystopia meant and I told him. Then he asked me what the worst one was, and without having to think about it I told him about this one called *The Road* about a dad and his son travelling across what I think is America. From the very beginning, I knew it wasn't going to end well and it didn't. I told him about it and he nodded as if I'd said something very wise instead of just given a quick outline about a story I'd read.

Maybe that's what happened in America, at the very end, he said. Maybe after the Exchange there were enough vigorous old bastards to bother to make that kind of horror happen.

I hope not, I said. And I meant it because that was a future no one should have to live in. Even people crazy enough to be part of the Limited Exchange.

Talk of the Exchange brought Dad back into the conversation, and because of that and the fact Mum had had enough to eat, the talk widened across the table as Brand asked what stories had been handed down to us about all that. Dad said no one knew who began it and that everyone involved, the ones that survived said it was the other lot. That was when the world was still talking to itself, about the last time nations worried about what other nations thought about them, before they all turned inward. Five to ten years later he said they just stopped talking. Brand nodded. That was very much like what he had been told by his father and mother.

This was about seventy years from the Gelding—threescore years and ten. A full lifetime, Bible style. I know that because one of the Busters sprayed it on the wall of the old church on South Uist and the weather hasn't quite undone it, though every year we pass it and it looks more faded:

THE DAYS OF OUR YEARS ARE THREESCORE YEARS AND TEN; AND IF BY REASON OF STRENGTH THEY BE FOURSCORE YEARS, YET IS THEIR STRENGTH LABOUR AND SORROW; FOR IT IS SOON CUT OFF, AND WE   Y AWAY. PSALMS 90.10.

I think whoever sprayed it was deep in the labour-and-sorrow phase of their life, because the lettering looks both shaky and angry at the same time. Bar says it's like a howl from the Lastborn generation.

By that time, the world's population had dropped dramatically. Dad set me the problem as a maths test, so I know the figures. At the Gelding it was about 7.7 billion. Like I said, threescore and ten years out from that it had dwindled to less than ten thousand people. I get vertigo trying to think about such large numbers, and how the size of our species just dropped off a cliff as sheer as the one at the back of our island. In seventy years, we were down to precisely eight and a half thousand in fact. Except of course the mortality rate must have been worse because there was plenty of other stuff going bad.

We know less of those more recent events like the Exchange, or the Convulsion or the Hunger for that matter, than we know about what came long before that, because all the reliable history we know comes from books, and we have no shortage of them. But after the Gelding, the supply of books became scarcer and then petered out, just like the world's population did, as if people lost the point of writing for the future when there wasn't going to be one. Or else they were writing on the internet, which was a spiderweb of electric networks that no longer survive. So the real stories of the last years are the ones told by mouth, and though they are closer in time, they seem more like myths and legends than the things that happened before them, because those earlier things were written down as history. This is why when strangers meet, the talk is always about those last days of the Before—the Long Goodbye—as people compare their versions of what they have been told, hoping the newcomer might hold a fresh piece of a jigsaw that in truth will now never be fully completed.

And the stories that come down through our family don't have a bird's-eye view of events because of course they only saw the edges of things, or heard of them at a distance, and for some of that time they were kept away from the world anyway, not quite in camps but not quite free, until the Busters decided that there was no use in studying them to reverse the Gelding, or trying to repopulate the world with them because they were so few. That's when Dad's parents came here, on the margin of everything, keeping out of the way of the world until it departed. I think they did that as much out of manners as anything, because Dad said he remembered his mother saying how the Busters, who by then were all well north of fifty and heading for the exit door, used to look at them with their youth and unwrinkled skin with something strange in their eyes, something that flickered between grief and jealousy and a usually—but not always—controlled anger.

They opened the gates and let us go, she had said. And though they emphasised we had of course always been free to leave, the fact they took the trouble to say so told us the opposite was true. So we went, and we kept on going until we'd put land and sea between us, and then we sat it out.

Sitting it out on an island isn't so strange a thing, nor was it crazy, said Dad.

Brand nodded, and of course we all knew the sense of it: travelling by land became less and less reliable and then more and more unsafe in the final throes of the Before.

But the sea is a road everywhere, said Brand. There was a kind of pride in his voice as he said it, as if the seaways were his own particular kingdom. But then he had by his own telling sailed halfway round the world, so maybe he had a right to the pleasure in it.

These islands were not so remote before the land was tamed by the roads, said Dad. Once they were like a great thoroughfare for the really ancient world.

He often told us this. That's why one of the early Christian god-people came and built his home on what now looks like the most remote place in the world, south of here on an island called Iona that I had heard of but never visited. He didn't do it to get away from it all: he was planting himself in the middle of a busy waterway. That's true. That's history, and I know it not just because it was one of Dad's favourite stories, but because I read it, not once, but in many of the books we have.

The talk turned to all the strange belief systems and sects and crazes that grew up in the Long Goodbye. First off, Dad said the crazies got crazier, and the ones with the biggest sticks got the most impatient and that led to things like the Exchange. The Exchange meant goodbye to oil from the Middle East, from the hot dry countries that were now hotter and drier. Then there were, maybe later, the Neatfreaks who wanted to leave their affairs in good order in case it could help any that remained. Or any life that happened upon our planet after we were all gone, if that was the way the story ends. They left things like a big seed vault in Svalbard, and various gene safes they called Arks scattered about the world, but they also started collecting things like the car piles.

And they did at least try to make the ageing nuke plants safe, said Brand.

That didn't go so well, not everywhere, I said, though I did not yet know what that meant in reality. When I was little, and before I read much, when they said "nuclear" I thought they were saying "new clear" and couldn't understand why they were worried about something that sounded so fresh and clean. Then I learned nuclear meant something old and dirty. Very dirty. And very, very long lived.

Those Neatfreaks were the opposite of the Bingers, from what I heard, said Brand. Damn Bingers just decided to use everything up because who the hell was going to need it when they were gone?

They ate all the pies, said Dad. Which is an old way of saying they were out-of-control greedy.

They're probably the ones who ate the dogs in the end, said Bar.

That's a horrible part of the Before story I don't quite believe, though Ferg swears Mum told him her mother had seen it happening, and that was why dogs were almost as rare as we are. Though it doesn't explain why bitches are even rarer.

I was told they got poisoned as the cities became emptier and people got scared of them running in packs and turning wild again, said Brand. I don't know which story is true.

Neither is good, I said.

The talk kept on down this darker path as Dad and Brand compared their families' versions of the past. What both agreed was that some people took their own lives, gently mostly, often together, to avoid the pain and helplessness when they got too old and there were no able-bodied younger people to care for them.

Or maybe they left early just to avoid the rush? I said, which is a joke I had found in an old book. It wasn't a joke that quite made sense to me, because I'd never seen a crowd, but I knew from the context how it was meant to be funny, and I suppose I was trying to seem clever to this new addition to my world.

Brand and Dad looked at me and neither smiled. I shrugged at Bar. She rolled her eyes as if I was a child that shouldn't have been trying to join in the elders' conversation.

And then others just clung on, tough as limpets, said Brand. Waiting to at least see what Armageddon looked like before going into the long dark.

And now they are all gone, I thought, and then found Brand looking at me as though he was reading my thoughts. He nodded.

The last wave, the Busters, broke, he said. And this is the New Dark Age. Maybe, probably, the Last Dark Age. Then he smiled broadly, as if to break the solemnness that had taken over from the holiday mood.

You wanted to know what a hot country's like? he said to Bar. I can show you.

He reached into the bag again, and this time didn't have to rummage too much. He came out with a squat glass jar of something as tawny and red as his hair. I could see it was a jelly and not another liquid, like the Akvavit, because as he tilted it the darker strips of whatever was suspended in it didn't move. It reminded me of the single amber bead Mum has round her neck, the one with a bit of insect trapped in it. Backlit by the flames in the grate, it looked like someone had reached into the sky and taken a lump out of a setting sun and bottled it.

Is it jam? said Bar.

Sort of—but not, he said. It's marmalade.

Like the cat? said Bar, looking at me. Like the one in the book?

Bar used to read us a picture book about a marmalade cat. It was Joy's favourite when we were small—that and a book called *D'Aulaires' Book of Greek Myths*—and it was so loved it fell to bits and had to be held together by an old bulldog clip. I don't know what happened to it. Maybe someone hid it so as not to be reminded of Joy. I hadn't thought about it for years. The memory of it tugged something inside me and made my eyes sting.

Bet you never tasted it, said Brand. Marmalade.

It's made of oranges, said Bar, chin tilting up, keen to show she knew stuff.

Ever tasted an orange? he said, looking round at us all.

We shook our heads.

Warmer up here than it used to be, said Dad, but still not warm enough for citrus.

Citrus. Dad didn't like people thinking he didn't know stuff either.

Brand unsnapped the lid and held it out.

This is what a hot country is like, he said. Fill your noses first.

We all leaned in and inhaled. It was something I'd never smelled before: clean yet spicy. It had a tang, a cut to it, and yet it was also, in some way I then thought was a miracle, sunny.

You have bread and butter, he said. We will have marmalade sandwiches as a dessert. A treat. As thanks for your hospitality.

And then he smiled, wide and white in the dense red of his beard, and waggled his eyebrows as if the whole world was a fine joke and we all lucky to be in on it together.

And to sweeten you up, because tomorrow I will take you to my boat and show you the converter and then try and make you give me much too much fish and food in trade for it. I may even see if you'll let me have that fine bitch there.

Bar snorted.

Over Griz's dead body, she said, matching his smile.

Oh, it won't come to that, he said. Was just a thought. She is a very fetching dog though.

We'll find something to trade it for—if it is the right converter, said Dad, and it came to me that the edge in his voice was because he was not quite liking the fact they were smiling at each other.

Your friends on Lewis said it was, Brand said. But you will see for yourself. Tomorrow.

The bread was cut, a smear of butter laid on each piece, and then Brand spread a thick layer of orange jelly on them.

What are the bits? said Bar.

The peel, he said. I cut it myself. I made it according to an old recipe book. I made it when I was in Spain, where there were no people but too many oranges. I found sugar in a ruined hotel and used that. It's sweet and yet sour. Even if you don't like it, you'll know what the south is like when you taste it.

The taste was shockingly intense, rich and more complicated than anything I had ever eaten. As he had said, it was sharp and yet sweet, but not sweet in the way of honey: it was an intensity that seemed to fill the whole mouth, but I could not taste the sun in it because the sweetness caught on the tooth the ram had chipped, and sent a lance of pain into my jaw.

It felt like the mouthful had bitten me, and though I winced no one saw me because they were all enjoying this new treat in their own ways. Bar was laughing; Dad had his eyes closed as if shutting out the world was making the experience all the more powerful. Brand was looking at my mother.

I folded the bread over on itself and palmed the sandwich.

Amazing, said Bar. It's like a mouthful of summer.

Tastes like it smells, said Dad. Thank you. It's wonderful.

Better than the firewater, I said because everyone seemed to be expected to say something.

More, have more, said Brand, reaching for the bread. Once you have opened the jar the taste goes very quickly. It will taste of slop tomorrow. We must enjoy it while the magic is still in it!

I excused myself, saying now I too needed a piss. Ferg was in the darkness outside, where he had been listening, and before he could ask I handed him the sandwich. He grinned and punched me on the arm, which was his way of showing affection.

Then we walked behind the house and he ate it. I watched his face as he did so, and saw the happiness it gave him.

It does taste of sunlight, he whispered. It's wonderful.

It hurts my tooth, I said. I'll sneak you more when I can, or hide it till he goes to sleep. He says he always sleeps on his boat.

Hope he's tired, said Ferg, pulling his coat tight round himself. Because I'm getting cold out here.

Don't know if Dad trusts him yet, I said.

That's Dad being Dad, he said. But that's okay. You go back in before he wonders where you've gone.

When I returned, Brand was talking to Dad about the converter, and Dad was smiling and yawning and saying tomorrow was soon enough to talk trade. Bar was chewing her way through her second sandwich, and Mum had fallen asleep.

Bar and I cleared the table and I pocketed the sandwich they had left me. Bar saw and silently nodded. She knew I was saving it for Ferg. She did not know I had not eaten mine because of the tooth pain.

Dad yawned again and said it was time to sleep, and began to take Mum to their bedroom, shaking her awake and leading her ahead of him. He told Brand he was welcome to sleep ashore, but Brand said he'd stay and chat with Bar and me and then sleep on his boat, as was his habit.

Bar was also yawning by this time, and as Brand and I talked further about the books I liked and the ones he had read, her head dropped and she went to sleep at the table beside me. I carried on talking, and now I know one of the reasons was because I was enjoying this new friendship, a new friend being something every bit as exotic to me as the marmalade was for the others.

As we talked, Brand ruffled Jess's hair, scratching behind her ears. She leant into him as he did so. I felt another tug inside me, but dogs are open-hearted and it doesn't do to be jealous of an animal's affections, so I pushed the feeling away and started laying out the bowls for breakfast. I can't remember exactly which books we talked about, and the talking went on for a while, almost as if we were each waiting for the other to admit they were tired, but neither wanting to be the first to say it. I do remember talking about a line in another book called *The Death of Grass* that perturbed me. It wasn't in the later part of the story where society fell apart and people began killing and raping and turning back into something feral. It was in the early bit of the story, before the grass and the wheat and the crops started dying and the famine began. It was a simple line, something like "the children came home from half term and they drove to the sea for a holiday". It was so different from my After world, that Before world where children were sent away from their home to go to a school. All the learning I had, and there was a lot because Dad's Leibowitzing meant he insisted we filled our minds with what might be useful and shouldn't be lost, happened in or in sight of my home. And going to the sea for a holiday? I've never been out of sight of the sea, not for a whole day. I don't know what that would be like. Sea's in my blood. Brand nodded and reached over and bumped fists with me. I told him I didn't know how easy I'd breathe if there was not at least some water glinting on the horizon.

Amen to that, he said.

That's the last thing I remember either of us saying because then I must have yawned and fallen asleep right there and then, foolishly warm in the fire and the sense that I had made a new friend.

I didn't know I was wrong. Or how soon I would find out exactly how easily I'd breathe away from the safety of the sea.

Chapter 6

The theft

I knew something was badly awry the moment I woke. My head was hurting and, as I staggered up to my feet in front of the cold fire, it was as if my legs had forgotten how to walk in time with each other. The house was silent and there was no one else awake. But outside there was a noise that drew me stumbling to the door and out into the thin slant of rain.

The red-sailed boat was not at the mooring.

It was just rounding the headland at the south of the bay, so nearly gone from sight that its bows were already obscured by the rocks. Brand was at the tiller and he saw me in the instant I saw him and, just before he too was swallowed by the jagged bulk of land, he smiled, his teeth flashing unmistakably white in the red of his beard, and he half shrugged and half waved and then was gone.

Two things stopped me in my tracks, beyond the fact that he was leaving without a farewell or any attempt to trade for the much-boasted converter. First was that he was wearing my father's rain jacket, the good yellow one with the peaked hood, which made no sense. Second was a delayed recognition of what his smile and shrug and half-wave had meant: it had been a farewell and a strange and almost good-natured admission of guilt. Honesty ran one way through the gesture, while dishonesty crossed it at right angles, like the warp and weft of Ferg's weaving. Brand was in that moment two things at once. But only one thing mattered.

He had stolen my dog.

I knew that with cold certainty the moment I saw Jip alone in the water, barking and swimming far out in the bay, so far out that he must have fallen or been thrown off the boat in whose wake he was struggling. I saw his head bobbing and heard the shrillness in his bark and knew that Brand had taken Jess, who was nowhere to be seen.

And then I was shouting to wake the others and running for the dory. He had not cut our boats loose, but he had thrown the oars into the water and the tide was slowly dragging them out to sea.

As I ran, I noticed without stopping that the racks that had been thick with drying fish were now empty. He had stolen our food too.

The chill in the water bit at me as I dived out to get the oars, and then I splashed back into the dory and was about to unshackle it to get to my boat—which was moored in the lee of the rocks behind which Brand had disappeared—but as I took a breath I saw Jip was going to make it ashore under his own power. I had a second thought: what was I going to do when I chased Brand down? I had not had to think at all about setting off to get Jess back: that had been a natural reflex. My first thought had been to scoop Jip out of the water and then get the *Sweethope* under sail and start the chase without waiting a moment longer, knowing every moment of delay was putting more sea room between me and my quarry.

Then I realised I might need a weapon, so I left the dory shackled and ran back to the house, intending to get my bow and a long gun. As I ran, I was gripped by a sudden dread that the others were dead because I could not see anyone moving or responding to my shouts or Jip's barking.

They weren't dead. They were drugged and—once shaken awake—vomitous and disorientated. Brand had poisoned them to sleep by putting something in the marmalade. That stubborn ram that had chipped my tooth the day before had actually saved me, because without the pain from the sugar I too would have eaten enough marmalade to be as drugged and useless as they were. Brand would have got clean away and we would never even have known in which direction he had gone, or how to begin chasing him down.

There would be days ahead when I realised that might not have been the worst option.

But right then, in the moment, full of adrenaline and anger and betrayal, all I could think of was getting after him as soon as possible. I tried to explain to Bar who was the least affected by what had happened, and as I did so I grabbed food and stuffed it into a bag. Then I kissed Mum, who looked at me blankly but seemed to squeeze my hand back as I said I was going but would be back with Jess, and I took Ferg's gun, and made sure he was lying on his side so that he would not drown in his own vomit before waking. Then I grabbed arrows and my bow from the hook by the door and ran for the dory where Jip was waiting, barking at me to hurry up.

Dad tried to stop me, stumbling after me and mumbling that he would come, that I should wait until he could get his head straight, and then he bent over and threw up what looked like everything he had ever eaten and I said I could not wait and he may or may not have heard me because he stayed doubled over, retching as Bar came out and held him upright, and then I just turned and left them, sprinting for Jip and the dory, and within four minutes I had got to the *Sweethope*, tumbled the dog aboard, followed him into the cockpit and slung my kit over the companionway down into the small cabin space—and two minutes later I had unloosed from the mooring buoy and tacked out into open sea, my eyes scanning for the tell-tale, treacherous red.

I was so intent on finding the small scrap of colour now halfway to the horizon that when I finally did and risked a fast look back to wave, I had cleared the headland and could no longer see my home or my family.

I had left without farewell.

Or blessing.

Or knowing if they would recover properly.

You can fall out of your own safe life that quickly, and nothing you thought you knew will ever be the same again.

Those thoughts came to me later.

In that moment, in the wide empty world, all that mattered to me and Jip, who was quivering on point at the prow of the boat, was the tiny shard of red in the sea ahead of us.

That was how the hunt began.

That was when things were simple.

That was when we thought we were just chasing a dog thief. That was before we went into the empty mainland and found we were chasing something else entirely, something we didn't even know we had lost.

That was how I ended up going where I've been. Into the ruins of your abandoned world. Seeing what I've seen. Doing what I've done.

And doing what I have done is how I ended up here. Alone.

No one to talk to but a photograph of a long dead boy with his dog and his sister. Nothing to do but write this down for people who will never read it.

Solitude is its own kind of madness.

Like hope itself.

Chapter 7

Running before the wind

I couldn't see red sails. The wind was blowing out of the north-east, and Brand had got out of the wind shadow of the great cliff at the back of our island a good quarter of an hour before I was able to get the *Sweethope* loose from its mooring. She was a small enough boat, though you might have called her a yacht. One person could manage her if you were lively about it and knew how to do it, but in truth it always went a bit smoother with two, and the pair of bunks below always reminded me she was not quite designed for one sailor. But I was used to sailing her on my own. By the time I'd got out of the bay and rounded the rocks to the south, he'd been able to put on every scrap of sail he had and must have been running at full speed ahead of the wind, putting more and more sea between my dog and me as I struggled to get out into the faster air.

And struggle was the right word. It felt like the boat was dragging herself through a peatbog. It was my frustration, I knew, but the sea around us seemed sticky, like it was trying to suck at the hull to slow us down. I think Jip sensed something similar. He stood on the forepeak and barked his own frustration into the sea-waste ahead of us, looking back at me every now and then, as if our slow progress was something I could do more to fix.

Visibility was good, and I should have been able to see him as I cast around the empty sea in front of the boat, but I couldn't. Given the strength and direction of the wind, it only made sense that he would be running south, and so I concentrated on getting up our speed and making sure I had as much sail spread as the boat would bear, and then, when I finally felt the kick of the strong air catch the canvas and heard the water begin to really fizz past on either side of the cutwater, I ducked below to grab the binoculars.

Jip must have seen Brand before I did, because he'd stopped barking and was just standing stiffly on the bow, still on point, back legs shivering with what Dad called terrier-shake, which I always took to be a controlled excitement. I found the dark sails a minute or so later, far ahead of us and racing for the horizon.

Something happened in my stomach when I finally saw them, a sort of flip and a dropping sensation. I think if I had not seen the sails again then Brand and his theft would have become a nightmare that would have haunted me for the rest of my life. Though maybe that life would have been longer than the one I'm now facing. I would have begun to think his disappearance was too sudden, too impossible to be real and perhaps even begun to wonder if he had been something supernatural. That was half of what was behind the flip and drop I felt inside—relief that the careful walls I had built around my sense of the world had held. Maybe in your busier world with more distractions like the internet and football matches and other people, you never felt the tug of the uncanny the way that I did. Now I am alone and stuck here with little to do other than write all this down and think,

I realise how much time I used to spend with my head in a book, filling the emptiness of my world and letting the pages distract from the darkness in the shadows behind me. I put a lot of effort into not letting myself believe in the supernatural. I think we all did. Of all the stories we used to take turns reading out loud around the fireplace, none were ever ghost stories. I know that was no mistake. Every empty house we passed might easily have been full of ghosts, if we chose to see them that way. But Brand disappearing into thin salt air would have been just the kind of thing to put a fatal chink in that protective wall.

The other thing in my belly was fear, not so much fear of Brand himself, for my blood was still up and against him, but a fear of what I now had to do. The truth was I had no plan. I had an aim, which was to get my dog back. My eye caught the long gun and the bow I had thrown down into the cabin. The fear was not for myself. I was young and angry enough not to feel that, though this wasn't courage: young and angry is not the same as brave. I was not scared of Brand at that moment, and that was a further stupidity. The fear was fear *of* myself. Of how far I would go.

You, in the picture I found, have nothing but sunshine and laughter in your face. Your eyes shine with it as you hang there caught in your star jump, forever lighter than air, caught between grass and sky between a sister and a dog who love you. Your thoughts can never have borne the sudden dark burden I felt when I looked at the gun.

A sea chase with the wind at your back is a long thing, and there was plenty of time for thinking as the miles flew past. In the open water that stretched between the last of home and the southern islands and mainland proper, it was also cold. I had a long sleeveless coat in the cabin, made from three sheepskins stitched together, with the wool on the outside. I got it and cinched my belt around the middle to hold it close around me. The smell of the wool reminded me of home. So did the cap I pulled over my ears, a stretchy knitted thing Bar had sewn for me made from an old jersey we had found preserved in a plastic bag at the back of a tall cupboard in a low house on Eriskay the summer before. The yarn was more than a century old, and Bar had overstitched it so many times to keep it together that it was easily as much stitch as sweater, but there was something of her in each of those tacks, so I felt a little less alone when I wore it. I'd watched her painstakingly working on it over a winter month and had come to secretly covet it as she did so. Then she unexpectedly and casually gave it to me, as if it were nothing.

You need a hat, she said. And that was that. Except that for a moment, and in truth a long time after that, it was everything. Bar didn't talk much, but she did a lot. It was in doing that she showed what she thought. That kept me as warm as the hat itself.

Thinking of Bar made me duck back into the cabin and get the mackerel line. There was no telling how long this might go on, and Bar would say there was no sense in going hungry. I could do more than one thing at a time.

Not well, as it turned out, because in grabbing the line I felt a sharp stab as one of the hooks went deep into the side of my finger.

There was no choice other than to grit my teeth and get out my Leatherman. The Leatherman goes everywhere with me, same as the dogs. It's my prized find, a long small and still stainless steel rectangle that unfolds into a pair of pliers and a wire cutter with knives and saws and screwdrivers and all sorts of useful tools that are tucked away in the handles. I found it in the rotted glove box of a car on Eriskay. It's a wonderfully useful thing. Swearing at myself for the stupidity, I pushed the hook all the way out of the pad of flesh on the side of my finger until the barb was clear, and then snapped it off with the wire-cutters. Then I was able to pull the hook back out without tearing myself up with the barb.

The long mass of the next two islands ahead was looming when I was done with my de-hooking, and I put the mackerel line overboard. I had to keep half an eye on the distant red sails which suddenly became camouflage as the land ahead became background. By the time the gap between the islands had revealed itself, cutting the long mass in two, I had thirteen gutted fish in the bucket at my feet and my hands were bloody with the work.

There's an old lighthouse on the shore and as I passed it I realised that I was now as far south as I had ever been in my life. The island on the other side was another like Barra, to be seen and not landed on. When we had come this far south before, we were looking for turbine parts in the fallen thicket of windmills on the north end of the island. But the sea was suddenly humped with bobbing corpses of seals, maybe thirty or so. We had smelled them before we saw them, and when we did see them Dad had simply turned the boat for home, saying the sea was sour here. And the sour sea was why we never came down this way again.

I had been small when that happened, and excited to be going on an expedition. I had thought I would return home with some exotic find of my own, maybe viked from the little harbour township said to be on the eastern side of the island. Instead I took home something equally unfamiliar—the memory of the fear I saw flash across my father's face before he remembered to hide it.

The sea didn't look sour, nor were there now any sea-bloated seal bellies to be seen. The air was fresh and the wind kept its strength up. Only the light was beginning to fade as I made what was really the choice that changed everything. It seemed small enough at the time, a matter of navigation, just the best way to sail through the sound ahead without going aground. Because I'd never crossed that southern limit of my world.

Somewhere in the back of my head, a voice told me that this threshold was a place to turn back. I looked at Jip and thought of Jess. She was every bit as tough as he was, but where Jip always kept the tiniest bit of himself reserved, even when allowing himself to be scratched or when choosing to sleep tucked in close to me in the winter months, Jess gave herself without keeping anything back. Her tail wagged that bit faster, and she was always a step ahead of him when running to greet us when we returned home. The voice in my head wondered if it was maybe that less guarded nature that allowed Brand to grab her. But thinking of her sweetness was not doing anything other than making the tears prick behind my eyes, so I pushed the voice away, far out of hearing, and watched the unknown passage ahead for shoals or skerries. And so, by concentrating on the job on hand, I sailed past the known boundaries of my world without noticing the exact moment when it happened.

Through the sound between Coll and Tiree, everything changed. The sky darkened and the wind, which had been constant at my back, now shifted and became difficult. As if he too sensed that some invisible boundary had been crossed, Jip finally dropped his head and curled up on the bench next to me. He didn't close his eyes, just rested his head on his paws, sighed and then stared fatalistically into the blank wall of the cockpit in front of him. His look was a little dispiriting, but the companionable warmth against my leg was welcome.

The *Sweethope* had been cutting smoothly through the powerful heave of the regular Atlantic swell, but passing within the protection of the barrier islands, the boat's motion changed and began to toil as the water around us changed to a queasy wind-blown chop. Visibility had been good for most of the day, but now it was as if several squalls of rain had been pinballing back and forth on the other side of the islands, waiting for our arrival. Within five minutes, one blew across the gap between us and the red sails in the distance, and then we were lashed with a short but vicious hail of rain that hit so quickly it seemed to have materialised out of thin air. There was so little warning that I barely had time to get my oilskin coat on over my sheepskin. Jip dropped off the bench and slid and skittered his way into the better shelter of the cockpit where he lay nose to tail on a slab of fishnet, positioning himself so that his eyes remained fixed on me through the narrow hatch.

On the other side of the squall, the visibility cleared enough for me to see that the red sails had been swallowed by a larger bank of rain ahead of us. I pushed back the dripping hood of the oilskin and stared into the weather, for the first time in the long day unable to see what we were chasing. I knew it had to be there—I had been unsighted for a short amount of time but not nearly long enough for Brand to have got away—so its absence unsettled me.

Looking back on it, I can't really believe how stupid anger had made me. Other than arguments with my family, which were as natural to us as water is to the fish that swim in it, I had no experience with a serious confrontation with a stranger who wished me ill. Bringing the gun meant I had some unconscious awareness that there was danger ahead, but the bow and arrows always went where I did, much as you would have carried a telephone wherever you went in your more crowded world. It's quicker to shoot a rabbit than it is to lay a snare for it if you're caught foodless away from home, and shooting for the pot was second nature to all of us both on and off the island.

Not having the red sails in sight was alarming, but also jolted me out of my one-track mind. I had to think of other possible tracks that my future might be about to go down. Although the last glimpse I had had of Brand had been that infuriating smile, I had to think that he might hurt me. But I didn't think he would. If he had been that kind of monster, the kind I had read so many stories about, he would just as easily have killed us in our sleep and pillaged our home at his leisure. But he had just stolen from us and tried to slink away before we woke. So a thief. But not a killer. But a thief when confronted might turn violent.

Setting out on a chase without a good plan is a very stupid thing to do, as it turns out. Almost as stupid as thinking you're clever. If I had been clever, I would have either turned back for home, or sailed after him until we were close enough to talk. And then shot him. I was not someone to give up easily. But I was not a killer.

I'm still not one of those things.

My clever plan was to fight fire with fire. I had no confidence in being able to talk him out of his thievery. And I would not be able to best him if it came to violence. So fire with fire meant stealing from the thief. Which meant stealth and cleverness. I knew I had one: I thought I had the other. And ideally it meant not being seen. Which is not an easy thing on the open sea. But as I looked around me, I realised that we were no longer on the ocean, but within the inner islands. The sun was dropping behind me, and would be directly in Brand's eyes. Better still, the dark loom of Coll and Tiree were also at my back as the sun set behind the low hills. I would be hard to see. And having seen the last fingernail sliver of waning moon over the familiar crags above my home yesterday, I knew the coming night would be moonless and dark.

Looking ahead, I could make out the long hummock of the next island and the mainland beyond stretching away on either side of the squall in which I knew Brand was hidden. Seeing both ends of the island, I was confident that I could see if he went to the right or left of the land, and this knowledge made me try something I thought at the time was the cleverest thing.

I took down my sails and threw out the drift anchor. Now, as the cone of material filled with water and the line went tight behind me, I could keep the boat stable against tide and wind, and hopefully pause and watch, camouflaged by the dropping sun and the land astern. Brand would think I'd lost him, or maybe been too scared to follow him between the two islands.

My plan, clever as it was, was based on the fact that no one would sail at night, especially where we now were. I knew Brand was a liar and a thief, but I also knew he was not a fool. These inner waters were rock-strewn and skerry-toothed, and sailing in the dark would turn into drowning in the dark before you knew it.

The *Sweethope* lay low in the water, and even though my bare mast stuck high into the air above me, I found I was crouching down with a knee on the companionway, as if that would help me hide. Jip saw something was up and got up off the bed he'd made on the nets to come and stand next to me.

I kept the rudder hard against my thigh, feeling the way it pushed against the twin forces of wind and tide, keeping us steady. And then, as the sun dipped and the world instantly seemed to get colder, the squall worried off to the right and the visibility cleared enough to reveal Brand's sails moving round a headland I had not seen against the larger mass of the island behind it. I thought, in my cleverness, that he was running to lay up in a hidden bay for the night, maybe even trying to hide from me as he did so. I stood up. Jip whimpered. I put a hand on his head and asked him to be quiet. Sound can travel far over the water.

I was excited. What was happening was of course just an accident of timing, but in my cleverness, in my hubris, I thought he was falling into a trap I had set him. You probably already know what hubris means. I had to look it up in a dictionary the first time I came across it in a book. But if you don't, it means getting such a big head that you miss the bad thing creeping up behind you.

I was so excited that the moment the red sails disappeared I hauled mine back up and forgot the sea anchor and nearly got knocked off the boat as the scurry of evening wind that always comes in the moment after the sun goes down hit the sail and caught me unprepared. The boat tilted and the boom swung and smacked so many stars into my head that I thought my skull had been cracked.

I swore and Jip did bark and I let him as I struggled back to my feet and got busy sorting out the mess I'd made of the boat. Three minutes later the dog was quiet, the sea anchor was aboard and I was underway, heading for the small island ahead.

I made it across the water before it became too dangerous in the dark, but in truth it was not a great spot to drop an anchor. It was on the weather side of the land, and there were skerries all around, hungry reefs waiting to snag the boat and take the bottom out of it. In the end I decided to drop two anchors to hold the boat a little further out than I might have done if the light had been better. I decided I would unstrap the kayak and paddle across. I would leave Jip, which he

would not like, but the stealthiness I was
one that would be helped if he were to bar

I thought this was a thing I would do be
So. Cleverness. Hubris. And the sketchies
What could go wrong?

Chapter 8

The bay at the back of the ocean

Later I found the name of the bay I had anchored in on some old charts, but from the water it didn't look significant enough for anyone to have bothered giving it one. I could hear Jip's reproachful growling behind the cockpit door as I slipped the kayak over the stern and held it there in the darkening water while I carefully got aboard and pushed off. I'd decided to leave the gun because there was no guarantee that even if I was forced to pull the trigger the bullet would fire. The ammunition we have was made long ago, and about half of it hangs fire and just goes click. I decided that if I took the gun I would be risking going click at someone who might well then take it amiss and retaliate with something more than clicking.

I was not interested in violence. The worst stories I read were the ones that ended in violence. When I was little I had a stash of old illustrated magazines about superheroes. I loved them for a bit, because they were so bright and drawn with a real joy for movement and design, some so vividly that the people seemed to be about to burst out of the page and into my world. They tended to walk around in really tight clothes and however much the writers tried to hide the fact, and however much they appeared to fret about what to do, all the stories ended up in a huge fight. Dad said they were written for younger boys really. I liked them despite that, until I didn't. And when I realised I didn't, I also knew that it was because everything was always a set-up for a punch-up. As if the only way you could solve a problem was by hitting it. Maybe your world liked fighting so much that it thought it had to prepare kids for that by telling them those kind of stories. Or maybe it was the other way round and your world liked fighting because those were the stories you were given when your minds were young. I didn't want this story to end with a fight. I just wanted my dog.

I didn't feel much like a hero, super or otherwise, as I pushed off from the flat stern of the *Sweethope* and began to paddle around the rocks lining the curve of land. My mouth felt sticky and my heart was thumping so loudly it almost drowned out the noise of the wind in my left ear as I paddled. My bow, which normally hung across my shoulders so naturally that I never noticed it, now seemed to be digging into my back with every stroke, like a sharp-boned elbow trying to remind me of something I'd forgotten.

My eyes are good in the dark, better than Bar or Ferg's ever were, but the light was failing fast. I could see the obvious things to avoid, but I scraped the kayak on a rock lying in wait just below the surface as I cautiously rounded the low headland. The tides had luckily worn it smooth enough that there were no sharp jags of stone to tear the bottom out of the boat and end my plan before it had begun. I paddled on for a few more strokes and then let the incoming tide take me round into the channel without doing anything more with the paddle than keep myself upright. I didn't want any splashing to alert Brand to my presence if he was on the lookout over the small bay that was revealing itself to me as I quietly drifted into it.

He wasn't, and the bay turned out not to be there either. Instead I saw a deckled channel of water separating the smaller island from the larger landmass that loomed on my right. I could see no sign of his boat in the water. My first thought came from a fear, and it was that he had fooled me by sailing straight through the channel and then turned back up the other side of this smaller island. I had a moment of panicked clarity in which I knew he was aboard the *Sweethope* right now, laughing at me and stealing Jip too, and my muscles had begun to turn the kayak before my mind kicked in and told them to stop, because my eyes had seen something.

If Brand had not gone ashore, I would have never seen the boat in the darkness. As it was, I caught a strange splash of light from within a building as he explored, and the light was strange because of the window that framed it. It was big and old, old not in a hundred years or just before the Gelding way but old in the way of many centuries past. It looked like a castle window I'd seen in books, not just because of the tall arched shape of it, stark against the night, but because of the stone walls and high-beamed roof I saw for a brief instant as Brand splashed the light of his lantern over it. It wasn't a castle of course. It was a church. An abbey even. But right then it was more than that. It was an opportunity. Because the other thing that this moment of light appearing like a shape cut out of the darkness with a pair of sharp scissors did was silhouette the mast of his ship on the foreshore. He'd sailed in beside a stone jetty and made fast to it, tucked in so tight that I could easily have paddled past in the blackness and never seen it.

But now I felt my spirits rise. I could see he was off the boat, and all I had to do was paddle across, tie off to his taffrail and get aboard quickly enough to get Jess out of the cabin where I was sure she must be locked up, then get back to the *Sweethope* without him knowing what had happened.

I moved fast, not needing to think much. The kayak moved easy and quiet across the water. Truth is the thing was so much a part of me that I didn't really think about how to make it go where I wanted any more than you would have thought how to swim or run.

I slipped in beside his boat and held myself there, soft and quiet, balancing the tug of the tide with my hand flat against the hull. No sound other than wave-lap and wind riffling through the rigging above. I put my ear to the hull, but could hear nothing below decks either.

I carefully walked the kayak hand over hand to the stern of the boat. Making sure not to have it bang noisily against the hull. And then I tied it off with a knot I could release with one quick tug.

Walking onto his boat was strange. It felt wrong. Uninvited. Unwelcome. Even though he had stolen from us, this was his home. I pushed the feeling as far away from the front of my mind as I could, crept across the cockpit towards the companionway and put my ear to the hatch, which was closed. There was no noise inside. Not a man's, not—and this was what I had been hoping for—a dog's. My fear had been that Jess should get a smell of me and start whining or—worse—barking. I popped my head back up and looked over the cabin towards the island, just in case Brand was silently on his way back, but the light in the church window was still there, and so, I figured, was he.

I risked a low whistle through the door. There was no answering noise from Jess. Which was not surprising, because once I had eased open the hatch and ventured a look inside, there was no dog, no Brand—but plenty of everything else. The cabin was jammed with things—boxes, bottles, lumps of machinery and sacks that, from the smell and size of them, contained our dried fish. There were bags hanging from the ceiling. The only clear space was a chart table. I would not have liked to be stuck in this cabin on a frisky sea. I ducked below the bags and made my way to the fore-cabin, behind a small door in the bulkhead. The thought came to me that if I was going to pen up a stolen dog while I went exploring on the island, that was exactly where I'd do it. On the other side of that thin wood door with its slatted metal grill.

I whistled again but there was no noise or movement on the other side. He must have taken Jess ashore with him. My fingers found a padlock with a key in it but it was unlocked, and when I lifted it clear of the hasp the door swung open into more darkness and a worse stink. I could see nothing at all, and something in that deeper stench made me unwilling to blunder in and feel my way around. I dropped the padlock back in the hasp and crouched in the darkness, feeling the soft rise and fall of the sea beneath me, trying to ride out my disappointment. My easy plan was sunk. I couldn't yet see what to do next. In fact I couldn't see anything much, deep in this unfamiliar, crowded cabin with a moonless night outside. Could have been the smell of the sacks of stolen fish, but I felt like what's-his-name in the belly of the whale. Did you know that story? Not the Bible one—the better one. He was a toymaker, and his little boy wasn't what everyone thought he was. He was a wooden puppet. Pinocchio. That's what the boy's name was—not the old guy's in the whale's guts. He was a liar and his nose got longer every time he told one. He wasn't bad though, the boy-not-quite-a-boy. Not mean. Just not grown enough to have a heart yet. I liked that story when I was little. Bar said it sort of fit me, especially after Joy was gone and we did what we had to do to adjust.

Anyway, what with the fish stink and the darkness, I got

an attack of what Brand had called the get-me-outs, and had to un-panic myself for a moment by concentrating on calming my breathing right down. Bar taught me that. She also taught me the difference between fear and panic. Fear's not a bad thing. It's quite a useful thing in the right circumstances, where it's a good response to something dangerous. Panic's not useful for anything at all except thrashing around and—likely as not—running smack into the very thing you're scared of.

I really couldn't make anything out in the cabin. I felt my way back towards the cockpit, barking my shins on something sharp-edged. Then I tripped on something else and went sprawling across the map table as one of the hanging bags clouted me on the side of the head on the way. The map was clipped to the table with magnets and it shifted and tore a little as I hit it. I steadied myself on the cabin wall and then I put my other hand out to brace myself, felt a pain like a bee sting and found I'd jabbed the needle end of a pair of those things you use for making circles on paper into the fleshy part of my thumb. I yanked them out with a bad word and sucked the tiny but painful hole they'd made.

As I stood there, I had time to think. The paper that had moved under my hand gave me an idea. The map was important to him. It was how he found his way around. So I would take it. I carefully stood and folded it, shoving it inside my jerkin, and went back out into the cockpit. I thought it might be good to use the knife which I seemed to have drawn from the sheath on my belt and start cutting all the rigging around me, maybe even slash the sails. But breaking things does not come natural to me. Too much of my life, of our lives, has been spent making and mending and trying to rescue broken things and make them useful again. And a good boat that works, even the boat of a bad man, is still a thing I could not feel right about damaging. That's what's called a scruple. But there were other ways to slow him down.

I ducked carefully back into the cabin and picked my way back to the fore-cabin door, taking the padlock. Keeping a close eye on the still-illuminated window on the shore, I crept along the side of the boat until I came to the anchor chain, which I pulled on until I got enough slack to padlock it to a ringbolt set in the deck. If things got to the state where he was chasing me and tried to get underway quickly, he'd have a lot of trouble doing so with an anchor that wouldn't lift. I smiled as I thought about it. And though I didn't damage the boat, I did allow myself the small pleasure of dropping the key into the dark water on the other side of the grab rail.

I thought about taking more time to ransack his lair, maybe to take things to bargain with him for the dog, if it came to that. But I felt unclean being on board. I know that's a funny word. It makes no sense at all, but that was how I felt. Not because I was trespassing. More because of something about the boat itself. That smell in the fore-cabin wasn't just a smell you sensed with your nose. There was a story in it, and though I did not know what that story was, I did know it was sad as much as it was bad. As I said, I didn't believe in ghosts or made-up things like that. But I do believe in atmospheres. And the atmosphere on that boat—on that night, in the deep dark with no one else aboard and no friendly moon in the sky—that atmosphere did feel more alive than it should have. It felt like it was watching me, waiting for me to do something wrong. It was just an atmosphere, a feeling maybe—but it had better night eyes than I did.

I got off that boat before it made me feel any colder in my bones, though the night was mild for the time of year. The mooring knot didn't come loose with the single jerk I had planned for it, and I took longer than I was happy with sorting out the mess I'd made, and then I was floating free, and with relief powering my arms I paddled to dry land—which was actually wet and slippy with treacherous bladder-wrack and strands of kelp covering the rocks below. Solid ground came as a huge relief, even though I now had to stalk Brand in the dark, with no clear plan as to how to confront him or—better—steal Jess back before he noticed.

I pulled the kayak into the grass above the tideline. Looking around, I wasn't able to see where Brand had put his dinghy, but there were so many humps and hummocks in the darkness that I could have wasted a lot of time looking, so I dismissed a half-formed plan to cut it loose and headed for the church.

Moving quietly was easy as the grass was soft under my feet. But even if I had been louder, I still would have heard the noise that stopped me in my tracks.

I knew it was music, but it was not the kind of music we made when we sang around the fire, and it was not the kind of music that Bar made when she played the tin whistle she had found still wrapped to the instruction book it had come with in the old art centre shop on Uist. It didn't sound like Ferg's strumming on any of the guitars he'd salvaged.

It sounded like angels crying.

I know angels don't exist any more than ghosts do, but if they did and they were mourning something big—like the passing of the world perhaps—that's what it would sound like. Because angels are meant to be pure, and this noise, this music was lots of things I had never heard before but most of all it was pure. The tune was high and sharp and it rose and swooped back and forth above everything, and then all the bright notes that had been gathered up so high to dance with each other tumbled down with a kind of desperate and inevitable sadness that made a hole high in my chest, a void like a lump I couldn't swallow no matter how hard I tried. It made my eyes wet. And as I blinked I thought of Joy. I had felt that heavy hole in my chest once before and that was after she fell out of our world. Hearing the clean, terrible grief echoing in the stone cavern of the church didn't just bring her back to me. It made me feel treacherous because I had let time dull the sharpness of her loss. Forgetting is a kind of betrayal, even if it's what happens to all grief. Time wears everything smoother as it grinds past, I suppose.

I was too short to look in the high window and see what was making the beautiful sound, so I snuck round the corner to the door, which was cracked open, letting a lance of light spill across the grass beyond. I kept close to the wall, feeling the old stonework as I edged round and looked in.

The noise was, of course, Brand. He had a lantern at his feet and he'd lit a small fire on the paving stones at the centre of the cavernous space. I'd never seen a ceiling as high. It was so high, it kept disappearing as the firelight below flickered and threw shadows across it.

Brand was wearing my father's coat and had a violin tucked under the long flame-coloured spade of his beard, and he was half turned away from me as he played it with a long bow, sawing slowly back and forth across the strings. His eyes were closed and he swayed as he played, his long hair falling forwards and backwards as his head moved in its own separate dance. It was like the music was a dream he was both making and getting lost within.

Because his eyes were closed, I let myself watch him longer than I meant. Because the music was so beautiful, so unexpected, so something I had never heard before, I stopped—for a moment—thinking about Jess and getting her back.

Lost in music. That's what they used to call it. On Eriskay there was a house with a shelf that was not full of books, but these thin brightly printed cardboard envelopes with big black plastic discs inside them. Dad said they were records with music trapped on them, but the playing machine stood on a table by a broken window on the weatherward side of the house. It was cracked and the mechanism had rusted out, so we could never free the music on those discs. Instead I spent a day pulling them out and looking at all the covers. One was called *Lost in Music* and I remember it because there were four people on the front and they looked like me, or at least I thought they did. I mean, not like me exactly, but they had normal-coloured skin like us. Not pale and cold like Brand, whose skin and sea-coloured eyes always seemed at odds with the warmth of his hair.

Music—even that wonderstruck violin music—is just as bad a place to be lost in as anywhere as it turns out, because if I had kept my bearings I might have heard the thing that crept up behind me before it snarled and barked and hit me between the shoulder blades, knocking me forwards into the immoveable end of the open church door, sledgehammering me into darkness before I could do more than grunt in surprise.

Chapter 9

I own her

The world came back, and it was on its side and it hurt. There was a great weight pressing my hip and my knee to the stone floor, and it was this pain as much as anything else that hooked me back out of the dark and laid me sideways, staring into the firelight, my cheek flat on the paving stones. I had a throbbing tightness in my forehead where it had hit the edge of the door, in just the same place that the boom had smacked it earlier. It felt as if my skull had cracked.

When I tried to feel it and see if there was any blood, I discovered my hands were stuck behind my back and I couldn't move them. That's when I did panic, and I thrashed around trying to get up and free them, and then the great weight—which was of course Brand—finished tying my wrists to each other and stood up.

The relief to the side of my knee and my hip was good, but the look he gave me as he stepped sideways wasn't, not a bit. It was cold and fierce and as dangerous as the knife he picked up off the chair by the fire. I knew it was razor-sharp because it was mine and I sharpened it every time I used it.

Where are they? he said.

Who? I said. Before I could think better of it.

The others, he said. Your father. Your brother. The rest of you. You wouldn't have come alone.

The fire crackled. My blood thumped in my ears. My head felt like it was going to split open.

They're outside, I said, now having had that time to think better.

He looked at me.

You stole my dog, I said.

How many came? he said. And don't lie and don't call out or I'll cut out your tongue.

Given that choice, it seemed like a good idea to do neither of those things. So that's what I did.

How many? he said.

You shouldn't have taken my dog, I said.

He looked at me some more, but his head was cocked and I could tell he was listening for something outside.

About then was when my head cleared enough for me to remember what had happened on the other side of the blackness I'd just been hooked out of and I began to wonder about who exactly had hit me from behind while I was watching Brand play all the sad magic into the night air. The Brand in front of me now seemed like a completely different person from the self-contained musician lost in the dream of his own creation. This Brand was on edge, all his nerves raw on the outside of himself, listening with more than his ears.

He suddenly put two fingers in his mouth and whistled. Loud. Shrill. Twice.

There was an answering noise from out of the darkness beyond the doors. A bark. But not Jess or Jip. Not a bark like a terrier barks, sharp and hoarse at the same time. A deep bark, as much rumble as woof. The noise a big thing makes.

Something big enough to hit a person in the back and knock them hard into the edge of a door.

Brand looked at me.

You stay. You don't move. You don't shout. Do that? Maybe you keep your tongue, he said. And then he slipped out of the church in a low ducking kind of run and left me staring up at the fire shadows dancing across the great vaulted ceiling overhead.

Liar, I thought. Thief and liar.

His dog was not dead at all. But where was Jess?

It didn't make sense. He'd stolen her. But she wasn't on the boat. And she wasn't here. She'd have barked if she smelled me. I wondered if they'd done something terrible to her. Or had she jumped overboard and tried to swim home and drowned? Had I been so set on following the distant red sails all day that I'd missed a small and loyal dog's head in the waves as I passed it? Had she barked in relief as I got closer to her and then watched the *Sweethope* sail past, leaving her alone and bewildered on the wave waste as the cold took her?

All of those thoughts kept repeating in my head, images that got worse and more detailed every time they came around. And the more I tried not to think of her last moments, the closer I seemed to get to them. I could easily have missed a dog's barking in the sound of the wind. Jip could have missed her scent. As my head whirled round and round on it, I became more and more convinced. We had betrayed her. But me most of all.

It hurt like losing Joy all those years ago, worse really because that loss had not been my fault, and by the time Brand came back after what felt an hour or more I had persuaded myself that she was dead and had died in the terrible way I had imagined.

He walked in taller than he had left somehow. Slower, calmer—not ducking any more. A big dog padded in at his heels, a dog with thick grey and black fur and a white face and the least doglike eyes I have ever seen. They were blue as Brand's own eyes, but not then nor ever after did I see them go warm in the way his could; they were always cold, and would never look away from you. Dogs don't like holding your gaze. Saga was different. Saga could outstare a rock.

Good dog, Saga, Brand said. Sit.

The dog sat in front of me and watched. Brand had made his fire out of chairs. He had a good supply of this firewood. There were lots of them in rows behind him, waiting for a crowd of believers who would never come again. He picked the nearest one up, stomped it to kindling and used it to feed the fire that had gone to embers and ash in his absence. There were lots of matching red books stacked on a shelf on the wall and he tore the pages out of one and fed the coals with them, using the empty cover to fan the fire back into crackling life. Then he kicked another chair to bits and added that to the new flames.

He took a chair and brought it close to the fire so he could sit over it and warm his hands and watch me at the same time.

You came alone, he said. Didn't expect that.

I kept quiet.

Don't need you to tell me I'm right, he said, nodding at the dog. Saga and I criss-crossed the island. It's not big. And she'd have smelled them if they were there. The others.

I don't know if you ever had your wrists tied together when you were alive. It's a horrible feeling, especially when they're trapped behind you. You've lost your hands and everything about you is open and exposed. It makes it hard to breathe normally. Brand looked at me and did the unnerving thing he could sometimes do, which was seem to hear what your head was saying to you. He smiled. Not a nasty smile, one of his good ones.

You can talk, he said. He took my knife from his belt and stabbed it into the seat of the chair beside the one he was sitting on so that it stood there, stuck in the wood, reflecting the firelight at me.

Not going to cut your tongue out, he said. That'd be a horrible thing to do to a person. Just said it to get your attention. Needed you to keep quiet.

I stayed that way. Like I said, hands tied behind you makes you feel powerless and the only thing I did have control of was my words, so I looked away and clenched my teeth to stop them getting out.

Was just a threat, he said. Don't take it bad. It's like when you tell a lie, it's always better to put a grain of truth in it to make it stick, eh? Thing with a threat is you have to put a little picture in it, something specific so that it catches in the head. You add that little picture, the person you're threatening has more to chew on in their imagination, and chewing makes them digest the threat properly and then before they know it it's a part of them and they believe it much more than if it's just words outside them, you see?

I didn't. But I did wonder who in the whole wide empty world he had learned this from. Or done this to. Maybe it was something he read.

My silence unsettled him, I think.

Say something, he said. Are they coming after you?

Saga barked at me and the shock of the deep noise and her teeth so close to my face sort of jumped the words out of my mouth without me meaning to let it happen.

Where's Jess? I said.

Who? he said.

My dog, I said. The dog you stole.

Jess, he said. And he leant back, smiling a little, scratching Saga's ears, rewarding her for frightening the words out of me.

I didn't know her old name, he said. I was going to call her Freya.

What have you done to her? I said.

She needed discipline, he said. She bit Saga.

Good, I thought. Good dog, Jess.

Locked her in a shed over there, he said, pointing into the dark. Small room, no food, hard floor. She'll be better behaved come light, or she'll stay hungry.

That was a relief. It flooded through me like warm water, washing away the images I'd made of her lonely death in the waves.

This was a holy place, he said looking around. That table up there was the altar. Where they made their sacrifices and such. There's a metal board with writing on it out there by the shed. It explains it all. If you can read. Not just the church. The whole island.

I didn't want to listen to him talk. Especially in the way he'd started to, all easy and friendly, like he hadn't recently threatened to cut my tongue out.

Just give me my dog, I said.

I own her, he said.

No, I said. You stole her.

He looked at me oddly. And then he grinned and threw back his head and chopped out a short laugh.

No, he said. The name of the island.

And he grinned some more and spelled it out.

I-O-N-A, he said. Iona. Not I-own-her.

And then his eyes got cold and serious again.

Though I do that too, he said. That's just a fact you need to get used to.

I want my dog, I said. You stole her.

You keep saying stole, he said.

I do, I said. You're a thief.

It sounds like I was being brave, writing down what I said then, in that dark echoey place by the fire. That's not true. I was angry and scared and felt very unprotected with my hands tied behind me. All I had for a shield was words.

A thief now, is it? he said. And he said it as if this was a word he had never heard before. A thief? Well now. That sounds bad.

Don't mind what it sounds like, I said. Give me my dog. And the fish. And my dad's coat.

He smiled then, looking down at the yellow oilskin.

It's a good coat, he said. But it's mine. I traded for it. Same as the dog that was yours and is now mine.

You did not, I said.

And how would you know? he said. Seeing as you were asleep at the time.

His eyes were level. Open, even. There was no real accusation in them. Maybe a bit of disappointment.

Ah, Griz, he said. I thought we were friends. Your father is a man who understands the nature of a proposition. There's more to a trade than like for like. He really wanted that windmill part. And while you were sleeping, we came to an agreement.

Just for a moment I let the warm smile and the soft words make me doubt myself. Had I rushed off before anyone could tell me I had grabbed the wrong end of the stick? Had I missed the turbine offloaded and waiting on the shore? Had everyone been too sick to stop me with the truth?

And a liar, I said. Thief and liar.

Ah, Griz, he said again. Words like that can poison a friendship, you know?

I know you're lying because if you had made a deal, you

wouldn't have run off so scared, asking if the others were there, I said. An honest man wouldn't have done that.

To his credit, he didn't drop the smile much.

Well, he said. Well. No one likes to be badly thought of.

They are coming, I said. They were right behind me. So you better let me go.

He shook his head.

Two liars now, he said. And us in a church. Double the poison, don't you think?

I didn't answer. None of the replies bubbling up in my throat made sense enough to be let out anyway. He stretched and then prodded a chair leg deeper into the fire.

They poisoned the dogs, you know? he said. At the end. They gave them something harsh and vicious to their wellbeing. That's why there aren't more of them. Why they're rare.

I kept quiet. He didn't like quiet. If he had a weakness—and I still don't know if it was really a weakness—it was not liking quiet when there was company to be had. He liked to talk. He liked being the centre of any attention that was going. Maybe because he was on his own so much. I had lived with four—once five—others. I had no need to be heard. If I wanted to know what I sounded like, I had Dad and Ferg and Bar to listen to. They sounded just like me.

Brand carried on. The old bastards were frightened of dogs turning into dangerous packs, he said. So they dosed them.

I could have asked him how he knew that. Because of course it can only have been a story he had heard from long before either of us were alive. A traveller's tale. A rumour. A lie. A story. I didn't say anything.

Whatever they gave the dogs did for the bitches more than the males, he said. Way I see it, what bitches remain have litters with fewer females in them than they used to. So, fewer females, fewer dogs in the long run. Males on their own don't breed. Males in a pack with no breeding to be done? Well, Griz, you can see how they'd get mean. You're tall enough for a person to think your body'd be telling you what I'm talking about, but then you haven't started with the hairs on your chin yet, so maybe it hasn't come on you yet, the wanting and the not having. But when it comes on you, you remember what I say. Men with no breeding to be done are the meanest creatures in the world.

I didn't like the look he gave me then, but it passed quickly, like he was as surprised by it as I was uncomfortable, and he just shrugged it back into whatever box it came out of.

So anyway, he said, scratching away at Saga's ears again. What dogs there still are may be thinner on the ground, but they're more dangerous. It's like as if in trying to cure the problem they boiled it down and made it thicker and darker. Like a bone broth.

I'd never heard that term before, but I knew what it meant. We always had a stockpot on the go by the range, and the thought of it came hard, like I could smell it, and like a smell it took me on a short cut right back to a place where I had been safe and happy enough. A place exactly the opposite of where I was: in deepest danger with spirits low enough to match it.

And maybe dosing the dogs was not a story. Maybe it was true. Maybe not. Mucking up how a poor creature can or can't have a normal litter seems awfully like what happened to humankind. If I'd been of a mind to talk to him I'd have said that the Gelding was a much more likely cause of there being less dogs than there should be. I didn't think old dying mankind—the Baby Bust—would have had time or inclination to go about poisoning dogs just for the meanness of it.

I didn't know then exactly how mean some Baby Busters found time to be. I just thought, who would want to poison dogs? It didn't make any kind of sense. But then I'd grown up on an island. I hadn't seen what a bunch of dogs or wolves could do when they were hungry and their blood was up. That came later.

He reached behind him and pulled a pack close enough to yank a sleeping bag from it.

I'm sleeping now, he said. You do too. A night sleeping on the stones here by the fire won't do you much harm. And if you get cold, you've only yourself to blame. You keep to your side of the fire and don't try anything because while I might not be a person who could cut another person's tongue out, Saga here would take your throat out in a heartbeat. Seen her do it. And that's not a lie.

And simple as that, he laid down on the bedroll and closed his eyes, and the dog lay down between us and kept hers open and looking straight at me.

I knew I was too uncomfortable to sleep, so I concentrated on calming my breathing and watching right back.

An hour later I was more uncomfortable than I had ever been in my life, and my hands seemed to be going numb.

I thought about waking him and telling him, but then just when I knew I'd never sleep again, I did.

Chapter 10

Paddling blind

Waking wasn't a bit good. I was so cold and stiff I heard my joints crack as I tried to sit up. I ached everywhere. And the pain in my head was worse. My eye had swollen half shut and was so gummy it took a lot of scrunching and stretching to get it open at all. But there was thin warming light coming through the arched windows even though the fire was now grey ash. And Saga was gone.

Brand sat on a chair, packing up his bedroll.

So here's what's going to happen, he said, and I stopped breathing for a couple of heartbeats as he pulled the knife out of the chair. I must be on my way, and just in case you're telling the truth about the others being behind you, I'd best be going soon. Dawn's up and there's light enough to see the rocks in the water.

He used the knife to quickly gut a couple more of the red books and put them on the embers. Then he kicked another chair to bits and put it on the fire.

You blow on that, you'll get it going again, he said.

I could see he was in too much of a hurry to fan it back into life for me.

I'm not a monster, he said. But I cut my own way through this life, Griz, and that is a truth. I don't want you or yours following me. You all stay up here, away from the world. You've got a safe enough thing going. Just sit tight. World might come by and take a few things from you every now and then, but mostly you'll be fine. You know what a tax is?

I did, but I shook my head.

Well, it was a thing people used to pay, like a money sacrifice. They paid it to be left alone and helped to live easier, I was told, he said. So when I come by, or someone else does, what we take's like a tax.

That made no sense to me at all. I was much more interested in the way he was weighing the knife in his hands.

I see you moving about before I go, I will take it badly, he said.

You can't leave me tied up, I said.

It's just rope, he said. And I'll not even take your knife. There's a graveyard you maybe came through on the way up? There's one stone unlike the others. I'll leave the knife there. You won't find it till it's full daylight, but you will find it. Stone catches your eye because it's different. I'm not a monster.

Saga clinked into view behind him. She clinked because she had Jess joined to her with a length of rusty chain, neck to neck, just enough play in it to let the bigger dog bite the littler one if she wanted, just enough to allow Jess to run hobbled alongside Saga, two steps to the one. Jess wouldn't be able to bite back because she was wearing something on her snout that kept her mouth covered.

It wasn't tight enough to stop her whining excitedly when she saw me, and her tail began wagging so hard her whole back end waggled from side to side and buffeted Saga. Saga snarled and bit her, not once, but twice. The muzzle didn't muffle Jess's yelp of pain. She tried to bite back, because being a terrier that was what she had to do, not having an inch of back-away in her, but all she could do was punch her muzzled nose into the side of the dog towering over her, and all that did was get another snarl and a single precise bite in the same place as the other ones.

Shackle the new dog to the old dog, said Brand. Teaches them how to be. Won't take long till she's broken to our ways.

Seeing the pain and confusion in Jess's eyes was worse than the image I'd created in my head, the one of her drowning alone. She stared right at me and the question in her look—why aren't you helping me?—could only be answered one way and my body was answering before my brain knew what it was going to do. I lunged to my feet and tried to get to her and then Brand stepped forward between us and straight-armed me in the chest with the open palm of his hand which hurt bad and winded me worse. It knocked me back so that I stumbled wildly to keep my balance, suddenly aware that without my hands to help me I could easily dash my brains out on the hard church floor.

As if he realised this, Brand jumped forwards and caught hold of my sheepskin. For an instant, we were eye to eye and I thought about hitting him in the face with my forehead, but then Jess yelp-snarled and tried to lunge at him, defending me, and Saga bit her again and then turned and ran, dragging Jess out of the building.

Again, Jess's instincts were better than mine, and again it was the worst thing I'd seen, Saga just yanking her alongside her like a broken limb.

Brand sat me on one of the chairs. Then he shouldered his pack and picked up a long case that I guess held the violin and his other self.

Breaking her doesn't mean she'll be damaged permanently, he said. Just means getting her head right, knowing who to be loyal to now. And don't fret. I'll be good to her while I keep her. She's full of piss and vinegar, same as you. I like that in a dog.

The cloud came back over his face.

Doesn't mean I want to see it in you. In fact I don't want to see *you* at all. Ever again. Because if I do, young Griz, if I do, things will go badly and there may be some dying to be done. So you stay in here until the sun's full up and I'm over the horizon.

He pointed with his chin.

You just find your way home and stay there. World's not what you think it is, but that needn't bother you out there on the edge of it. It is empty enough though, so don't you go looking for me. Once I'm gone, I'm gone.

You stole my dog, I said.

That all you can say? he sighed. Doesn't get better the more you say it.

And with a half-wave and the ghost of his earlier smile he turned and walked out of the room, leaving me alone with the chairs, the mouldering pile of books and a fire I could not be bothered to work on. Instead I got up and walked around the church looking for something to get the rope cut.

There was a glint of metal behind the altar table, but it was just a cross on a stand and the metal had no edge sharp enough to help. I tried rubbing the rope against the corner of the altar but the stone was too dull and the rope too tough to get it done.

And then I got angry again and found I was standing in the door looking towards where the boat had been moored and looking at nothing but water. I decided there and then that if I couldn't see him then he couldn't see me and so I went out of the church and looked for the graveyard. It wasn't as overgrown as I thought it might be, and the reason was obvious, though it gave me a shock when I first saw the sheep move out of the corner of my eye and thought it was Saga. There were wild sheep on the island and three ewes and a ram watched me suspiciously as I walked carefully into the garden of gravestones. It was a smaller graveyard than I expected, but then it was a small island and what buildings remained intact apart from the church wouldn't have supported a big population.

The stones were all rectangular and weathered and I didn't bother to read names as I usually did when walking past grave-markers on the Uists. I just made my way to the one different grave which was a round boulder, not shaped by anyone.

There was writing carved into it, writing that told me I was standing on the grave of someone who had been called Smith. My knife was in the grass in the shadow of the boulder, and I used Mr. Smith's stone to carefully sit on, and slid down so my hands could find the knife behind me. Then I used it again to lever myself upright. I said a silent thank you because even though ghosts aren't real and when you're dead you stay that way, it seemed the polite thing to do.

I returned to the church and very carefully backed up to its thick wooden door, pressing the tip of the knife into the grain as hard as I could. Then I carefully put my wrists on either side of the blade and began to saw.

The knife fell out twice and I had to awkwardly pick it up and stick it back in before I got my hands free. And when they were my own again I gave a yelp and ran to the top of the slope that crested the island to check on the *Sweethope*.

It was gone.

He hadn't taken it in tow, because I could see his red sails in the distance, but he must have cut the anchors loose. Maybe in retaliation for my locking up his anchor chain. I saw the

Sweethope closer in, but still too far to swim for. And it was moving away on the drift of the tide.

My heart began to hammer again, but I was not too worried as I ran back down the slope to the other side of the island where the kayak was. I could move fast when I paddled, faster than the tide, and though it would be a long pull I knew I could reach the boat.

And I had to. Not just because it was my boat. But because Jip was locked below. If the boat got away from me, he would slowly starve and die of thirst. Alone. And believing he had been forgotten.

That thought made me run faster, which was a mistake because I fell and twisted my ankle and then had to hobble the last hundred yards.

Brand had found my kayak. And he'd been annoyed by it. The paddle lay snapped on the shoreline, as if he'd thrown it in the water which had then floated the parts back to shore. He'd also stamped through the kayak, putting a foot-sized hole in the top covering about where my knees were.

I cursed and turned the kayak over to look at the hull. And then I breathed a deep sigh of relief. You could see where his foot had smashed the bottom of the boat against the rocks, but it had not made a hole.

My heart was thumping badly and my hands were trying to move too fast and I fumbled and dropped the bow as I slid it out of the kayak. I left it on the ground and retrieved the broken paddle. Again I was moving too fast and nearly sliced my thumb open as I cut the mooring rope that was coiled in the bottom of the boat and used it to start lashing my bow as a splint between the two broken parts. My fingers seemed to have forgotten how to tie the right knots as the anchor knot kept slipping loose and making the whole lashing come loose.

I closed my eyes and made myself count twenty very slow elephants. Then I cinched the beginning of the lashing so tight it hurt my hands as I kept the tension on, and wrapped the bow into the paddle. I took extra care with the finishing knot, and then tested the repaired paddle. It felt clunky in my hands but solid.

I didn't waste time looking back at that church; I just gritted my teeth, told myself I was fine and not hungry or thirsty or hurting in all the wrong places, and dug in.

I paddled around the point and scanned the sea ahead of me. No sign of the red sails, which was not such a bad thing, but also no sign of the *Sweethope*. Which was. I began to feel that rising panic again and looked around to get my bearings, trying to work out where I'd stood on the hillock that divided the island, and then remember the rough direction the boat had been drifting.

As I did so, I realised that one reason I maybe couldn't see the *Sweethope* was that I had been looking from a higher angle on land, whereas now I was sitting at sea level. And then again the sails were down which made it harder still to spot.

It's almost impossible to stand up in a kayak, but I did. Very, very carefully. And then I saw the mast, and then the hull, and then as I sat down I realised I could still see them both. It was as if the panic had blinded me. Like I thought I'd lost them, so I did lose them.

The wind was getting stronger and blowing with the tide, which I didn't like. I fixed my eye on the *Sweethope* and began the chase into the choppier waters between the bigger island and the mainland beyond. I kept an eye on the hills in the far distance and made a point of keeping track of the direction the *Sweethope* was drifting by using them as markers. I decided if the gap between us lengthened because of wind or my arms tiring I should still be able to find the boat by keeping on its bearing.

When I made the plan, I felt it was one of the ones you make for luck but you're never going to need. Maybe an hour later I seemed no closer and my arms were shaking and my shoulder sockets seemed to have grit in them.

Then a sudden squall blew in from over my shoulder and I took my eye off the boat to look at the hole in the kayak top, wondering if the rain would fill the hull. I decided maybe I should take off my sheepskin and stuff it down there to prevent water getting in, and then when I looked up I couldn't see either the *Sweethope* or the mountains beyond.

I decided once more not to panic.

But I did want to.

Instead I closed my eyes and concentrated on feeling the kayak and the current.

If you paddle in open water, there's always a tension between you, the sea and the boat. You want to go to A, the sea's pulling you towards B and your body feels the tension between those two destinations with every stroke as it fights B and angles the kayak towards A. I'd been paddling hard for more than an hour, maybe two even, and without noticing it my body had got into a habit and a feeling. I concentrated on getting that tension back—recreating the pull of the water and the balancing pressure as I pushed the kayak where I wanted it to go.

I was literally paddling blind.

It was like a game I used to play on the big wide beaches on Uist: close your eyes and see how far you could walk before you opened them. On the hard-packed sand, it was a matter of counting steps and feeling the slope of the beach so you didn't veer into the shallows. It was always easy to start with and then you began to wonder if there was some treacherous loop of seaweed or piece of drift-garbage that was going to trip you at your next step. Eventually, a kind of horizontal vertigo would grip me and I'd open my eyes to find the beach clear ahead and all the snares only in my mind.

I counted to a hundred, then another and then halfway to the next hundred I felt the rain stop and I opened my eyes and there was the *Sweethope*, almost dead ahead. I grinned and felt good. Then I realised it was much closer than I'd expected and felt even better. And then I heard a distant barking, and felt worse as my thinking brain caught up with my excitement.

The *Sweethope* was turning slowly, and the reason it was closer than I had expected was that it was caught on a skerry. Shallow banks of sharp-toothed rocks are common around the islands, lurking just below the water, ready to rip the bottom out of any boat too blind to see them. As the *Sweethope* continued to yaw around, it revealed a lick of white in the water behind it where one of the treacherous outcrops was just breaking the surface.

Fear surged through my shaking arms and gave a boost of energy I didn't know was still in me. The barking got high-pitched and urgent as I approached, and that helped too.

When I was about a hundred yards out—and just beginning to think everything was going to be all right—there was a cracking noise and the boat slewed drunkenly in the opposite direction to the one it had been going. The current had twisted it off one rock and snagged it on the next one. I had visions of the scene inside the cabin if the hull were holed and that noise meant water was now gushing in, and I started shouting and whistling so that Jip would know help was on the way.

Brand had been in a hurry to get going, and so had only

cut the anchor ropes in order to set my boat adrift. They were whipping the side of the hull in the freshening breeze, and I snapped my hand out and caught the flailing end of one and used it to pull myself alongside. I shouted to Jip and banged the boat and as his barks mounted in excitement I threw my paddle into the cockpit and awkwardly scrambled aboard, almost losing the kayak as I did so, and then as I sprawled to keep hold, I nearly fell back into the water myself.

It's okay, Jip! I shouted. It's okay.

But it wasn't. Even as I manhandled the kayak over the taffrail, I could feel the keel grinding on the rocks below. I wondered whether I should lash the kayak down as I always did, or if I should leave it ready for a quick exit if the boat was holed and started to sink. Habit won and I tied it off with a quick-release knot, jumped down into the cockpit and tore open the cabin hatch. Jip hit me like a furry cannonball, jumping up, tail thumping away as his paws scrabbled at me, yelping and barking happily. Like all terriers, he wasn't usually a soppy dog but he had clearly been scared by his confinement and the absence of a familiar person as the boat had swept away on its own.

Sorry, boy, sorry, I said and hugged him to me.

I allowed myself to bury my face in his fur while he licked away at my neck for a long moment. I think we both needed the physical contact with something familiar, something that loved us.

Then the boat lurched and I pushed him away and ducked into the cabin. I really needed to see if we were taking on water. A quick check seemed to show the hull was intact. The floor was dry all the way to the bow compartment. That was good news. But the grinding noise was worse below deck, where it had an added resonance that came through the soles of my boots. This close to, there was an ominous creaking undertone below it, like something was bending under the boat. I thought it was the keel and that it might be jammed in a crack in the rocks. It seemed to me there was every chance it might snap off or rip straight out of the bottom of the boat. Jip was standing in the hatchway looking at me, panting.

I grabbed the old saucepan we used as bailer and dog bowl and filled it from the canteen. He scrabbled down the steps and lapped the clean water greedily. I told him I'd feed him later and stepped up into the cockpit, ducking below the boom and looking over the side opposite the tide, trying to see exactly what we were stuck on.

It wasn't rocks. I think if it had been rocks then maybe the waves would have smashed the *Sweethope* more than they did. What the boat was stuck on was a moveable object, itself drifting with the tide. At first I thought it was a boat, half sunk and drifting below the surface, but its sides and angles were all flat and right-angled. Then I realised it was a big metal shipping box, the size of a small house. There was one of them on Eriskay, mostly rusted out, on a wheeled trailer by the causeway. The majority of the paint on this one had gone and it had a thick beard of barnacles and seaweed dangling off its wrapping, which was a tangle of nylon fishing net. I crossed to the other side of the cockpit and saw the net was snarled round a second metal box floating end-on, nose down in the water. The first box must have had air trapped in it, making it more buoyant. It seemed like the keel of the boat was wedged in the gap between them. Because the boat was above water, the wind was trying to make it move faster than the current that was moving the boxes below, and that was what was twisting the keel.

I was going to have to cut the netting. And there was a lot of it. And the wind was getting up. So I was actually going to have to get it done before the keel snapped off. If the keel went, the bottom could rip out of the boat, or the boat could just capsize.

With the boathook and my knife, I set to work. I hooked the tangle of netting and pulled it to the surface and just started sawing at it. I didn't have a plan of attack to begin with, but as I worked the twist of the current and the movement of the boat kept it taut and I was able to cut down the same row, strand after strand. The plastic your people made was strong stuff. We find so much of it now—I wonder if it will outlast us entirely. The netting bit back as I cut it. Sharp strands parted suddenly and scratched at the back of my hands as I worked the knife, and the palm of my right hand got blisters which then burst and stung in the salt water.

I don't remember much from that afternoon, because it was gruelling, repetitive work and my side hurt from lying on the deck and leaning out over the water, and my back hurt from being bent over the gunwale all the time. I do remember stopping for water and making a lanyard for the knife because my grip was so painful I was worried about dropping it into the sea, and I do remember doing exactly that several times as the light began to dim all around, each time yanking it back up out of the depths and carrying on sawing away at the hard plastic strands. I also remember how the net suddenly untwisted at one point, slashing the side of my arm with a garland of sharp-edged shellfish that had colonised it. I've still got those two scars. And then—maybe because the part of the net that had been closest to the sunlight had rotted more than the strands I had started on—the thing suddenly came apart, and the heavier, nose-down cargo box dropped into the depths. Because it was already underwater, there was no noise and it was a strangely final but undramatic moment as it disappeared. The other one was more lively—freed of the counterweight, the air trapped in it bounced it higher in the water and though I moved fast, it still took skin off the back of my forearm as the rough tidemark of barnacles rasped across it. I swore and pulled back onto the boat.

The floating container rolled slowly on the surface like a lazy whale showing its belly to the sky, and then began to drift away as if it had never meant us any harm at all.

Cut loose, the *Sweethope* immediately felt different under my back. It bucked more in the chop—suddenly frisky—as if it really wanted to get moving again. And though I wanted to lie there and sleep for a while, I knew the boat was right and I had to get sails up and find somewhere to moor for the night.

Again, I have little memory of the rest of the afternoon, except I know I got the sails up and caught the wind and that Jip reminded me to feed him. And I know that the boat steered a bit differently to the way it always had, but I put that to the back of my mind. And most of all I remember that though I had the strongest heart-tug to turn her north and head home, I headed south-east, for the mainland. At the time I thought it was because it was close now, and so provided the best chance of a safe anchorage. Now I think I always knew I wasn't going to give up on getting Jess back. And then again, I had never once set foot on the mainland itself. Curiosity, you see. It doesn't just kill cats.

Chapter 11

Tilting at giants

I didn't find a great place to moor, but the thin scrape of cove I did find was protected enough for a mild night. It was just luck that I still had Ferg's anchor on board that I'd spent the day rescuing before Brand sailed into our lives, because without it I'd have been in trouble, the others still being on the sea bed to the west of Iona. I took that as a good omen and felt a little better as I made sure of my knots and dropped it over the side and waited anxiously until I was sure it had bitten into the bottom and was holding us steady. Then I went below and lit the lamp and did the two things I had been wanting to do all day. I ate some of the oatcakes and wind-dried mutton I'd grabbed from the kitchen at home, and I reached into my jerkin and took out the map I'd stolen from Brand's boat and spread it out on the table.

Jip jumped up on the bench next to me and curled up with his chin on my thigh as I examined it. When he did that back at home, Jess would often take up a similar position on my other side, so that I was bookended by my dogs as I read. As I scratched his ears, my other hand automatically reached for hers before my brain told it she wasn't there. It gave me a bit of a lurch, and so I concentrated on what was in front of me instead: it was a map of the mainland. It was printed on both sides, the top half on one, the bottom on the other. The land bits were crowded with place names and printed lines showing roads in different colours. The clear sea around it was covered in handwritten notes and numbers, none of which made much sense to me. What I only noticed when I flipped it over was that the lamplight winked through lots of tiny holes pricked all over it. The holes seemed to be random until I flipped the map back over and saw the pattern that made sense of it: the pinpricks matched places on the coast on each side, which of course meant that half of them appeared to be scattered randomly across dry land if you looked at them on the wrong side of the paper. I thought of the sharp set of dividers I'd jagged myself with in the dark. This was a map of where he'd been or where he was going—or both.

Most interesting of all, there was a multiple speckling of holes in one specific area. It was in the middle of the sea on one side of the map, but on the other it nestled right above what I had as a child—when I thought the mainland looked a bit like someone sitting down, seen from the side—thought of as the country's bottom. There was nowhere else with that concentration of holes, and nowhere else with so many different coloured pencil lines radiating from it. When I looked closer and read the word *Norfolk* printed across the land next to it I felt a little jump of excitement. He had said he'd been raised on the Norfolk Broads.

I remembered his words when he was trying to apologise for saying he was going to cut out my tongue. He'd said when you tell a lie it's always better to put a grain of truth in it to make it stick. I decided he'd salted the lie of his life story with a grain of truth. And Norfolk was that grain. The lie was about having left it and never gone back there. Maybe I wanted to believe something to make sense of trying to find him, maybe I needed that excuse to go exploring. I've had time to wonder about that, and I think that's true. But then I just knew—again maybe because I had to know something to stop me drifting off anchorless and rudderless—that those holes were his home. The place where he was taking my dog.

I fell asleep on the bench with Jip at my side, and I slept well despite everything. My body was exhausted but my mind—having made a decision—was calm enough to let me sleep long and deep.

The nearest hole in the map—the first a pencil line went to—was a city a long way south of where I was. Blackpool. When I woke, I again had that tug to go home, but the wind was from the north and Jip was on the prow with his back to it, as if he knew where Jess was going, and so we followed.

That journey is a blur to me now. I knew little of navigating by a map, because all my life I had sailed a small chain of islands by sight, never venturing beyond a seascape I knew. But I could read a compass and knew where the sun rose and set and with the map now pinned to the table in the cabin I thought I could feel my way down the coast, and feel is what I did, in more ways than one.

I still hadn't set foot on the mainland, remember, but the further I got from home the more it crowded in on my left shoulder, like a presence that was watching us, waiting for me to look squarely at it and notice how irresistibly it was beckoning me. It was like the dark pull of a magnet, always there. Always invisible. Impossible to ignore.

If I'd had sea charts and not a map of the roads crisscrossing the once crowded land, I probably would have kept my bearings better. Two days of fast running slipped past. I spent a night at the tip of a wide firth that cut back north around a big island and led beyond that, I think, to the river that Mum and Dad had gone up a lifetime ago to collect the *Sweethope*, the one where they had slept in the library and closed up the doors as they left to save the books. Again, I felt a tug to go and see that, and I nearly did but Jip was on the bow looking south again and so we followed his nose instead.

Passing houses and small villages on the shore was odder than doing the same thing on the familiar islands. There I knew every house was empty. I found myself less sure of it the more houses I saw. Some of the buildings still had unbroken glass in the windows, even after all these years of neglect, and they would wink the thin sunlight back at us as we passed. Every time that happened, I had the strangest feeling that they were trying to get my attention. I could often feel the hairs going up on the back of my neck as we went on, as if they were doing something behind me. Like laughing. Like they knew I was making a big mistake.

On your own it's easy to let unsettling thoughts like that get under your skin. Did you—in your crowded world—have those kind of quiet moments where your own mind had room enough to stalk you and play games? Or were there too many other people to let you hear the songs it wanted to sing to you—the bad ones as well as the good ones? I still had no idea how full of others your world was at this stage, not having begun to walk the remains of it, but I felt the loneliness it now radiated sharply enough to take the picture of you out of my rucksack—where it lived as a bookmark in whatever book went with me—and pinned it to the map, maybe so I had some company other than Jip. I had no pictures of my family, so you had to do the job for them, I suppose. Just having another human face to look at helped.

Because some of the sailing was monotonous and the mind likes to drift, I found myself jolting out of a daydream on more than one occasion convinced that I'd dropped my guard and that the feeling of being watched was more than real, that it was some sixth sense telling me that Brand was out there. He was hidden against the dark land mass, stalking me, instead of the other way around. When that happened, I'd scan wildly about me, raking the sea and the mainland shore for a sign of him. But he was never really there, not where I could see him. He was only in my mind.

Jip's day was always the same. Wake, stand on the bow until we got underway, then sit in the cockpit by me, with breaks for eating and shitting and pissing. He was suitably embarrassed about these last two things, which he normally disliked doing while anyone was watching, but we made a deal where I pretended not to notice while he was doing it and then he pretended he couldn't see me sluicing the piss away with seawater or flipping the turds over the side with the rusty trowel I kept on the boat for just such embarrassing moments. I went over the side, taking care to keep the wind behind me, pissing or crapping, and Jip studiously ignored my contortions in his turn.

The cuts and scrapes on my arm from the shellfish weren't healing as fast as I would have liked, which I put down to the salt in the seawater and the constant spray off the waves. When I covered them with sleeves it was worse, so I kept them bare and hoped the air would eventually dry them out and let them scab over. I thought the clean seawater would at least stop them getting infected. It certainly stung like it was doing something.

Halfway between a big island that I thought might be the Isle of Man and the mainland, I found a strange sight. There was a tilted forest of broken windmills like the ones on the islands back home, except these ones were in the middle of the sea. When I first saw them I couldn't think what they were. I remembered that story about the old Spanish man who thought he was a knight in armour and that windmills were giants and went off to fight them on an equally old and bony horse. Except these weather-bleached windmills looked more like the bony horse. Maybe like giants' skeletons—with the occasional unbroken propeller blade jutting into the air like a sword.

I sailed close to this forest of metal tubes and slackened sail so I could drift past it and look up at them towering above me. It was a strange, quiet moment as the sun bounced off them while we passed through the tiger-stripe shadows they cast across the sea all around us.

Jip barked at some of them. They didn't seem to mind.

Whatever they might have been defending, if they really had been the giants of my imagination, was long gone, but in my mind now they still stand as gatekeepers, because after I had passed them a whole new world of wonders began to unfold.

When I turned away from them to look at the mainland, I saw something that made me tighten the sails and tack towards it. A huge tower jutted above the biggest scrabble of houses and buildings I had ever seen. A city, I thought. This is what a city looks like.

As I got closer, the sun was already dipping low in the west and the light did that thing of reddening everything it fell on, giving the world a golden glow. The tower was made of metal and looked a bit like the one I'd seen pictures of in Paris. But the one in Paris did not rise out of the roof of a brick palace like this one did. As soon as I saw it, I knew I was going to climb it, just to see what the world looked like from up there. Just to see what a bird sees.

You probably wouldn't have been so excited by a tower. You had aeroplanes after all. And helicopters. For me, it was the closest I would ever get to flying. You also would have known that this wasn't a city either. Just a town.

It was high tide. A long metal fence stretched away in front of the buildings sticking out of the water, and lamp posts and flagpoles jagged into the air all the way along behind it, their feet in the water too, some of them leaning drunkenly like the windmills behind me, but most of them more or less upright.

A big jetty stuck out into the sea and I thought I would sail there and tie up to it. When I got closer in, I realised it had once had buildings on top and a deck that had all been gutted by a fire. There was some kind of giant metal wheel that hung bent and melted off the side of the jetty half underwater. I took real care drifting in beside it in case there was debris just below the surface, but there wasn't, and I tied off to a stanchion that seemed to have enough metal in it beneath the flakes of rust to hold.

And then, after all my excitement about finally putting my feet on the mysterious mainland—I didn't.

I sat on the side of the boat with Jip and looked at it all and tried to make sense of it.

The sea lapped the front of the buildings behind the sunken fence rails. That wasn't too surprising. I knew the sea level had been rising for years. Maybe if the Gelding hadn't happened they'd have built a wall to protect the city, I thought. Now the buildings on the front were themselves that wall. I let my eyes travel along it, wondering what it had looked like when those doors let in all sorts of different people instead of just the sea. Some of the frontages had had letters on them, but they were mostly gone or illegible, and those that remained made up nonsense sentences—_ALLROOM _UNHOUSE! COM_DY __USE_EN__! _OAT _RIPS _AS_NO __ACH _OURS I__ _REAM _INGO! _ROUPS WE_COME.

I read them out loud to Jip. He didn't seem to be able to make sense of them either.

About half a mile down the front was another crazily melted assembly of criss-crossed metal that seemed a bit like the giant wheel beside me. It ran round the perimeter of a group of other structures that I could make no sense of, dipping and swooping and loop-the-looping as it went. It wasn't as high as the tower, but it was very tall at the top. I wondered what kind of thing needed a giant fence like that. The wind that always comes off the sea as the sun dips whickered at my neck. I pulled the sheepskin tighter around me. Away in the distance something screeched. It might have been a bird.

Tomorrow, Jip, I said. We'll go ashore tomorrow. In the light.

Chapter 12

Landfall

I didn't remember and the bowstring didn't care.

The arrow took the big rabbit just forward of where I was aiming at the shoulder and smashed through the neck bone, killing it instantly. It was a good shot but I wasn't congratulating myself. I'd forgotten that the cuts and grazes on my forearm still weren't healing properly so instead I was swearing and holding my arm where the loosed string had ripped at the scabs and salt blisters as it passed, raking it raw and painful again.

Later I'd skin the rabbit before cooking it, but right then it felt like I was the one having a taste of being flayed.

The big rabbit wasn't a rabbit when I got to it. I think it was a hare, and if I'm wrong about it, it's the kind of rabbit I've been calling a hare ever since—longer ears and much more powerful legs. I've only managed to shoot a couple other than that first one as they're harder to catch unawares than normal rabbits. Maybe longer ears hear better. Jip has run his heart to bursting trying to catch a lot of them but never managed to kill one for himself, which he takes as a personal affront.

Every time he's gaining on a hare, it notices and boosts for the horizon, or maybe they like teasing terriers, because they have an extra kick of speed that they can turn on whenever they like.

I now knew the structure that I'd seen the night before was not a giant fence but a rollercoaster because when I got into the shadow of it there was an old sign saying what it was, and though it was blistered and corroded it was still readable. And I knew what a rollercoaster was because I had seen them in a book about American holidays. They had carriages you sat in which whizzed you up and down and people put their hands in the air on the down bits and screamed. I mean, in the picture they were smiling and shouting, but the words said everybody screamed in excitement.

Nobody was screaming now. The place was quiet apart from the creaks and clanks the wind teased out of the old metalwork and the rotting buildings beneath.

I had thought we would climb the tower first, once we came ashore, but when the sun came up the tide had gone back out to sea and the *Sweethope*'s keel was scraping the sand below. Worried that if the tide went further out it might snap, I threw out the anchor and loosened the lines attaching it to the jetty so it could float a little freer. Then I took my rucksack and my bow and arrows and climbed carefully along the side of the jetty towards the shore. I had the map folded into the pack too, because I thought if I climbed the tower it would help me get my bearings if I compared what I saw with it. Taking the pack wasn't anything special, though as it turned out it was a lifesaver. It's just how we were. We carried our own water, packed our own food and always kept the basics to light a fire or tend a wound close by. No one else was going to help us if we got into trouble. It was just second nature. I also had two of the big plastic water bottles looped round my neck to fill up at the first opportunity.

Fresh water and food, those were always the priorities on any trip, but on this day I had thought to break habit and celebrate my first steps on the mainland by climbing the tower and looking out over it. Jip had other ideas, and wouldn't be carried easily. Negotiating the skeleton of the jetty was tricky enough with pack and bow and two water bowsers clunking round my neck, so I dropped him in the water and he swam happily to shore under his own power.

The retreating sea had left the strip of ground in front of the houses standing a few feet above the waterline. Wet sand spilled into the open doors and windows, and the half-buried hulks of old cars were scattered along the whole length of the sea front. Some were just humped roofs, lurking like giant beetles; others had been tossed by the storms and were showing rotted wheels and rusting axles to the sky. Jip walked out of the water, shook himself, looked back at me, wagged his tail and turned to sniff his way into this whole new world of unfamiliar and exciting smells.

I followed him ashore with a little more difficulty. The jetty had been gutted by fire and I had to test my footing every step of the way to dry land. When I took the last—or maybe that's the first—step onto it, I dropped the water bowsers and looked about me. The tower dominated the skyline to my left. The palace it grew out of was not golden in the morning light but red-bricked. It seemed vast. Until then the biggest building I had been in was that church where Brand had played the violin. This palace building was many churches big. Jip had, however, followed his nose to the right, down the sea front, towards the rollercoaster. Though at that point in my mind it was of course still a mysteriously giant fence. I took out an arrow and fitted it to the bowstring in case we startled a rabbit, again out of habit, and followed. It wasn't really a hunt because I couldn't keep my mind on it. There was too much distraction. The place had a funny smell, not a bad one, but a bonfire, charred smell. I decided it must be the jetty, though the smell stayed all the way down the front as I looked into the broken windows and up at the bits of old signs that hinted cryptically at what the different buildings had been for. On closer inspection OAT RIPS were offering boat trips and the suggestion to USE EN was actually amusements—the big sand-floored room with the low ceiling bellying ominously down over it didn't look that amusing, though the rows of corroding, burst machine cabinets jammed in beneath had wild cartoony drawings on them that had once clearly been brighter and more colourful than they now were.

There were no footprints on the sand other than mine behind me, only paw prints that Jip had made ahead, and I followed him towards the looming jumble of structures surrounded by the rollercoaster.

We both stopped by the open doors of the _AS_NO which other smaller signs explained was a casino. I knew what that was too, and wanted to see what a place where people had come to be glamorous and lose their money looked like, but there was a smell of something powerfully dead in the lobby. Jip turned away from it and again, I followed him back out into the clean air. Things die and things rot. And you don't always have to go poking at them.

The enclosure that the rollercoaster ran around was a Pleasure Beach, and there was more sand on the ground to prove it. There was also a wall with a huge skull wearing a Viking helmet three times the height of me snarling a warning at us as we approached. It was probably funny to your people. And I knew that. But to me it seemed a grim snaggle-toothed presence, full of real malice. The Pleasure Beach was a strange village full of grotesque things like that skull. There were oozy-looking gingerbread houses built purposely askew to loom alarmingly over you. There were all manner of metal cages and decaying machines—most with once bright but now weather-bleached plastic seats hanging off the end of them, things presumably meant to hurl people around, though that looked like it'd be torture and not pleasure at all. There was a lot of broken glass and so I trod carefully. Moving so slowly let me creep up on an animal I hadn't seen before, and I nearly put an arrow through it until I realised it was a half-buried teddy bear.

I saw a pair of giant birds like ostriches standing very still among some greenery and though I quickly realised they were made of plastic I still nearly jumped clean out of my skin when I looked slightly to my right and saw a giant lizard the size of a horse crouching amongst some ratty shrubs, watching me with an evil look on its face, showing just enough teeth to promise a nasty end if it leapt for me. I instantly went very cold and still. Jip walked up to it and cocked his leg on its tail. It was only then I saw that it was just another statue, made of concrete. The look Jip gave me seemed to say "so much for dinosaurs".

It hadn't been real. Of course not. Dinosaurs are even deader than you are. But the shock it had given me was. I walked over to the base of the giant tangled-looking fence where there was more light, and that was where I found the sign that explained that it was a rollercoaster, and it was while I was reading it that I felt Jip go hunting-still beside me, and that was when we saw the hare lollop out of the bushes and pause to twitch its nose towards the sea.

Once I'd shot it and hung it off my pack, Jip got very

interested in following its scent trail back into the undergrowth that had invaded this corner of the Pleasure Beach, while I climbed the rollercoaster. To start with, I only meant to go a few feet above ground to see if I could watch his progress, but it was sturdy and didn't move at all as I went higher, so I kept going. I climbed onto the track and walked very carefully up the thin footplates that made a flight of steps alongside it. Probably not the most sensible thing I could have done, but I always kept a hand on the rail. Things built sturdily in the old world have had a long time to start coming to pieces again in the After, and I did not want to end my adventure by falling through something broken. And yes, it was an adventure. I was still determined to get Jess back, but even though that fierceness was in me, I was also excited to finally be putting my hands and my feet and my eyes on a world I had only read or heard old unreliable stories about. And the higher I climbed, the more I felt that streak in me begin to open up and breathe better in the newer, cleaner air. It came to me that I hadn't known I had been being less than I could have been until then, when I saw there was so much more of the world for me to be myself within.

There was a carriage parked on the very top of the rollercoaster. If there hadn't been, I might have turned back before I got there. I don't think that would have made a difference, but it might have. As it was, I looked up at it and thought it would be good to get to it and sit there and rest a moment, looking out at the view opening up before me.

Jip was back at the base of the rollercoaster, barking up at me, eager I should see the rabbit he had lying on the sand in front of him. I waved and told him I'd be down in a minute. The wind had picked up again, and the sky was darkening, but I was really concentrating on looking at the step in front of me and then the next one. I didn't need to look at the clouds gathering behind me; I could feel there was a good chance of rain coming, smell it even. I'd just sit at the top and rest a moment, then come down before it started. Mainly I was trying not to look down, because then my balance wavered a bit and I felt queasy. Like being seasick on solid ground.

I got to the top and that's where I found him. Slumped on the floor of the carriage, a rattle of old bones themselves weathering away to powder in the rags of what had once been his clothes, strands of long grey hair coiled like a nest by the skull. There was one rubber boot, cracked and perished with a leg bone still in it, and a backpack. The pack was thick plastic, black and with a roll top. The straps were gone but the pack itself had been designed to be very waterproof. Maybe because it had been stuffed under the seat and was protected from the worst of the weather it seemed to have survived with its contents inside.

There was also a gun on the floor among the bones.

The weather had rusted it into a useless lump, but it was there. So were the holes in the skull. Small one in the bottom of the brain pan where the muzzle would have pressed against the top of the mouth, and a big chunk blasted through the scalp. It told a sad but clear story. He'd climbed up here for a last view of the world and then blown himself out of it.

I told the bones I was sorry, and then opened the pack. It cracked stiffly as I did so, and then I saw I was wrong. It was full of photographs, a lifetime of pictures—but on top of them was a lipstick and pots of make-up and a small mirror and a hairbrush. There was also a sort of metal urn, which I thought might have something interesting in.

I opened it and found it didn't. It just had ashes inside, grey and gritty. I could understand why this woman would have decided to die with her best face on, looking good for whatever came next. There was a sort of defiance in it that I could admire. But I didn't know why she would have climbed all this way carrying something as meaningless as an urn full of ashes. I hefted the canister. It wasn't light. And she must have been old, from the grey hairs she'd left behind. I don't think I'd have made better sense of it if I'd had time to sit there and think about it, but I didn't even have that luxury.

Something made me look behind myself, back up the mile of beachfront to the tower. Even at this distance and from this height you could see how much taller it was than the rollercoaster. It seemed to be almost touching the grey clouds closing in above it. It was only dwarfed by the black cloud rising off the sea below it.

Except it wasn't a black cloud. It was smoke. And at its base was a fire, and the fire was the *Sweethope*.

I should have run down the steps, except I could see that in the time it took me to run the mile back to the jetty it would be too late, way too late. I sat down and stared at the disaster.

Because that feeling I'd had about being watched? Maybe some of it was imagination. But one part of it had been real. I'd come looking for Brand. But he'd found me.

I couldn't see him. I couldn't see his boat. I couldn't even see where on the wide, exposed stretch of coast sweeping north to the point it might be. There was nowhere for him to hide it. Unless there was an inlet behind the point. I couldn't see his damned dog Saga, and I couldn't see Jess.

All I could hear was Jip's bark getting more urgent as if he sensed what he could not possibly—from where he stood—see.

Scratched in the sand by the jetty end was a message. Big enough for me to read even a mile away, clear beneath the smoke pluming off the funeral pyre of my boat.

I TOLD YOU, GRIZ. GO HOME.

Chapter 13

The tower

Six words in the sand proved that Brand could write. But I don't think he'd read the same books as me. If he had, he still might well have stolen my dog, but he wouldn't have burned my boat.

That's what I think now, after all that's happened. Then, sitting in shock at the top of the rollercoaster, watching the *Sweethope* burn, I just felt numb. And guilty. And scared too, of course. I had done a stupid thing—a chain of stupid things—and this was the result. I hadn't thought it out. I'd rushed off without preparation, on my own, despite my dad trying to stop me. I hadn't listened to him. I hadn't listened to anything but my heart and my anger and I hadn't used my head. Most of all I was stupid because I hadn't used my head. And now Bar and Ferg and Dad would think I was dead for a long time because a long time is what it would take me to get back home without my boat. Even Mum would notice I was not beside her in the evenings. I was sure about that. At some level she would notice I was gone. And what if they came looking for me? How would they find me? How could we *not* miss each other in this huge world? They might come to harm just searching for me. Home might just fall apart. It was all my fault. Dad had been right, all the times he called me wilful and headstrong. Brand had just stolen a dog and some fish. Brand was just one of those bad things that life throws at you, like a storm or a sickness. A Brand was just something you toughened up and coped with. You couldn't argue with a storm or a fever. It didn't know any better. It just was.

Me? I knew better. And I'd betrayed everything.

If there was ever a moment to cry, that was it. And I wanted to. I felt the sharp spike of tears wanting to come. My throat was tight with the sobs waiting to be set free. No one would ever know. The old lady on the floor beside me wouldn't. She wouldn't hear. She wouldn't see. She was just bones, eyes and ears long gone. But I didn't cry. Maybe because *I* would have known. Maybe because Dad was right and I am too stubborn for sense. But mainly I think because it wouldn't have done any good. The milk was already spilt.

I took less care clattering down the steps of the rollercoaster than I had going up, but still enough not to run and risk tripping and injuring myself. When I got to the bottom, Jip pretended he was more interested in eating the rabbit he'd caught until I hoisted my pack and picked up my bow, and then he picked it up and ran with me as I headed back to the jetty. Maybe I should have been more careful. Maybe I should have worried that Brand might have set the fire to lure me back so he could ambush me or something. But the thing about maybes is that you can get lost in them and end up going nowhere. I needed to be doing.

And I knew, though I don't know how, that he was gone. If he'd been setting a trap, he wouldn't have needed to write the words he had left for me to find. Still, I kept scanning the scene ahead for a glimpse of his red hair as I thumped my way up the mile of hardpack back towards the jetty. But he was long gone. He'd left the message. He didn't need to stick around to tell it to me himself.

He'd also left my kayak.

That surprised me. That stopped me short when I got up to it. That almost undid the whole not crying thing. That kayak was as much part of me and home as the *Sweethope* had been. It was lying on the sand below the words he'd written, and the mended paddle was leaning across it.

It was another message. He was saying he wasn't a monster. That always seemed important to him. And maybe in his own mind he wasn't. I guess no one's the monster in their own story. Monsters are just a matter of perspective.

The *Sweethope* was burned to the waterline but still belching black smoke, a dead boat still floating. Sails torched, rigging gone. Unsalvageable. The fire had burned the ropes mooring it to the jetty but it had swung in and got snarled up in the great melted tangle of the fallen wheel. He must have used something to set the fire in the cabin and then just walked away. From the burned rubber smell and the persistent black smoke, maybe a tyre. We burned brittle old rubber tyres to send smoke signals in emergencies. The thought made me doubly homesick.

I sat and stared at the dead boat for a long time. I don't know how long, and I don't remember what I thought of, not precisely. I do remember what I felt, which was hollowed out and rubber-legged. I felt like I'd better stay sitting and watching in case I stood up and the wind just blew me over.

Jip sat on the ground and looked at me, the remains of his rabbit still in his mouth. He always loved rabbits after he'd killed them and would carry them around for ages as if he was as proud of them as he was for having caught them. He'd lick them, like he was grooming them. Sometimes it could get a bit macabre.

Eventually he whined at me. Or maybe he'd been whining, trying to get my attention for a while. Shock had put me in a sort of stunned cone of temporary deafness. He wagged his tail and nudged the rabbit with his nose.

Good dog, I said. We're going to have to do a lot of hunting from now on.

Something had eaten the day without me noticing the passing of time. The threatened rain had never arrived and the sun had swung across the sky and was dropping into some new ominous looking clouds towards the horizon.

All my dried meat and fish and oatmeal was burned away with the rest of the boat. I had enough food for a couple of days in my pack, and of course I had the hare.

Watching Jip with his rabbit reminded me of this, and that made me get up on legs that were no longer rubbery but now stiff and unhappy to be moving after such a long time spent sitting still. I made myself go across to the smooth roof of one of the buried cars and use it as a table to spread out the contents of my rucksack so I could take stock of what provisions and tools we had for whatever was ahead of us.

I had the map and my notebook—the one I'm writing in right now. And I had the picture of you, of course. And I had more food than I'd expected as there were some oatcakes at the bottom I'd forgotten about. I had a waterproof and a folding knife, fire steel, binoculars, extra socks and a sweater. I didn't have my bedroll and I would definitely miss that. I would also miss the big compass on the boat, but I had the small brass walking-compass that was always pinned to the flap of the pack instead, so that was fine. North is north, no matter what size your compass is. And I had my first aid kit. So I had the map, a compass, provisions, tools, dry clothes and, with you and Jip, a couple of friendly faces. I told myself things could be worse.

Things could be worse, I repeated for Jip's benefit. He thumped his tail on the sand and kept licking away at the rabbit.

I looked around. The new incoming rain clouds. Still no sign of Brand. No sign of a red-sailed boat. I looked up at the tower.

Come on, boy, I said. Let's get some perspective.

Before we went into the red-brick palace to try and find the way up the tower, I thought I should pull the kayak further up the beach in case the tide took it while we were exploring.

That's when I discovered the bedroll. He'd taken the trouble to stuff it inside the kayak before torching the boat. I was glad to see it, but also strangely put out that he thought I was so soft that I couldn't do without it or so useless that I wouldn't have been able to vike the materials to make myself a new one if I wanted.

Patronised. That's the word for how I felt. Like I was an annoyance and not a threat.

Still a monster, I said as I hauled the kayak higher up the beach, above the tideline. Still a monster.

The doors to the palace were warped and stuck, so they didn't open until I'd taken a lot of my frustration out on them with my boots. Jip watched me patiently as I hacked at them, and then trotted inside with his dead rabbit friend, without waiting for me to lead the way.

The floors were covered in debris from the bits of ceiling that had fallen down, but it still was a magical, cavernous space. The lobby was pillared and big enough, and then when we followed a faded sign into the ballroom it was huge beyond anything I'd imagined. It had two layers of curvy balconies all around the sides, no straight lines, all scrolls and waves, some fragments of the original gold paint still picking out the details, though most of it was mottled and grey. The floor was buckled wood where it wasn't rotted, and where it was rotted a few hopeful saplings had taken root, thin scraggly things reaching up out of the gloom towards the broken hole in the roof and the light beyond. Something had fallen through the skylight, and now the weather was getting in I saw that sadly the whole building would go before long. Dad used to say that all you needed to do to the old houses on Uist was make a fist-sized hole in the roof and they'd be down in two years.

It was the first time I'd been in a building like that, like something in a kid's fairy-tale book. There was a stage at the far end with tall pillars on either side which framed it and supported an elaborately and even more curvy top. When I got close to it and my eyes adjusted, I saw there was a woman standing on it looking down at me.

Again, that was my first proper statue, so the cold chill that went down my back and froze me is understandable. Once I'd seen she was made of flaking gold plaster and was missing half an arm on one side and was holding hands with another arm that had broken off what I imagined had been a fallen sister on her other, I relaxed.

I still said hi.

Which got Jip's attention, but not hers. He trotted over for a look and a sniff. There was enough of the lettering that had been carved below her for me to read "I WIL_ ENCHANT". And for a moment she had cast a spell that had frozen me, so it wasn't a lie. I felt her eyes on me as I picked my way back to the doors, through the debris of broken glass chandeliers that had fallen all around the saplings, as if put there to protect the fragile new growth.

I went back to the lobby and rubbed away at the signs until I found one pointing me to the right door for the tower. It took me halfway outdoors and we began to climb the steps that switched back and forth up the inside of the latticed metal body.

When things had worked, there had been a room on cables that must have lifted people up to the top, but without electricity it was leg-ache to the top, or nothing. And by the time I'd got halfway up the thing, my legs were definitely adding their complaints to the list which included the large cuts on my arm (not healing), my head (bruised, now throbbing all the way round to my ear) and my tooth (still aching in twinges). Even though I was inside the rusting cage of the tower, it still felt exposed and dangerous. And the higher I climbed, the more the cool breeze became a cold wind. I paused and listened to it whining through the metalwork around me. Jip had gamely climbed this far, but when I started back up the steps he just looked at me and went back to grooming his dead rabbit friend.

I was sweating and breathing hard when I got to the door at the top. It had a glass window claiming to be the "tower eye" through which I could see a big enclosed room with more glass windows all around. It was also locked, or if it wasn't the catch had corroded and wasn't moving a bit. It had been a bad enough day already. I wasn't in any kind of mood to have a stupid door make it worse, not after pushing myself up all those steps. I braced myself on the handrail and kicked the handle, hoping the impact would unjam it. I kicked it really hard, several times. Then I tried it, giving it a really aggressive jiggle.

The lock held. The hinges didn't. The door fell awkwardly out of the wrong side of the frame, twisting as it came down. I managed to get my arm up and protected myself as best I could, but it was a heavy door and it slammed me into the side railings, whacking my head as it fell past, going end over end and smashing down into the angle of the landing below.

I shouted all the worst words I knew. But when I got myself to my feet and checked for any permanent damage, I found it wasn't as bad as it felt. I now had a bang on the other side of my head to balance the black eye, and when I put my fingers there to touch it they came back with enough blood on them for me to know I'd got a graze to match. But again my pride had taken a bigger hit than my body, and I made a mental note that I was just going to have to be more careful from now on. Whatever happened next, I was definitely going on a long journey and nobody else was going to be around to stop me doing stupid things to myself.

I then immediately betrayed all that sensible thinking by walking up the last steps and stepping into the room above, looking out at the huge view beyond the wall of glass. If I had ever seen a bird's-eye view before, I'd have paid more attention to the floor.

I had both feet standing over thin air before I knew it and when I looked down there was nothing between me and five hundred feet of air, straight down to the hard sand on the seafront. My survival instinct kicked in and my legs flexed and I stamped down, throwing myself backwards with a yelp of horror. I landed hard on my tailbone, scrabbling with my feet until my back hit the door-frame and then I stopped. And only then did my mind click in and start to flail around, trying to understand the miracle of how I had pushed hard against nothing but thin air and yet still managed to power myself back to safety.

I crawled forwards and looked down. The outer strip of floor was glass. Just like the windows, except where the windows had taken decades of weather head-on, not to mention the streaks of seagull shit that striped them, the floor—protected and pointing straight down—was relatively clear. I reached forward and tapped it. It was really thick and rock-solid.

Looking straight down through it gave me my first real experience of vertigo, much stronger than the queasiness I'd felt on top of the rollercoaster. I decided not to tread on the middle of it again. Although the glass was obviously designed to be trodden on, I had just seen how treacherous the metalwork of the frames holding it in place might be.

I walked round the room and found the other side of the central block. Someone had once camped out here. There was a pile of blankets, a couple of chairs and even a table with a camping lamp and an old music player with speakers. There were empty green bottles, neatly lined up along the glass wall. The lamp had corroded into uselessness, but there was also a plastic box. The catch snapped and the hinges cracked off when I opened it, because most old plastic gets brittle and shards really easily, but inside there were four candles. They and the blankets had survived so long because the room at the top was basically a sealed glass and metal box and no rats or mice had been able to get to them. Candles were a real rarity. There was also a pair of crutches, which I thought was odd. The climb was tough enough without needing to crutch your way up there. I decided at the time that whoever had come here must have really wanted to see the view. I was strangely cheered by the fact that people had once camped out here in the sky, listening to music and drinking. It seemed a life-enhancing thing to have done, presumably as the world was dying around them. I pocketed the box of candles and hoped they'd had the time of their lives. It didn't occur to me until much later that the reason they hadn't needed to take the crutches with them when they left is that they wouldn't have needed them if they'd taken the short way down after the wine was gone and the music stopped.

There was a last flight of steps up to an open viewing platform above the room, and the door to that was stiff but scraped open enough for me to slip through it and out into the wind. Once there had been high metal railings all around the walkway, metal bars that rose above my head and then curved back on themselves, but now almost a whole side—the one facing north—was missing. From the condition of the other metalwork, which was burst and shaling flakes as if the rust consuming it was a fungus, it had probably rotted off and fallen into the ballroom below. Maybe that was the thing that had broken the hole in the roof, and had let the saplings in.

There was also another thing that made me feel sad in the same way the bundle of rags and bones on the rollercoaster did, though this pile of clothes was not especially ragged and there were no bones at all. There was a pile of surprisingly well-preserved clothes that had been neatly folded and placed under a pair of boots wedged beneath the bottom of the railings, right next to the gap above the distant hole in the roof. It may have been nothing more than a pile of clothes and a pair of old boots, but my imagination created a man—I think it was a man from the size of those boots and the red hooded jacket beneath them—stripping off like a swimmer and standing naked in the wind before taking a long final dive through the ballroom roof far below. I have that kind of mind, the one that makes fantasies from scraps of evidence. When we were little, Bar used to put us to bed, and after she had read or told us a bedtime story she would give us three things to weave our own stories about as we went to sleep. She always chose odd, unconnected things, like a seal, a mountain and an umbrella for example, and I would begin making a story that soon turned into a dream and a good night's sleep.

Something moved in the breeze on the edge of the railing where it had broken off. It was a chain, like a necklace, made from lots of silver steel balls linked together. There was a pendant hanging from it and it was this, twisting in the wind and reflecting the light that had caught my eye. I unhooked it and looked at the pendant. It was a small rectangle with rounded edges, with a stubby tube jutting down off the bottom end of it. The tube was solid, but stippled with random holes of different sizes which dented its surface like tiny craters that caught the light. It must have been stainless steel to have lasted this long without tarnishing. It was an odd thing, and although I immediately added it to the story I had made of the final moments of my imagined naked diver—as he took it off and left it hanging there with the clothes he left behind—it did not feel like a sad or a bad thing. In fact I took it as a good luck sign, because the symbol pressed into the centre of the rectangle was my lucky number, 8. And the 8 was surrounded by a circle from which arrows radiated outwards to all the points of the compass. The little story I made up for myself about the pendant was that it was lucky, meant for me and as it seemed to be my special number inside a symbol that meant "you can go anywhere", I should definitely take it and wear it. Not least because if I was to find Brand and Jess in this whole unknown world I was marooned in, I would need every scrap of good luck I could lay my hands on. So I took it, looped it over my head and put it under my shirt.

Of course I know it's foolish to be superstitious, and that in this world you have to work hard to make your own luck, but I was on my own then and in low spirits and was looking for something, anything to stiffen my courage. Even as I did it, the sensible part of me knew I was clutching at straws, but when you're in danger of drowning you will grab at anything that might just keep you afloat.

Behind the palace there had once been a town and that was where the burned smell that had been competing with the sea breeze all day was coming from. The sprawl of buildings and the vegetation which had re-colonised the streets between had caught fire, and done so quite recently, since there was no new green in the grey-black scar that stretched away inland. Sometimes, back on the islands, a lightning strike will set a fire among the heather, and then the wind will take the flames and blow them across the slopes, leaving dark wounds which green over the following spring and in a couple of years grow right back into the landscape, leaving a patchwork that time fades and adjusts and—after a while—erases. This had the same wind-fashioned shape and was new burn, definitely this season's fire if not quite this week's or this month's. The blaze had stripped away the green covering that still blurred the outlines of the unburned streets which remained to the north-east, and it had revealed the pattern of the old roads and buildings that lay beneath the softening leaves and grasses like a hard skeleton. The long lines of houses marched up the slope away from the sea, following the billow of the low hills behind and snaking up the valleys between them. The procession of burned-out shells were too regular and straight for nature. And they also seemed determined to hold hands in a long chain. Like there was an extra strength in companionship as they hugged the land for comfort. That's what I thought then, anyway. I had, after all, just taken a bang to the head.

The streets had burned too. It must have been an inferno. Last year and the year before had been drier than ever, though Dad always said every year got hotter, which was the reason the old jetties on the islands were mostly underwater, whatever the tides. The rains came less often, he thought, but when they did they were harder. So on the one hand they were more violent, and on the other more or less the same amount of water landed on the islands every year. The burns ran and the springs sprung and the small lochans that laced the island were still there. And though the heather and the grass might get drier sooner in the summer, the islands were almost as watery ashore as the sea they were surrounded by.

Lack of water wasn't going to be an immediate problem on the top of the tower either, because as I was looking out over the burn scar, trying to make sense of the landscape beyond, a matching dark cloud slid over us and began to spit and then pelt with rain.

I retreated inside and listened to the shower lashing the windows. The sea below was beginning to stack up with long incoming white-topped rollers. I was pleased to be under cover. I had wondered if I could see all the way back up the coast towards home, but I couldn't: it was too far and the shape of the coast and the islands didn't correspond with what I remembered of them at sea level.

A big gust of wind blew the door shut above and I got a shock from that, but as I sat there and felt the walls and the floor around me I was reassured by how solid it all felt. I'd begun to wonder if the tower might fall down because someone was moving around on it after all these years of rust and wind, but strangely the storm reassured me. The viewing room was waterproof and there was no hint of shake inside. If it had stayed up for all these years, more than a century since anyone painted it, I thought the likelihood of it falling down on this night of all the thirty-six and a half thousand nights in between was so tiny that it wasn't worth thinking about.

Also: tree houses. I had read a couple of books that had other kids having houses in trees to play in. I used to dream of sleeping in a tree, with the leaves moving around me in the wind, like waves. The problem with the islands is that there are no trees on them. Not really. The wind scours everything down to heather height, and those that do find purchase are seldom much taller than a person. And certainly not tall enough to climb, let alone build a house in. The viewing room seemed like the best tree house in the world.

The people who had left me their candles had stayed up here for fun when things must have looked terrible for the world as it aged and died all around them. Looking back, it does seem a bit crazy of me to also have been thinking about doing something because it was fun then, at the very moment when everything else had just got as un-fun as anything had ever been in my life.

I heard Jip bark from below and went to tell him I was okay and I thought we might spend the night up here. There were blankets enough for both of us to be comfortable. When the storm cleared, I intended to spread Brand's map on the floor and see if I could match what I could see of the landscape with the shapes on the paper. So, I told myself, there was also a practical, sensible reason for my night in the sky.

I'd dumped my rucksack on the landing halfway down, not wanting the bother of carrying it all the way, so I went back to get it and to lead Jip reluctantly upwards.

He spotted the glass floor immediately and really didn't like it. He kept to the inner section where it was solid and lay there looking at me like I was the biggest fool in the world for bringing him there.

The storm arrived full force about then and was quite a thing. It dimmed the sky and then got darker still as the air filled with grey curtains of rain. I could see them distinctly as they swept in across the water beyond the lines of white tops marching towards the shore.

I wish I'd been alive when you could go in a plane. Not just to look down on land and sea, but to soar around the clouds and look down on them too. Did you do that? Go on a plane. See what the top of a cloud looks like?

I made a pad of blankets and waited until Jip settled in next to me, and then wrapped another two round us, and sat and stared at the lightning forking down over the sea in the far distance. Jip never liked thunder, and barked back at it from under the protection of the blankets, pressing closer to my leg as he did so. I put my hand on his neck, into the familiar wiry hair, and told him it was all right, and that everything was going to be fine in the morning.

That calmed him enough to turn the barks into growls. I just wished I believed it. I thought I'd probably feel better if I ate something, but then exhaustion took me and I fell asleep alongside him.

The thunder was still rumbling when I woke, but the rain had stopped and the noise was now coming from far in the distance. The gaps between the lightning flashes and the noise were long enough for me to know the storm was now worrying away at the landscape more than ten to twelve miles away. Jip shifted in his sleep. I took care not to wake him as I moved to get more comfortable and looked down at the jetty.

The sea was still heaving, but the clouds had lifted enough to let the sliver of moon throw enough light to reflect off the surface. I thought I could see the remains of the *Sweethope* still tangled in the great melted wheel, but maybe I was imagining it. It wasn't there when the sun came up. But by then I'd made my choice and seeing it wouldn't have done more than confirm me in it. The sea had also washed away the words of warning Brand had written in the sand. Seeing them wouldn't have changed anything either. As I said, all they did was prove he could write. Not that he'd read the right books or learned the right lessons. Maybe if he had done so he wouldn't have burned the boat and told me to go home.

You burn boats so your troops stay and fight, because they can't run away home. Aeneas did that when he brought those who had survived the fall of Troy to Italy and founded another empire in Rome. And the Spanish explorer whose name I can't remember did that when he arrived in South America with his troops. He ended up taking the whole continent and all its silver and gold with a handful of violent men with guns who couldn't go home. I'm not violent, and I'm not a man and I didn't have a gun. But Brand had burned my boat. And in doing so had made my choice for me, no matter what he thought the message he was sending was.

I wasn't going home. Not then, not yet, or not to *my* home anyway. I was going to go to his home. I was going to get my dog. I was going to take his boat. And then, when and only if I did that, I would go home.

Like I said.

Bang on the head.

Chapter 14

A glimmer of light

That wasn't the whole story. There was another reason. And in fact maybe the whole burning the boats thing is something I made up for myself afterwards on the journey as we walked. I certainly had plenty of time to think as I did so. And enough reason, as things got more complicated, to knit myself a nice excuse for all the harm in whose way I had put myself. Ever bang your thumb with a hammer? Hurts worse than a normal knock because you did it to yourself.

Before it got light, but after the storm had gone and the distant thunder had rolled away, taking the lightning out of sight beyond the hills to the north, I woke again, needing to pee. I went up the stairs and out on to the rain-slick platform where I added to the wetness on the ground, taking care to allow for the wind direction. It was when I was straightening up that I saw it and stopped everything.

There was a light in the darkness. A tiny pinprick on the horizon to the south-east, so small it could have been a star on the point of setting. Except it was orange and I'd never seen an orange star and the clouds were battened down overhead, so that no other stars were visible to compare it with. I clattered down the steps to get my binoculars and the compass, which woke Jip. I made him stay because I didn't want him falling off the open side of the viewing platform, and then I went back up.

The light was still there. But it was a long, long way off. The binoculars couldn't pull it closer, not enough to have any idea what it was anyway. The compass was useless in the blackness of the night. Dad gave it to me when I went off on my own for the first time. It had been his as a child and he said the markings once used to glow in the dark, but now they had worn out. I went back down and got a couple of the green bottles. Back out in the darkness, I sighted them carefully with my eye, so that the tops lined up with the distant orange spark. I then went back down and slept surprisingly well, knowing that when the sun came up I could look along my homemade sight line and see what was at the end of it.

I dreamed too, gentle happy dreams of walking into a village, which in those dreams looked like the one that always featured on the last page in a series of comic books I had loved as a child, an ancient thing with a stockade of wooden spikes and happy villagers sitting around a big fire having a feast while the village musician was always tied up somewhere in the picture, looking very annoyed because they didn't like his music. What these villagers really liked was having punch-ups with Roman soldiers and eating roast boar. Except in my dreams the village was not just full of strangers, but Bar and Ferg and Dad and even Mum was there, laughing and handing out food, and there was a small girl with a kite running round and round the fire until she saw me and dropped the kite and sprinted towards me with her arms wide open and then I woke up.

At least that's what I think I dreamed. Remembering dreams is like picking up small jellyfish—they slip through your fingers—and you never know if it's a dream you had or if you added to the dream in the remembering. Sometimes it's hard to know if you're remembering a dream at all, or just a dream about remembering a dream. And if that doesn't make sense, well, neither do dreams.

There was nothing at the end of the sight line. I was bitterly disappointed when I looked again in the light of day. But there was no unexpected settlement full of welcoming villagers waiting to help me. I wasn't, of course, really expecting Mum or the girl with the kite, but I had gone to sleep wondering if there were people living in the empty landscape, people we had not been told about. But there weren't, or if there were there was no sign of them and, since the one thing that hasn't changed since the end of the world is that everyone still needs breakfast, the absence of smoke from a cooking fire seemed to seal the end of the hopeful delusion I had gone to sleep beneath.

There was just a slightly raised bump on the horizon, too far away to see if there was any building on it. I unfolded my map and used my compass to orientate it. Then I took a bearing on the line I had marked with the bottle tops, and then I used the straight edge of one of the crutches to draw a line from the tower, right across the map.

And then—since the orange light had been broadly on the way to where I had decided Brand was based—I knew where I was headed. I could check it out, and keep right on going until I got to the other side of the land where I was sure he really had his home.

Jip was happy to get back to ground level. I pulled the kayak inside the hall of the palace. The building might be on its way to falling down now that the weather and the saplings had found a way in to the ballroom, but I reckoned it would take time, and the kayak would be safe enough for a while. Certainly until I walked back to get it on my way home.

I wonder if it's still there.

We set off inland. I wanted to look back, but I didn't because I knew if I did I'd start having doubts, and I had made my mind up. And there was quite enough to fill my eyes and my head as we walked through the charred skeleton of the town, Jip running ahead, quartering back and forth, nose to the ground on the hunt for new and interesting smells.

The shells of the broken houses leaned against each other as the road rose away from the seafront. The fire had burned the vegetation that had overgrown them right back so the old cracked tarmac had been revealed again, broken and buckled both by time and the bushes and small trees that had pushed through and which now survived as flame-stripped trunks and branches. The place smelled of fire char, but not a clean woodsmoke smell. More of a greasy, oil smell. Walking into your world, thinking of how many people had lived in this one street and then thinking how many other streets just like it must lie ahead did give me a strange feeling. But the blank window sockets didn't look at me in the same way the empty houses on the islands did. Maybe the fire had burned out the last residue of whoever had once lived there.

Where the burn stopped and the houses continued, some still roofed and more or less intact, it was different. Just as empty but more alive again. Going was slower because the snarl of small trees and bushes got in the way, but it was still easy walking, though I would lose sight of Jip for minutes at a time. When glass survived, it winked the thin sunlight back at me as I passed. I remember one house had GONE sprayed across the front in yellow paint in letters that were higher than me. Birds flew in and out of the upper windows where I imagined they had been building their nests now for generations. It was a cheerful thing to see, as were the squirrels that loped freely along the roofs and tree branches. Life was making use of what you had left behind.

I'd never seen a squirrel except in a book, but the moment I saw the long bushy tails, I knew they weren't rats. The speed and deftness with which they ran and kept their footing so high above the ground was exhilarating. At least to me it was. To Jip it was another affront, and he barked excitedly and tried to get at them, jumping up and even at one point trying to climb a tree. He didn't have much time for books, so maybe for him they really were just rats with fluffier tails. Either way, they immediately got added to the list of things he knew he was born to hunt. I wonder what they made of us as we passed beneath them. They can't have seen people before. It seemed like they were studiously oblivious to us as they hurtled smoothly from branch to branch—occasionally making wild and gravity-defying leaps from tree to tree, landing and carrying on as if they had not just performed a miracle of balance and surefootedness. I could have stood there and watched them all day. I decided I liked squirrels just as much as Jip did, but in a completely different way.

Once we left the edge of the town, the countryside sort of closed in, just when I would have imagined it would open up. The reason was, again, the trees. They got bigger and crowded in over the old road which was fully grown over, covered in moss and grass. As I said, at home on the islands there were no trees to speak of, and those very few that did survive were wind-shorn and stunted things, cowering behind whatever windbreak had allowed them to survive. There was one plantation of dwarfish pine on a hillside on North Uist, but it was a tangled and dark place into which I did not go.

Walking beneath real broad-leafed trees was something I had never done. And on this first day it was exhilarating. After an outdoor life spent under grey or blue skies, it was a novelty to find myself beneath a roof of green, and not just the one green, but so many different kinds of green. It wasn't just the variety of trees that led to the medley of shades and intensities of colour—it was the sunlight beyond that turned some of the leaves into bright tongues of emerald that outlined the darker mass of the shadowed leaves beneath. They were tall, the trees on that first stretch of road, broad-trunked and ancient. The spread of their branches supported a thick canopy which must have kept down the younger generation that was trying to burst through the old tarmac road beneath the moss and grass. As if to prove this, after a couple of klicks I came to a place where two huge trees had blown down across the road and, where they let the light in, a new tree had already grown taller than the shaded saplings around it. The roots of the fallen trees had ripped great discs of earth out of the ground when they went down, and examining them made me realise that there was a huge system of roots beneath the surface to match the spread of branches high above it.

It's a marvellous thing, a tree.

Rabbits had dug homes into the newly exposed earth, and Jip caught two before I could persuade him to come along with me. I was keen to get as many klicks behind us as we could before nightfall, and so I gutted them and hung them on my pack to skin later.

Good dog, I said. That's our supper taken care of.

Many of the houses we passed were roofless shells, overgrown with brambles or cracked apart by the vegetation that had taken root in them decades earlier, but there were others that seemed less affected by time and neglect, at least until I got a closer look. Stone-built houses seemed to stand up better than brick, and brick better than houses made of frames covered in plaster. The walls of these houses had burst with damp long ago and here and there the remnants of the plastic sheeting they had been lined with fluttered like white flags. I remember coming out of the trees for a section of road, and found myself reflected in the long glass wall of a building that was, I think, a place for buying petrol or charging a car. It was an odd thing to see myself so small in a landscape, Jip at my side. Of course I'd seen myself reflected in mirrors and house windows before, but this was by far the biggest window I'd seen, and it made me look very small against the landscape stretching away all around me. Just me, my pack and my bow and then trees that towered above and a patchwork of brambles and hedges and scrubland beyond. The world looked very big. I looked tiny. Jip looked even smaller, but he also looked like he belonged in the wildness more than I did. The scale of me was somehow wrong, too big and too little at the same time. I looked like something not quite myself, like a character in a story. As I walked on, I wondered if that was what it was like seeing a movie or a television—a small person in a giant frame. Dad said that's what people used to do, sit in the dark with lots of other people and watch a huge story take place on the screen hung in front of them. You'll have seen movies. I wonder what you'd have made of Jip and me.

The other thing I could see in the glass, plain as day, is that one of my arms was considerably redder than the other.

That made sense, since one arm was also itching more. The scraping I had given it on the netting had never really had time to heal, and the salt sores that had developed had not gone away. I wanted to keep going, but I knew I should take time to take care of it before it got worse so I walked up to the petrol station and found the rotted carcass of a vehicle that had rusted to the chassis. Just like many of the dead cars on the island, the axles and the wheels and the engine blocks had survived longest. I put the rucksack down and got my first aid kit out, using the engine block as a table to lay it out on.

You had what Dad called the "'cillins" in your time: antibiotic medicines that miraculously stopped things going infected and septic. Any 'cillins that survived had been manufactured long before the world died, and even the ones that were packed away in foil packs to keep out the moisture couldn't escape time. We found old pills every now and then when we were a-viking, but they had little effect. Luckily Dad had the way of other medicines from his ma, who he said was a wonder at healing, and so we all carried kits in our packs that could help us if we got hurt by ourselves. Unpacking my kit made me a little homesick, because of course everything in it had been made by Dad or Ferg or Bar. I remembered Joy boiling the cotton sheet we had found in an old house to make strips for the bandages, and I myself had gathered the honey in the small airtight metal canister. Ferg had made the ointment in the tin that had once contained a brown boot polish, but I had helped him gather the woundwort that went into it, stuffing bags made from old pillow cases full of the violet-flowered plant. Bar read in a herbal book that it was also called "heal-all" and "heart-of-the-earth". I opened the tin and smelled it and thought how far I was from the heart of my earth. Then I recapped it and washed my arm with some of the drinking water from my bottle. I let the wind dry it, and then I smeared the most livid patch of sores and scratches with the honey. As I did it, I felt the heat in my arm like a fire beneath the skin and knew I should have done this two days ago, and told myself I was a whole different kind of fool to the one I already knew myself to be.

I wrapped Bar's bandage over the honey, and tied it off. Then we set off again. Of course, now that I had taken notice of it and done the right thing, my arm kept intruding into my thoughts, itching and throbbing. Among the other things I had in the kit—like knitbone paste and staunchgrass—was some powdered red pepper from the plants Bar grew under glass. If the sores and the scratches were no better at nightfall, I told myself I would make a paste with that and put it in the wounds. The pepper paste burned badly, but it always seemed to make infection go away, especially if mixed with the garlic she also grew, but I had none of that with me. One of the family on Lewis had jumped off a rock onto the yellow sand at Luskentyre and impaled her foot on a razor clam. It had killed her in pieces, and the going was ugly and brutal as the infection had spread up her foot to the point where they had thought about cutting it off to save her, but because cutting a foot off your daughter is a terrible thing to do they had left it too late and the infection had spidered up her calf. When they did take her leg off below the knee they thought they had caught it, but she never woke up. Before the end of the world you had conquered infection, but it turns out all it had to do was outwait you. It waited until the medicine factories closed because no one was young enough to work in them, and then back it came.

I knew I was strong, and I wasn't too worried about my arm in the long run, but I was just worried enough to walk along with a niggle at the back of my head. At the time it wasn't a big thing, but it was annoying. Like a tiny stone in your boot.

Before I set off, I picked up a few small pebbles and put them in my right-hand pocket, and then as I walked I tried to count my paces. This was a trick Dad had taught us on the long beaches on South Uist. A klick is a kilometre and once you've calculated how many of your steps that is, if you count paces you can see how far you can walk in a day. Or you can look at a map and if you know what direction you're going and how far you've travelled, you'll always know where you are. That's the theory. I wasn't yet aware I was in the process of testing that theory until it broke. I was just trying to count to one thousand, three hundred and fifty, which is my count for a klick. There were a lot of new things to see as I walked and I had to concentrate on not losing count. To help with that, every time I reached one thousand, three hundred and fifty I put a pebble from my right hand pocket into my left, in case I lost count.

I walked twenty-five pebbles that first day. I remember that. It was a round number. I walked them along the grown-over road because it went almost exactly in the bearing I had taken from the tower, with my glass bottles and the orange light. Because I had known that once I was on the ground the ridge where I had seen the fire would not be visible to me, I had marked the nearest landmark that I could see along that line. It was a sharp needle that had looked small when I saw it, but as I got closer I could see that in fact it towered over the surrounding landscape. It was a church steeple. I supposed they were called that because they were steep, but of the ones I have since walked past, it still seems the tallest and the sharpest, scratching the sky with a tiny bent cross at the very tip of it. What became apparent as I got closer was that it was in the middle of what must once have been a city. As I write this I realise I don't really know the difference between a city and a town, except one is a lot bigger than the other. I suppose if I had a dictionary I could look it up. But I don't have any book other than the one I'm writing this in. If it wasn't an official city, it was certainly bigger than the town I'd left in the morning, and fire had not destroyed much of it. Or if it had, the fire had visited a long time ago and the living green had grown right over the char and ash it may have left behind. That doesn't mean the city was intact. It was definitely well on the way to turning back into landscape. Like I said, nature will take a building down if you give it enough time. The rain gets in, the cold turns water to ice in the winter, the ice swells the building cracks and then seeds sprout in the cracks in the spring and all you have to do is wait for the roots to push the walls and the roofs further apart to let in more seeds and rain and ice and eventually things fall apart just as surely here on the mainland as out on the islands.

I wonder if it would be sad for you to think that the wild is well on the way to winning back the world you and your ancestors took and tamed. I can imagine it might be, especially when I see the amazing stuff you all built. I have seen things I could not have imagined, not even from the pictures I used to pore over in the old faded books back home. I have walked in the shells of buildings that I cannot believe were possible to build. I don't know how someone could have got so much stone up into the air and left it so well made that it stayed there. And it's not just the buildings—it's the bridges and the tunnels. I am still awed by the power and the cleverness that went into building them, power and cleverness that must have been an everyday thing to you. But buildings are no different to trees really. Or people. Eventually they fall over and die.

I walked into the city and the ruins of the buildings seemed to rise and close in around me the nearer I got to the steeple.

It took me two pebbles to get there from the edge of the countryside. Animals had worn tracks which wove along through the grass and bushes that filled the gap between them, the gap that had once been streets. In the mud and the leaf mould I saw the tracks of pads—like rabbits, but some bigger, and I saw hoof marks, which surprised me. I shouldn't have, because we keep ponies on the islands, but somehow I hadn't thought there might be ponies on the mainland. I turned a corner and found myself face to face with a fox. He was big, the same size as Jip, and his fur was a deep orange, except for the flash of white on his chest and at the tip of his tail. He looked at me without surprise but with that great stillness that comes over an animal preparing to run the moment they think it's safe to turn their back on you.

He was standing at the foot of a great slope, which was the top floor of a building that had collapsed. All the floors had been concrete and there had been no walls. I think it had been made to put cars in. Anyway, the floors had fallen in and were stacked on top of each other like a tilted spill of oatcakes. The grey of the concrete was cut up into car-sized boxes by faded yellow lines which immediately looked like a giant ladder the moment the fox turned tail and ran for it, loping up the slope as Jip gave chase. The fox disappeared into a door faintly marked EXIT at the top of the slope, and Jip would have followed him had he not heard the sharp whistle I gave, and stopped dead. He gave me a reproachful look, pissed on the side of the exit door and then trotted back down to the road beside me.

I was itching to go a-viking in the huge buildings I was passing but I had everything I needed in my pack or on my belt, and I didn't want to distract myself from my plan. Or rather, I did desperately want to distract myself and go hunting through the lost bits of this new territory opening up all around me, but I wanted to get my dog back even more. I had worked out how far I would have to walk to get from the tower to the place on the other coast where I was sure—from the marks on the map—that Brand called home. If I could walk thirty klicks a day, I could be there in ten or twelve days. Twelve days was not so long. But I could do my viking on the way back, was what I told myself. Once I had Jess. I hoped that Brand was sailing straight home, and I believed he might well be as his boat had been loaded to the gunwales with things he had picked up on his travels. Of course I had no idea as to how I might rescue her, but I was sure that I would come up with one once I saw the lay of the land. There were a thousand things wrong with this plan, not least that I was basing everything on the map I'd stolen, and hanging every hope I had on the web of pencil lines that radiated from that single spot on the east coast.

So. No viking. And if I was to be true to the plan, I should have walked past the steeple and gone another five pebbles before making camp. But I was tired and the day of trees and then the mass of overgrown buildings was so new to me that I felt somewhere between stunned and dizzy with the novelty of it all. So I decided I could make up the distance tomorrow. I sweetened the decision by telling myself I should try and climb the tower that supported the steeple and check out the next landmark on the compass line. The church was easy enough to find, though I did have to lace my way to it through a maze of smaller streets where red-brick buildings were tumbling into the dense thickets of brambles choking the roadways between. When I got there, I found it stood on a sort of point, above what looked like a river of trees that forked away on either side of it. I could see a real river sparkling in the sunlight beyond that. What I didn't know then, but now do know, having seen a lot of country, is that the river of trees was actually the old railway lines, and the reason the tops were level with me was that they were in a groove that had been cut down into the land for them to run along. Railways fill with trees faster than roadways, perhaps because the rails were laid on loose stones, instead of the hard skin of a tarmac road. What I have found is that if you try and follow a railway on an old map, you make better time walking beside it in the clearer fields than you do trying to wind your way through the undergrowth that has enthusiastically recolonised the tracks. They're more like greenways than railways now.

The church doors were locked, or corroded in place. They were made of heavy wood that had seemed to have hardened instead of rotting. The iron railings around the church had corroded into an uneven and unwelcoming barricade, and the stone forecourt was buckling with weeds and saplings. But the windows were all intact, at least all the ones I might have reached were. There was a big round window at one end, like a giant stone flower with coloured glass panels radiating out from the centre. There were broken panes there, but no use to me in getting in.

I would have given up, but Jip chased something fast and sleek under the arch supporting the tower, and when I followed his excited barking I found he had chased the rat inside the building, through a door I had missed. The door was actually locked, but a gutter above had failed, so that water had striped down the side of the church in a years-long stain and pooled in a depression under the tower. That had rotted the bottom of the door, making a dog-sized hole that he had pushed in through. I pulled away at the wood until it was Griz-sized, and crawled in after him.

Inside was wonderful and awful. The windows that had looked drab from the outside radiated light and colour over the high-ceilinged interior. The glass showed bright pictures of bearded men in robes doing things and women with scarves over their heads looking up into the sky and holding babies. The ceiling was a complicated structure of wooden supports stepping up to the peak, and on every possible perch there were more statues of men in beards. When I was small, I read a children's Bible that told all the important stories, so I'm pretty sure most of the painted women were the Mary because their faces were the same, only the colours of their scarves and robes and the things they carried were different. Some carried babies, some odder things like wheels and flames. All of the beards can't have been the Jesus, but I know the naked ones nailed to the crosses were. The statues weren't just up on the roof supports. They were everywhere, big and small, free standing or hanging from the walls. The church in Iona had had one or two, but this—this was what a crowd felt like. It was the most crowded empty space I'd ever been in, and I had the nastiest feeling that they had all been waiting for me, or someone, to disturb their peace and quiet.

Although one end of the church was pretty untouched by time, at the other end there was a jumble of long metal pipes where something that I think was a musical organ had fallen down. In the books I read, people came to church for peace, or to talk to a god, or just to be with all their neighbours. I didn't think this was a comfortable place to talk to a god. There was too much pain in the statues, too much relish in the way they were made. I think relish is the right word, if it means a delight in something. It felt like the sculptors had made the statues with a real liking for the hurt of being nailed to that cross. Maybe that's my ignorance rather than their fault. Maybe loving the pain was a thing that made sense if you believed in invisible things like this god. I just felt... disconnected from the meaning of all that enjoyment. Like someone was giving the punchline to a joke I hadn't heard the beginning of. Maybe I should have read a grown-up Bible to see what the point of it all was, but we had no time for gods where I grew up. It had passed, they had passed, just like you all had passed. Gods are just stories now. Bar said that's all they really were anyway: stories to make sense of lives of those who wanted someone else to take charge of them, rather than cut their own way.

Bar read different books to the ones I did. Books of ideas, not stories, and practical books about how to do things or make things grow. They never interested me as much as a made-up book about people. But I liked the way her mind worked.

I found a small door that led up to the tower. The confined space made me a bit breathless, tightness rising in my throat as I ascended. I had the strange feeling of walking up into a dead end. I began wondering how I would get out of this narrow twisting stone spiral if the door at the bottom slammed shut and the one at the top wouldn't open. I would be stuck like a bug in a bottle. My calm mind knew the door at the bottom would not slam shut as the wind couldn't get at it even if there was a wind, which there wasn't, and there was no one else who would push it shut as the world was empty. My fear-mind had other thoughts. The door at the top did open, though I broke one of the hinges tugging and kicking at it. I stepped out onto a stone platform that ran round the base of the steeple. Looking up, I saw the height of it and the bent cross on the tip, and I felt the huge weight of stone balanced overhead like a threat. Did you ever go to the edge of a cliff and feel a kind of pull, something sinister but exhilarating making you want to jump? The mass of all those stone blocks seemed to hang there with a similar kind of tug.

Stay there, it seemed to be saying. Don't move. And we'll be down to squash you any time now.

I took a bearing on my compass. I could see a notch in the high ground looming in the distance, with a paler hill rising beyond it. If I kept the peak of the paler hill just to the right-hand side of the notch—like a gunsight—I would be on target. I took out the map and drew the shape on a blank bit of sea so that I wouldn't forget it. Then I went back down into the church. I had thought of sleeping in there, but there were too many eyes that would have stayed watching me as I slept. They weren't human eyes, and though the statues stared there was nothing in the way they'd been carved that reached out to you. Not like the woman in the yellow dress. But I'm getting ahead of myself. I did sit on the altar and share some dried meat and oatcake with Jip before we left, and as I sat there looking back into the body of the church, I realised I was probably getting the same view the god's priest had had when the rows of empty benches had been full of living people. I tried to imagine what kind of noise all those metal pipes now splayed like a giant's game of jackstraws at the other end of the room might have made. I couldn't, and when I left the building, the strongest memory wasn't the statues and the cruel torture they seemed to take such a grim delight in, but the glory colours of the glass windows all around them. They stayed in my mind like jewels.

The woman in the yellow dress lived in a Greek temple in the middle of the town, squatting ominously on one side of a stone-flagged square. Of course it wasn't a proper Greek temple, but it looked like a darker version of the white one in the book of myths Joy and I had pored over by the fireside a lifetime ago, where Zeus or maybe it was Athene lived. It had the same pillars in front, supporting a big triangle of stone, making a big porch, behind which were doors and windows. The windows had been shuttered with board, maybe to protect the glass. I spent a long time trying to work out what the letters carved in stone on the front of the building said. I think it was "TO LITERATURE, ARTS AND SCIENCES".

The doors were cracked open just enough for me to slide in after Jip. Inside were more doors, glass this time. These inner doors were what had kept the weather and the animals out. I pushed them open with some difficulty, and went in. The upper windows weren't boarded, so I climbed the stairs. It had been a museum. That's what I discovered when I read the labels on the walls. But everything in it had gone. Everything except in one room in the middle. It was another big and empty space, and in it was a chair and opposite the chair was a lady in a yellow dress, staring right at me. I say she was a lady because a lady is a fancier kind of woman, and the dress was as fancy as you could imagine, long and luxurious and the liveliest yellow with black bits on the edges. It wasn't a dress you could have done anything useful in. It was a dress made to get in the way. It was, however, a very good dress for lounging in and looking at people. And her eyes were doing a very intense job of looking. She was only one painting, but there was more life in her two eyes than in all of the blank Jesuses and Marys in the church put together. She looked right at me and I knew she was seeing me, just as intently as the artist must have seen her. She looked at you and you felt... connected. Maybe not connected with her directly, but with life. Because that's what the painter had caught, that's what the painter had liked. Her life. Maybe just life itself. I sat in the chair and looked back at her.

Hi, I said, I'm Griz.

And then I laughed at myself for talking to a painting and her look seemed to share the joke she had not been able to make. I hadn't been able to bear the idea of going to sleep with all the sculptures looking at me, but I decided that sleeping in this room with just her looking over me would be a very different thing altogether.

I think someone else had found it restful sharing a room and a look with her, and that's why the chair had been placed right in front of the painting. I expect one of the last of the Baby Bust had come here to see a young face after all the young faces had gone, dead or just grown old around him or her. It must have been so sad without a younger generation growing up behind them. I think they came to sit in that chair to touch that bit of life once again. I left my bedroll and went down to deal with the rabbits.

On the way, I got distracted by a room on the ground floor. The sign said "MUSEUM SHOP" and though from the mess and the dust overlaying it all it was clear someone—maybe many people—had gone a-viking through it a long time ago, there were interesting things left. It was mostly books, but also some pencils which I took and a little brass pencil sharpener with a steel blade that had not rusted. The books were mainly old picture books about art, too big to carry, but there was a tilted shelf of small books, about the right size for a pocket; they were guides to stuff like flowers and birds and rocks and things you might see on a walk and want to identify. I decided I could afford to add two of them to my pack without overloading myself. The obvious one to take was called *Food for Free*; it had a picture of blackberries and raspberries on the front. A quick look through showed it was a guide to eating things you found rather than things you had grown. It had lots of really good pictures to help identify the food that wouldn't poison you. If I was going to forage my way across the mainland, a book that told me what not to eat among the new plants I was encountering was nothing but a gift. The less obviously useful one was called *Trees* which I took because I liked it, having only really just discovered a world with proper big trees in it. Looking back, I suppose both books helped me survive. But only one of them saved my life. And it wasn't the obvious one.

I took a pile of the less portable books out with me to look at after I had made a fire on the porch between the heavy columns. I sat with Jip and paged through the larger books as the rabbits cooked, feasting my eyes on the colourful pictures that were still bright on the page after more than a century. I ate my rabbit while it was still hot, and Jip waited until his was just warm and then took it out onto the steps to eat slowly in the privacy he always favoured. Jess was different. She always ate fast, but kept looking up at you and wagging her tail, as if including you in the fun. I felt a pang at the thought of her and hoped Brand was feeding her properly and that she was safe, wherever she was. And then I remembered her chained to Saga and knew she wasn't.

As Jip ate, I carefully unbandaged my arm and inspected it while the light was still good. I decided it looked a little better. I put some more honey on it and equally carefully rebandaged it. If it didn't actually look better, I told myself, it didn't look worse. That was something. In the morning I would refill the two water bottles from the river I had seen, so I drank most of what I had left, pissed as I watched the sunset from the top of the steps and then went inside for the night.

You would have thought it was a very early time to go to

sleep, but then you had electric lights to keep the rhythm of your day as you liked it, not as the sun dictated. And it had been a long walk, as far as I had ever walked in one day and my feet were sore, my arm was still throbbing and the pack straps had rubbed a blister on one shoulder. I closed all the doors behind me and laid out my bedroll in front of the lady in the yellow dress, and lay down. Jip patrolled the edges of the room, ever hopeful for a rat, and then came and went to sleep beside me. I looked into the eyes in the painting and tried to think what her life had been like. There was kindness and intelligence and even a sense of humour in her face, but I wondered if she could ever have imagined while the painting was being made what would come of it, what would become of her. I didn't think she would have dreamed that her strong gaze would go on to outlive her many-greats-grandchildren, and end up looking at Jip and me as we slept on the other side of the end of the world.

And sleep I did. Long and deep, right into the heart of the night.

And then I was awake, and very still, listening to the low growl coming from Jip.

It was the kind of noise you definitely don't want to wake up to. It put a cold chill right down my spine.

It was pitch-dark, but when I put my hand out I felt he was standing rigid, hackles raised, quivering.

I sat up and found my knife.

I let my other hand stay on his back, telling him we were okay by touch and not sound. I wanted to listen for whatever it was that had roused him. He stopped growling, but he stayed on his feet and the bristle of fur at his shoulders remained erect.

There was something moving outside the windows, down

on the ground. I could hear a kind of rubbing and moving noise—nothing specific like footfalls or breathing, just the noise of movement, faint and almost inaudible, more like a disturbance in the air than an actual sound. But it was definitely there and it was the noise something larger than a rat or a squirrel would make. I edged to the window and tried to look down and get a sight of whatever it was, but the angle was too steep and I couldn't have seen what was there, even if there had been more light. All I could do was sense that the noise seemed to be travelling towards the front of the building. The front of the building with the unlocked door.

I went and got my bow and arrows as quietly as I could and took Jip with me out on to the stairhead. I told him to stay close, which is one of the suggestions he knows to follow from our time hunting on the island. He sat next to me as I knelt in the dark, facing the main door below. I nocked an arrow without thinking and laid the others where I could grab the next ones without looking, and then we both did a very good job of mimicking the stillness of all those statues and reached out into the night with our ears.

The thing (or the person—Brand even, because I was half thinking he had tracked me) scuffed its way up the steps and on to the portico. I swear I heard sniffing, and immediately knew they were examining our campfire and discarded rabbit carcass. There was a horrible sound of bones crunching and then silence, after which came more of the general sound of something moving, this time closer to the front doors. Then there was more silence, so long that I had to switch knees to stop getting cramp, and longer still until I began to wonder if we had imagined it all and relaxed enough to rest both knees by sitting on the top step of the stairs instead of kneeling.

Then there was a loud bump and a creak as something barged the front door and Jip took a step forward, fur bristling again, his warning growl rumbling low and unmistakable and I had the bow drawn and ready for whatever was coming in.

And then nothing did.

Just nothing and more nothing and then the sound of some bird hooting in the distance, a noise I knew was an owl, a noise so perfectly recognisable that even though I had never heard an actual *tuwit-tuwoo* there could be no mistake. And then more silence.

I don't remember relaxing, though I do know that Jip sat down after a very long time. And I certainly don't remember going to sleep in such an awkward position.

I woke with sun in my eyes and a bad crick in my neck from where I had slumped against the wall and slept half sitting, all crooked and folded in on myself.

I thought I would go and see that it was safe before I let Jip out, but the moment I opened the inner glass door he bolted through my legs and darted out onto the porch, casting left and right.

I felt strangely foolish peering out of the half-open door, bow held ready as I scanned the square for the night visitor, trying to see if he was lying in wait for us.

Jip had no such qualms as he raced back and forth, furiously intense as he tried to get the scent of it. He disappeared round the corner, and was gone for several minutes, then he came back looking much happier than when he'd left. He cocked his leg on the corner of the museum where we had heard the thing rubbing along, and then he trotted to the centre of the square, nose down, until he discovered a large pile of fresh shit. It wasn't recognisable as human, which I felt relieved by, but I had also never seen its like. Jip didn't seem to mind what kind of new and unseen animal it had been. He just cocked his leg and put his scent on it too.

He seemed pleased with his work, and I too felt cheered up by his attitude. With that and the sunlight, the night's fears seemed to disperse. If my arm hadn't been so itchy and tight it would have been the perfect beginning to the day.

Chapter 15

The fever

I said goodbye to the lady in the yellow dress, taking care to close all the doors behind me so weather and animals wouldn't get in to bring the museum down before its time. When I was far enough away to look back and see more of the building, I did notice that there was already a pair of saplings sprouting from one side of the roof, so that time was coming. If I'd had the *Sweethope*, I think I might have taken the lady with me. I would have liked Bar and Ferg to see her looking at them. Dad would have thought it fanciful nonsense. Mum might have liked her smile for company.

I didn't have to find my way to the river to fill my water bottles because we crossed a stream running down the middle of a street, and the water there was fast and clear. Sometimes when it has been hot and dry for a long time and then it rains, the water slides right off the land and doesn't have time to soak in as fully as it would do if it was landing on damp earth. I was bottling the rainfall from the thunderstorm I'd seen from the top of the tower.

We walked up out of the city, back into the countryside, heading for the distant notch in the hills. The land here rolled gently up and down. We were walking cross-country now, not following an old road, though we did share direction with a railway line for a few pebbles, marching alongside it.

Sometimes I lost sight of the notch as we dropped into a low valley, but it was always there when we climbed the other side. I gave myself landmarks that were closer but still in line with it as we went, so we stayed on course throughout the morning. The landscape was lightly wooded with broadleaf trees. The open spaces between them which had likely once been farm fields had become heathland, criss-crossed with wide strips of thicket that had begun their life as hedgerows. My new trees book told me they were mainly hawthorn, beech or hazel. And where they weren't, they were mainly bramble. Enough bramble for me to put my boots on. Though it was easy enough to negotiate the thickets because animals had worn their own paths through them over the years, and though I couldn't help but look for a human footprint among the hoof and pad marks, I never expected to see one, and nor did I. In between there were wide spaces of grass and bracken dotted with low shrubs. Jip loved this open heath because it gave good hunting and all the rabbits he could dream of.

He ran so hard I began to worry about him damaging himself. Dad said terriers could sometimes be so stupid they'd run themselves until their hearts burst, but I don't really think that's true. Now I'm far enough away, I realise Dad was a worrier who hid his fears in sternness and bouts of bad temper that blew in without warning or sense, like dark storms from out of a clear blue sky. Worrying about terriers having heart attacks was thinking out of fear, though fear of what I don't know. Maybe he was just worried about losing a valuable dog. But Jip brought back three rabbits before he tired enough to just walk alongside me, and when a hare exploded from a gorse bush we were passing he took an instinctive couple of paces towards a sprint after it, and then stopped and looked back at me, wagging his tail, tongue lolling from his panting mouth. He was happy in the sunlight, and so was I.

It was a hot day and the blister from the pack straps became uncomfortable by lunchtime, when the sun was at its highest. It was berry time of year and I'd been grazing and picking blackberries as we went. We stopped by a small pool and sat under a willow for a rest. I ate the berries I'd picked and some of the dried meat that remained. Jip drank noisily from the water, and disturbed something that splashed and then rustled off into the long grass and docks on the other side. Jip looked after it with his ears up, but then he dropped to his haunches and panted in the shade of a nearby hazel tree.

I looked at my arm, which seemed fine to me, and thought about how to deal with the painful pack strap. I'd seen tufts of wool on some of the brambles as we passed, and now wished I'd picked enough off to make a pad to spread the pressure. I decided to do so as soon as we set off. Since wool on the thorns mean there were sheep somewhere around, I also wondered if I should shoot one if I came across them. Fresh meat would be good, and I could perhaps smoke some to carry with me. But there were plenty of rabbits and berries everywhere, and killing such a big animal and wasting the bulk of the meat seemed a waste at the time. I did not intend to be on the mainland for so long that I would need to lay in stores, let alone carry them. I could live off the land as we went, I thought. I didn't know as much about hunger then as I do now. But at the time I thought I was moving fast and travelling light. I didn't know that some journeys are best taken slow. At that point, I even felt guilty for resting in the shade of the trees and using my new book to identify them. I felt I should be up and walking every hour of daylight.

I remember all these details about that stop by the pool very clearly. Even down to the bright colours of the dragonflies hovering and zipping over the water. I remember lying back and looking up at the blue sky through the pale green screen of willow leaves and thinking that rather than killing a whole sheep, maybe I could air-dry rabbit meat on my pack as we walked so that we had some food in the days when Jip might not be able to catch our dinner, or I shoot it. And then I remember we were walking towards the notch again, and I don't remember much about the next couple of days because it turned out that my arm was not getting better at all.

I walked in a sort of daze, counting paces and pebbles and sleeping under trees. I know we passed houses, lots of houses, but I don't remember going into any of them. I do remember realising I had forgotten to transfer pebbles to keep track of my pace-counting, even though I had not forgotten to keep track of my steps. I drank a lot of water and stopped talking to Jip. My arm had given me a fever, I think. All I do recall is the notch in the hills that seemed never to get closer, and the counting. And then I went to sleep one lunchtime under an oak tree and when I woke I was shivering and it was dark and Jip was barking at me. I got into my sleeping roll and stayed there. For a couple of days all I could do was sleep, shake, stumble out of the bedroll to shit and then when there was no food left in me to come out, I swallowed the last oatcakes and lay there thinking this was a very stupid way to die. Jip just stayed beside me, giving me his warmth in the nights and his companionship during the day. He'd disappear and return with rabbits, but I didn't have the strength to light a fire and so he ate them while I watched.

I don't know how many days I was sick, but I do remember when I decided it was time to go. I had crawled to the edge of the water to refill the bottles, and was doing so when all the noise in the world seemed to stop.

The birds went quiet and even the breeze seemed to slow so that the leaves above us were silent. I turned to look at Jip who was standing rigidly, looking into the bank of woods opposite. All the hairs on the back of my neck went up. I saw nothing and the noise slowly bled back into the world, but just for an instant I had the absolute conviction that I was being looked at. And not looked at kindly. And even though I was still feverstruck and retching out most of what I drank, the thought of remaining in that place became impossible. I stumbled back to my lair and the first thing I did was string my bow and lay an arrow ready. Then, keeping my eye on the woodland opposite, I re-stuffed my pack and slipped out from under the willows and slunk away on to the rising heathland. My head was splitting with pain and all the joints in my body seemed to have grit in them, so that any movement was both stiff and painful. But despite that, the feeling I'd had by the water was so intense that I had to get away from it as fast as I could.

Maybe there had been nothing there. Maybe it was the memory of the large unseen thing that had rubbed noisily around the corner below us in the night at the museum. Or maybe I had been looked at by something that saw me as prey, in much the same way that I looked at rabbits or deer. Or sheep.

Sick, shaking and stumbling, I walked the whole day with the bow in my hand and an arrow nocked and ready. When I finally stopped at nightfall, my hand had frozen into position and I had to massage it back into life.

I stopped at a house. I wanted doors and walls to be safe behind. It was brick-built with two floors and an intact roof, and it stood beside a big pond in the middle of a stand of trees which had overgrown whatever garden it had once been surrounded by. I climbed in a broken window on the ground floor and looked around. The trees had sprouted so close to the house that their leaves pressed against the glass that remained, making the interior dark and claustrophobic. The stairs were sound enough, and I carefully creaked my way to the upper floor where there was more light. There were two rooms and a bathroom. The bathroom had a fireplace. Strangely the bedrooms didn't. I was feeling terrible and was realising that the full day's walk was a mistake. I couldn't stop shaking. Jip must have thought I was in trouble, because he hadn't set off on the rat hunt that usually marked his entry into a new house. Instead he stayed close, looking up at me with his head cocked.

Sleep, I said. Just need sleep. And fire. Cold.

The sun had not set on what had been a warm enough day, but my teeth were chattering. I kicked a couple of chairs to bits and kindled a fire in the bathroom fireplace. The chimney drew well, and the flames took. I went back into the bedrooms and took the drawers from a chest of drawers and stomped them to more firewood, which I laid in a stack by the grate, and then I shook out my bedroll and, in a house with two bedrooms, lay down on the bathroom floor. I would have gone to sleep right there had my arm been itching as badly as it had been ever since I came ashore, but the very fact that it had stopped began to worry me and go round and round like a worm in my head. I wondered if that meant it had got worse, that the infection had poisoned the arm so much that it had begun killing off the nerves. I wondered if I had come so far, so impulsively, only to end up another unnoticed tangle of bones and rags on the floor of a house no one would ever visit again, friendless, forgotten and far from the sea.

I sat up and made myself unravel the bandage on my arm, painfully conscious I had not changed it for days. I think I expected to see blackened flesh and rot, but in fact the honey had begun to do its job. I knew I should boil the bandage before re-applying it, and while I was thinking about what to do and if I had the energy to in fact do anything at all, I did the only thing I actually was able.

I fell asleep. And I don't remember anything else except when I woke it was bright sunlight and my mouth was dry as old straw and something smelled dead and after a bit I realised that smell was me. I'd messed myself. I felt ashamed even though there was no one but Jip to see. He came over and licked my face to show he didn't care and was glad I was awake, and then went out, presumably to go hunting.

I drank deep from my water bottle and got up a little too fast which made me retch. My legs felt bendy in all the wrong directions, and the room swam alarmingly around me as I tried to walk. I took off my soiled clothes and took them downstairs with me, holding on to the wall as I went.

I climbed out of the window and carefully walked to the pond. It was fed by a small stream that came off the slope behind it, so it wasn't stagnant water. I drank some more and then set about cleaning my clothes. It took a lot of scrubbing and rinsing and doing it over again and again to get them clean, but I did it. The stink wasn't just the mess I'd made: it was the sweat with which I'd soaked the rest of my clothes, lying asleep in my fever. And of course it was also me. Leaving my clothes spread out on a bush, I got into the pond and washed myself too, ducking below the surface and giving my hair a good scrub as I did so. It was deep-bone cold but I've never swum in warm water so the ache and tingle of it was familiar and, in its own way, comforting. I turned on my back and swam to the middle of the pond, where I floated, looking up at the sky and feeling that great sense of exhilaration that comes when you've been so ill you had forgotten what well feels like. I wasn't strong, or even really over it, but I was definitely over the worst. On the mend, as Dad used to say.

You can work today because you're on the mend.

The warmth of the day was going, however, and the sun dropping. I realised as I floated there that I must have been asleep for almost a full twenty-four hours. And it would be dark again soon.

Jip brought a rabbit to the edge of the pond and dropped it with a bark that said it was for me.

I got out and took the rabbit and my wet clothes back to the house. I broke up some more furniture and got the fire in the bathroom going again. I was feeling well enough to poke around, which got me a couple of cooking pots and a good knife from the kitchen, and in the bathroom cabinet a curved plastic pot with a flat lid and a faded label that said it was DR HARRIS ARLINGTON SHAVING SOAP. It still had the ghost of a smell, clean and sharp. I decided there and then to heat water in one of the cooking pots and re-clean my clothes with some of this soap. The lid cracked when I opened it, but I still have a much smaller puck of the soap with me wrapped in a piece of cloth. I think the smell must have really gone but I sometimes take it out and sniff it and imagine I can get the faint outline of what it once was.

That night, I wrung out my newly fragrant clothes and hung them in front of the fire to dry as I slept. I boiled the rabbit meat with a sprig of rosemary I broke from a bush by the kitchen door. It didn't taste of much, but I ate it all and slept long and deep, waking once to see Jip lying across the door, facing the stairs, on guard just in case anything came in to see what we were up to. Comforted, I quietly told him he was a good dog and went back to sleep.

He was gone when I woke.

Chapter 16

Shooting the albatross

I got dressed and waited for him by the pond. And then I walked around whistling and then calling for him until my throat went raw. When waiting got to be unbearable, I left my pack so that he'd know I was coming back if I missed him, and then I took my bow and went looking for him seriously. I tracked back along the way we'd come, and then I returned and walked ever widening circles around the house, still whistling and shouting and listening. I froze many times, ears straining at a distant noise in the woods, convinced that at any moment it would turn into an excited crashing through the undergrowth that would end up with an exhausted but happy Jip bounding back to me. But that never happened. I ate berries when I remembered to, but I didn't have the heart to go hunt a rabbit or find anything else to eat, maybe because I couldn't think of anything sadder than the lonely meal waiting for me at the end of the day if I didn't find him.

But I didn't find him, and he didn't find me. All that did was a darkness that seemed to come earlier than I'd expected, and a long night back in the house without a fire. I didn't light it because I didn't want the crackling of the wood to drown any sounds outside that might be an injured dog trying to get my attention. But in truth I knew then that I'd likely never know where he went. Or why. Or if he meant to come back and couldn't. I told myself that accidents happen, even to terriers. Thinking of what that accident might have been kept sleep away for more than half the night.

I was awake before the dawn, waiting for the greyness to take over from the dark, but first light brought nothing but a short and depressing rain shower and no dog at all.

I was feeling physically stronger, but my spirits could not have been lower. I was so worried and sad that my thinking was nearly as muddled as it had been when I was gripped by the fever. Once the shower had passed, I sat on the stairs and listened to the water dripping sullenly off the trees pressing against the windows and tried to think realistically and practically. Again, I don't know if it was the right choice, but I decided to look for Jip again for one more day—and then move on.

In my heart, I think I would have waited for him for ever, if I truly believed he was coming back. But it wasn't just the house and the woods around it that I was circling. It was the nasty, heartbreaking truth that Jip would never run off and leave me. It was the very opposite of his nature to do something like that, and while he might stay away hunting all night, he would always have returned if he could. Nevertheless I spent hours walking around the woods, looking into rabbit holes, listening even, just in case he had dug himself into a tunnel he couldn't get out of. I'd seen how far he would dig into the sand dunes at home if he thought there was a chance of a rabbit at the end of it—ten feet or more sometimes.

It was while crouching silently by one of these holes that I looked up and saw the badgers. Two of them across a patch of nettles, staring back at me, unmistakable white heads with two thick black stripes running from either side of the muzzle up across the eyes to the ears behind. The first badger I saw was in a book about a rat and a mole that went on a great adventure. That badger was wise and tough and stern and a good friend in need. I don't know if these badgers were wise, but they looked tough and stern enough and while not unfriendly, they didn't seem especially concerned by the sudden arrival of a human. But they did look larger than I had expected a badger to look in the flesh. They not only looked quite big but more than sturdy enough to give as good as they got in a fight with a terrier the size of Jip. As they lost interest in me and shambled of into the undergrowth, I began to wonder if there were other ways Jip might have got into trouble than digging too enthusiastically.

I found the corpse at just about the time I was going to give up. I almost missed it, but the tail of my eye must have noticed the fur and the brown paw sticking up in the air against the grey-green trunk of a beech tree. Or maybe it was the geometrical regularity of the bones of the ribcage among the chaotic shapes of the undergrowth. Without thinking, my head swung back to see what I'd so nearly walked straight past and I felt my stomach flip and something unswallowable appear at the base of my throat.

I went very still for as long as I could manage, and then found I was moving towards the body, pulled by a magnet I couldn't escape no matter how much I wanted to.

Jip was more than my dog; he was my friend, my family, my brother.

He was not this freshly dead fox at the foot of the tree.

Relief hit me so hard that my legs went and I dropped painfully to my knees in the rough tangle of fallen twigs and beechnut shells. I found myself gasping for air as if I'd been holding my breath for a long time. Maybe I had. Since I was little, since Joy was taken from us over the high cliff at the back of the island, I've always prided myself on not crying when things hurt or get tough, so I don't think I was crying, but the sobs of air I took in might have sounded like it if anyone was watching.

I spent one more night in the brick house, which I had come to hate because it was where I had lost my other dog. I sat beside the bathroom fire on my bedroll and read the book on trees by the glow off the flames. That's where I learned the name of the beech the fox had died next to, and the fact that the little three-sided nuts spilling out of their hairy cases were called beech mast. And that they were edible. That's about all the good I got out of that night, and again I did not sleep well. There was a wind, and the trees that were slowly squeezing in on the house from all sides rustled and scratched away at the windows all night. When I did sleep, my dreams were full of things trying to get inside the house, and trees that walked, and triffids—which were from a book I read about a very different end of the world than the one you and I are on either side of. Your world didn't end because of meteorites that blinded everyone, or killer plants. Although Ferg said one theory he'd heard from the Lewismen was that what did it was something your lot put on the plants, something that got into everybody's bodies and then became infectious and stopped breeding happening. That was just something he said. To me that sounds as fanciful as triffids. Or krakens. That was another strange book by the same writer. Maybe if I'd been sleeping by the shore, I'd have dreamed of krakens. But I was far inland, and my eyes hadn't seen the healthy sea for days. I think I was as soul-sick for the sea as I was fever-struck. And now I look back on it, I also think my mind was reeling from all the new things I had seen, not just the novelty of bridges and churches and towers and trees, but the sheer, relentless immensity of what had been left behind. It was the volume of it all, pressing in on my head like the big bench vice in Dad's workshop.

I did a spiteful thing when I left the brick house. I feel bad about it even now, though I don't know exactly why I should feel like this, any more than I know precisely why I did it. I regretted it the first time I looked back and saw the column of black smoke rising into the still air behind me, but by that time it was far too late to do anything about it. I had walked four pebbles without turning because leaving a place that Jip had been and just might one day return to was so hard I think I might have broken and run back and waited—as I said—for ever. I had broken up the empty chests of drawers and left them spilling into the fireplace when I left, waiting until they had caught before leaving, hearing the thrum of flames vibrate through the ceiling above me as I climbed out of the downstairs window for the last time.

It was a cremation. A fire burial. A Viking funeral. An end, marked. A farewell signal put into the sky for what was left of the world to see, to honour a dog and then to be dispersed and blown away in the wind. Those were some of the high thoughts I had as I walked away towards the notch in the hills, definitely not crying. Then, when I did stop and look back, I saw it for the meanness it was. I had just hated the house for what had happened in it and had not thought of how it had sheltered me while I got better. I had burned it and the homes of the animals that lived in its walls and under its floors, and the birds that had nested under its eaves, and I had burned the crowding trees too. The trees had done nothing bad, other than grow where they could. A bad thing had happened to me in that house, but it had happened as blamelessly as the rain. The bad thing that had been done in that house, to the house, that was done by me. I walked onwards, sickened at myself, the nasty feeling that I had somehow called down bad luck on my future growing with every pace.

You know the rhyme about the ancient sailor that stoppeth one in three? Dad used to read it to us by the fire in the winter, and it chills me now to think of it as much as it did when he did the voices, and described the icebergs on the polar ocean and the other warm and sluggish sea that trapped them later, thick with sea snakes and ghost ships. It seemed to be describing another planet entirely. I felt just like that poem. Like that ancient mariner, in my case at sea in a land whose rules I did not quite understand until it was too late. I never understood why the mariner shot the albatross that had saved them, and I still don't know why I burned the house that had sheltered me. But I did. And I did it on purpose, in a kind of vicious lashing out at something just because I was scared and confused and sad. I didn't need to see the bright lick of the red flames at the base of the black column of smoke towering over the copse and the pond to know that, just like the rhyme said, I had done a hellish thing.

I had shot the albatross.

Chapter 17

Woe

I walked away from the accusing finger of smoke with the thumpity-thump delivery Dad had always read the mariner poem with pounding away in my brain. If you listen to someone reading a poem often enough, it hammers itself into your mind and makes it not only easier to remember, but also harder to forget. I would really have liked to have forgotten the lines that kept going round and round, the ones that said something like:

And I had done an hellish thing,
And it would work 'em woe:
For all averred, I had killed the bird
That made the breeze to blow.
Ah wretch! said they, the bird to slay
That made the breeze to blow!

Well, I told myself. At least I don't need breezes to get me moving. All I need is my legs.

And I did punish them, walking more pebbles in that first day than I had done in two before I had lost Jip. I walked hard to make my body ache enough to distract me from the heart-wrenching question of why I had set off on a probably futile search for one dog and then lost the other. In shame and self-loathing, I walked through the dusk and on into the darkness, lit by moonlight until the clouds came and then I rolled into an uncomfortable bundle beneath a little rounded bridge that had once taken a small road over a single railway track. It was dry and like a house without walls on two sides. I slept well and woke to the sound of birds in the trees all around me, and stepped out into the sunlight feeling that this was going to be a good day. The feeling lasted through most of the morning, and even raised a bit as my nose caught a whiff of woodsmoke blowing into my face as I climbed the first proper slope I had so far encountered on my walk from the coast. I knew from the direction of the wind that I was not smelling Jip's funeral pyre behind me. And I knew I must be close to the spot I had marked what seemed an age ago on the rain-lashed viewing platform on the tower, the source of the distant firelight I had seen winking at me in the storm, the spark of hope and mystery that I'd been so excited about when I had been confident and angry, and had a good dog to travel towards it with. Before I lost Jip and shot the albatross.

Some part of me must have been thinking straight and acting cautious, because I crested the slope with my bow in my hand, arrow ready.

The fire had not been manmade. Ahead of me was a burn mark just like the ones on the heather-covered slopes at home. It had blown through the bracken and gorse in the same long distinctive tongue shape. I walked the length of it, from the widest point to the narrow tip where it had begun. There I found a small stand of trees protected from the wind in a crease in the land just below the ridgeline, and half of them—on what must have been the windward side—were still green. The others were charred and it was easy to see where the lightning had struck and ignited the fire. One tree still stood—taller than the rest but dead on its feet, split in two by the strike. The halves leaned away from each other exposing the burned-out heartwood. It was somehow terrible—both the sight and the thought of the power it must have taken to do that, electricity jagging out of the sky. Even at the time, it seemed like another bad omen. I did not know that one day I would know exactly what the tree had felt like, riven in half by a bolt from out of a clear blue sky.

The burn scar stemming from the lightning tree was still fresh. No growth had begun to fill in. The smell was new and strong. The fire had been nature, not man. The spark of distant hope had been an illusion and the adventure it had lured me into was a mistaken ordeal instead. It had also killed my dog.

I was still as alone as I had ever been. I sat on the ridge and looked down at the countryside spread out below. I decided the best way to deal with the disappointment was to look at the map and try and work out how far I had come, where I was, and how far I had to go to get to Brand's hideout. I was thinking of it as that by then—a hideout. A place thieves and pirates took their plunder. It was fanciful, but at that point I was not seeing the world as it is, because I had still seen so very little of it. I know that now, now that I have had a long time to do little else but think. I was still seeing it through the lens of the books I had read about it before it died, and that coloured things. It was like the old pair of sunglasses that Bar used to wear when fishing, the ones that made the water look different. It's not exactly like that because Bar's sunglasses actually took away the reflection on the surface of the water and let you see what was happening below. My lens of books didn't seem to be helping me see any hidden things below the surface.

The map was both helpful and confusing. I had a rough idea of where I was, even though I had messed up my distance counting while I was feverish, on the days when I had futilely plodded away counting steps but forgetting to mark them with my clever-but-actually-not-so-clever-if-you-forget-to-do-it pebble trick.

Before I laid out the map, I climbed as high as I could, out on to the edge of an area of high moors, and looked down. My compass gave me north, so I was able to lay the map down at my feet and orientate it in the right direction. I weighted the edges against the wind and spent a long time carefully trying to match up the features that were so confidently marked on the map with the much blurrier details time and vegetation had overgrown. It took me most of the rest of the daylight to put it all together in a way that at least half made sense, but even as I went to sleep I was not sure I'd got it right. My plan was to walk to the curving line of trees about five klicks away and see if it was, as I guessed, one of the important roads the map showed and numbered beginning with the letter M. If it was the one I thought, then walking along it would take me to a very big city in the middle of the country, and then if I confirmed that I could make my way east by following the path of old roads and a railway line until I hit the coast more or less where I wanted to. It would be better than steering by notches in the hills. Especially because on the downside of this high ground there would be no more slopes rising ahead of me.

I woke and looked for Jip and then remembered he would

not be greeting me on any more mornings, and so I drank some water, checked the map and got going, my stomach telling me it needed filling and my legs wondering why they couldn't have a few hours more rest.

I hit the M road where it cut into the shoulder of the slope I was descending. The deeply cut sidings were a vivid slash of purple and green, and as I pushed through the head-high plants, the seed-pods snapped noisily, firing seeds in every direction. It made me jump at first, but then I decided it was quite a cheery thing and even whacked some of the plant heads as I passed, just to see the sharp little explosions.

Grass and moss had invaded the roadbed, but I could see it had originally been many cars wide and had once had a low barrier of metal and thick steel cables running down the middle of it. It made a sort of green road that ribboned away between purple banks for several klicks ahead and I wove my path along the old road, checking my compass every pebble to make sure it was the one I imagined it was, and wasn't a different road snaking me back the way I had come.

I saw two strange and differently wonderful things on that road, before the next bit of albatross luck happened. The first was a true marvel.

As the roadway passed through another deeply cut groove in the surrounding high ground, there was an impossible bridge. It was beautiful, as if made from two thin ribbons of stone which I expect were concrete. One carried a road that ran straight across the chasm, continuing the line of the slope that had been removed. The other ribbon supported it in a breathtaking arch that sprang from the right hand side of the cutting, barely seeming to touch the top piece before curving back down on to the left-hand side. It was obviously rock-solid, having stood there in all weathers for more than a century, probably a century and a half, but it was so light and joyous it seemed more like movement than something built. It was like a leap made from stone. A leap and a balancing act. Would it have looked so wonderful to you? Or would you have driven a car beneath it and not noticed? With so many marvels around you, did you stop seeing some of them?

The other wonderful thing was what was on top of the bridge looking down at me. It was a black bull. Or maybe a big cow. It looked male though, and it had stubby horns and a huge hump of muscle around its shoulders. It wasn't nearly as interested in me as I was in it, because as I walked under the bridge and looked back, it did not bother to come to the other side to watch me on my way. I had never seen a bull or a cow before. I didn't feel particularly frightened by it, though I definitely doubted I would be able to kill one with an arrow if it decided to attack me. A pony was the biggest animal I had seen thus far in my life, and the biggest one I had hunted was the deer. The bull was rangy and bunch-muscled at the same time. It looked like all it would have to do was flex those muscles and arrows would bounce off it. And if the arrows didn't bounce off, there was too much body between the outside and the vital organs within for even the most powerful bowshot to penetrate. I looked back at the empty bridge behind me and was glad that cows and bulls were plant-eaters. Something that size with a taste for smaller mammals would have been terrifying.

On the other hand, something that size would feed a person for a year if you could kill it and smoke or salt the meat. And there were other ways of killing and catching than shooting with a bow. Traps, for example. I was thinking all this as I walked, maybe because the universe sometimes has a warped sense of humour—or perhaps just a really sharp sense of timing.

Before the end of that day, I was the one in the trap.

It started with being hungry. The diet of berries was fine enough, though it wasn't entirely agreeing with my stomach. I reckoned I was about half a day's hard walking from the big city where I would have to take a turn from the M road and follow a railway line towards the coast—if I could find it. I had made good time so far and decided to see if I could find some rabbits to shoot. With that in mind, I waited until the road bottomed out into flatter land surrounded by heath that had once been fields. Then I turned off the road and walked parallel with it, bow ready. I saw a hare that ran too soon and too fast for me to fire at it, and then a couple of white tails turned up and ducked into thickets before I could aim properly. There was enough game around for me not to worry about firing at every opportunity. It just wasn't worth the risk of losing a precious arrow loosing off at anything but a certain hit.

I walked off the heathland onto a small built-up area beside the M road, this one connected to a similar collection of single-storey buildings on the other side by a bridge that was too thin for cars and which had buckled in the middle and fallen onto the roadway. I suppose it was a bridge for walking on. It was covered, like a big pipe you'd have to go through. Probably to keep the rain off. A huge rectangular canopy had fallen in and landed drunkenly on top of some rusted boxes that I recognised as petrol dispensers from the couple I'd seen back on the Uists. It was tilted up on one corner, propped on a tank. This was my first tank, and I knew it by the long gun-barrel and the tracks rusted to the wheels on either side. I don't know why an army tank would be on a petrol station. I climbed up on it and tried to open the big metal hatches, but they were corroded shut. I hopped down again and then froze as I saw a child's face in the end of the gun-barrel looking at me. And then I realised it was a toy doll's head that someone had put inside it. Again, I don't know why.

Before there was a tank there, this must have been a place that travellers came to eat and refuel when going along the M road. The low building smelled damp and earthy. I didn't trust the saggy roof, but through the broken window walls I could see the rusting skeletons of chairs and tables.

A faded plastic sign told me to try a Whopper.

I don't know what a Whopper was. Maybe you tried one once. I hope it was good.

I walked on, hungry, skirting the M road, still tracking it in the hope of rabbits. A few pebbles later I saw something in a stand of white-barked birches and stopped walking. It was a deer, smaller than the ones on the island, with a lighter coat and much shorter antlers. I carefully shrugged out of my pack and took two arrows. One I put through my belt at the back; the other I nocked as I began to carefully move into bowshot.

The wind was in my face so I knew I couldn't be scented and the deer seemed totally absorbed in cropping the grass between the birches. I moved slowly, keeping an eye on the ground in front of me to be sure I didn't tread on anything that would make a noise and spook my next week or so of meals. The deer moved away, and I thought I had lost it, but it had only decided to graze on a different patch of grass. I entered the birch wood carefully, trying to calm my breathing. Beyond the thin strip of birches was a taller mass of vegetation, a steep rampart of brambles and creepers rising above the silvery leaves like a dark thunderhead.

The pale deer was easy to see against it. It was entirely unaware of how close I was getting. I slowly raised the bow and said the silent apology and thanks that Ferg had taught me when he and Bar first took me hunting, the one that calms your breathing and brings good luck. And then I shot it.

I don't miss much. And the deer was close and perfectly broadside on. I saw the arrow feathers thump home exactly where I had aimed, just behind the shoulder. The deer gave a couple of instinctive steps forward, and then fell. I dropped my bow and the spare arrow and ran in, unsheathing my knife in case it was lung-shot and needed a quick mercy. Ferg said every second you left an animal in pain when you could end it for them was a curse on you. But the deer was heart-shot and dead, and looking as suddenly sad as all prey does when the life is gone. I said another silent thanks and promised the meat would not be wasted, which was not something Ferg or Bar had taught me, but something I had added myself when I shot my first deer.

I should have dragged it out the way I had come, but I would have had to step over fallen logs to do so, and there was an animal track winding through the trees that looked clearer. Because I wasn't paying too much attention to anything other than the light and whether I would have enough time to gut and butcher it before dark, I didn't see the boar until it was too late. Jip would have seen it. He would have warned me. But Jip was gone.

I heard the huff and growl before I saw the small eyes and the large tusks turning towards me from the brushwood just ahead. I went still and the eyes and the tusks raised themselves off the ground as the boar stood up. And up. It was much bigger than I had imagined a boar could be. Not as big as a bull, but just as solid and hard-muscled. It just looked like trouble. I don't know what you would have done if you had met a giant boar on a remote woodland track, but I do know that whatever the right thing was, I didn't do it. I kept looking at it, and backed away slowly.

It's okay, I said, putting all the soothe I had in me into my voice. It's okay.

The boar huffed and grunted some more, pawing the ground. Its eyes looked really angry. I didn't know boars got so big.

I didn't know how fast they could run either. There was a spit of dirt as it launched itself at me. I twisted away and ran and everything that happened next happened in a jumble I still can't quite get straight in my head. I ran and there was no room really, nowhere to run to. I felt the boar's breath on the back of my leg and tried to dodge sideways. I hit the trunk of a tree that I hadn't seen and then I was on my back, and the boar was sort of turning round in its own length and charging at me and then I was on my feet and instead of the boar's breath I heard its teeth snap together and felt the tug on my leg as it bit at my trousers, and I stumbled because though the bite had missed my flesh it had tripped me. And then as I corkscrewed to my feet, brambles ripping at me and trying to keep me pinned in place, the boar leapt at me and hooked its tusk into my thigh. That tusk must have been keen as a shaving blade because I felt the air on my leg as the material was cut from knee to inner thigh as I was jumping in a forlorn and desperate attempt to save myself—and even though I was going up and away from the boar's head, the tusk punched into me like I was being hit with a sledgehammer. It wasn't a sharp feeling like a cut. It was a horrible dull punch and I knew the damage was bad even as my fingers found the branch above me and I swung out of the animal's way. It turned and twisted, ready to slash me again, but somehow I lifted myself high enough so my feet were clear of it. And then, with a last grunt of pain, I swung one of my legs across and got a precarious toehold on another branch and held myself there, shakily parallel with the ground,

Where the tusk had got me was close to the big artery on my inner thigh. In that moment, as I held myself in an awkward horizontal position, stretched between two thin branches, I knew that blood loss would very soon make me lose my grip. And I knew that the position in which I was desperately clinging to safety was also ridiculous and undignified. Maybe that's always the way death comes. I made myself look across at my thigh.

There was no sheet of blood. Just a ruined trouser leg.

It made no sense. I had felt the blow. And then I craned round to see what the boar was making such a noise about, thrashing this way and that below me.

He had my little book of trees and my tin of beeswax impaled on the tusk. I'd been carrying the book in my front pocket so I could identify what kind of trees I was walking past. I took advantage of the fact he was so occupied with clearing his tusk and scrambled closer to the trunk of the tree, where I managed to get the right way up and climb higher.

There was blood, but it was not mine. And it was the thing that had made him angry enough to attack. He was hurt. Something had taken a great scoop out of the flesh on his back leg, close to the tail. It was nasty wound. I could see the dried blood on his leg from haunch to trotter, and as he shifted I could see the torn up and exposed muscles flex and move. I didn't have much time to feel sorry for him because he finally got the book and the tin off his tusk and started circling the trunk of the tree, looking up at me and butting it. It wasn't a very big tree, and I don't think his butting and rooting at it had as much effect on it as my weight as I scrambled around getting on the other side of the trunk from him. To my horror the whole tree began to tilt alarmingly. Very aware that I had used up any good luck that was due to me with the trees book, I knew it wouldn't be very long at all before this tree fell over and dumped me right back at tusk level. As the tree began to topple towards the cliff of brambles, I scrambled as high as I could and then leapt desperately towards it.

Hurling yourself into a bramble patch is not to be recommended, not unless the alternative is dropping into range of a murderously angry wild boar in so much pain that nothing will do but inflicting even more of the same on you. I know the thorns tore at me because I still have some of the scars, but at the time I felt nothing, fear numbing me as I grabbed desperately at the high bank of greenery and briars. It must have been ten metres high. Even as I had jumped, I had a vision of myself tumbling into the centre of it, the briars ripping at me but too insubstantial to hold my weight. Instead I hit something so solid it nearly jarred both wind and consciousness out of me. I held on and scrambled into the bramble cliff, half stunned and unsure what I was seeing.

The Neatfreaks were the Baby Busters who tried to tidy things up and leave the world in an organised fashion. I think it must have been them who had stacked so many old cars on top of each other. I had hit a rusted axle end and used it to crawl further in to safety. I lay across an old drive shaft and got my breath and my senses back. Inside the wall of brambles there was a three-dimensional maze of corroded car bodies. There were some creepers and briars twining around within the structure, but most of the growth was on the outside where the sun was. It was a strange space, broken up by the ribs and spines of the long dead cars, and the covering of vegetation gave it an underwater feeling. It would have been peaceful if there hadn't been an angry wounded boar snuffling around just beyond the wall of thorns.

When I moved, the car skeleton shifted slightly. Something broke away from something else and fell noisily through the remains of the five or six cars below, hitting a bit of each one on the way down. The car pile was not a wholly safe place to hide. As I clung there and looked around, I was able to see how far gone most of them were. The solid panels had mostly corroded off. Where they survived, they were laced with holes, well on the way to crumbling into nothing. The frames of the cars were thicker metal and they and the wheels and axles were what was keeping the pile intact. The floors of almost every one I could see were either gone or clearly not suitable for treading on. The seats had long rotted away, right down to the springs, which were themselves rusted. There was nowhere you could trust yourself inside the whole pile. I had the strong sense, as I shifted again and heard the grinding noise that accompanied the movement, that the whole structure was just waiting for an excuse to fall in on itself. And even if that didn't happen, there was an equally uncomfortable possibility that I might fall through the tangle of sharp rusty metal and impale myself on something, or that an axle or an engine block might drop out of a hulk above me and finish me like that.

I clung on and tried to figure out what to do, other than stay still. I had seen what the boar's snout was capable of, pushing at the thin tree trunk. If it started jostling away at the foot of the car pile, I definitely thought it could destroy the balance and bring it all painfully and fatally down. I peered down at it and decided that it was mean enough to do that out of sheer spite and anger. I could see my bow and an arrow lying in the undergrowth beyond it, but there was no way I could get down and past it to get to them, and I was pretty sure it was too tough to kill with a single arrow unless I was unbelievably lucky.

It seemed like my only option was to stay very still, lying on top of the axle until the boar got tired and went away. The boar didn't seem to have any plans to do anything else, however, and stayed where it was, huffing and snuffling with what I first thought was anger but that—the longer I listened to it—I realised was pain. I tried to think of good things, like the miracle of the tiny book of trees that had saved my life. I told myself it could be worse.

And then it started raining, and it was. The metal got slippery and, badder than that, the car above was one of the few that still had some bits of bodywork intact, a roof that was angled just right to catch the rain and then funnel it in a small waterfall, right on top of me. It was miserable, cold and dangerous. And the more I tried to stay still, the stiffer I got, and the longer I waited, the more I started to notice the stings and aches of all the scratches criss-crossing me, the ones I'd got from throwing myself to this precarious almost-safety inside the cliff of briars. Once again, I thought what a fool I had been to rush off alone after Brand. And that thought led to the worst thing which of course was not dying alone, because I supposed when that happened I wouldn't know much about it, but the losing of Jip. That was my responsibility. If I hadn't come inland, away from the sea that I knew into this country I was so ignorant about, Jip would still be alive and by my side.

I closed my eyes and tried to think of something else, something that would stop me feeling like I was going to slide off this axle and cut myself to shreds on every exposed bit of corroded metal below me. But I couldn't. Jip wouldn't get out of my mind. It was like a haunting. Every time I tried to distract myself, he was there, like a ghost. Happy memories of simpler times? Jip was there. Setting off on this foolish journey in the *Sweethope*? Jip was there. Sitting by a warm fire in the safety of an island winter? Jip was there. He was so there that I imagined I could hear him barking.

The boar stopped snuffling and went very still.

The only sound was the rain. And Jip's barking.

I opened my eyes. I wasn't imagining it. Jip was barking and he was getting closer. It was unbelievable and it was unmistakable. Jip was alive, he was coming and the excitement in his bark told me he had scented me. My heart leapt. Then the boar huffed and turned and trotted towards the noise and my heart plummeted. Jip had the heart of a lion, and didn't know to back off a fight, but he had the body of a terrier and the boar that was trotting towards him was much bigger and heavier and was equipped with tusks that would rip his belly open in a single twitch.

No! I shouted. Jip, no! Run! No, Jip! Go away!

His barking raised in excitement at the sound of my voice.

My guts turned to water.

No, Jip! I yelled. Bad dog! Bad dog! Get away with you! Bad dog!

I heard a squeal of anger and swear I felt a tremor in the earth below as the boar must have seen him and kicked into a charge

I heard Jip's answering snarl.

NO, JIP! I shouted, launching myself off my axle perch, half scrabbling, half tumbling down through the car carcasses to the ground, some forlorn hope moving my body before I knew what I was doing.

NO, JIP!

There was a thunderclap.

And the world bucked.

And the boar's squealing stopped dead.

I froze. No sound but the rain and the car chassis rocking against each other overhead, disturbed by my sudden descent. I stared at the wall of brambles between me and the fate of my dog.

And then there he was, barking happily at me on the other side.

Once more I forgot about the thorns and burst through and then he and I were together and he was jumping up and curving round me, barking and licking excitedly, tail thrashing and I was trying to hug and stroke and scratch him all at the same time and we were such a tangled mess of happiness I forgot about the boar and then my hand got snagged in the rope round his neck and before I could quite realise what it was and wonder at its strange out-of-placeness I heard a twig crack and looked over his head and my eye followed the long loop of rope and at the end of it I saw her.

I saw the hooded figure and I saw the pale horse she sat on, and I saw the long double-barrelled gun she was holding, pointed up at the sky like a knight's lance.

She saw me, nodded and then her eyes kept moving, scanning the undergrowth around me, carefully, inquiringly. Finally her eyes came back to me and she spoke.

Eskeelya doe-travek voo? she said.

I could tell it was a question.

Eskeelya doe-travek voo? she repeated, eyes again looking behind me.

I had no idea what it meant.

I don't understand what you're saying, I said.

I did understand what the gun meant when it lowered and pointed at me, and then beckoned me out of the trees as she backed the horse away back into the open. She pulled the rope for Jip to come. He resisted. I stroked him.

I wondered if she could hear my heart thumping over the noise of the rain.

She gestured again with the gun, and then grimaced as if my not responding was causing her actual pain.

Veet, she said. *Veet*.

Okay, I said. Okay. I'm coming.

Chapter 18

John Dark

The boar was dead. The gun had blown an ugly chunk out of its face. It was just like the chunk blown out of its backside, only fresher. I didn't know then but I found out soon enough that this wasn't a coincidence. She had tried to kill the boar the day before, but only wounded it. If Ferg was right about the curses that piled up as long as you left an animal hurt before finishing it off cleanly, then she was drowning in them. And there was nothing clean about the way the boar had been finished off. It had tried to disembowel me, but now I looked at its poor hacked-about body I felt sad. It had been in pain. A human had caused that pain. I don't blame it a bit for attacking the next human it saw.

But I didn't spend a lot of time looking at it, or even thinking about it. There was too much else to take in. Her horse. The other two horses behind her, riderless, roped together, with great bundles hanging on either side. They were all pale grey, dappled with whiteish blotches and long white manes. They were much bigger than the little ponies we had on the islands. They stood very calmly, not even that interested in me.

Oo son lays owe-truh? she said, pointing around the landscape with a questioning gesture. She grimaced again and I realised that she was actually in pain.

I don't understand, I said.

The rain was easing and she pushed the hood back off her head. My first thought was that her hair matched the horse's—grey, strong and wild-looking as the wind blew it round her face. My second thought was that she had a face that was really two faces, the first old and weather-beaten but one that had also kept alive within it the second, younger face it had once been.

She grimaced again and pointed at the dead boar.

Sallo! she said, spitting at it. *Pew tan de sangliay.*

And she spat on it again and then turned her horse so that I could see the other side and the thing that made her grimace every time she moved.

The side of the horse was pink with blood. My first thought was that it was injured, but as I followed the irregular fan of blood back to its source I saw the wound was in the woman's side, a gash in her buttock that she had tried to bind with a sash.

I had not expected to meet anyone on the mainland, or at least not until I got to Brand's home. I had been brought up in the sure and certain knowledge that the mainland was empty. It made sense to me. I had, as I said, been made to do the maths to calculate how vanishingly few people remained in the world. And there was an unspecified sense that something had happened there that made it mysteriously hostile to man. I had in fact seen nothing that supported that on my journey so far, and had been wondering if it was really true or just a story our grandparents had told to make sure we kept safely out of the way, on the fringes of the world as the Baby Bust died away. I had been a dutiful enough child, but maybe all children have an urge to go where they're forbidden, or to touch the things they have been warned away from. I think that was how my secret wanting to travel and see the forbidden world began. Even though I was now grown, I had still felt a sense of excitement as well as righteous anger as I'd set out on this journey. And though I hadn't expected to meet anyone, I had of course thought about what it might be like if the unlikely happened. But of all the things I had imagined, I had not anticipated that we would not be able to speak to each other.

You would have thought of this possibility, coming from a world still crammed with people talking in a whole mish-mash of different languages. In fact, when I now look at the photo of you, I realise I don't even know if you and I would have been able to talk if we had met. I had just assumed you spoke the same language as me. But maybe you were from somewhere else, like she was. This mainland was no more hers than it was mine. As I eventually found out, she came from across the sea channel dividing it from the bigger mainland to the south. She was French. But before I knew that, I knew three much more important things about her: she was badly hurt, she needed help and she was extremely bossy. I think the long word that describes her best was imperious. She carried herself—and her gun—as if she were in charge of the world. And she hated to be seen with any kind of weakness.

Communication was hard at first. She seemed both frustrated and slightly offended that I didn't speak her language, which was an odd thing since later she had me dig a small book out of one of the packs: an English/French dictionary. She wouldn't have brought it along with her had she not anticipated the problem. Once the book was found, we moved from communicating by sign language alone to doing so by sign language and pointing at words in the dictionary.

But that was long after she had showed me how to put up her shelter and had managed to painfully get off her horse.

The shelter was a rectangle of oiled cotton, with metal-ringed holes in it from which hung long strings. She showed me where to tie it off between two trees, and then she threw me some aluminium pegs so I could pin down the back to make a sloping roof. Then she waved me away, again with the gun, and got off her horse. She dismounted on the other side of the animal, and I think she did that so I wouldn't see her wince and cry out as she did so. Imperious meant that she was proud before she was anything else.

I went to help her, and again she waved me back.

She took two steps towards one of the horses, obviously intending to get something from the packs, and then she stumbled and yelped and fell hard, and then lay there.

She'd fallen on the gun and was panting with the pain from her wound. I leapt across and yanked the gun out from under her. It wasn't the gentlest thing I could have done, but I wanted it out of the way quickly in case she grabbed at it.

She gasped and then growled and glared at me as if she wanted to scorch me with her eyes as a punishment.

If I'd been a really good person, I would have looked to see if I could help before doing anything else, but I'm not a really good person. I'm just me. Not bad. Just good enough. So the first thing I did was take out my knife and cut Jip free. The second thing I did was check to see why he was limping. It wasn't deep, but he had a cut running three quarters of the way around his foreleg, as if something had caught it in a noose. He licked my hand in thanks and looked at the woman and then back at me.

I know, I said.

I opened the gun and saw there was only one shell in it, and that was the one she had fired to kill the hog, so she'd been bluffing when she ordered me around with it. Hadn't really felt like she was threatening my life anyway, but it was good to confirm that was so. I left the gun on the ground and went to her packhorses.

She started shouting at me, but her voice was weakening and I ignored her. I found her bedroll and placed it under the shelter she'd had me put up. Then I pointed at it and used sign language to try and tell her I was going to help her get to it. She batted my hands away when I first tried to get hold of her. I stepped back and made calming gestures with my hand, the same gestures I used to make when approaching the half-wild ponies on the islands when we needed to get a halter on them. I said the same things to her that I said to them, using the same calming voice.

It's okay, I said. It's okay. I'm not going to hurt you.

Maybe it was the tone but she allowed me to drag her across to the shelter. I laid her on her bedroll and tried to look at the wound. Again she batted me away, pointing at the horses. She wasn't talking much now and maybe that was because she was gritting her teeth to deal with the pain. I got that the horses should be unburdened and that they should then be hobbled and left to graze. The packs took some unbuckling, but the hobbling ropes were on top and the horses let me slip them on their legs with very little fuss, being used to it. They wandered off and began munching the grass noisily.

More grunting and pointing had me going through the right pack and finding her medical kit and the dictionary. The stuff in her medical box was different to mine, but there were clean strips of bandage and a lot of herbs and ointments I didn't recognise. She snatched them from me and started to try and deal with her wound. And that was the problem, because she couldn't twist around to get at it. She'd been able to tie a loop of material around herself and cinch it tight, but the gash was behind her.

I indicated that I would have a look. She shook her head in irritation. I picked up the book. Although I used it hundreds of times after that, I remember the first word I looked up. The English was "infection". So was the French. I grunted in surprise. When I showed it to her, she stared at it and the side of her mouth twitched microscopically.

Infection, I said. If you don't clean it you will get infected. And you can't reach it.

Anfecksee-on, she agreed.

I took the book and found the next word. I pointed at myself, then at her, then the word. She squinted at it.

Ay-day, she said.

Yes, I said. I will *ay-day* you.

She looked at me with those eyes that were both old and young.

Okay, she said.

Okay, I said.

She beckoned and I gave her the book.

She pointed to the word for clean. Then at the word for close. I must have looked confused because she tutted and found another word.

Sew.

She pointed behind her. And grimaced.

Sew.

She rummaged through her medicine box, tutting as she did so. She was looking for something that wasn't there.

I walked away and found my pack. I brought back my honey and showed it to her.

Okay, she said. She said other things in French but I was too busy building a fire. After a bit, she watched me and said nothing. Her face was getting as grey as her hair now, and the night was coming in. I wanted to get this done while there was still light enough to do it by. The wound was long and deep. I was going to have to clean it and then see if I could close it. There would be lots to do before dark.

She stopped barking commands at me after a bit, I think because she saw what I was doing and approved. I got the fire going and used two of her cooking pots to boil the water we both had been carrying. When it had boiled for ten minutes, I put her bandages in and boiled them for another ten. While that was happening, I made a rack out of birch twigs and used it to stretch the bandages on to dry in the heat of the fire as I let the boiling water cool. I speeded that up by pouring the water from one pot to the other, letting the air get at it.

It was still just warmer then blood temperature when I started. I pointed at her trousers. I indicated they would have to come off.

Pew-tan, she said, and took out a knife. Before I could stop her, she had reached round and cut through the waistband just over her hip, wincing with the effort. Then she started trying to peel the two sides apart to expose the wound. The blood had dried and the material was stiff and glued to her skin. She winced and looked paler.

No, I said. I'll do it.

I felt sick when I saw the damage close up. The boar's tusk had cut long and deep, deep enough for me to see the different colour of fat and muscle. It was worse than any cut I'd seen before, and the thought that I might have to sew it up gave me a feeling like vertigo.

First things first, I said. First things first.

I helped her roll from her side to her stomach. Because I imagined this would hurt about the same as having a bone set—which was something I'd seen Dad do for Bar—I went and found a branch a little thicker than my thumb and cut a short length from it. I gave it to her, making a dumbshow to let her know she should put it in her mouth to bite down on for the pain.

Pew-tan, she said again, rolling her eyes. But she shrugged and put it between her teeth and turned away.

The wound didn't smell, and the blackness within it was dried blood and not anything worse. I used the lukewarm water to soften the bloody trouser material enough to free it and swabbed the revealed buttock as clean as I could on either side of the horribly gaping slash.

I put my hand on her shoulder. She didn't turn round.

I'm sorry, I said. This will hurt.

She nodded and said nothing while I sluiced the wound with the clean water. Her whole body tensed, and I realised how strong and wiry she was under the clothes that hid it. I tried to get it done as quickly as I could. The only sound I heard was the wood of the branch crunching between her teeth.

Cleaning it just made it look worse really: fresher but also easier to see where the flesh had started dying. If it had been a gash on an arm or a leg, I might have thought of just trying to hold the wound closed with a really tight bandage, but being where it was there was no doubt it would have to be sewn up.

I realised that I had been staring at it for so long, trying to work out what to do next, that I had not seen her turn her head and stare back at me.

Anfecksee-on? she said.

Not yet, I said. And then I held up the jar of honey.

Ah, she said. Ah *bon*.

She nodded her head and turned away.

I cleaned the needle by boiling it. It was the needle I always carried for mending things that might rip, like bags or sails or clothes.

I almost scalded my hands washing them, and I used my shaving soap to clean them. She watched me do all of this with her head craned round as she lay on her stomach. I showed her the needle with an apologetic grimace.

Mared, she said.

Pew-tan? I said.

It was the first time I saw her smile properly. The stern face cracked and let out a little unexpected sunshine.

Wee, she said. *Pew-tan*.

And she picked up the stick, bit down on it and turned away.

I think it would have been easier if she had fainted, but she didn't. Pouring the honey into the wound made her buck and flinch, but that was the first, not the worst of it. I've done some horrible things in my life, but sliding that curved needle in and out of living flesh and then making knot after knot in it, pulling the wound closed and leaving a thin and badly puckered gash is one of the things I still have nightmares about. I am not a good sewer at the best of times. At the end of things, it looked more like a length of barbed wire than anything else. But I got it done as fast and as neatly as I could, and when there was no more wound to cinch tight, I poured a line of honey over it and carefully laid a strip of clean bandage on top to hold it in place. Then I made a pad to put over it and was going to ask her to lift her hips so I could wind the long bandage around it to hold it in place when I realised she was asleep. Asleep or passed out. She was breathing though, so I left her undisturbed and just watched in case she woke and tried to roll over on the wound.

Jip came and sat with me, and for a long time that was all I needed in the world. He licked my hand and I scratched him, and then I buried my nose in the familiar roughness of his neck fur and he let me hold him and tell him how much I had missed him and how bad I had felt when I was sure he was dead and it had all been my fault. And then we just stayed leaning against each other and watched the sky and the sleeping woman. The horses cropped away. It got darker. When she woke, she did try to roll but I stopped her. Then she drank some water and went back to sleep.

Before it got full dark, I hung the pig upside down and cut its neck so that if the blood had not already settled it might run out during the night. Then I collected the horses and tied them to a tree each. And then I went to sleep too. I didn't know if what I had done would work or if she would take an infection and die. As I lay in the darkness and listened to the unfamiliar sounds of the night starting up, I wondered if it had been the right thing to do. I decided I didn't know if she was as dangerous a person as Brand. Then I thought some more and decided she was probably as dangerous, but that she had saved me and found Jip and that, all in all, I probably had done the right thing. And then I slept.

I woke in the early morning, dew beading the trees and the grass. She was poking me with a stick. She needed to piss. Helping her up was a complicated effort. Holding her up while she squatted awkwardly keeping the wounded leg straight so as not to put pressure on the stitches was even more so. When I got her back on her bedroll, she looked white.

Door may, she said, nodding at my bedroll. Then she went straight back to sleep.

By the next time she woke, I had slices of hog sizzling over the fire and the three horses were untied and grazing again. I had also been through her packs. I could make no sense of the things she had clearly collected on her travels, some of which were useful—like tools—and others of which seemed just to have caught her fancy because they looked interesting, like a small bronze head, or a homemade doll, sewn together with buttons that nestled in an old box full of shiny necklaces.

She was looking at me, her face unreadable. Then she gave me a nod, as if I'd done something right.

Mare-see, she said. *Mare-see*.

I brought her some of the boar. She rolled onto the unwounded side and ate propped up on one arm. She finished the slice and belched, deep as Dad did. She smiled, as if pleased with herself. She picked up the dictionary and flicked through it, found a word and showed it to me with a raised, questioning eyebrow.

Name?

Griz, I said. My name is Griz.

I pointed at her.

Mwah? she said, eyebrow still raised. She shrugged her shoulder as if names weren't important to her, as if she was above having just any old name like everybody else had one. Then she made a face as if just picking one of her many names.

John, she said.

John? I said.

Wee, she said, nodding. John Dark.

Chapter 19

A bond

Even though we didn't speak the same language, I liked John Dark. Even though that wasn't her real name, only what it sounded like. And the name it sounded like wasn't really her name either, I discovered. It was a joke, and as good a name for a French woman as any. Though I didn't get the joke until it was explained to me long after our ways had parted.

I remember that first day and night very clearly, but the days that followed blurred into one another. I was torn, wanting to be on my way to find Brand, but not being able to leave her until she could at least get up and piss for herself. There would have been no point sewing her up just to leave her in a pool of her own mess. Would have been a waste of good honey, not to mention the not-quite-so-good needlework. And of course I wanted to know her story, why was she here, where had she come from, what had she seen, what she knew. She looked like she'd seen a lot.

She got my story out of me first. Using the dictionary and lot of eyebrow raising she asked, Where from? and I showed her on the map—not exactly, but roughly. I didn't quite trust her enough for that exactly. Family? was easy. Four fingers answered that. So was Alone? That got one thumb. Why here? was harder: I laboriously pointed out the words for "a man steal my dog; I go find him, get dog". She made me do it twice because she couldn't believe it. I added "red beard" the second time, hoping she might know about Brand, but her eyes didn't flicker a bit in recognition. Where? was easier to answer. I just showed her on the map. And since I had it open, I showed her where I thought we were. She made me get a map from her own bag and, though hers was better, being backed in material, it showed the same landscape. And we agreed we were just outside the big city in the middle of the country.

We established she came from France which was not a surprise by then, having read the cover on the grubby dictionary. What was a surprise was when I asked, Where boat you? and she shook her head and made it clear there was no boat. She pointed to the horses and rolled her eyes. How could she get them on a boat? Then she made walking movements with her fingers. I shook my head and pointed at the sea. She snorted and pointed at another area on the land and traced it across the narrow channel. Then she snapped her fingers and demanded the dictionary. She found the word for "tunnel" which was another word like "infection" that was spelled exactly the same. I didn't believe her, because even if there had been a tunnel under the sea, I'm sure it would have filled with water after a hundred years or so. And that's assuming the rising seawater hadn't submerged the entrances and filled it that way. However, she was emphatic that she had ridden under the sea to get here, with an oil lamp that she showed me hanging off one of the baskets.

I didn't mind that she was lying. I hadn't quite told her

exactly where I was from either. I did like the swagger of her lie. Ferg once said to me that if I was going to lie I might as well make it a big one as a small one, and I think that's what she was doing. She didn't want me to find where her valuable boat was laid up.

I asked why she had come here. Her face did flicker then. Her finger found "family" again. Then "daughters". Then a word that I first read as "pest" until I realised I was reading the French word and that there was an *e* on the end and in English it meant "plague".

I'm sorry, I said.

She shrugged, but her eyes were elsewhere for a long moment.

I wanted to ask more questions, but I could see she was sad and tired and so I went off with Jip to refill the water bottles from a stream that came tumbling down the slope behind us. As I did so, I wondered about the plague she had spoken of. I decided it was probably just a normal disease that likely once would have been easily fixed with drugs we no longer had. After all, a plague is a disease that sweeps through huge populations, inflicting terrible damage. There just wasn't enough population left to have a plague in. I think I was wrong and she was actually being very accurate about the symptoms, but that's what I thought then.

She spent most of the day sleeping, and when she wasn't she always seemed to be looking at me with her head on one side, as if I was something that she could not quite make out. It was late that afternoon, or maybe the next one when she told me the other reason she was here. She thumbed her chest, then pointed to the dictionary: I. Look. Someone. Too.

Someone? I pointed back and raised my eyebrows in imitation of her questioning expression.

Kel Kun, she said. *Kel Kun Demal.*

Whoever this Kel Kun was, he made her eyes go away again.

I changed the dressings morning and night, and there was no smell of infection, though the wound line was crooked and red and was, for the first two days, worryingly hot. I kept using the last of my honey on it, and she dosed herself with the contents of her medical kit, and between the honey and the powders and leaves she ingested, the wound did seem to be healing.

She had several habits that were odd to me, things she was emphatic about. Maybe everybody else's habits are odd to strangers. One was the *loo garoo* sticks. These were long torches, made from wooden handles which had spools of material wound round the head, material that had been soaked in sticky pine pitch. She never lit them, but she insisted that we kept them laid close to the fire at night. When I tried to ask why, she just pointed out at the darkness, at the three horses hobbled close by and the blackness beyond.

Poor lay loo, she said.

I made a question with my face. She smiled.

Lay loo, she repeated and then made a mock-serious I'm-trying-to-scare-you-but-not-really face.

Lay loo? she said, waggling her eyebrows. *Lay loo garoo.*

So the torches became the *loo garoo* sticks, and were—to me—a sort of quaint pointless ritual she liked. Until of course they weren't.

Several things became clear as we waited for her wound to heal. One was that Jip had got caught in a snare she had set for rabbits around her camp. I found a bunch of them, made from the thin wire in one of her bags. She pointed at them and then at Jip's leg with a shrug of apology. Another was that she had seen the burning house I had left behind us and had ridden to see what it was, in much the same way that I had been drawn to the fire I had seen from the tower. Like me, she had been drawn to a possible sign of other people—but unlike me she had found it was so. She said she had thought the fire might have been Kel Kun Demal.

One afternoon she pointed at the horses and asked, by miming, if I could ride one. We don't ride the ponies on the island, just use them for carrying and walking beside them. But since I had ridden them as a small child, perched between the panniers carrying the peat, I nodded.

The next day, we ran out of honey and she decided the wound was knitting well enough for her to start walking and trying the horse. She was grey-haired but she was tough, and now that the pain had subsided and the infection—if it had been infection—had gone, she was energetic again.

By a mixture of mime and dictionary-pointing, she made it clear that she wanted me to go with her into the city, where she had seen a big nest of bees. She pointed to my jar. She wanted to repay me by replacing the honey that had healed her. I was in a strange state of mind—in a hurry to get to Brand, overjoyed to have Jip back, but also not wanting to go our separate ways, and since the city lay more or less in the right direction I nodded. She spent the day reorganising the packs, and then she put one horse-load's worth on a tree, close in by the car stacks where she indicated she would find it when she returned, and then made me get up on the second bag-free horse and ride around a bit.

Jip barked to see me riding, and the horse snorted in something between ridicule and frustration, as if it could sense how suddenly nervy I was, but she said something to it and her words seemed to work like a spell and calm it right down.

There was light left in the sky, but after a couple of wide circles to get used to the feeling of being carried across the landscape on such a high and swaying seat, we returned to the camp and spent a last night feasting on boar and berries.

She didn't look so cheerful the next day as we saddled up and set off down the hill. Her face was set and sour as the horse lurched over the rough ground, and once again I saw her teeth set against any sound of pain that might try and escape. It was a misty morning, and she rode with her hood up. Jip criss-crossed the slope ahead of us, surprising some early rabbits, but his heart was more in chasing than killing and anyway we had all eaten well the night before, him included.

By the time we descended to the old M road, the sun had driven away most of the mist and as the day warmed, so did she. She dropped back to ride beside me, watching me with a disapproving eye. By the time we had gone five klicks or so, she decided that the various instructions she had communicated in mime to me—things like sit up, squeeze with your knees, relax your hand, don't pull the reins and so on—had turned me into a slightly less disappointing rider than I had been at the start of the day and she grunted in approval.

Bravo, Griz, she said.

I don't know which made me more surprised and unexpectedly happy. Her approval or the fact that she'd used my name for the first time.

She rode ahead, leading the pack horse. My horse was happy to follow as they wove in as straight a line as they could through the saplings and larger trees that were invading the old M road. It's a strange thing, riding another animal. I hadn't really thought about it when I had been given rides on the peat ponies, but now I felt it strongly. It wasn't so much the sensation of moving along without doing much—that was familiar enough from being driven by the wind on the sea—it was the fact that the motion which carried me was obviously the particular movement of another living thing. It was a controlled lurch, always—or so it seemed to me—on the point of tripping or at least losing its own special cadence. But as the day progressed, I stopped fighting it, and then by forgetting to worry about it I relaxed and slowly began to feel a part of the horse, rather than apart from it. Which probably doesn't make sense unless you rode horses and felt what I was feeling. But you probably drove around in cars instead. Did that feel as exhilarating, or were you always worried the engine might run away with you, the same way I had worried about the horse stumbling?

As we headed onwards, the city slowly started to rise around us, as if it were a growing thing crowding in on either side. Once again, the scale of who you were, the sheer number of you, began to wash over me. There were hulks of long, low buildings that must have been factories, and then mazes of regularly divided vegetation that must have been more overgrown streets of identical box houses and then in the distance, converging with us, another raised roadway striding across the intervening wasteland of shrubs, trees and tumbledown buildings on stubby legs of concrete.

What did your cities sound like when these roads were full of cars? Was it a whine or a rumble or a growl? Or a roar? Did all the different kinds of car and lorry sound different? Could you tell what was coming without looking? And seeing all the roads there were, how did you stop bumping into one another if you were travelling at the speeds I've read about?

I couldn't keep my wits about me or stay alert to danger,

and I was just riding one horse. If I had been able to, maybe I wouldn't have ridden right into it.

But then not all danger looks bad on the outside. We were just going to get some honey.

Not everything sweet is good for you.

Chapter 20

Kel Kun Demal

It started off as a great day. Sun was high but not too hot, the birds were making a lot of noise and enough rabbits were running to keep Jip happy as we wove our way closer to the centre of the city.

Birdsong like this was still a new thing to me. On the islands, there were occasional shrieks and caws and the lonely piping of single birds flying across the moor, but the birdlife was too thinly stretched to make anything at all like the constant noise that you get on the mainland. To begin with, I found the songs of the different birds was like a tumble of conflicting sounds, none of them particularly loud on their own, but relentless in the way they pecked at your attention from all sides—a coo here, a tweet there and a warble from somewhere else. And because they were all different noises, I kept twisting around, trying to spot where they were coming from, to see what bird made which noise. And then after a bit the fact the noise was always there seemed to blur those distinctive bits together into a wash of sound, like the sea. It became background and not something I spent any more time trying to unpick into the individual parts it was made of. By the time I met John Dark, the ever-present din of the birdlife all around me had become—like the sea too—a comforting noise. I had also got used to the fact it sounded different at dawn to the way it did as the light left the sky at the end of the day. And although I hadn't got very far with identifying the various species, I had worked out which birds were pigeons and which were magpies from the small book I'd found in the museum shop.

There was one different-looking bird that had sandy feathers mottled with darker brown ones that flew across our path as we rode down a sloping ramp that took us off the raised M road. I think it was a song thrush. It made a happy piping sound as it flew high above us, and when I looked over at the woman I saw that for a moment she'd lost her stern mask and let the younger face she kept hidden behind it have a moment in the sun as she too watched the bird jink and climb over our heads into the clear blue sky, looking as if it was singing and flying just for the joy of it.

Then her mask came back down and she nudged her horse forward towards a gap in the overgrown ruins ahead of us. She knew where she was going, and my horse just followed her lead. A brick-built building had given up trying to keep standing tall at some time in the recent past and had slumped across the narrow alley, filling the space with an untidy jumble of bricks and glass. John Dark sucked her teeth in disapproval and turned her horse to the side, finding a narrower alley to go down. I don't think she wanted to risk the horses cutting themselves or stumbling on the new rubble. One thing I had noticed by then was the way you could easily tell what ruin was new and what had fallen down a long time ago by the way the vegetation overgrew it. New rubble shifted under your feet, but as soon as moss and grass and the roots of plants had taken hold, it quickly became stable as the plants and the dirt bound it together.

We emerged from the alley and pushed our way through an area of scrubby bushes that were all about as high as the horses' shoulders. This had been an open area in the middle of the city, and once there had been light poles to illuminate it. They were corroded into sharp stubs, or had tilted and fallen, pulled down by the weight of the creepers that had overgrown them, but they were regularly spaced, which made it easy to spot them once you had seen the pattern. There were also trees that had grown randomly among them, and after I had ducked beneath one as we passed, imitating John Dark just ahead of me, I straightened up to see the three men standing in front of me.

They had their backs to us, and the one in the middle had his hand raised in greeting so that I instinctively looked beyond him trying to see who might be waving back at them. But there was no one there, not even them really: they were just statues facing a great tangle of wreckage where one end of a huge stadium had collapsed a long time ago, making a hill of massive concrete slabs and twisted metal pipes, all now well bound together by the encroaching plant life. The statues were men and all wore short trousers and had their arms around each other, like brothers. One of them was bald and had a football held against his hip. When I guided my horse around the front of them, I could see they all had expressions that weren't quite smiles, but more like they were expecting something. Whatever it was, it had either come and gone, or perhaps just had never arrived. All they had to look at was a ruin now. Not that they seemed upset about it. Brambles had grown around the block of stone they stood on, but I could still see one word carved in it. It said "BEST". So I expect these were the best players in the team. I was looking into their faces, wondering what they had looked like in real life, when John Dark whistled at me.

E. C., she said, and stopped her horse.

She grimaced as she got off, and had to catch hold of the saddle to stop herself stumbling to her knees. She didn't like that I'd seen the weakness, and made a great show of teaching me how to hang the horse's reins over its head so they dragged on the ground in front of it so that it wouldn't walk off, and then took things from her saddlebags and beckoned me to follow her up the hill of debris.

I left my horse and did so. There was broken glass beneath the moss, so we both trod carefully, but the building had been down long enough for nature to have bound it back into the earth and made it stable. And then, following her footsteps, I found myself at the top of the greenish hill the rubble was now turning into, looking down into what had once been a football field. It was now a hidden oasis of deeper green, with a stand of what I now knew were oak trees at one end, and a thicket of flowering hawthorn in the middle. Rabbits darted among the long grass around the trees, turning tails as white as the May blossom when they ran away at the sight of us. Jip immediately set off like an arrow, his mindset on serious business as he plunged into the undergrowth.

The other three sides of the stadium were in better shape than the one we were standing on, but on two of them the jutting roof that had once sheltered watchers from the rain or sun had dipped and collapsed in on the endless rows of faded pink plastic seats below. Trying to imagine the number of people this arena must have held, what that looked like, what that must have sounded like, made my head hurt. Does absence have a weight? I think it does, because I stood there feeling crushed by something I couldn't see. It was a much stronger feeling than the one I had when looking at a landscape full of empty streets. Perhaps it was because so many people had once chosen to come and squeeze in close to each other in this single space. Again, there are no such things as ghosts. It didn't feel haunted. But it did feel like something. Like it had once been peopled—and very densely peopled—and now it just wasn't. It was unpeopled, in the same way something can't be undone unless it has first been done. This was the atmosphere I had been trying to understand ever since I stepped on to the mainland, and it was a very different feeling to just being empty. It was more like loneliness, not mine from finding myself alone in this world, but this world's loneliness without you. It had known you, and now you're gone—and maybe this is just for a while, perhaps until the signs of you having been here are worn away and your houses and roads and bridges and football stadiums have been swallowed back into nature—it will miss you.

Or maybe I'm going a bit mad thinking like this and then taking the trouble to write my crazy thoughts down so that a long-dead boy who will never read them will know what my theories are about a world he can never visit. Maybe that's what happens when you spend so long on your own, like I do now. Maybe I'm just talking to myself.

Anyway, the rest of the afternoon was a very good day. Until it wasn't.

Once she had got moving, John Dark seemed happier about the pain from her wound and walked much less stiffly.

She led me into the middle of what had been the field and closed her eyes, holding her finger to her lips. I listened. And then I heard it, just as she opened them again and looked a question at me.

It was a low humming noise, a gentle sound that filled the background and seemed to stroke the ears. Bees were thriving in the huge walled garden that the stadium had become, and there were a lot of them.

There were two fallen trees that had begun to rot from the middle out, and beside them was a strange kind of wooden shed on wheels. Maybe someone had, at the end of things, decided to come and live here behind the protection of the stadium walls. Maybe she kept the bees. Her shed on wheels had become a kind of huge beehive, and there were bees in the fallen trees too. It was a very protected space, and the meadow that the field had become must have been a ready supply of bee food.

John Dark pointed at a recent campfire and pointed at herself. I understood she had been here not long ago. This was how she knew about the bees. She then pointed to one of the fallen trees and grinned. We were going to get the honey from inside the trunk.

We worked together more or less in silence, and she was able to show me with deliberate movements what we were going to do. I don't know if the silence was in order not to stir up the bees, or just because in doing something physical it was easier to mime, but it was a strangely calm and intimate way to spend time with another person.

I felt closer to her in those few hours than I had to anyone outside my family, now I look back on it. Even when working with the Lewismen, there was always a distance. Perhaps because we were two tribes—working together but supported by the others in our own family who also shared our difference to them. With one person, all those barriers went away, and we just talked with our hands and eyes.

Like I said. Intimate.

She built a fire on the ruins of her last one, and fed it until it got going. Then she moved the burning coals using her knife and the flat of a small hatchet and held them in front of the opening in the fallen trunk, right against the wood so that it began to scorch and smoulder. She fed that baby fire, indicating that I should keep the mother fire going as she did so. Then she started putting damper material on the smaller fire making it begin to smoke. The trick was to keep the core of the smaller fire hot enough and then to damp it with just enough material to keep it smoking heavily. Then she had me go into the stand to break off a plastic chair bottom. I shattered a couple because the material had become brittle with age, but on the third try I got a rough square and came back. She then had me fan the smoke plume so it entered the rotten hole in the trunk.

I should say that before we did all this we wound some sacking material she had in her saddlebags around our heads, and fastened our clothes so there was little chance of any of the bees getting in and stinging us. She had gloves too. I wound more material around my hands instead. I once read an old comic about an Egyptian god who came back from the dead as a mummy. That's what we looked like. Half grotesque and half ridiculous. And me waving the seat back and forth, trying to create a breeze that would force the smoke in and the bees out. But of course there was no one to see us or laugh at the spectacle we must have made amid the smoke and the swarm of bees beginning to exit the trunk and buzz around us, out where the air was less thick.

She took her hatchet and began to hack efficiently at the rotten wood, enlarging the opening and exposing the honeycomb. The bee's nest was formed in great rounded lobes of beeswax that looked fleshy and a little unearthly. I think it was the organic shape of the lobes that were in contrast with the geometric regularity of the honeycomb from which they were made. There were still big clumps of bees crawling over the fat lobes, which made them seem alive. We moved the fire closer and fanned the smoke until most were gone or just drowsing. And then, without warning me, she reached in with one hand and chopped a couple of the lobes free. The bees got angrier and less drowsy at that point, and some flew into the slit in my face covering that I'd left to see out of.

One of them stung me on the eyelid. I tried to keep fanning but the pain was like a hot needle had been stabbed into my eyeball. I gasped and staggered away, dropping the seat.

I heard her laughing and stumbled after her. The bees were buzzing louder as we emerged from the protective haze of the woodsmoke, but amazingly we weren't followed by a large cloud of them trying to sting us in revenge for our theft. We stopped and sat on the crumbling cement steps at the far side of the field.

She looked elated, and carefully put the stolen honeycombs on the grass at our feet. Then she looked at the smoking tree trunk in the distance.

Mared! she said.

And then she took her largest water bottle and walked back into the smoke and the circling bee cloud. I thought it was a heroic thing to do. And it was the right thing too. I liked her for doing it. She kicked the fire away from the entrance to the trunk and poured water to douse the smouldering end. Having stolen some of their honey, she made sure that their home was not burned down at the same time. She even picked up the seat and put it on top of the hole she'd widened, giving them a new roof. Then she half ran, half danced out of range of the bees, laughing as she came. Once more, she looked younger than the face she normally wore. She sat next to me and unwound the sacking strips, using them to wrap the first piece of honeycomb which was about the size of her head in circumference, though flatter from the side. Then she clicked her fingers at me to take my bandages off to wrap the second piece. My eye had swollen alarmingly so that I could only see out of the other one, and she looked surprised when she saw it—though whether at what it looked like or at the fact I had not made more fuss about it I never knew.

Because at that point, the other—unsuspected—bee that had got inside my layers began to vibrate angrily against my neck, and everything began to go wrong fast. As I tore open the fastenings at the neck of my shirt, she saw something and her eyes widened. I saw it and thought for a moment that she had seen my secret, but then I checked and she looked away, and I knew it was not that but something else, something she was hiding. And because I was relieved it was not the one thing, and because my eye was really hurting quite badly, I did not take time to think too much about what the other thing she was reacting to might have been.

She rummaged in her bag, and took something out which she shoved in her pocket before turning back to me. She leant down and broke off a piece of honeycomb, squeezing the gold honey on to the finger of her other hand.

Then she pointed at my eye and held up the honeyed finger.

Bon, she said. *La me-ay say bon poor sa*.

I let her reach over and daub the honey on my bulging eyelid. It felt sticky and warm and then things suddenly got confusing and fast and then shockingly painful. Not the eye, but my neck, because on what was, because of the eye, my blind side she pulled the thing that she had shoved into her pocket out again and looped it quickly over my head and tugged it tight.

The thin copper wire of one of her rabbit snares bit into my neck as she leapt behind me and yanked my knife from my belt. It happened so fast I was frozen in confusion for a second, and then I was choking and trying to get my fingers under the noose so I could free myself. And then she hissed in my ear and jabbed the tip of my knife into the base of my skull, not hard, not enough to break the skin, but enough to warn me to be still.

She said a lot, very quickly, spitting and hissing the words out in a long stream of anger. I don't know what she was saying, but it was not good. And then the knife hooked under the silver steel ball chain of my pendant. She worked it round until she could hold the pendant and look at the lucky eight in its circle of arrows.

She went quiet. I didn't move. I was sure I could feel blood dripping from the wire around my neck. It could have been sweat.

All I could hear was the hum of the bees in the distance, that and my heart thumping away in my chest, like a panicked secret trying to punch its way out into the open air.

Pew-tan, she spat. There was wonder and disappointment in the way it came out. And anger. A lot of anger.

She yanked the chain so that it snapped. She hefted my pendant in her hand, staring at the symbol pressed into it.

My lucky eight, at the centre of all those arrows going everywhere.

But like I said, not good luck.

And with the wire round my neck, and the very angry woman keeping it cinched tight—not going anywhere either.

What? I said. My voice sounded ragged. What?

She held the pendant in front of my good eye and unleashed a torrent of words, only three of which I got as she showed me the symbol, too close to my eye to really focus on.

Ooh ate eel? she said. *Ooh ate eel?*

Chapter 21

Key ay voo

The pendant was a key. I'm not spoiling anything by telling you that. I only know it was a key because she showed me the word in her dictionary later, when she was trying to get me to tell her where I had found it and what had happened to the person I had taken it from. It doesn't spoil anything because whatever the key was made to open remains a mystery. This story is not about a mysterious journey that ends up opening a wonderful door with a magic key. It's not that kind of story. I'm writing this on the wrong side of a locked door, has no key and I don't know if it's ever going to open.

And I only have her word, I suppose, that it was a key anyway. It didn't look like any key I'd ever seen. And she was less interested in the fact it was a key than in how I'd got it and who from. I tried to explain I had found it on the top of the tower, but my answer seemed to make her even more angry. She didn't believe me. She kept asking where the man was. Her finger kept stabbing the words "where man?" And whatever I managed to communicate to her was just wrong—no man—what man?—found key—found key on tower—not know—all the answers seemed to rub salt in some wound I couldn't see.

She shook me angrily and looked deep in my eyes.

Ay voo? she said. *Voo, Griz. Key ay voo?*

All I could do was shrug, still bewildered.

I don't know what you want, I said. But I'm not an enemy.

She tied my hands behind me with more wire, and then she loosened the noose around my neck. It was while she was tying me to the flaking metal holding the seats to the stadium steps that Jip came back, looking suddenly confused as he dropped a rabbit at my feet and then looked at us both, sensing something was wrong. She straightened up and spat some words at me, and then went away, towards the horses.

Jip looked at her and then at me and whined, confused by the fact I hadn't picked up the rabbit or ruffled the fur between his ears.

We're in trouble, boy, I said. I pulled against the wire binding my wrists but stopped as it bit into my skin.

Jip saw me wince. He trotted up the steps and looked at my hands, pinioned behind my back. He whined, unsure of what was happening.

It's okay, I said. It'll be okay.

He licked my wrists. I scratched his neck with my fingertips. As best I could. Then he moved away and barked.

It'll be fine, I said. She'll calm down.

She didn't. She came back, leading the horses and set them to graze on the overgrown pitch. Then she carried my bag up the steps, past me, and into a doorway where the steps disappeared inside the stadium. The landing made a square concrete-lined cave in the slope of the arena. She made her camp there, lighting a fire and unrolling her bedroll. If I scrunched round, I could sort of see what she was doing.

She was talking to herself, low and angry. She undid my pack and tipped all my possessions on the floor in front of her. Then she painstakingly spread them out and sorted through them. I don't know what she was looking for, but she didn't find it. That made her even more angry and she squatted on her haunches and looked at me as if everything in the world was my fault. Her silence and the flintiness of her stare was unnerving. There was no trace of the younger version of herself, the one that she had let out earlier in the day before the light began to fail.

As it got darker, the concrete roof and walls of the landing in which she had set her campfire made a warm square in the surrounding darkness, but all that did was make me feel the chill of the evening coming in. It was colder than it had been, and you didn't have to have a dog's nose to smell the rain in the air. Jip walked up the steps and looked at her. She ignored him. He sat down and barked at her. She might as well have been deaf for all the attention she paid him.

She gave me no food, no water and just left me sitting against the seat frames. I tried sawing the wire against the old metal stanchions, but it was too painful and, from what I could feel with my fingers, all I was doing was cleaning the corrosion off them, taking it back to the smooth metal beneath. The wire seemed no closer to breaking and I stopped. If anything was going to get sawed through, it was my wrists. I had no choice but to sit it out. Literally sit, because she didn't bring me my bedroll or allow me to lie down. I've spent uncomfortable nights in strange places, and can sleep almost anywhere if I'm tired enough, but that started out as the worst night of all. Then things went downhill. And then—with the visitors—they fell off a cliff.

To begin with there was the physical discomfort. The longer I sat, the less of me there seemed to be to provide some kind of padding between the cold concrete and my bones. Then there was the awkwardness of sitting with my hands behind me. It made my shoulders and my neck ache, and it made my arms numb. I kept wiggling my fingers to make sure I wasn't losing circulation. The least uncomfortable position was to let my head lean back until it rested on the plastic seat bottom, which left me staring up into the night sky, but did rest my neck a little.

It didn't rest my brain though, and it was that as much as the physical discomfort that kept me awake. I tried to keep it calm, but I had no luck with that. It raced away, whirling furiously round and round like a windmill in a high wind. I kept replaying everything that had happened since I encountered John Dark. I had thought we had a sort of trust between us. She had certainly helped me—rescued me even—and I in turn had helped her with her wound. I had imagined we had also found a way to understand each other with our miming and pointing at words in the dictionary.

It had seemed a bit of a cruel joke to meet one of the very few people left in this wide and empty world only to discover we couldn't talk because we spoke different languages, but we had made the best of it. And the worst of it was that I had liked her. As I have said before, I did not have a lot of other people to compare her with, but she did not seem untrustworthy. She just seemed like herself. She had never tried to make me like or trust her. I had taken her to be what she appeared to be: gruff, tough, definitely rough-edged, but straight. Brand, in retrospect, had been too much of a storyteller for anyone more experienced in the ways of other people than I was to trust. He was putting on a show. I rescued a book once called *Modern Coin Magic* by J. B. Bobo, and I spent one long winter practising the tricks inside. One of the things that made them work—apart from having nimble fingers—was making the people watching you look at the wrong hand at the right time, and so miss what you were actually doing. That's what Brand did: his smile and his stories were all showmanship making you look over there while his other hand was picking your pocket over here. John Dark was not like that. And this was the uncomfortable thing that kept whirling around my head. How had I got her so wrong? Had I misunderstood something vital in our halting communications? Why did she seem to suddenly mistrust me as deeply as I mistrusted Brand? The looks she had given me and the way she had spat her words after she had discovered the key round my neck definitely seemed like she felt fooled or betrayed. But by what? What did the key have to do with this Kel Kun Demal? Or had I been wrong from the very beginning, and had she always been dangerous to me? It didn't feel right, the thought that she'd been baiting a trap for me ever since we met, but maybe she had? Maybe she had just needed a separate pair of hands to sew her up. But that didn't make sense. None of it made sense. All of it churned round and round in an endless loop in my head, wiping out any chance of sleep or rest.

I'd smelled the rain coming, but I didn't see it when it finally did arrive because the overhanging cloud had blocked out the stars and the moon. Instead I felt it, full on my upturned face as the first fat drops fell heavily out of the darkness overhead. I blinked and squeezed the unexpected wetness out of my eyes, and then instinctively bowed my head as the rest of the following downpour hammered down after them. In seconds I was half drowned, rain hitting the concrete around me so hard the drops seemed to bounce back up to have a second go at soaking any bits of me they might have missed on the way down.

I heard Jip barking at the downpour, and then I felt hands at my back and heard a lot of what I took to be French curse words as John Dark took pity and freed me enough to drag me up into the dry warmth of her square cave. She refastened my wrists, but in front of me this time which felt a lot better, and then she pushed me down to sit on my own bedroll against the wall on the other side of the fire from her.

Thank you, I said.

She grunted and leaned back, eyes as hard as the concrete she was resting against.

I don't know what I've done wrong, I said.

Door may voo, she said, and mimed closing her eyes and resting her head against her hands. *Door may.*

Whatever the words meant, it was clear she wanted me to go to sleep. I had no real objection to that plan. I was exhausted by the whole day and the ugly turn that things had taken but—as I said—my brain was whirring too fast to let the rest of me slow down and rest. Her eyes bored into me across the low flames of the fire. That became too uncomfortable to bear, so I slumped down and closed my own eyes so as not to have the added problem of whether to stare back—and so perhaps provoke her further—or to look shifty by avoiding her gaze. Unexpectedly this did help me slow down a little. Unable to see anything, I listened instead, and the regular hiss of the rain slamming the concrete all around was in its own way almost as restful as the sea-noise I was used to falling asleep to, and though my back remained damp, the heat from the fire that I could feel on my front dried me out and made me feel almost comfortably drowsy. Jip came and leant against me, and the warmth of his sleeping body added a bit of comfort and made everything just a little less grim and a lot less lonely. And with all that, pretending to be asleep could so easily have turned into being asleep, if it was not for the one remaining thought that would not stop scratching at the inside of my head every time it went around.

Why did she want me to go to sleep? What was she going to do when I was unconscious? I didn't think she was going to hurt me. Or kill me. She had had a chance to do both of those things the moment she disabled me with the wire noose around my neck. But then I had not thought Brand would steal from us, and he had not—until he thought we were all asleep. Mistrusting sleep is a horrible thing. Brand had not just stolen from me; he had left his own unpleasant gift in its place, a gift that goes on taking even more from the receiver, because it stops the one thing that you need to rest and re-gather your energy. I read something somewhere about someone "murdering sleep". That's what Brand's deception has done for me. My sleep is not quite murdered. But ever since he stole from us, it has been fitful and getting worse—sometimes too much, never restful enough. I opened my eyes to find she was still looking at me. And now her look seemed to have an air of satisfaction about it, as if she had caught me red-handed in a dirty trick, pretending to sleep.

She pointed a finger at me.

Voo, she said. And then she seemed to speak English. Just two words, but definitely almost English. Freeman *voo*?

It didn't quite make sense.

Voo, she said, and this time she held up the key and jabbed it at me. *Et voo an Freeman?*

This time the two words seemed to slide together into one.

No, I said. I showed her my wrists, wired together. No, I'm not free.

She shook her head as if she didn't believe me.

Pew-tan, she said. And then she put a couple more bits of wood on the fire and slid a little further down the back wall so that her eyes were hidden by the flames.

The rain didn't ease up for at least an hour. And when it did, the noise it made receded and let the other sounds it had been masking be heard. The main noise was water rushing down the sloped stairs and walkways of the stadium, and the splattering noise of the run-off dripping all around us. But the best noise was John Dark's breathing. Although it was more than breathing because breathing alone would not have been loud enough to make itself heard over the wet noise all around us. It was her snoring.

Maybe if it hadn't started raining so suddenly she would have repacked my bag after she'd searched it. Maybe not. Maybe she would have just swept my things into a big pile against the wall. Out of my reach. But she hadn't. They were just strewn over the floor. And though the fire had died down to a reddish glow now, there was enough light for me to be able to see the glint of my Leatherman.

Jip woke the moment I moved. I felt his body tense and willed him to keep quiet. I twisted round and put my hands on him, stroking him, letting my touch tell him everything was all right. I didn't want him making any noise that might stop the regular snoring on the opposite side of the fire. I rolled down onto my side and squirmed round onto my stomach. Then, worming my body along the cold concrete floor, I inched forwards on my elbows and knees, heading for the tool and, I hoped, freedom.

Something brushed past me and I froze, but it was only Jip, walking to the edge of the landing to look out and take a sniff at the night air. The slight clicking of his claws on the hard floor seemed horrifically loud to me, but the snoring didn't lose a beat, and I relaxed.

If I had not been so focused on reaching the Leatherman, I might have noticed Jip going very still. And I imagine that if there had been more light I would have seen the hackle fur on his back bristle and rise. But although the clouds had moved on and allowed some moonlight back down onto the pitch, I was not looking at him. I was holding my breath and reaching for the multitool. Metal scraped against concrete, again a tiny sound that seemed catastrophically loud, and then I had the familiar heft of the well-used steel in my hands and found I was able to open it quite easily, despite my wrists being bound, turning the thin rectangle of steel into a pair of pliers.

If I had not been so worried about dropping the pliers as I awkwardly reversed them so that they pointed towards my elbows, I might have heard something moving on the field below us. There must have been some noise, however small.

And if I had not been so elated by the ease with which I was able to slide the open jaws of the pliers down the channel between my wrists, far enough to put the wire binding them together into the sharp indented blade of the wire-cutter waiting at the bottom of those jaws, I might have noticed the snoring had stopped.

If I had not been so focused on freeing myself, I might have noticed what was about to happen. But I was, and I didn't.

I leant forward on my hands, my chin on the damp concrete, putting the whole weight of my body behind my fingers which were squeezing the handles of the Leatherman.

There was a click like a gunshot as the wire-cutter severed the wire. And then the thing that happened happened and what happened was really three things and they all happened at once.

Jip barked and hurtled into the night.

John Dark said *pew-tan* very angrily.

And a horse screamed in the darkness below.

Chapter 22

Loo garoo

There was a fourth thing, but it happened a moment later.

It was a wild, high howling, a noise that shivered a deeper crack in the darkness itself. And it seemed to be in answer to Jip's barking. And it was followed by snarls and growls that made the hairs on my neck stand up just like a dog's. I'd never heard it before, but my ancestors and yours had, and maybe that left some memory of what it meant deep in the back of my brain, because the sound of it made my gut flip and go watery so that I had to clench so as not to piss myself.

Son day loo! said John Dark and plunged the *loo garoo* stick into the fire. The pitch-soaked material blazed into light and she literally jumped right over me as she raced down the steps towards the noise, carrying her gun in the other hand.

She either did not notice or she didn't care that my hands were free.

A boom like a thunderclap split the night as she fired her gun at something that set off a new series of howls and yipping and then I was on my feet, grabbing my bow and arrows. I strung the bow in one fast tug, and quickly looked around for my knife.

Then I heard Jip bark again and then snarl, and followed John Dark hurtling down the steps towards the light of her flaming torch that was now arcing back and forth on the pitch below.

The steps were very wet and slick with rain and moss, but I kept my footing by a miracle until I tried to stop myself at the bottom and slipped and half tripped to a halt on one knee, hitting it so hard that I later found I'd ripped the knee out of my trousers. I snatched an arrow and nocked it and only then—panting and shaking but finally still—was I able to make sense of what was happening.

At first I thought they were dogs. They weren't. Nor were they anything you would have expected to find roaming free on this island when you were alive. As a kid, I read a whole book about how they returned to the country after centuries of being extinct, but that was a fantasy. They were something much older than the tamed land you knew, older still than the empty one that we have inherited from you. But there's no question they do fit the wilderness that time is turning it back into.

Wolves.

In the circle of light cast by the flaming torch in her hand, John Dark stood with the horses, one of which had a sheet of blood washed down its flank. A dead wolf lay in front of her. And Jip stood at bay beside her, snarling out at the loose ring of wolves circling them. The wolves moved all the time, never still for long if they did stop, always pacing and watching. I could see the glint of their eyes on the other side of the horses, behind John Dark. The circular movement masked the fact that they were slowly but definitely getting closer. She seemed to realise this, and kept on turning herself, cutting fiery swathes through the night with her torch, trying to force them back. The horses were terrified, eyes rolled wide in their heads, but they stayed close to her. At first, I thought it was because they trusted her to protect them. Then I remembered she had hobbled them so that they wouldn't stray.

There was one wolf that was bigger than the others, and where they circled left, it circled right, which added to the confusion and the difficulty in keeping track of them. It kept its belly close to the ground as it moved. John Dark was trying to keep her eye on all the wolves at once. Jip just watched the big wolf. The dog was stiff and quivering with bottled-up tension, almost fizzing with the fight building up inside him. It was a look that terrified me almost as much as the wolves themselves. It meant Jip had decided that when the wolves got too close, he would kill the big one first, before going on to the next and the next. That was how his mind worked. He was born without an inch of back-off in him, and I think—being a terrier—he always assumed he'd win and would never stop until he did. Until he didn't. At which point he'd be too dead to care much.

It was a big wolf. About the size of two, maybe two and a half Jips.

I realised there was a sort of plan to the way the wolf pack moved. It kept John Dark just distracted enough trying to keep track of them all so that they could each move a little bit closer every time her back was momentarily turned. I wanted to shout a warning, but didn't want to distract her. Now I realise that I too was getting mesmerised and immobilised by the movement of the pack.

I was certainly distracted enough to miss the first lunge the big wolf made at the rear of the already bloodied horse.

Jip was un-distractible. He hit the wolf broadside on, like a small snarling battering ram that bit into the wolf's neck as the momentum of his attack knocked it over and the two of them somersaulted across the grass. The wolf threw him off and rolled to his feet before Jip did. Now Jip was stuck between the big wolf and the others. The big wolf snarled and stepped towards him as two smaller wolves slunk behind Jip, into his blind spot.

John Dark swung the torch towards the big wolf who turned and looked at her, just in time to see the gun come up and point at his head.

It went click.

Any ammunition that remains from your time is so old and unreliable that it is always less likely to shoot as hang fire, which is why I was raised to the bow. The look the wolf gave her, even as it cringed away from the swinging flames of the torch, was almost human in its contempt.

Then one of the wolves behind Jip darted in to try and bite out the hamstrings in his back leg, and as Jip jumped and turned so fast that I heard the wolf's teeth clash on the empty space where he had just been, the big wolf twisted away from John Dark as if it had had eyes in the back of its head all the time, and sprang for the back of Jip's unprotected neck.

The wolf jerked in mid-air and hit Jip solidly in the back, hitting him like a sack of bricks, just as heavy—and just as inanimate. The back of the arrow stuck out of the base of its skull, buried to the fletch. Even if I were to touch a bow again, I'd never make another shot as good as that. And the funny thing is that I don't remember thinking I should fire, or aiming, or drawing or loosing the string. All I remember is the arrow in flight and the sure knowledge that it was not going to miss, and then the sound of it hitting which was like the noise an axe makes when it bites into the wood. It must have severed the spinal cord at the very top, killing the wolf as it leapt, so that it was dead on landing.

Jip must have known the wolf was dead before the wolf did, because he didn't even try to fight it as it landed on him.

Instead he shrugged the body off and scooted beneath the horses' bellies to take up his previous position, keeping guard with John Dark, watching the bits of the circling pack she couldn't keep track of.

She looked across the darkness at me. If she was surprised to see me free and with a new arrow nocked and ready, she didn't show it.

On core de fur, she shouted, gesturing with the guttering torch. *On core de fur!*

It was clear what she meant. It was also clear that her eyes were not the only ones now looking at me. I turned and pounded back up to the campfire as fast as I could. I grabbed the other *loo garoo* sticks and lit one.

I heard her shout from below.

Veet! she shouted. *Veet!*

Jip barked to underscore the urgency of whatever she was saying.

I went back down the steps three at a time, and when I got to the bottom I didn't stop, but hurdled the fence and ran at the wolves with the fire held in front of me, waving it back and forth like a scythe. They parted and then I was inside the ring with Jip and John Dark and the three horses. There was no need for talking. Her stick was dying in her hands, so I handed her the other one and took over keeping the wolves at bay while she lit it. Jip barked at me, exulting in the midst of all this danger. I think he was happy because even though there was a bigger pack out there, now he had his own pack with him.

We were together, but the night was still going to last longer than the remaining two torches. John Dark fumbled with hers, holding it in the same hand as her gun which she broke and tried to reload with two more cartridges. I understood why she was doing it, but took little comfort from it when she snapped it closed again. There was no guarantee either of the things would fire, and the illusion of safety is a danger all of its own. Out of habit I went to retrieve my arrow from the big wolf. I swung my torch to keep the others back and flipped it on its back with my foot. It was solid and much heavier than I expected. It looked doglike enough for me to feel a pang of something close to guilt as I reached down, put my foot on its neck and pulled the flat-headed arrow all the way out. The other wolves seemed to growl a little deeper as I did so. The shaft was red from tip to butt by the time I got it out, and I snapped my wrist to clear the blood off the feathers, sending a spray of red arcing towards them. This seemed to enrage them further, and two began to howl.

I risked a quick look at John Dark and caught her wincing as she moved. Her wound was obviously hurting. Maybe the stitches had torn open. The torches were burning down and we were running out of time.

I knew what we had to do.

There! I shouted, pointing at the red cube cut into the darkness above. We take the horses to the fire!

She stared at me. I pointed at the horses and did my best to mime that we should all go up the steps to the safety of the concrete box and the fire within.

It will be safe, I shouted. There are walls! The fire will last longer than—

She shouted something angrily at me, but she was nodding agreement. I think she was telling me she understood and I should shut up and we should get on with it before the last two sticks of fire began to gutter away and leave us blind and undefended in the darkness.

She stepped quickly across and gave me her torch, then quickly unhobbled the horses. She took the reins of all of them in one hand, slinging the gun over her shoulder before she reached for the torch. Then she nodded up at the square firelit cave.

Al on zee, she said.

Slowly and awkwardly, with the wolves following all the way. John Dark led the horses over the barrier, which they didn't like, and up the narrow, steep steps between the endless lines of seats, which they liked even less. Jip came with us, doing his own kind of circular patrol around us, keeping close but growling at every wolf who ventured a little nearer than the others. I brought up the rear, walking backwards, trying to keep the wolves in front and to either side of me within the edge of my vision. I had my bow slung on my back, but in my free hand I carried an arrow, ready to stab at anything that leapt at me. Other than the low growling, there was very little noise apart from the scrape of the horses' progress up the wet steps. I backed into one of the horses as we went and it whinnied and lashed out at me with its hoof. It missed, but the side of its leg made glancing contact and knocked me over, so fast and unexpectedly that I fell awkwardly, face down with one arm tangled in a seat. I heard something snap and for a moment knew for certain it was my arm, then realised it was the arrow. The torch lay on the concrete steps below me, half rolled under one of the plastic seats that was already beginning to catch fire from it, and beyond that two pairs of wolf's eyes gleamed hungrily, low to the ground and getting closer.

I felt wolf paws on my back, and knew I was done for, and then I heard the wolf on top of me bark warningly at the two pairs of eyes that then slunk back a bit, and I knew it was Jip defending me and not a wolf at all. I scrambled to my feet and darted forward to retrieve the torch.

Jip stayed close to me for the rest of the clumsy retreat up the terrace, as if he didn't quite trust in my ability to take care of myself, which was probably an accurate assessment of the situation. He kept up a low, almost subsonic growl all the way. I found the rumble of it next to my leg was quite comforting. There was one final spasm of ungainliness as John Dark had to yank and cajole the already very spooked horses into the confined space of the landing, and then we were in—protected on three sides by solid walls with a staircase behind us that we'd have to keep an eye on, and only the open end of the box to defend.

We stood there, panting hard, suddenly immobile and not sure what to do now other than wait.

Mared, she said.

The horses had not liked being led to the back of the landing, past the fire. They were crammed in next to each other, still skittish. John Dark said something else, something I missed but that sounded irritated and worried. I followed her gaze. The fire was not as big as I'd remembered. And there was certainly not enough wood to keep it blazing until dawn.

It's okay, I said. I've got it.

The plastic seat I'd accidentally set fire to was still burning halfway down the terrace. It backlit the wolves who were now arranged in a lumpy half-circle among the lines of seats sloping away below us. The prickling on the back of my neck and the growling that Jip was directing up into the darkness above the mouth of our cave made me sure the circle was a full one and there were wolves up there waiting to leap if we ventured too far.

I pointed out the burning seat to John Dark, then pointed at the seats beyond the mouth of the cave. Then I unslung the bow from my back and put an arrow in, ready. She understood my sign language and nodded.

As she walked out and lit two seats on either side of the steps below, I watched her back by keeping my arrow trained into the gloom above us. No wolf sprang down on us then or later in the night as we made more forays out to light more plastic beacons when the first and then the following pairs guttered out. It might have been that there were no wolves circling above us. It might have been that those that were there were so impressed by my marksmanship that they were too scared to try it. Or, and I think this is the real truth, the noxious chemical smell of the thick black smoke that plumed above the burning plastic made them run somewhere safer, downwind.

We made it through until first light, protected by the fire. Safe, but at the cost of a foul chemical taste and smell that stayed in my mouth and nose for days afterwards. I understand why there's still so much plastic in the world, still pale fragments of who-knows-what-it-once-was washing up on the beaches, or just junk slowly weathering away like all the seats in the stadium. If you'd tried to burn it all on a rubbish heap, you'd have choked the world to death.

The dawn was accompanied by a complete absence of wolf, except the dead one down on the old playing field.

John Dark and I had taken it in turns to sleep. The light came while I was dozing and I woke to find her poking at me with her boot and nodding towards the field.

Eels on two party, she said. *Lay loo. Eels on two party.*

I think *lay loo* means wolves. But whatever that meant, it was good, because it was her younger happier face saying it.

Then a serious look came over her.

Eel foe parlay, she said. *Tew nay pars un day Freemen. Okay. May eel foe parlay day Freemen.*

She pulled the key from her pocket, looked at it and showed it to me.

Okay? she said. Okay, Griz?

I nodded. At the time I didn't really know what she meant, but at least she wasn't trying to tie me up. I sensed things were better between us now. After our shared ordeal, I felt she knew I had saved her and the horses, and that whatever the misunderstanding about the key was, it was at least now agreed to be a misunderstanding, and that we would sort it out.

Maybe it was the sunshine peeking over the edge of the stand opposite, but everything felt more secure. More optimistic. Safer. Trustworthy.

Turned out she wanted to tell me a story.

And we already know how safe those things are.

Chapter 23

Freemen

The story of the Freemen came in fits and starts over the next few days as we travelled. It was told in a mix of mime and pointing at words in the dictionary, and because of that I might still not have it quite right, but I think I have the general idea. I do know I have the specific reason John Dark came to this place looking for the one Freeman in particular. I know what her grudge against him was. He had killed her daughters.

But before we get to who the Freemen were, or maybe even still are, I should put us on the road again. After the night of the wolves, we left the stadium, taking our honey and the horses. The one that had been wolf-bit seemed almost unaware of the damage to its flank until John Dark put a thick wipe of honey across the wound, and then it flinched and whinnied and tried to bite her. I was holding its head and the convulsion nearly pulled me off my feet.

She had quizzed me at first light about the way I had found the key. As best I could, I explained about the tower and the pile of clothes and my feeling that the person—who she called "Freeman"—had killed himself by jumping off the platform.

She asked me about the clothes and I told her about the boots and the red-hooded jacket. The jacket seemed to confirm things for her.

It also untethered something behind her eyes, and she sat for a long while, not looking at me but not looking away either, as if she had forgotten I was there while she watched whatever it was that had been pulling her away. I think knowing that the Freeman she was hunting was dead was not a simple release for her. I think she had filled whatever the hole was inside her with the quest to find him, and now that was not possible, she didn't feel satisfaction, but a different kind of loss. I wonder if that explains why she rode with me. She suddenly had no purpose. Maybe she rode with me while she worked out what her new purpose was going to be. Maybe she just wanted company. Maybe she knew more about where I was going than she let on. But she did ride with me, and I was happy with the company, and grateful for the horse to ride on. And as we rode, as we camped, as we sat by fires and streams, this is what she told me, in the most halting and patchwork way.

She and her family lived away from the sea, near the mountains between what used to be France and Switzerland. She said it was good farmland and there was snow most winters. There was a big lake on the Switzerland side and they went there and fished in the summer. They were horse people like we were boat people. That part of the story was easy enough to understand. They lived there because of the Freemen, although none of her family had ever seen a live Freeman. The Freemen had once lived there, because of the "brain circle" underground.

That's where our trouble with communicating made things a little hazy. She said there was a big circle, underground, and it was said to be full of a brain. That seemed wrong, so after some back and forth with the dictionary we agreed that by brain she meant machines, or a computer. She had never seen them as they were locked away in a circular tunnel a hundred metres under the ground, but they must be long dead as there was no electricity to wake them up and make them remember things. Her father's father's father had gone down into the rock and seen the endless curve with one of the last Freemen. He had said it hummed. And then the Freemen had turned off the lights and it had stopped humming and they had left it and locked the entrance as they went.

It was a story her family told, that they had come here when the last of the old people who worked on the big underground machines were very old, and had helped them until they were gone. Those old people were Freemen. They had worked until they died, trying to make the underground ring remember so much about what humans had discovered so that it became human too. They had tried to teach her great-grandparents their secrets, but it was too late. They were already horse people and farmers. They were not science, she said. That's what John Dark said, and it was what she had been told: they were farmers, and not science now. Her family had been told that the underground brain was just one of several across the world. She said there were once other groups of Freemen trying to do the same thing.

Life, she said by pointing at the words in the book. Life in machine. Body die. No babies carry new life. Freemen try make life go in machine.

And then she found another word, and her blunt finger stabbed it to the page.

Freemen mad.

Freemen say: life in silicon.

I asked her what that meant.

She shrugged and said it was something her great-grandparents told her it was what the Freemen said a lot.

Freemen say life bigger than people. No babies. No new bodies. So life not in bodies. In silicon.

Silicon is a kind of rock. Life in rock?

It made no sense then. It makes less sense now even though I know a little more about the Freemen and the scientist who they named themselves after. But I got that part of the story in plain English, later, from my worst enemy. And even though that helped it sort of make sense, just thinking about the size and the ambition of what they tried and failed to do leaves me feeling sadder and more alone somehow. Definitely more helpless.

You had an internet. You lived in a web that linked you with all the answers that ever were, and you carried them everywhere with you in a glass and metal rectangle that was pocket-sized but could talk to satellites. You never needed to be stupid, or not know things about everything.

We're out here on the wrong side of a dying world trying to piece together the story of what's happened from torn fragments that we can only snatch at as they flutter past us in the wind. Like with the army tank with the doll's head in the gun-barrel under the fallen petrol station canopy, I will never know why everything happened. Or what it meant. I will never see the big story.

She said there were other Freemen and though the tunnel was locked away, her family always remembered where the door was in case one of the other Freemen came, but they never did. Not for three generations, by which time it was quite clear the Baby Bust Freemen were long gone.

And then the Freeman came from the east, riding out of

the mountains, carrying the key that matched the symbol on the door of the Freemen's cave. The key that I had thought was a pendant. The man who killed them all.

He came from far away across the mountains. He was not one of the old people. His family learned from the Freemen. They did not become horse people. Not farmers. Not only farmers. They learned what their fathers and grandfathers learned. To be what he was. Electricians. The word in the dictionary was almost the same in French as English, only with an *e* instead of an *a*.

Understand machines not, she said, pointing at the words. Only know turn on power.

So I think the electrician and his family had been taught how to maintain the power at a place where other Freemen had buried a brain machine, and had passed that on down the generations.

Power electrician home not work, John Dark indicated. Bad time. Electrician come find family me.

So maybe when the underground computer brain his family had tended all the long years had died, he came looking for one of the other ones to make that work.

Except he couldn't and it didn't.

Brain dead, she stabbed. Power dead.

She was crouched beside me over a campfire in the dark when she told me that, because I remember she had to tilt the pages to catch the light from the flames as she did so.

Ordy natoor footoo, she said out loud, and spat into the flames.

And then he had killed her family. Not on purpose. But when you're dead the how doesn't matter as much as it does to the ones you left behind. He brought a disease.

La pest, she called it.

Maybe that's what made him come looking for another

Freeman settlement. Maybe his family died of *la pest*. Anyway, he brought it with him, because she saw the boil scars under his arms when he bathed. And his were healed but the ones that her family got didn't.

Jay duh la sharns, she said, her face twisted and sour as she spat into the fire again.

Sharns, as she later showed me in the dictionary, is spelled "chance" and means lucky.

The sour twist in her face meant she wasn't.

He left while she was nursing the last of the people she had loved, and then when she had buried them, she followed him with nothing in her mind but the need to send him after them.

I understood without her having to put a name to it, but before she put the dictionary away for the night, she showed me anyway.

Vengeance is the same word in both languages.

Chapter 24

An itch between the shoulder blades

She showed me her armpits. After she told me about *la pest*, she showed me there were no boil scars. She wanted me to know she had not caught the disease and was not carrying infection with her the way the electrician had. She meant it to be friendly, to show things were okay between us and that was the way she wanted them to be from now on. Up until that point, I had not thought ahead enough to worry that if he had infected her family, she might be carrying *la pest* in the same way. It didn't quite stop the worry she had now raised in my mind, because I didn't know much about how diseases worked or how the germs went from person to person. I wasn't that clear on what germs actually are and if they all work in the same way.

So we rode on together, and now I worried a little bit about whether I was going to catch *la pest*, but not enough to leave. I decided that however it was that germs went from person to person, if it was going to jump from her to me it would have already happened, probably when I was sewing her up, my hands smeared with her blood. But she looked healthy and strong and after a couple of days I forgot about it. There were other things to fill my head by then.

The higher ground began to slope away to the east, and we entered a new area of vegetation. The scrubby moorland, overgrown and extensive as it was, was nothing compared to the huge swathe of trees we now found ourselves descending into. What had been the midlands of the mainland was now really a great forest of broadleaf trees, mainly beech and oaks and sycamores. On the map, the land ahead should have been full of towns and villages, webbed together with roads and railways. It looked clear enough on the map, but as we looked down on it, it was now hard to make out how the variations in the patchwork of forest matched the confident—but much more than a century old—marks on the paper. We were looking down on a wilderness of treetops. Maybe this was what looking down onto clouds looked like. Only green.

This was when my compass really came into its own, because when we entered the wood, there was no more chance of navigating by landmarks. We rode in among the trees and it was immediately a very different world. Because of the sun filtering through the high canopy of leaves, the dappled light all around us was green. It was almost like being underwater. But it was most like being in a story, one from my childhood, the one about the hobbit that Ferg read us one winter when the weather outside was too fierce to do anything in for weeks on end. It was a story I loved, but I had had to imagine the woods and the forests and the strange creatures that peopled them because, as I said, there is no real woodland on the islands: the only dwarves there are the trees themselves, which are stunted things it would be easier to trip over than fall out of.

But this greenwood was deeper and greener than any I had imagined. There was more birdsong. More insects, like the big shiny black beetle that gave me a shock scuttling past my head when I leant back against an oak tree on our first halt. It had mouthparts that looked like the antlers on a deer and was as big as my thumb, like a metal toy. And then there were butterflies. I hadn't really imagined a wood would have butterflies, but they were all around, orange ones, purple ones and my favourites which were black and white and appeared to flap less than the other butterflies as they glided silently between the trees, seeming to use no effort to do so.

The lack of a distant horizon made me much more aware of the sounds close by me. Not just the horses' hooves on the ground, or the small branches breaking or whipping back once we'd pushed them aside in order to pass: it was the more intimate noises, the horses' snorting, and my breathing. And John Dark's humming. She was always humming when she rode. It was not exactly tuneless, but it was no single tune, and no mix of any ones that I recognised. It was more the idea of a tune, but with important bits left out. I don't know if she was even aware that she did it. It was mostly okay, but sometimes I found it annoying. Usually when I was tired and hungry, which was when almost anything was annoying.

I know having the fanciful thoughts about the hobbit story may seem strange because I was on as serious a journey as I could imagine, going to get my dog back from someone who was likely to be ruthless and wholly opposed to my plan. Not the time to be thinking about a child's book with wizards and elves. I had thought what getting Jess back might involve, and I knew that in the last resort, if it came to it, I would use force. And since Brand was bigger than me, using force likely meant doing it at a distance with my bow, and using my bow meant maiming or maybe killing. The chance of an arrowhead finding an artery even if I didn't mean it to was real, and I wasn't cocky enough to think I could just bluff him.

So a bad second choice of violence likely lay at the end of my journey if my first better choice, stealth and theft, didn't work out. I was really holding on to the fact I was good at not being seen when hunting.

My fantasy was that Brand would be there (not a guaranteed thing) and that I would sneak up on him (this in my mind's eye meant darkness) and that Jess would be calm enough when she realised I was there (wholly miraculous if it was to happen) that she would then let me sneak her silently away. This would neatly pay Brand back, giving him the rude awakening he had given me: a new dawn and the knowledge he had been outwitted. In some of the daydreaming which I allowed myself, I stole his boat too and sailed home, leaving him arriving at the beach or jetty just too late to do anything than shake an aggrieved fist at me. Or in other versions, he smiled that white dazzle of his and shook his head like a good loser, acknowledging he had been viked and outsmarted by a better pirate. But I was pretty sure that honour among thieves was just a pretty phrase I'd read, and not something that existed in the real world. So daydreams apart, there would be blood at the end of this journey. And I didn't know how I felt about that. I'm ashamed to say I had felt fine about it in the flushes of anger that Brand had provoked me to—the theft of Jess, the poisoning of my family, marooning me on Iona and the burning of my boat—but violence is an ugly thing and in the calmer moments I racked my brains for other ways to get what I wanted. Better a brain than a fist. A brain can hold anything, from giant things, like distant stars and planets, to tiny things we can't see, like germs. A brain can even hold things that aren't and never were, like hobbits. A brain can hold the whole universe, a fist just holds what little it can grab. Or hits what it can't.

I wondered if the man who wrote about the hobbit had ridden through the greenwood like this. Despite the bird noise it was a peaceful place that lulled you. Without the compass it would have been easy to get lost. It was a maze without walls, just tree trunks and bushes, and animal tracks beaten through them. John Dark rode with her hood up and the grey hair escaping it, astride a similarly grey horse. From the back, there was something a bit wizardish about her, and it was easy enough to imagine there were other eyes in the forest watching us from behind a screen of leaves or brambles. It was even easy to imagine the bigger trees looking down on us and noticing us passing. I thought a lot about that book as we wove east among the oaks and beeches, and that is certainly why I called the house we ended up taking refuge in the Homely House, because that was the name of the house the travellers in the story made a much needed halt in. And the Homely House we found ourselves in did, in its way, contain a kind of magic, though the magic was in truth just the kindness of long dead people, not immortal elves.

The woods had swallowed everything on this side of the mainland in a way they hadn't in the west. I don't know why there was a difference like that—but it made it a strange journey. Often I'd look at a stand of brambles and realise it was the body of a house, and then look around and realise I hadn't noticed we were weaving through a collection of buildings in a village or on the edge of a town, surrounded by houses that had collapsed into mulch, or become roofless shells out of which trees now grew to a height of a hundred feet or more. Often the clue was realising the thinner "tree trunks" were old street-light poles that had remained upright and unrotted. Brick and stone houses of course lasted better than the ones built with plaster and wood and plastic, but again most still had roofs that had fallen in and were now just shells full of healthy rot and vegetation.

On this side of the mainland in the great forest it was much harder to see the hard edges of your world.

One afternoon we found ourselves riding alongside an enormous cliff of dark green that I later worked out was a yew hedge, and when we came to a gap in it we saw the ash trees on the other side were growing around a pale stone church. The gravestones were mostly tumbled flat, and I only noticed the first one that gave the clue to what all the others were because my horse slipped on it. I looked down, saw the writing "Gone to my Father's House" and knew it was a graveyard. The squat church still had its roof. It looked hunkered down somehow, like a squat blockhouse determined to fight the encroaching trees, most of which were at least the height or higher than its stubby tower.

Light was just beginning to fail, even though there were a couple more hours of visibility left in it, but John Dark was tired and made a noise and a gesture that indicated we might as well stay the night here, pointing at the door of the church. I was keen to get on, but not so keen that I didn't, for a moment, think of agreeing. Even if we couldn't force the door, the covered stone porch would have made a good dry cave to sleep in.

Then we heard Jip growling. The air went very still. John Dark suddenly had her gun in her hand, her head swivelling back and forth, trying to see what it was that Jip was reacting to. I unslung my bow and nocked an arrow. A purple butterfly went past between us, but apart from that, nothing else seemed to be moving in the wood. And that itself was ominous. It had suddenly gone very quiet. No birds sang.

It was so still that Jip's growl seemed to vibrate the air around us.

I couldn't see anything. But I had the same sense of something large, of something aware of us that I had had in that museum, when we'd slept with the lady in the yellow dress and had woken to feel as much as hear something rubbing round the corner of the building in the street below us.

Pa bon, said John Dark quietly, and backed the three horses out of the graveyard. We both kept our weapons ready and continued on our way, very aware of every noise and movement around us. After ten minutes or so, the ground began to rise and the birds began to sing again.

I don't know what had alarmed Jip. I don't know if it was something about the church, or if there was some animal watching us that he took exception to, but as we rode away he kept up a rearguard action, circling back and standing in our trail, staring down the way we came, hackles still raised and nose testing the wind behind us. It was unnerving in one way, but in another way it was comforting to know he was there to sense the things we couldn't see.

Griz, said John Dark. I turned to see she had paused her horse beside a beech tree. She pointed at the trunk.

The grey-green bark had been shredded, and recently. Something had hacked and dragged sharp scratches through it, exposing the vigorous orange of the underbark and the paler sapwood below it. They were deep, angry gouges, and whatever had made them was not just strong but big, because even the lowest of the slashes were started about five or six feet off the forest floor.

Pa bon, said John Dark and made her hand into a claw which mimed slashing at the tree.

Gross griefs, she said. *Pa bon do too.*

And then she mimed keeping eyes and ears open, and led on. I paused by the clawed tree trunk and felt the gashes. They were deep and they were still wet. This had happened recently, which meant that whatever had done it was not far away. Maybe it was the thing we had sensed by the church among the ashes.

Jip peed on the tree in a defiant and matter-of-fact way, and we moved on. Maybe it was a boar like the one that attacked me, I thought. Maybe the gouges were tusk marks. But that would still mean a giant boar, which was not a cheery thought as the night came on. Even less cheery was my real thought which was that they were claw marks, and I had no idea which of the animals I had thought were native to the mainland could have made them.

Zoos. I've read about them and I've seen pictures. Places you put animals when their natural habitats got swept away by farms and mines and things. Were they good? Did you go to zoos? Did it feel like visiting the animals in a prison, or was it exciting? Do you think the animals knew they could never go home because home had been cut down and burned and turned into something else, full of people and machines and not them? Maybe they would have been grateful then, happy that you found somewhere for them to be instead of just killing them all. Or maybe they just went a bit mad. I saw a black and white photograph in a book and the chimpanzee was behind the bars and the look in its eyes was just like a person, lost and frightened, even though it seemed to be grinning like a maniac. Maybe it was just showing its teeth.

Anyway. Zoos.

I thought about zoos as we rode away from the church and the slashed beech trunk, and what I thought about them was this: what happened to the animals as the world slowly aged and died? Did you kill them in their cages, or did you let them go, to fill up the world that was slowly emptying of you? I thought a dying world would have had more on its mind than shipping wild animals back to the places they'd been taken from, but perhaps I'm wrong. I thought it was most likely that you let them get old like you and then die or maybe put them gently to sleep instead. But there was another thought that stalked me as we rode onwards, which was that maybe someone had let the animals out and left them to find their own way home. And if so maybe some of the animals had just decided to stay. After all, the world was hotter than it had been. The mainland had not been a good habitat for them when their ancestors had been stolen and brought north to the zoos in the first place. Maybe the climate changed enough to make it good for them. I was thinking of tigers and lions but it could as easily have been bears. I hoped if it was something it was bears because bears did not, as far as I knew then, stalk people and horses.

And, like Jip who kept looking back down the trail, I couldn't quite lose the itch between my shoulder blades that told me something was watching them every time I turned my back.

Chapter 25

The Homely House

John Dark had the same itch between her shoulder blades. She didn't check behind her, but she looked from side to side much more often than normal, and she never put the gun back in the scabbard that hung from the saddle in front of her knees. I think she didn't look back because she knew Jip and I were bringing up the rear, behind her and the packhorse. It was a kind of trust. The packhorse between us was also getting jittery. And again, it may have been because it was the end of a long day of travel, or it may have been that it could sense something out there stalking us, but the spooked horse made me more aware of the shadows lengthening around us as the light dimmed.

Jip suddenly burst into action, plunging into the undergrowth and barking wildly. We both stopped and swivelled in our saddles, listening for what our eyes couldn't see. Jip crashed through the undergrowth, still barking, getting further and further away. It was hard to hear if he was chasing something and if so, what it was. And then the faint barking was cut off short and there was no sound of movement that I could hear.

La pan? said John Dark, and mimed rabbit ears over her head.

I shrugged and turned back to listen, peering into the late afternoon dimness, ears straining. Jip suddenly bolting away like that was unsettling, and the barking stopping so abruptly was worse.

I whistled and waited, then whistled some more.

I was just about to turn back when he trotted out of the bushes, head up, tongue out, looking very pleased with himself.

John Dark looked pleased too, but I noticed she quickly tried to hide the smile as soon as I saw it.

Jip, she said, tapping the side of her head, as if testing whether it was cracked. *Eel ay foo.*

By this time, I had worked out that *eel ay* is French for "it is". The other word was clear, in context, given the tapping of the head.

Yes, Jip, I said, shaking my head at him. You are *foo.*

Jip just kept panting and smiling, tongue lolling redly out of his mouth as he did so. His air of satisfaction, given the fact he was not carrying a new dead rabbit friend, made me think he had chased something off, rather than chased something down. I don't think Jip could have chased off a lion or a tiger or even a bear, unless it was a very small and unusually timid one, but as we proceeded the itch between my shoulder blades seemed to have gone. And given the fact that neither of us had actually seen anything stalking us, it is possible we had invented the stalker and so brought it along to shadow us only in our minds. We both relaxed a little and pressed on.

The next halt came about half an hour later when John Dark pushed up through a stand of low hazel trees and pulled her horse to a stop. I emerged beside her and followed her gaze.

The Homely House sat in a clearing on the edge of a steep slope, with trees crowded in behind, but an open glade in front of it. The trees weren't green, but a dark purple, which looked closer to inky black in the failing light. They were, I knew by now, copper beeches. They made the stone with which the house was built look pale in contrast. It was a big two-storeyed house, and would have been old even when you were alive. It was wide rather than tall and felt tucked into the crest of the slope, as if it had been comfortable there for centuries, watching the world change below it. There was a high wall on one side of it, and a couple of lower buildings to the other side, built of the same aged stone.

Bon, said John Dark. *E. C.*

She rode on, up to the high wall. There was an oak door, grey with age and studded with big nailheads the size of limpets. She dismounted and tried it. It was stiff and the hinges graunched alarmingly as she pulled it towards her, kicking down the grass tussocks which had grown in its way since it was last opened. And then she stepped through the door in the wall and disappeared. I got off my horse and took a moment to stretch and scrabble the hair between Jip's ears, and then I heard her calling and followed her in.

It was—had been—a walled garden. There was just enough order left to see that once there had been a neat grid of fruit trees at the centre of it, and glass houses had been built against the two walls that caught the sun. One of them had collapsed, but the other was more or less intact, and John Dark was standing in it. Her mouth was smiling and dripping with wetness. She had a half-eaten fruit in her hand. I thought it was an apple, but she beckoned me and pulled another off the tree scaling the wall behind her. The day had been a long and hot one. As I walked over to her, I was engulfed in the thickest, headiest smell I had ever experienced. It was sun and it was warmth and it was clean sweetness—all distilled together. Nothing on the island smelled like that. And the apple? Wasn't an apple at all. Its skin wasn't shiny, but matt and furry, and it was yellow and pink, almost red.

John Dark grinned and bit some more out of the one in her hand.

Pesh, she said. *Pesh bon, Griz, pesh bon*.

I bit into the fruit. It still held the heat of the long day's sun and was much softer than an apple, though the only apples I have tasted come from the walled garden on Eriskay, and they are small, hard and sour. This tasted big and generous, and sweeter than anything I had ever tried. It didn't have the sharp bittersweetness of Brand's marmalade. It had a shape that filled your mouth, a rounded and warm sweetness that immediately made the saliva run and mix with the juices in anticipation of the next bite. It tasted just like the smell around us, but more so. It was like tasting a smile. You'd have thought this fanciful, I expect. Your shops would have been full of *pesh* and other things even more exotic. You probably wouldn't even have been able to remember the first *pesh* you ate, among all the different tastes you were used to. And of all the glories and riches in your gone world, that's one thing I don't envy you for. That's something I have that you didn't: the glory of that first *pesh*, taken in the warm sun at the end of a long, tiring day. It was perfect.

Not many first times are perfect. That was.

We turned the horses out to graze, hobbled for the night, and then we faced the house. The windows were narrow and made of stone with diamonds of glass held in place by lead strips, like the house I had left in flames, but this house seemed much older than that one. The memory of having burned it out of spite made me feel a bit bad, but the words painted and still visible across the door of this new place made me feel better.

WELCOME, STRANGER

It was the same kind of once bright spray writing that had been used to put the Bible verse on the church in South Uist, but the hand that had written was firmer and more generous. The original colour of the paint had faded to almost white, but the message was still clear.

John Dark looked at the words and then at me.

Okay, I said.

I stepped past her and tried to open the door. It was also oak, like the gate in the walled garden. I could see from the thick crust of moss that had grown across the bottom gap that it had not been opened in living memory, and I was fully expecting we would have to kick and shove at it, but it didn't even squeak too loudly as it opened with just the smallest resistance. This was unusual enough for me to look back at John Dark and exchange a look with her. She made a face and shrugged.

Okay, I said. *Bon*.

Wee, she said. Good.

I walked in. The room was low and broad and had an immediate generous feel to it. The walls were panelled with wood. There was a wide staircase leading to the floors above. There were carpets laid out across the hall, dark rectangles on the lighter floor, with complicated patterns on them. The colours were muted both by age and the layer of dust that covered everything. The only sign of neglect was that layer of dust. The house had been left in good order, and that had been done on purpose, as we were to find out.

Griz, said John Dark.

I turned and found she was standing at the big table that took up the centre of the room. There was a frame, like for a painting, and behind the glass someone had placed a couple of sheets of paper covered in big letters.

WE HAVE GONE.
WE ARE IN THE BATHROOM AT THE TOP OF THE STAIRS.
DO NOT WORRY ABOUT MOVING US
WE ARE HAPPY THERE AS WE WERE HAPPY HERE IN LIFE.
PLEASE MAKE YOURSELF AT HOME.
FOOD IN THE WALLED GARDEN.
FIREWOOD IN THE SHED BY THE BACK DOOR.
TAKE WHAT YOU NEED. USE WHAT YOU CAN.
STAY AS YOU PLEASE OR GO AS YOU WISH.
BE WELL. BE HAPPY. BE KIND.

I read it twice, and then I cleared my throat and tried to translate it for John Dark. It made me feel strange, reading something directly meant for me, written to me from the past. I mean, I know it wasn't written for me, Griz, but it was written for anyone who came into the house and found it and that was me.

When I had made it clear what it said, we headed upstairs without needing to agree to do it. It just felt the right thing to do. Paying our respects.

They had gone neatly, making as little mess as they could, and they had gone together. They were just bones now, tangled together in the giant metal bathtub which had feet like a dog's which lifted it off the ground. Their skulls leaned together, companionably, one bigger than the other. The water had evaporated over time, leaving a flaking, rusty tidemark that was probably not just rust. There was a knife lying on the floor beneath the bath. Looking round the room it was hard not to imagine their final moments. There were saucers everywhere, full of puddled wax that had once been candles, and where there were no candles there had been vases and buckets full of flowers and branches, of which nothing remained but dry stalks and twigs that crumbled to dust when I touched them. There was a green bottle of wine with a foil around the neck, and there were two glasses lying unbroken among the bones. It looked like the big one had held the smaller one lying against him. I supposed they might be a man and a woman, but I do not know what the difference is in skeletons. They had filled the room with candlelight and flowers, and then they had got in the bath together, and drunk the wine and then I think they had gently cut their wrists perhaps in the warm water and I hope that they had just felt they were going to sleep in each other's arms. It didn't feel a sad or a creepy room at all. Bones are just bones. And it didn't feel haunted. Like I say, there are no such things as ghosts. But it felt like we were intruding.

I think John Dark felt the same.

Eels etay day john four, she said. *Tray four*.

Then she nodded and walked out of the room. She went downstairs to hunt around, and I walked along the corridor looking into the rooms on either side. They had covered everything with sheets, to keep the dust off I think. They had been there so long that they had caught drifts of dust, and I was coughing because I had just moved the sheet aside to look into a tall cupboard to see if there were any good clothes or boots to vike when I heard a noise that sent an immediate spike of fear down my spine.

It was a high-pitched woman's scream, long and wavering, and it wasn't John Dark. And then there were suddenly other voices, more voices than I had ever heard in my life.

The sound almost made me pee in shock.

And then I heard John Dark shouting for me.

Chapter 26

Tannhäuser

It wasn't a woman screaming, and there weren't other people downstairs. There was just John Dark and a blocky sort of box with a handle on the side. The box was covered in a skin of mottled material that might have once been made to look like leather, but it was worn and frayed and the thin plywood beneath poked out at the edges. Its lid was open, and inside a disc like a big flat black plate was turning around and around despite the fact a sort of tubular metal arm like a goose's neck appeared to be clamped over it. When I had time to look closer, I saw that in fact it only touched the spinning disc very lightly, with the end of a needle that went along a tiny groove that spiralled from the outer edge to the inner circle. The centre was a round paper label, a dark red and gold thing.

The screaming was singing, as were the other voices. And the noise flowing under them was music. Big music. I had not heard your music before. Not like that. I had heard music, of course, but it was all little music—Ferg's salvaged guitars or Bar's tin whistle, and I had been transfixed by the lone sadness of the violin Brand had played in the chapel on Iona. But those were all one, at most two instruments at a time, and I had heard the music as it was being made. It was good but compared to this it was thin. This was music so large and deep that I could not really imagine what the instruments were that made it. It was shocking. And frightening. It was exhilarating and all those things in between because I was touching your reality as you would have experienced it. I wasn't poking through overgrown ruins and sorting through the cracked and rotting stuff you left behind, trying to patch together your world from the rubbish pile. This was like a time machine: the sound I was hearing was the same sound you would have heard if you had turned the crank on the player. These musicians were long dead, but the sound they made together had outlived them and all the generations following, through the Gelding, through the Baby Bust and right on up to now.

I know you had all sorts of ways to record sound and moving pictures of people. But the devices you used don't work now. The electrics have not lasted; they've corroded and died and your screens, big and small, are only useful to us as glass surfaces if we need something perfectly flat. This machine didn't work on electricity. I opened it up carefully later and found it ran on a big spring that you wound tension into with the handle. As it unsprung, it turned the plate on which the disc sat, and the needle somehow picked up the sound from the disc and sent it out into the world through what must have been a noise box mounted on the head of the goose neck.

This was older tech, and it had outlasted the electric music machines. It was a magic trick, this disc, catching voices in time and then holding them across much more than a century and then releasing them into our ears at the drop of a needle. The sound was sort of crackly, as if it had been captured next to a fire that spat and popped as they played and sang, but through it you could hear the music loud and clear. I didn't see the picture of the dog on the label until it stopped spinning. It was sitting looking into a cone attached to another kind of music player. It was a terrier like Jip and Jess, white where they were black. Whoever painted the dog had caught the way they listen when something gets their attention, head cocked to one side. At first I thought the label meant the music was called His Master's Voice, but when I read it and found the other discs with the same label but different writing I figured out it was the name of the company that made the discs.

We both agreed it was *bon*.

We kept the music going as we searched the house, going from room to room, taking the note on the hall table seriously. Whenever a disc finished, one of us would go back and put a different one on, sometimes the other side of the one we had just heard, sometimes something completely different. Some music slowed you down and made you want to sit and listen to it again and again; other kinds of music made you want to jump up and move around to it and dance. This all would have meant so much less to you, I think. You wouldn't have thought it a kind of magic. You probably had hundreds of different bits of music you could listen to. I doubt you were any more amazed at the ability of a machine to capture musicians' performances and hold them through time for you to enjoy whenever you wanted than you thought there was anything extraordinary about a car that moved, or a plane that flew. What a luxury, to get used to magic like that.

I found a bigger compass that unfolded and had a round mirror and a kind of sight on it. It was designed for walking, I think, because it hung from a string you could put round your neck. The kitchen had knives, and even better, a sharpening rod that looked like a pencil that would fit in my pack without adding weight. Because of weight, I only took two knives, one made from a single piece of stainless steel, with black dimples bored into the handles for grip. In the study, I found a drawer with folding knives in it. I took one with a chequered dull silver handle which had a red shield and a white cross on it. It wasn't as good as my Leatherman, but it was great. It had a saw and a spike and a screwdriver as well as a blade and it was scarcely tarnished. The blade took a good edge when I sharpened it. I also found a really powerful pair of binoculars. They had "Trinovid" stamped into them and the lenses were still clear and uncloudy, which was unusual. I took them to the window and they made the distant trees leap forward almost into the room itself. I was pleased to have them because of the power they gave me over distance, to see where I was going. I didn't know they would be the root of my downfall.

And then there were the books. There was a room lined with bookshelves from floor to ceiling next to the one with the music box in it. John Dark wasn't interested in it, because the books weren't in French, but because the room had been dark and dry and sealed they were in great shape. I made a mask out of a square of material tied round my face and began to explore the shelves. Book dust seems to be the worst kind of dust in my experience. I didn't want it in my lungs, making me cough all night. I found a few books I knew which was like meeting old friends in a strange place, amid a multitude that I didn't know. In another life, if I had not been on my way to get my dog back, I think I would have stayed there for a long time, just reading books and listening to music and eating *pesh*.

There was a book on the shelves whose title caught my eye. It was called *Surprised by Joy*. It was partly the title that reminded me of my lost sister, and partly the name of the author whom I recognised because he had written books

Mum had read to us when we were little. They were the kind I had liked, about a group of people on an adventure—children who went through a wardrobe and found a land of magic and talking lions and an evil ice witch. This didn't seem to be that kind of book, not a story but a memory about the writer's own life. But it had a poem inside it which had the same title as the book. I can remember the first lines as they gave me a pang of extra familiarity:

Surprised by joy—impatient as the Wind
I turned to share the transport—Oh! with whom
But Thee, long buried in the silent Tomb.

Joy had always been in a hurry, trying to catch up with our older siblings, determined to do exactly what they did even though she was much younger. And the wind had taken first her kite and her over the cliff at the back of the island where the water was certainly a deep and silent tomb. I read it several times because I don't quite have the way of poetry in my head and also because when I come across a "thee" in a book I know it's old words and probably not written for me in the now, so my brain seems to wander off, but the rest of the poem unravelled itself. In the end, I realised it was about mourning someone and being betrayed by a second of happiness that makes you forget your loss for a moment, and then feeling worse because that unthinking instant of happiness ends up feeling like a betrayal of the lost one.

We made a fire in the fireplace and sat with the windows open, watching the light die on the landscape below. The music we found ourselves listening to was like the house itself: just the right thing at the right time. The label said it was called "The Overture" from *Tannhäuser*. I remember the second *a* had those two dots over it. Must be a foreign name. And wherever *Tannhäuser* is, I bet they have fantastic sunsets, or maybe dawns, because the music fit them both. We sat—eating *pesh* and fire-roasted boar—and played that record again and again until it was dark. It started very slowly and confidently, building a gentle but quietly powerful tune, and then a different instrument, I think a violin, maybe more than one, swirled slowly in and seemed to ask a kind of mournful question answered by more violins steadily building and then the whole thing developed into a kind of strong upward cascade of sound that had rivulets of violin tumbling down out of that building cliff of noise, in a way that reminded me of the hundreds of tiny burns and streamlets that sprang down the slopes of the island after a heavy rain. Half the music swirled you upwards, while the other bit tumbled away in sharp, ordered fragments. That won't make sense unless you ever heard "The Overture" from *Tannhäuser* and know what I mean, and since you don't exist anywhere except inside my head, I suppose it just doesn't make sense to anyone else except me. And maybe you too, I suppose, since you're the one I'm talking to, trapped inside here with me.

Watching the red sunset glow and then fade to blue over the great forest with this music playing again and again is something I will not forget. I don't know what the birds and the animals all around made of the noise. They were probably as startled as we were. None of them would have heard anything like it either.

We slept in the music room, with the fire playing shadows on the ceiling. And when I woke, the red was back in the sky and I played the disc one more time, and that is how I know it works even better as the sun rises. It had more hope in it. I took that as a good omen.

As I went out to check on the horses, I heard John Dark put on some different, faster music, and when I came back I caught her doing a kind of jigging up and down and shaking her bottom which stopped as soon as she heard me. She turned and her face was young and her smile not a bit embarrassed.

Dance ay, she said, beckoning me. *Dance ay, Griz. Say bon*.

And so there in the house that I was already calling the Homely House, John Dark and I danced. As we danced, Jip came in and began to prance around us, barking. His tail was wagging, but I don't know if he was joining in or telling us we had gone a bit mad. We danced to something called "Tiger Rag" and then we danced to someone called Louis Jordan and then I must have overtightened the crank because it wouldn't play, and that was when I took the player apart a bit. I was terrified I'd turned the spring too tight, maybe broken it, perhaps trapping all that music back in the disc, never to escape again. I had a horrible cold feeling of guilt as I sat and used my new knife and the Leatherman to unscrew the top and tilt it so I could see the mechanism. I jiggled and poked and nothing sounded broken, and then John Dark, who had been sitting and watching me with interest, disappeared and came back with a little can with a spout and a plunger.

Wheel, she said and pressed the plunger. A little drop of golden oil appeared and fell to the floor. She handed it to me. I used it to make the mechanism slippy again, and worked some into the hole where the crank handle went. And then I put it all back together and by a miracle it worked again.

We didn't do any more dancing though. I looked at the sky and saw it was towards midday already. I didn't want to leave, but I knew staying was a trap. A nice trap, and well meant by the people who had lived here and sealed it all up so as to preserve it as a haven for those who might come after. But a snare all the same.

I made it clear I wanted to leave.

Say bon E. C., said John Dark.

I know, I said. But I have to go.

I pointed to the east.

I have to get my dog.

Mime and pointing at the dictionary followed and then she went for a walk in the walled garden and I went to hunt rabbits with Jip but they were all gone or sleeping far underground. I sat with Jip looking out over the sea of trees to the west and south of us, and listened to the birdsong and the murmur of the wind. He rolled on his back at my feet, which is not something he does very often, and I took as an attempt to cheer me up. I scratched him on the special place on the side of his ribs and his leg jigged up and down as it always did.

And then we went back into the house and found John Dark with a pile of fresh *pesh* and a finger pointing at the dictionary, jabbing at the word for tomorrow.

Okay, I said.

Okay, she said.

We both made separate passes through the house before it got dark, looking through the neatly laid out objects stored away for those who came later. I decided to take a different set of books about trees and plants, and a couple more pocket-sized leather-bound ones that had thin paper like onion skin. Big, but light. They were books I had heard of from reading other books. One was *The Iliad*, one was *Treasure Island* and the other *The Odyssey*. Looked like a lot of reading in those slim volumes, and I thought we had many nights ahead of us.

I also took a hat and a long oilskin raincoat. Its collar had been eaten by something, maybe a family of moths, but the greeny-brown oilskin was thick and heavy. It would double as a groundsheet on wet ground.

We played *Tannhäuser* as we watched the sun go down,

and then we stoked the fire and turned in, anticipating a big day come morning. I slept deeply and don't remember any dreams, prophetic or otherwise. I woke with first light and found John Dark was already up and packing away her stuff and loading up the horses. I had a last look round the library, trying not to think of all the wonderful stories I was abandoning there, and then made my own preparations to leave.

Chapter 27

False start . . . or there and back again

The day began early and was tinged with sadness from the very start as we saddled the horses and strapped on their packs, and then said goodbye to the Homely House.

I hoped if all went well that I might pass by there again one day, but the world—big and empty as it is—still contains more surprises than you can imagine, and so even before what happened happened to me, I knew returning to that happy place was not something to rely on.

We had—as invited—taken things that were useful to us. We had enjoyed the comfort and calm atmosphere. We had argued about whether to take the record player, but in the end had decided to leave it. One day, someone else might find their way to the house and the rooms would again fill with music. I think the couple in the bath deserved that.

As John Dark was packing the horses, I took a bunch of lavender which I had cut from the hedge of it that divided the walled garden and went to say thank you. I know it's an odd thing to do for an iron tub full of long-dead bones, but the fancy took me and I did it quickly and quietly, not wanting to have to explain it to John Dark. I wasn't ashamed or embarrassed or anything. It was just too complicated a thing to explain in sign language and by poking at a dictionary. I wasn't even quite sure why I was doing it, only that I should. Jip came with me up the stairs.

John Dark had been there before me. She had taken the dry stalks out of one of the vases and left it full of newly cut roses, big pillowy ones that grew on the sunny wall of the house. The smell of them already filled the room. I grinned at Jip and cleared another jug of dry stalks, half of which went to powder in my hands as I did so. Then I put my lavender in and nodded to the bath.

Thank you, I said. We were happy here too.

Only Jip heard me say this, and he didn't seem to find it too stupid. I closed the door on the way out and we walked down the stairs. John Dark was waiting. She saw the remaining dry flower stalks in my hand and grunted. I don't know if she was embarrassed by me having seen her roses, or thought I was shy of being caught with the evidence of my own parting gift, but we never talked about it.

Al on zee, she said briskly. *Foe part ear*.

We closed up the house and made sure it was as weatherproof as we had found it. And then we mounted up and headed east.

In the end the Homely House was a place of death, but its lesson was the dangerous and seductive one that death might not be terrible, but instead nothing more than a long-needed rest, an endless and gentle sleep. Those were the thoughts I had about it as I rode away, and though they weren't exactly bad thoughts, I knew they were not useful thoughts for a person to have, not someone who had things to do in the world. They were later thoughts, to be filed and retrieved when I was older. They were thoughts that dulled the edge, and I still believed at that stage that I had years ahead of me full of unknown terrain through which to cut my way.

Ends happen fast, and often arrive before you've been warned they're coming.

Jip ran happily in a big circle round us as we descended the slope and entered a flatter country that was not as thickly forested as the tract of land we had come through. It was still well wooded, but just thinly enough to make out the shape of old fields here and there, given away by the straight hedgerows that had towered into something more like natural fortifications. In the first hour, we had to double back on our tracks twice because we'd found ourselves bottled in on three sides by impenetrable blackthorn thickets.

And then we came to an open meadow that was passable, but totally overgrown with giant hogweed. I didn't know what it was called then but between what happened next and where I now find myself there were enough lonely nights by the campfire for me to have found it in one of the books I'd brought from the Homely House. If you ever saw cow parsley, you'll know what it looked like, only much, much bigger. Ribbed stalks thicker than my arm, bristly and purple-blotched, rose maybe three or four metres above us: these stalks supported a wide bowl-shaped spread of white flowers, like an upside-down umbrella, each about two metres wide. All the flowers faced up into the sky. It promised a clear enough passage, with plenty of width to weave our way through the stalks, and Jip bounded happily ahead of us. But John Dark pulled up short and turned to me. She pointed at the stalks and said:

Mal.

Which by now I knew meant "bad". She mimed itching wildly, and then pulled up her hood and yanked her sleeves down to make mittens to cover her hands. I did the same. We were about thirty metres into the plantation of hogweed, and I was looking closely at the ribbed and bristly stalk of a particularly thick plant as I passed, wondering if it was the hairy bristles themselves that were *mal*, when there was a crack and a yell and then a horrible crunch and thud, heavy and meaty enough to feel it through my horse's hooves, and I turned to find John Dark had disappeared off the face of the earth. I looked around the other way in case I hadn't seen her cut around me, but I was alone beneath the strange-looking plant heads.

Then Jip barked and ran across and began to paw at the rim of what I now saw was a hole in the vegetation covering the ground. John Dark and the horse had not only vanished from the face of the earth, they had fallen into it.

I dropped off my horse and ran to the edge of the pit. They were both still moving and still alive at that point and, though it was hard to see down into the darkness, even before my eyes adjusted I could tell it was very bad. Even before the horse started screaming. Even before I saw it trying to stand on brutally snapped front legs, struggling to get itself off the vertical length of rusty pipe that had gone straight through it as it landed.

Someone, long, long ago, had buried a water tank in the field. A big one. It had stayed there as the field turned into a wilderness of hogweed, and then it had corroded and waited and then John Dark had taken the wrong way round a stalk and fallen through the roof, jolted off the saddle as her horse impaled itself, landing in about a foot of water.

I could see her face looking back up at me, fish-mouthing in shock. So I knew she was the right way up and not about to drown. I ran for the packhorse and grabbed the rope she kept in one of the panniers. I looped it around the base of the thickest hogweed stalk I could find and ran back to the hole.

Jip was barking and John Dark was shouting my name, though the splashing and the screaming of the horse made it impossible to hear what else she was saying. I quickly tested the rope to make sure it was anchored, said a prayer to a god I don't believe in and slid down the rope into the tank, which made Jip bark even more urgently.

Everything in the tank happened badly, and it happened fast, and even now I can't quite remember the order of things. It's like a broken pot in my head. I can see the shards, but they're not quite joined up into a complete object any more.

It was dark in there and the sky above the hole in the roof was bright, so my eyes kept trying to adjust to the stark contrast in light levels.

It's probably good that I couldn't see everything clearly, but seeing it in fragments and flashes made it even more like a nightmare.

John Dark had blood streaming from her head, and her nose was mashed sideways. She was trying to crawl through the black water towards the horse, but something had happened to her leg.

I tried not to think of the horse, but it was stuck and struggling on its spit of rusted pipe and its front legs were bent in all the wrong directions.

It huffed pink bubbles of blood and foam as it panted and screamed.

Its rolling eyes were the whitest things in the world. Brighter than the sky above.

I stumbled through the water to John Dark. She had managed to throw herself across the horse's neck.

It bucked and twisted in her arms.

I thought she was trying to comfort it. I wanted to shout at her.

I remember I was angry. At least I think I was angry, for a flash.

I wanted to tell her it was beyond comfort. Tell her what we had to do, what I had to do now, fast, before anything else. But I didn't have the words. I just had the knife, already in my hand, without knowing I'd drawn it.

Even now I can see it as a living nightmare. Like I'm still there.

A fragment of her face staring at me.

I think she doesn't understand.

Non, Griz! she shouts.

I think she doesn't want me to do it. I think she doesn't understand how very, very terrible the hurt to the horse is.

Then I see she isn't trying to comfort the horse. She's desperately trying to reach her arms round it. She can't. Her fingers point for me.

They shake with the tension; they stab at what I should be seeing, what I should have thought of.

I hurl myself across the tank and try and pull the gun from the scabbard.

At first it won't come, then the poor horse spasms as it tries to stand one more time and the gun slides free.

Veet, Griz! she screams and buries her head in the mane of her horse, looking away.

Veet!

I lean over her and jam the barrels awkwardly behind the horse's head, where the spine meets the brain. It's an awkward position. I don't have the butt properly seated on my shoulder. I don't have time for perfect.

I pull the trigger.

As I said, it's not unusual for old ammunition to just go click and not fire.

In this case that prayer to the god I don't believe in must have found an ear, because the metal tank bucked and exploded in a thunderclap. The butt of the gun jerked off my shoulder with the recoil and smashed into my cheekbone.

The horse dropped and went slack as the death twitches set in.

I was deaf, ears ringing. I didn't know yet that the recoil had split the skin over my cheekbone. I didn't know yet that I would have a black and bloodshot eye for many days to come. I still don't know if the faint sobbing I could hear was me or John Dark.

It was probably both.

Getting her out of the tank was almost impossible. If she hadn't had the rope on her packhorse, it would have been. Her leg was broken, and she'd taken a really heavy blow to her face and head when she landed. She was also as soaked as was I from the foul water in the bottom of the tank. There was only about of foot of it, but every bit of it stank, and now it had the horse's blood in it too.

Thankfully she passed out the first time I tried hauling her out of the tank with the rope looped under her arms like a sling.

Lifting someone's deadweight is brutally hard, and I couldn't do it by myself. I lowered her back down, wincing as she ended up slumped across her horse's body. I untied the end from the hogweed anchor and knotted it to my horse's saddle, then walked the horse away.

It took some trial and error, and I'm afraid she took some more knocks as I tried to manage the horse and keep the line taut enough to run back along it and grab her before the horse moved and lowered her out of my reach.

Finally, I snatched hold of her hood and managed to get her out of the hole before the horse backed up again. She got some extra scratches and grazes as I did that, but she ended up in the air, breathing oddly, eyes closed like she was never going to wake.

I didn't know what to do about her leg. I didn't know what to do next. She was alive though. Doing something is always the best way to think, so I dropped the rope down again and went back down to get her saddlebags and rescue the gun, and also the knife I had dropped, which took a bit of finding in the water.

Her horse had stopped twitching by then. I patted its warm neck in apology and left it there as I climbed out. She was still unconscious.

There was no neat and tidy way to do what I had to do next. So, hoping she'd stay unconscious, I went into the wood that edged the field and cut some straight poles and brought them back to her. I measured them against her leg and cut them to length. I had seen this done when one of the Lewismen had fallen off a roof on North Uist. I had been small, but it was a simple thing. I took off my belt, and I took off hers. I made some new holes with the point of my knife.

And then I hurt her badly. She whimpered and flinched and at one point opened her eyes without seeing anything as she made a deep groan like a man might make. But she didn't wake properly as I slit her trouser leg to see the damage, and then felt for the break and laid it as straight as I could. Then, not sure if this was right, I braced myself and pulled her leg until the broken bits seemed to line up as best as I could get them. She moaned a lot as I did that. And then I lashed the poles on either side of the leg to keep it straight. Once I'd used the belts to cinch the first two poles tight, it was easier to tie the other poles around it, so her leg was held in place and protected in a bundle of rods.

I looked down at her face, wondering if I should try and put her nose straight while she was unconscious too, but I didn't have the nerve for it. I was sweating with the effort and fear of it all. I decided if I was going to wake her it should be while doing something useful, because I probably had one chance. So I brought the packhorse over and rearranged the saddlebags on either side so their tops made a kind of flattish bed at right angles to the spine of the horse. And then I used the last of my strength and luck to lift her on top of the horse, and lash her to it. I used the rope and criss-crossed her body with it so there was no chance of her falling off.

I turned my horse's head around, with the packhorse following, and headed back across the hogweed field, towards the Homely House.

It started to rain. Either the god I didn't believe in had a fine sense of fairness and was balancing out the good luck of the gun firing first time, or it had a malicious streak. Or maybe there's more than one imaginary god and that one liked matching the mood to the weather.

I didn't bother about keeping myself dry, since I was already soaked from the water at the bottom of the tank, but I pulled the oilskin mac I had intended as a groundsheet over John Dark to keep the rain from her face. As I did that, I had the nastiest thought that I was wrapping her in a shroud, like a corpse, and wondered if she would still be breathing when I next took the cover off her face.

We retraced our tracks back to the Homely House. It seemed to take three times as long as it had coming down. Jip no longer patrolled round us as we went; instead he trotted beside me, looking up every now and then as if to see how I was. I told him I was okay but my voice sounded woolly and trapped inside my head. The trees kept some of the rain off, but not much and as my hearing came back I heard nothing but the trudge of the horses' hooves and the dripping of the water off the leaves. Then we climbed the final open slope in the full pelt of the rain, and although the horses didn't slip much on the rain-slick grass, they felt shakier and less surefooted.

I stumbled when I dismounted in front of the door we had left sadly but hopefully that morning, going down hard on one knee. Jip barked worriedly and came and licked me. I got back up and went to see if John Dark had survived.

I pulled back the tarp and saw her eyes were wide open and unblinking. My legs began to go again, but then she blinked.

Okay, I said. It'll be okay.

She didn't look at me. She just closed her eyes and turned away.

She must have known I was going to hurt her again. Getting her off the horse was easier than getting her on, but not much. I took the door off one of the tumbledown sheds in the walled garden and propped it at an angle against a table I dragged out of the house, making a kind of ramp. Then I untied her and tried to pull her on to the top of the ramp without jerking her leg too much.

I tried to be as gentle as I could, but again I was manhandling deadweight. She didn't make much noise in protest at my efforts to start with. And then she didn't make any at all because I think the pain made her pass out again. Or perhaps it was the hit to the head.

I got her on the door. And then I dragged the door across the ground, up onto the porch and—skinning my knuckles as I just managed to squeeze it through the doorway—into the house, out of the rain.

I used a big padded stool to balance the door on so that she was level with the long deep sofa in front of the fire, and then I slid her off it and onto the cushions. Her eyes flickered as I took off the wet outer clothes as best I could. This revealed more ugly bruises on her body. I think she had broken ribs too. I looked at her nose, mashed sideways. Dad had straightened Bar's nose when she slipped on a rock and broke it against the gunwales of the *Sweethope* two summers ago. I knew it had to be done as soon after the break as possible. And half a day had gone, so it was now or never. I think if she hadn't have been breathing so weirdly I might still have left it, but I thought it might clear her nose enough to stop the snuffing heavy snorts that she was occasionally racked by. So I put my hands on either side of her face, gripped the nose between my thumbs and told myself this was a little thing compared to setting the leg, and that if I was going to do it I should do it once, hard and sharp and decisive. And then I gritted my teeth and twisted it back into the centre of her face. She growled in shock and her eyes snapped open for an instant, but then fluttered closed again. The graunching feeling as I did it made me feel a little sick, but when I took my hands away I was happy that it now looked more or less in the right place and wasn't so obviously smeared across her cheek. And then when I put blankets over her she seemed to sleep again, though I had no idea of the difference between sleep and a coma.

I wanted to lie down on the other sofa and sleep too, but I got a fire going first, and then I went and took saddles and packs off the horses and left them sheltering under a tree.

I ate some food because I knew I had to keep my energy up. There was no pleasure in it. The *pesh* just tasted sour, and the smoke-dried rabbit was so tough it hurt my teeth as I tried to chew some of the goodness out of it. And then I put a covered pot with some water and boar meat in the fire to cook away as I slept, and changed out of my dirty wet clothes.

I hadn't been naked in a long time, not since swimming in the pool behind the house I'd burned. And I hadn't been naked in front of anyone who was not my family ever. I was tired and wet and cold and exhausted and I thought, in my heart, that John Dark was probably in a coma she wasn't going to come out of any time soon, if ever. What I really thought, especially after seeing the bruises on her broken ribcage, was that she was dying. I had no idea what internal damage she might have suffered, and certainly no hope at all of healing it, whatever it turned out to be. So bone-tired, wet, cold and sledgehammered by the day's events, I stood in front of the flames, naked, my hands braced against the high lintel of the mantelpiece and let the fire warm me.

Her eyes were open when I turned to warm my back. She stared at me. I stared back at her, and then I twisted away and pulled a blanket around me. When I looked at her again, her eyes were closed and I don't know if she saw anything.

She didn't say anything about it the next morning, or indeed anything for the next two days. She hovered between a dull unhealthy sleep and a waking that was pained and undignified. I fed her when she was awake, *pesh* and the broth from the boar meat, and between bowls and pans and wet cloths to clean her up with and a tarp under her blankets to lie on, we coped with her need to piss and shit despite being unable to move. It didn't worry me, but she hated that part of it.

The only good thing was the swelling on her nose got better, and although both her eyes remained yellow and purple and bloodshot, they were on either side of a more or less symmetrical face again.

I think I understood her silence. She was like a terrier that had been hurt. She had just gone into herself to heal. I came back into the room on the first morning, bringing more firewood and Jip had climbed on the sofa and lay against her, giving her his warmth. He looked at me.

I said it was *bon*.

Chapter 28

Onwards, alone

It all comes down to pissing and shitting in the end. That's what Dad used to tell us about getting old and ill, or looking after those who were injured. He wasn't wrong.

Now that things had taken a turn for the worse, I began getting more and more worried that Brand would arrive at his home and then leave before I got there. I resented the time I was losing by nursing John Dark. And I could have left her and gone after him at any time I suppose, but she wasn't able to move off her bedding to take care of herself, so I would have been condemning her to dying in her own mess. I couldn't do that.

Days passed in a blur of sameness. Feeding, helping her do what she had to do, cleaning her up when she did it while she was unconscious, again and again, day after day. It was harder because she either couldn't or wouldn't talk, and I began to worry she couldn't see either because sometimes she squinted and sometimes she stared with wide-open eyes that didn't seem to react to what was happening in front of her.

She wasn't dead, but maybe she was just dying slowly. She certainly didn't seem to be getting any better. I filled my days when she slept by reading books from the library, but the pleasure I normally took from it was damped, because I knew I should really be on my way to Brand and Jess. Too much time to think made me second-—and third- and fourth-—guess my belief that he would be there. I went back and forth over my reasoning as to why I had been so sure the marks on the map meant that Norfolk was his base, and every time I did I came up with more reasons that I had been a fool to set out on such a crazy quest on such thin evidence. I punished myself for chasing an illusion just because I had wanted to take action rather than accept the impossibility of my loss. I told myself I should have stayed home and looked after my family and been satisfied I still had Jip.

But I kept coming back to the same thing.

Brand had stolen my dog. I didn't actually have a choice. He had to expect me to come after him. It was a matter of loyalty. Even if I never found her, I had to try. I had to give it my best shot. I knew in my better moments that I was doing this because I wouldn't have been able to live with myself—or Jip—if I didn't.

And so, on the principle of planning for a better future, even if it seemed unlikely, I kept my mind calm by keeping my hands busy. That worked better than just sitting and reading and living in my head with all the echoing doubts bouncing around inside it. I made John Dark a pair of crutches. Then I dug a hole just outside the door to the garden, as a toilet, and I knocked the bottom out of a sturdy wooden chair that had armrests and planted it over the hole. I filled a bucket with wood ash from the fire and left it by the chair.

I wondered about making her a chair with wheels, but none of the wheels I could find turned any more: they were corroded in their axles or the rubber tyres had perished to nothing. I started getting jealous of the attention Jip paid to her. That was stupid and mean-spirited, but I felt it. I began smoking meat in the large fireplace and when done I hung a good cache of it from the walls. I found as many pots and pans and bottles as I could and filled them with water, leaving them round the edge of the room.

I don't know if she knew what I was doing. She watched me and her face gave nothing away. The bruising was fading to all the colours of a pale rainbow, and as it disappeared her skin was now always as grey and washed out as her hair.

I lived those days like I was slowly drowning in despair and a large part of that was because I didn't know how to do two things I knew were the right thing to do, two things which cancelled each other out.

In the end, she showed me.

I woke to find her gone. The dawn light was watery and the fire was cold and long gone to ash. I sat up and looked around. The crutches were gone too. So was Jip.

She was on the seat over the hole in the garden and she was crying. I think it was partly from the effort to get there, and partly out of frustration, because one of the crutches had toppled away into the grass and she couldn't quite drag it back into her reach with the other one. She looked away as I came out onto the dew-soaked grass, and I picked up the crutch and gave it to her without speaking. After a bit, I realised she was sitting motionless because she didn't want me to see the effort it was going to take to get back on her feet. I went back into the room, but watched her from behind, through the window. She got shakily upright, and then swung herself precariously to the door, where she leant and panted for breath. The effort of keeping her splinted leg off the ground was exhausting. She was trying to use muscles she hadn't used for many days, maybe even weeks. I had stopped counting because the mounting tally of wasted days felt like it was pressing down and slowly suffocating me.

She looked at me and nodded. I helped her get from the door to the sofa and she lay down and went straight to sleep.

She didn't exactly get better then, but she got more mobile. I think she knew something was wrong with her head and something else was wrong with her body inside. I would see her wince in pain and hold her hands to her temples until whatever was hurting her went away. It made me think of Dad wanting to drill the hole in Mum's head when she'd cracked her skull. I couldn't see any fluid coming from John Dark's nose though. And I certainly didn't go looking for a hand drill.

She asked for things by pointing. I brought her the dictionary and I brought her a pencil. She pointed at the record player and I put music on. Then she waved me away, wanting to be alone.

I went hunting with Jip. He caught a rabbit and I shot two, though I missed another and spent an irritable half-hour searching for my arrow in the middle of a tangle of brambles.

When I came back, she was sleeping. She woke and ate and then went back to sleep. I read until it was dark and then went to bed myself.

Dawn came with a poke in the ribs.

She stood over me, jabbing with her crutch. I sat up and she handed me a note. She must have spent all the time I was out hunting stitching the words together from the dictionary. She didn't know how verbs work in English, but it was painfully clear what she meant. As I unfolded it, she swung herself out into the garden and made noisy use of the hole in the ground.

I know this is exactly what she wrote because I have the note still, folded into the book I am writing in.

YOU TO GO TO FIND YOUR DOG NOW.
I HURT ME NOT TO BE BETTER.
I NOT TO WANT TO BE SEEN LIKE THIS.
I TO BE HAPPY TO LEAVE ALONE WITH MY MEMORIES.
WATER. MUSIC. FOOD. HOLE IN GROUND. THANK YOU, GRIZ.
TO GO QUICK. NOW. IMMEDIATE.
BEST WAY TO SAY GOODBYE.
TAKE HORSES.

If she believed she was going to get better, she would have said take one horse. It was telling me to take both that made me wipe my eyes.

But she was right about a fast goodbye. There was no point lingering or arguing. She had given me permission. She had solved my problem for me.

She came back and stood leaning in the doorway.

Bon? she said.

I nodded.

Veet, she said. *Allay veet.*

I left her the saddlebags full of stuff from the packhorse. I dragged them inside and put them close to the sofa. She nodded. It wasn't just useful things she had collected, there were memories in there she had brought through the tunnel from France. Then I picked her a basket of *pesh* and took a bag for myself and saddled the horses.

I gave her the basket when I went back in to say goodbye. I caught her scratching Jip behind the ears, which he was enjoying, though she pretended she hadn't been as soon as I entered the room. I found I didn't know how to say goodbye properly. She beckoned me closer and suddenly hugged me so tight I think she wasn't just hugging me but all the ones she had lost.

Or maybe she was making the most of her last moment of human contact.

Then she spoke English. She must have learned it from the dictionary. Her voice was ragged and raw, and the words sort of twisted in her mouth and came out with a French flavour, but it wasn't hard to understand.

Griz, she said. Griz. Thank you, friend.

I squeezed her back and said "friend" too, then the rest of the words I wanted to say got choked up and stuck and we both stayed like that until we had composed ourselves. Then she let go and pushed me back firmly. She held out another folded piece of paper.

Not to read now, she said carefully.

And then she kissed me on both cheeks and sat back down on the sofa, avoiding my eyes and waving me away with a hand gesture as imperious as a queen.

I rode away with that familiar unswallowable lump of loss stuck behind my breastbone. As I did so, I heard the record player start to play the fast and happy tune we had laughed and danced to, and I knew she wasn't dancing but putting a brave face on what was to come and trying to cheer me up. I heard it three times and then either she got too tired to wind the player again or we had got too far away to hear it any more.

Jip kept looking up at me and then stopping and looking back at the house, and then running to catch up and look at me again, as if asking me a question I had no good answer for. Once the sound was gone, I picked up the pace, moving faster than we had before. Now the decision was made, there was no good to be had from taking any longer than necessary.

We got many klicks beyond the hogweed field before night

fell, and found ourselves on the edge of a more varied terrain that stretched away flat and featureless ahead of us.

I watered the horses in a pond and hobbled them for the night.

Only when I had eaten and laid out my bedroll did I take out the note. It was too dark to read by then, but I poked the fire back into a blaze and turned myself so that I could read it. It didn't say much, but in a way it broke my heart and made me feel terrible about leaving her all over again. I still have it here in my other hand as I write this.

YOU TO LIE TO ME, GRIZ.
IT OK. I TO UNDERSTAND.
BUT I TO KNOW WHY YOU ARE SO STRONG.
YOU TO REMIND ME OF MY DAUGHTERS.

And yes, my eyes were stinging as I closed them to start chasing sleep that came in unsatisfactory fits throughout a long cold night. And no, it wasn't because of the woodsmoke.

Chapter 29

First sight

I know reading has made me sentimental. Dad doesn't read much other than practical books that don't have stories in them, and apart from sometimes sitting with Mum and holding her hand by the fire when he thinks we aren't watching, he is not a needlessly tender man. He's brisk, often curt, and decisive. He gets things done, like he has a list in his head that he is always adjusting, adding to and ticking things off.

I made myself more like him as I rode away from the Homely House and John Dark. I stopped myself from wondering each night as I made the campfire if she had died during that long day, if she was lighting her own fire as I lit mine, or if the Homely House was quiet again, and now the home of a new corpse. I didn't read any of my books, not even the new ones. I told myself I didn't need to soften myself with distractions like that, but that if I succeeded in my wild quest I would allow myself as much reading as I liked as a reward. Instead of reading, I just used the map and the compass and tried to make sense of where I was, to keep on track for where I was going.

My biggest piece of luck was looking for shelter one night

as the rain set in again, and finding what I took to be a big metal lean-to, overgrown with creepers. There was room for me and the horses under it and it was only when I lit the fire that I saw the underside and the giant writing and realised it was a large, miraculously still legible road sign which had fallen and ended up tilted against the trees that had grown up around it. It took a night of lying there thinking, but once I worked out what to do it made it very easy to get a sense of where I was: I just looked at the distances to various towns, and used a piece of string to measure those distances against the scale printed on the bottom of the map. Then I found the towns named on the sign and drew circles of the right diameter to match the distances—and where they all met had to be where I was.

Knowing my position gave me an added sense of purpose as I pressed on. I ignored the houses that I passed and wasted no more time viking through any of them. I slept under the stars, or under John Dark's tarp shelter, and I disciplined myself to focus only on what lay ahead. I suppose it was like what being a soldier must have been, preparing to go to war. Not wanting to fight, but getting your head straight so you were ready and as unsurprised as possible in the face of whatever fate held in store. Every morning, I woke and practised with my bow, fifing three quivers before I ate and moved on for the day. At midday, I fired three more. At night, just before dark, I fired a final three. Jip often stood and watched me, as if wondering why I was hunting tree trunks, or how many times I expected to bury arrowheads in one before I killed it.

I sharpened my mind by trying to remember every moment I could of those I'd spent with Brand, so I would be able to read him better when we next met. I practised the arguments I might have to make. I also sharpened my knives.

I tried to make myself go cold inside, methodical and

unemotional like my dad. Jip made that difficult because he was having such a happy time, running all over this new terrain, exploring the sights and the huge variety of new smells that the changing landscape must have presented him with. Even with a simple human nose, I could tell things smelled different: for him the mainland must have been like me discovering the bigger music on the record player. The islands are simple—sea, salt, heather, wildflowers in the machair. They were like music made with a guitar or a tin whistle, or Brand's single violin. The mainland with its variety of plants and flowers and trees must have been like a huge orchestra for him. *Tannhäuser* through the nose. He hunted with me and he slept close, sharing the warmth. His happiness was infectious. He brought me rabbits and a rat and early one morning chased a hare over the low ridge ahead of me, and when I crested it, ten minutes later, he was standing, hare-less, silhouetted by the still rising sun, nose to the light breeze, tail stiffly behind him, staring at what should not, according to my map, be where it was.

It was a sea marsh, and beyond it, sending a tang of salt even I could smell, was the sea itself. Much closer than the map had led me to expect it might be. The land had gone, swallowed by water that had risen as the world had got hotter. On Eriskay, you can swim and look down on the old ferry jetty sunk a metre or so below the waves. On Berneray, you sail in and moor your boat to the chimney stack of houses that used to line the foreshore. So although the world is still a big place, the dry bits of it are, I suppose, smaller than in your time. And the flat lands on the east, one bordering the North Sea, had now gone under it.

Which made sense of the map which had put Brand's base so very far up the river from the estuary. Because now it wasn't hidden away so far from the sea at all. The sea had come and found it. That explained lines I had thought slapdash, the ones that "flew" over dry land. Because that land was not dry now, but marsh or seabed. I got off the horse and found the new binoculars, steadied them on a low tree branch and took stock of the terrain ahead. The trees thinned out and gave way to a sort of in-between land where dry spits and peninsulas jutted into the marsh. The marsh was covered in great expanses of reeds in some places, like flat islands in the water, dotted with wading birds, and in other places you could see the shape of the huge fields that had once been here by the skeleton remains of old hedgerows with their feet in the shallower water. The carcasses of several old buildings were tilted and half collapsed in the water here and there all across the marshscape, looking surprised to find themselves shipwrecked. Some of the old giant electrical pylons had survived a century or so of storms and the power cables they had supported as they marched in heroic swags all the way across the land curved down into the water here and finally lost themselves in the incoming waves.

The sound of gulls was distant, but immediately recognisable, and the noise sent a treacherous wash of nostalgia through me to soften the hardness I had been practising. I've read that smells are the most evocative things, but the right sound can take you out of yourself too. For a moment my mind went away, back to Mingulay and my simpler life. And then Jip barked and I jolted back to the present.

He was looking up at me, head cocked. Like I was missing something. Then he barked again and looked out at the landscape again, nostrils flared, tasting something on the wind.

I pulled out the map and tried to make sense of what I was seeing the marks the map makers had made, but it was very hard, especially because I had only a sketchy sense of where I was. I took the time, because I was still on slightly higher ground. Once I approached the new coast, it was all going to be flat and wooded and impossible to make out any remaining landmarks.

It was the low sun that gave the overgrown town away. I saw a flash and looked at it, and saw the house windows dully reflecting the light back at me through a stand of willows, far in the distance. It was so far that I hadn't been able to see the river beyond. But once I fixed on the houses and the overgrown ruins beyond, I scanned slowly around them and saw two things. The first was a wind turbine turning very slowly. And then, just beyond it, there were uprights that were too regular to be trees that I first took for headless light-poles, and moving further on from them I saw another dull flash of water, which must have been the river, and just seaward from that I saw the thing that made me realise the light-poles were masts and I was looking at a mooring along a river's edge.

I was thinking it was perhaps not more than a morning's ride away when I saw the sails further along the bank.

The red sails.

Chapter 30

Be careful what you ask for . . .

It was always a gamble.

Ever since I'd stolen the map, a little part of me had known I might be making a huge mistake. The lines that radiated from the place I was now overlooking might not have been Brand's home at all, and even if they were, there had never been any real guarantee he was heading back there. He might have been off on another years' long voyage to other unexplored parts of the world. Or they might not have been lines that marked his comings and goings at all—they might have been someone else's lines, some long dead sailor's tracks left on an old map that Brand had later viked.

As I had travelled down across the broken spine of the mainland, I had certainly had enough lonely nights and days to consider these possibilities. I'd begun to ask myself whether my quest was more to do with what I wished than what I could rationally expect. And as the wear and tear and the losses had mounted up—not just the loss of Jess that began it all, but the *Sweethope*, and even John Dark—I had started to dread rather than wish for the moment of arrival. I had reason enough to suspect very strongly that my luck had gone, but since my boat was burned I had no choice other than to try and finish what I had started. And then when the accident with the buried water tank happened, I think I knew for sure that fate was against me. And still I had plugged on, not really through doggedness or the courage of my convictions, but because I didn't know how to make sense of those horrible losses—other than by playing out the hand I'd chosen, clinging to a wild hope. Which is another way of saying I was too stupid to know what else to do and I should have cut my losses, but I didn't know how.

I had always been bad at card games. Ferg or Bar almost always won because I usually held on for a bit too long, forever sure that the next or even the final card would be the one in fifty-two chance I needed to complete my own winning hand.

Hope less, count more! Bar would say.

But keeping a tally of cards like it was a maths problem never seemed like a game to me. It was more like a chore. And so I enjoyed playing for the companionship of it, but seldom won. Though on the rare occasions when I did beat them, the infuriation that it sparked in my more careful siblings made victory all the sweeter.

Seeing the red sails was like that. A hoped-for but actually totally unexpected win. Very, very sweet. So sweet that I shouldn't have dropped my guard and stopped expecting it to turn sour.

I had to get closer. I had to lie low and spy out the land. I had to be clever and quiet and match the headlong recklessness of my decision to set out on this hunt in the first place with a cautious and well-thought-out plan to make it end well. I had to not squander this unlikely turn of luck.

I went forward carefully now, making sure the horses and I stayed in the woodland and didn't expose ourselves in the open areas. I wanted to get close enough to lie up and watch before I did anything else.

Now I kept Jip close by putting a long rope on him. As I did so, I explained we needed to be quiet, that he shouldn't bark and this was just to stop him running off on a hunt and giving us away by mistake. Of course I was really talking to myself, but I had always spoken to the dogs and explained things, and I think even when they didn't understand the details, they understood the tone in my voice. Jip hated being leashed, but after a bit he gave up tugging the line taut and trotted beside me, the rope slack between us. Every now and then, he would look up at me as if to ask if it was time for this game to stop, but I shook my head and told him it was necessary.

After a couple of hours of quite slow progress, I hobbled the horses and climbed a tree. You probably climbed lots of trees. Maybe you even had a tree house. For me this was a first. Jumping into a tree to escape the boar didn't count. I tested each branch as I hauled myself higher and higher, and then I stopped, held myself steady with one arm around the trunk and peered east through the thin screen of leaves. Towards the mooring.

Again, at first I thought I had gone astray, because I couldn't find it. There was a light breeze, and the branches moved in a slow heave like the sea that made the clouds of leaves all around me murmur and rustle. It was quite peaceful. I took another look through the binoculars and this time I found the sails and the buildings, which were closer than I had expected.

In the distance, at the very edge of my hearing, I thought I could hear a dog.

I climbed down the tree as fast as I could, worried that Jip would start to answer the distant barking and give us away.

The wind was coming over our shoulders, and down on the floor of the wood the noise was more muffled, so he didn't get a smell or hear any sounds that might set him off. However, I was determined that he shouldn't give us away by mistake, so I retraced our steps about a klick and then—greatly to his mystification and outrage—tied him to a solitary tree and left him with the packhorse. The tree was an old and very tall pine. Its red bark zigzagged into the sky and supported dark green shoals of needles and cones that were moving gently in the breeze. Older brother and sister pines had fallen around it, their greying trunks and roots making a kind of natural stockade around its base. It would be an easy landmark to find on the way back, and would be far enough away for Jip's protesting barks to remain unheard. I left him a pan full of water and then I knelt and ruffled his neck fur with both hands as I looked into his eye.

I'll be back soon, I said. It'll be okay. I can only do this by myself.

And at the time, I meant every one of those three lies.

I felt odd setting off without him. Naked almost. He always came hunting with me. Not having him cutting back and forth in front, looping forward to see what was ahead and then coming back to check on me, felt odd. Like I was missing a limb. Like it was making me walk funny. Self-conscious. Unnatural even. I felt lopsided. And unprotected.

But I pushed on, carrying my bow and keeping my eyes and ears open.

I was just scouting. I wasn't planning on doing anything rash. This is what I kept telling myself. Though I did think if by some miracle Jess came to me we would make a run for it and trust that Brand, who wouldn't have horses, would never catch me in the wide maze of emptiness and ruin that lay between me and home. In my mind, even if I couldn't find enough of a boat to mend and retrace my steps back once on the west coast, I could ride to the ruin of the old Skye Bridge and swim across to Skye with the dogs. From there it would be easy to get to the westernmost edge of the big island and start burning things until Dad or Ferg or Bar—or the Lewismen even—came over the water to see what was going on.

Hope can keep you afloat in troubled times. It can also drown you if you let it distract you at the wrong moment. I was enjoying thinking about how surprised they'd all be to find me waiting on the beach with both dogs, when the tree in front of me spat bark shards into my face as an arrow thunked into it.

Don't move, said a muffled voice ahead of me. Or the next arrow is yours.

On the plus side, it wasn't Brand. On the other hand, I had been wrong about the horses: there were three riders, faces hidden by old gas masks and scarves. One had a gun with a long and curved magazine underneath it; the others had bows aimed right at me.

Okay, I said.

They stared at me. Not being able to see their faces was unnerving, but they somehow seemed just as unsettled as I was. Like they didn't know what to do either.

I'm Griz, I said, and raised my hand in the beginning of a wave.

Don't move, said the one with the gun. And don't talk.

I had the strongest sense he needed quiet to think what to do next.

I nodded.

Are you sick? one of the bowmen said. His voice sounded younger.

Yes, said the gunman. Good. Are you sick?

No, I said. Just tired.

Have you been sick? said the other bowman.

Not especially, I said.

Where are the rest of you? said the first bowman.

There's just me, I said.

The gunman snorted.

And where have you come from? he said.

North, I said. I come from the north. Who are you?

Shut up, said the gunman as the second bowman began to answer. He turned to me again.

Leave your weapons here, he said.

I hung my bow and the quiver full of arrows on the tree.

All of them, he said.

So I took my knife and then my other knife and left them sticking in the tree too.

No more knives? he said.

I shook my head. My Leatherman wasn't really a knife. I could pretend I forgot it if they searched me.

But they didn't search me. They didn't come any closer than they already were.

Who are you? I said. I don't mean any harm—

Plenty of time for talking later, said the gunman. He reached into his saddlebags and threw something at me that thumped into the grass at my feet with a clink of metal on metal.

Put one of those on each wrist and close them until I hear them click, he said. Don't play games.

They were two pairs of handcuffs made to hold your wrists together. One was silvery, the other a dull black.

Why? I said, wondering if they would get me if I turned and ran, or if that moment had passed.

Because I'll shoot you if you don't, he said. I'm sorry, but I'll have to.

He did sound sort of sorry, but he also sounded like he'd shoot me anyway.

I bent and put them on. The hinges were oiled and they clicked into place, and I stood and showed each pair dangling off a different wrist. It wasn't clear to me why he wanted me to do that.

Now click the cuffs together, he said.

That made sense: I would have found it too awkward to cuff myself with one pair of cuffs, because my wrists wouldn't have bent that way, but cuffing myself with two pairs was easy.

They'd done this before.

You don't want to get close to me, do you? I said. That's why you're using two of these. Otherwise you could have come over and cuffed me with one pair. What are you scared of?

We're not scared, said the second bowman as if I'd insulted him.

Don't waste your breath, said the gunman. Like I said. Plenty of time to talk to him if he survives.

If I survive what? I said.

Quarantine, he said.

Chapter 31

Quarantine

Quarantine was a cell, half underground, in a bunker. Or maybe it was the cellar of a building that had fallen down. Maybe a police station. Maybe an old army barracks. It was quite a distance from the mooring with the red sails, although you could see the masthead and the settlement next to it from the windows of the cells on one side of the bunker. There were six cells, three on each side of a hallway, facing each other.

The distance from the settlement was on purpose. It was quarantine. They didn't want to catch whatever I might be carrying. If I was infectious. Which I wasn't, of course.

They made me walk ahead of them as they shouted instructions, guiding me through the trees and into the edge of the old overgrown town towards the bunker building. Then they dismounted, and the bowmen made me walk down a flight of steps and then one made me stand as far as possible from himself as he opened a barred gate and stepped away as I was ushered through it by the other. They made me go to the far end of the hall before they approached the gate and re-locked it.

The six cells all had heavy doors with slits in them so jailers in the old days could have looked in on the inmates to see how they were doing.

Don't you close those doors, said one of the bowmen, his voice indistinct as he backed up the stairs. You close them, you're stuck for ever because we don't have the keys. Use the toilet in the end cell on the right. The old drain's clear but you flush your business away with a bucket

of water.

Wait, I said. What are you scared of?

Not scared, he said. Prudent. Last visitor but one brought a plague killed three people. Fucking Freeman... You'll stay here a month; we'll see if you get sick. You're still alive after that, we'll be happy to let you join us.

He doesn't want to join you, said a voice from the deep shadows in one of the cells I had taken to be empty.

The voice sounded tired, disappointed in me, and chillingly familiar.

He just wants his bloody dog, it said.

I turned and peered into the gloom. His beard split in a thin smile, showing me a flash of white teeth.

I told you to go home, Griz. I did warn you.

Brand. I felt winded and couldn't speak for a moment. I heard the door at the top of the stairs slam shut and then the noises of the horsemen leaving.

Brand didn't get off the cot in his cell. And he didn't say anything else.

I went into the cell across the hall from his and sat on the cement ledge staring at him, framed in the two doorways. It felt like a lot of time passed in silence then, and maybe it did. But eventually all that silence seemed to be sucking the air out of the cells, and talking seemed like the only way to keep breathing.

Where's Jess? I said.

She's fine, he said.

Where is she? I said.

Took the chart, he said. That's how you got here, right?

Where's my dog? I said.

You find another boat? he said. Is that it? But then—how likely is it you found a boat that was ready to sail? You find a boat these days, you got to cannibalise twenty more to get enough lines and sails and tackle that work to make it go. No. You didn't find another boat. You walked.

He got off the cot and came and stood in the slant of light falling across the doorway and looked at me closer. He shook his head and grinned.

I wanted to kill him. I don't like violence. I think violence is a kind of stupidity. But right then, for that grin, I think I could have killed him.

You're a tough kid, he said. Stubborn. I mean, you're like an irritating little cough I can't seem to get rid of but I give you that. You have my admiration.

I don't want it, I said. I just want Jess.

Jess is a commodity, he said. A bitch that can have pups is a rare thing.

Bitches have puppies, I said. It's what they do.

No, he said. No, that's not so.

I glared at him some more.

You walked across the mainland? he said.

I didn't nod.

Never saw a pack of wild dogs, did you? he said. Strange that, no?

I shrugged.

Sure we talked about this back on your island, didn't we? he said. The Baby Busters put some kind of poison out for the packs of hungry dogs they got scared of once the population got small enough, and that poison messed with the bitches' ability to have pups. Least that's what I heard.

The thought made me look away. It had the nasty finality of an unwelcome truth. I felt ashamed of being human.

Dogs were with us from the very beginning. And of all the animals that walked the long centuries beside us, they always walked the closest.

And then they paid the price. Fuck us.

Maybe the Gelding wasn't an accident. Maybe it was just desserts.

That's what makes her a commodity, he said.

What's a commodity? I said.

I knew. Sort of. But I wasn't sure he did. And I wanted time to get my thoughts together and get away from the sad thought of the millions of dogs that must have wondered why they couldn't have litters any more.

It's something you trade, he said.

And you're a trader, I said. When you're not being a thief.

Sometimes, he said, nodding. Mostly I'm just a traveller. I don't meet enough people to trade with.

But you meet enough to thieve from, I said.

Do I? he said.

Yes, I said.

That converter. For the wind turbine. The one I came to trade with your dad, he said.

What about it? I said.

You came aboard my boat, he said. Like a thief yourself. No invitation. Took my chart.

That's different, I said.

You see that converter while you were there? he said.

I let the silence suck a little more air from the room as I thought.

I wasn't looking for it, I said. It was dark.

You didn't see where I left it on the beach on your island then, he said.

I stared at him. He grinned some more and then shrugged magnanimously.

I mean, fair enough—you came after me like your arse was on fire, so you probably didn't have time to have a good look around, he said.

But, I said.

And you were well asleep while me and your dad were still up talking by the fire, he said. So you don't really know what deals were done. Do you?

Dad would never have given up Jess, I said. Jess is my dog.

Sure about that, are you? he said. Sure your dad would never make a deal where he sacrificed one thing to save a bigger one?

Jess is mine, I said. She's not anyone's to trade.

Okay, he said. If you say so.

Liars lie. That's what they do. That's what he was doing. Lying, and in so doing trying to make me lie to myself. Trying to make me not trust my family. Liars lie by cutting you loose from what you thought was so and persuading you this other thing they are waving in front of you is the new truth. You will have come across many liars in your crowded world. I expect you knew this from the get-go. I imagine you were prepared for them, and knew how to deal with them. I hadn't met a liar until Brand sailed into our lives. But I already knew this about how they work and what they feed on. Liars want you off balance and alone, so you can drown in self-doubt.

Brand already had me halfway there before I noticed what he was doing.

If you're doing so well, I said, what are you doing in here?

That, he said, is a good question. But before I answer it, you answer my question. Man to man. Are you going to try and kill me?

What? I said. His directness had again winded me.

You're glaring at me like you are going to leap at me at any moment and it's a small enough space we seem to find ourselves in, and we should get this out of the way, otherwise it's going to be exhausting. So I'll ask again. Man to man. Are you going to try to kill me?

You're bigger than me, I said. And violence is stupid anyway. And you stole my dog. You didn't kill my family.

I paused for a moment and wondered if they had recovered. I had after all left them distinctly vomitous and grey-faced.

So? he said, blue eyes glittering.

So, I said. Man to man? I won't kill you.

He nodded.

Okay, he said. Well, that's reasonable if we're to be locked up in here for a while.

Especially if you give me back my dog, I said.

He didn't quite know what to make of that. He decided to hang a smile on it, but it hung a little more lopsided than normal and I had the satisfaction of knowing he wasn't quite sure of me.

So what are you doing in here? I said.

It's as they said, he said. A lone traveller, a Freeman came through carrying a disease that raised boils in the armpits and killed three of them after he left and went north.

This had to be the same traveller John Dark had told me about. The one who caused *la pest*, the Freeman whose key I wore round my neck.

So the Cons have decided anyone from outside has to sit in quarantine and not be ill for a month before they let them into the compound, he said. That's why they were wearing the masks and scarves. They don't want to breathe our air until they know we're clean.

The Cons? I said.

Conservators, he said. It's what they call themselves. They're not the nicest people in the world. They don't have much of a sense of humour. They have a mission instead. But though they don't travel much now, they are great traders for the few of us who go about the world.

What's their mission? I said.

They want to conserve the human race, he said. They want to repopulate the world. They want to fix what has changed because they think that "changed" is the same as "broken" and that the glories of what once was must always be better than the excitement of what might be in the future. Great breeders they are, and they want to put the clock back, and there's no telling them it can't be done. They're stubborn—like you. But with less heart.

That was typical of Brand. Unsettle you and then slide in a compliment to make you trust him a little bit.

And that was never a good thing to do. As I was about to find out. Again.

Forewarned is not always forearmed. Sometimes you spend so much effort looking out for the trap you know is there that you miss the other one you didn't know about.

Chapter 32

Visitors

I had to tell them about Jip. I figured he would be all right for a day maybe even two, but the pan of water I had left him wouldn't last, and it would be better for them to have him than for him to die a long nasty death of thirst. And then the packhorse had to be unhobbled too, taken in or allowed to roam free.

I decided, however, that I would wait out that first day in case I could find a way to escape, that Jip would forgive me this. I did, after all have my Leatherman. They hadn't searched me because they had been scared to touch me.

Have you tried to escape? I said to Brand.

Why would I? he said. They'll let me out eventually. I haven't got the plague. They feed me well here. It's quite restful. I catch up on my sleep, nothing to worry about. And they like me.

So they don't know you very well, I said.

Again that flash of white parted his beard, the little grin that now put my teeth on edge.

They've stopped travelling, he said. They used to. But then the three best sailors among them went off on a fine summer's day, dropped over the horizon into a dark storm that lasted a day and a night and never came back. My guess is the sea took them. And now those that remain, they think it's too dangerous. So they like me because I can go out into the world they're scared of and bring them back useful things.

Like my dog, I said.

Well yes, he said. They like the idea of being able to breed guard dogs. And then he sighed. There have been wolves around that attack their sheep and they worry that one day the wolves might attack them, which is stupid, because wolves don't attack people. I read that in a book.

I didn't tell him he was wrong. Maybe one day he'd trust a wolf, believing the lie he'd read, and that would be as good a way for him to get the nasty surprise I wished on him as any other.

I'm going to try and escape, I said.

Don't, he said. It'll just make them angry.

If I escape, that won't be my problem, I said.

You won't, he said. Why don't you just sit down and tell me about your journey? I like a good story.

Me too, I said. But this one hasn't finished yet.

So we had some more silence, which I didn't mind and he didn't like.

I passed the time looking out of the three different cell windows on the sea side of the bunker. I could see the top of his boat's sails. And there was a smudge of smoke, about the size of a cooking fire, beyond that which marked the Conservators' settlement. I could see some movement beyond the trees that screened it, but just flashes. The bigger movement was the sails, which kept dropping and then rising.

What are they doing to your boat? I said.

He came across the hall and into my cell, and looked out of the window next to me. I was uncomfortable having him this close to me. I don't know why. He smelled of sea and woodsmoke. And he had something about him that was always dangerous, like the dark pull of a cliff edge.

I stepped aside.

He sucked his teeth and made a snapping noise with his tongue. It sounded like he was swallowing some irritation.

I'd say they're monkeying around with it, he said. I'd say one of them is trying to learn how it works.

Maybe they're not all scared of the sea, I said. Maybe when they learn to do what you do, they won't like you

so much.

He watched for a while. I could see he wasn't too happy with people touching what belonged to him. Ironic, that.

They're all scared of something, he said. It's how they work.

How many of them are there? I said.

Now you want to talk, he said.

I watched his back.

I'll trade you, I said. I'll tell you how I got here if you tell me about them.

He turned and looked at me.

I want to know about them, I said.

You don't, he said. Really you don't. It won't make you happy.

I'm already not happy, I said. I haven't met many people. I'm interested. I was told there was no one left living on the mainland.

And if you found there were other things you were told that aren't quite true, you'd be even more unhappy, he said.

No, I said. I'd be less ignorant.

You want to know about them because you're planning something, he said. And it's pointless. Just wait. What's going to happen will happen.

How many are there? I said.

You don't give up, do you? he said, and sat back down on the concrete ledge.

No, I said. Not really.

I think there are nine, he said. But they keep some of them away in another locked place.

A bunker like this? I said.

No, he said. Not like a prison cell. Like a private area. Behind a fence.

If there aren't any people left in the world, who are they trying to keep out? I said. They can't have built a fence just for you.

It's not to stop people getting in, he said. It's to stop them getting out. I think.

Why? I said.

It didn't make any sense to me. It's not like there were so many loose people on the planet that you could waste any useful bodies by locking them away.

Because that's where they protect the breeders, he said. That's where they keep the girls and the women.

Breeders? I said.

Their word, he said. Not mine.

I felt a coldness in my gut. It made me feel a little sick. I sat down and looked at my feet until it passed.

I guess I was wrong. They weren't wasting any useful bodies.

I felt his eyes on the back of my neck.

Feeling happier yet? he said.

You said they were great traders, I said. What do they like to trade?

People, Griz, he said, and there was a kind of sadness in his voice, as if he were telling me this for the second time, as if it is something I should have gathered from what he had already told me. They like to trade for people. Especially girls.

And then he made me tell him about the first part of my journey, chasing him from the chapel to the pier where he'd burned the *Sweethope*. I told him the bare bones, and though it was the last thing I wanted to do I did it for two reasons. Firstly because he refused to tell me more until we'd "traded". And secondly as I remembered and spoke about it, I was able to take my mind off what he had told me.

I stopped my story at the point he'd burned my boat, and told him it was his turn. And in this way he gave me the story of the Cons, and I told him about my journey south across the mainland. I didn't tell him about the wolves or about John Dark. I don't expect he told me everything about the Cons either, but in the give and take of it all, this is what he told me.

As far as he knew, the Cons were the only people left living on the mainland. They were the largest group he'd come across on his travels. They believed their mission was to repopulate the world, as he had told me. And they believed the mission was so important that it justified them in doing things that were not good. Brand thought that if there had been more of them they might have gone raiding and rounded up entire families, bringing them back to what they called the Conservatory, forcing them to live and work there like slaves. But thankfully there weren't enough of them to do that, so instead they did something else. The ones who could sail went on journeys, and when they found families they would offer to trade. No one normal would trade a child, but they always offered because they saw themselves as good people doing a good thing, even if others didn't understand it. Then they would come back, preferably in the dark, and steal the child if they could and disappear over the horizon before dawn. It was a theft, but it was for the greater good. That's how they justified it.

And then their sailors had set off and never come back. Maybe the storm Brand talked about is what got them. I thought it was just as likely they'd tried to steal a child from the wrong family, and had been caught and dealt with. That was a happier ending, to my way of thinking.

After that, the Cons had stayed home, fearful of venturing further to sea than was necessary to fish the shallow waters around them for food. Instead they relied on what Brand called Sea Tinkers. He was one, he said, and he knew of two others, though had only met one of them. People like him, moving back and forth across the waters, looking, trading, restless, yet always happy to barter stuff they'd found for food or other things they couldn't find on their own. Like companionship.

Companionship sounded like a word loaded with more than one meaning. I didn't push it, and he glided past.

The Cons had a supply of pre-Gelding medicines that still miraculously seemed to work for the most part. That was valuable and worth trading almost anything for. They also grew a plant that could be smoked or cooked with, which made the world lighter and eased pain and worry for a while. They told the Sea Tinkers they wanted girls for their mission, and would pay well for them. They didn't mind if it was trade or theft that brought them to the Conservatory, and they tried to smooth everybody's conscience by pointing out how well looked after the girls were. Treated like family.

Brand saw my face.

I know, he said. And for what it's worth, Griz, I never took them up on the offer. But I know at least one of the other Tinkers did. And you know what the worst thing about all this is?

Right now, it sounds like a long list of things, I said.

He nodded.

The worst thing is that the Cons still think they're good people.

And then we heard a noise outside the window and got up to look at what was coming.

It's food, he said. They'll feed us well. You'll see.

There were three of them. I recognised one from his gas mask, but the others were new. One was wearing a different kind of gas mask; the other had a scarf across the face and a pair of goggles.

They had old plastic baskets on the end of long poles. They came close enough to push the baskets against the bars of the window and then moved away fast, as if even touching the building we were in with the end of a long stick was potentially dangerous.

How are you feeling? shouted the man I recognised.

Fit as a fiddle, shouted Brand. He made his voice light and cheery, as though he had not a care in the world.

I hope you stay that way, shouted the man, like he was a friend.

Well, we'll know soon enough, said the other. He didn't sound as if he liked Brand as much as the other. Tomorrow night's the inspection.

That reminds me, said Brand. Would you be kind enough to bring me my fiddle from the boat? It's at the foot of my bunk. Black case, you can't miss it.

We'll bring it later, said the friendlier man. And look forward to hearing it.

Well, said Brand, we can at least share music without fear of infection.

Indeed, said the man.

Oh, said Brand, just one thing...who is monkeying around with the sails on my boat?

Oh, said the man. That's Tertia. She just wants to see how it works. I can tell her to stop if you like.

That'd be good, said Brand. My boat is my home. I would not like it broken.

Of course, said the man. She's too inquisitive for her own good anyway. But she's doing a fine job of looking after your dogs.

Thank her for me, said Brand, glancing quickly at me.

They walked away and Brand, who was taller, reached out and brought the food and the water inside.

I won't have people jiggering around with my boat like that, he said.

Tertia, I said. Never heard a name like that.

It's old language, he said. A number. They use numbers to name themselves.

Why? I said.

I told you, he said. They like the past. That's why they'll do anything to make it happen again. But I reckon giving you a number instead of a proper name makes people feel they're things, not people, if you ask me. That one speaking is Quintus. Means five.

What does Tertia mean? I said.

He shrugged.

I don't know, he said with a shrug. Four? Three? Doesn't matter. The women's and girls' number names end in an *a*. That I do know.

He looked at me.

What's the inspection? I said.

Oh, it's nothing, he said. They just stand and look at us and see if we've got boils yet, to see if we're infected.

Where? I said.

Over there, he said, pointing to the bars at the end of the

passage. We just stand there, turn around, show our armpits and our crotches. It's no big thing. They do it every night.

So we have to take our clothes off? I said.

Yes, he said, but they don't prod you around or anything. They just stand back and have a good look to make sure. Now cheer up. Let's eat. The food's good, and everything looks better on a full stomach. They're not going to poison you.

Chapter 33

The truth will set you free (and other lies)

Some poison goes in by the mouth. Other poisons go in at the ear.

And Brand was always a good talker, able to sweeten his words with a grin or a joke to make you miss the tell-tale taste of something that was going to eat you up from the inside later on.

The food was good: bread, potatoes, some green leaf that was pleasantly bitter and mutton—salt marsh mutton, he said. You could taste the sharp tang of the sea in the meat, as well as an underlying sweetness. It tasted a bit like the sheep did at home, and for a moment I went back there in my head, wondering what they were eating and what they were talking about as they sat round the table. And even though Mum would not be joining in the conversation, I had such a pang of longing just to be next to her and holding her hand by the fire that I stopped eating.

I'll finish that if you've had enough, said Brand.

I shook my head and forked more mutton into my mouth. Chewing meant I didn't have to talk until I was ready.

So you lied, I said.

Did I? he said, raising an eyebrow. That seems unlikely.

You said you were raised here. Back at home. When you were telling your traveller's tales, you said you grew up on these marshes on an island in an estuary, and that your family died and you went off travelling the world. So either you were lying then, or you're lying now. Either you didn't grow up here, and are lying. Or you did grow up here, and you're one of the Cons yourself.

He looked at me.

I like you, Griz, he said. I like the way you don't give up. I also like the way you make me feel... uncomfortable. Like with that question.

It wasn't a question, I said. It was just a statement of what must be true.

There you go again, he said. Did I tell you about the archipelago in Sweden and the pale girls?

Yes, I said.

That was home, he said. And they were my sisters.

Were? I said.

Maybe they still are, he said. But if you tell the Conservators about them, I will kill you. Understand?

When he didn't smile, when he looked at you and his face went like a rock and his eyes turned into unblinking blue ice, he was someone entirely different.

Yeah, I said. If what you told me about them is true, I understand why you wouldn't want them to know about your sisters.

And you understand I'm not joking? he said.

I don't know, I said.

The lines in the crag that was his forehead rearranged themselves.

What? he said.

You're a really good liar, I said. You know how to use stories to get what you want. And telling me you'd kill me if I told anyone you came from this archipelago thing is a really good way to try and make me believe it's the truth.

His face went much more serious, colder, flintier and then the great red spade of his beard split open again and was full of white teeth and the pink inside of his mouth as he threw his head back and roared with laughter.

Griz, he choked, and punched me hard on the shoulder—not to hurt, but to show some strange affection. Griz, I do like you. I like you a lot. You're just a kid, but you're no fool, that's for sure.

I'm not a kid, I said.

When your beard comes in, that's when you'll be a man, he said. Nothing wrong with being a kid.

You're right, I said. But my beard isn't coming in.

Not yet, he said and punched my shoulder again.

Not ever, I said. And if you punch me again, I'll punch you back and it won't be the shoulder.

I meant no harm, he said.

I know, I said, but for a cunning man you're pretty stupid.

Stupid, am I? he said.

Just as stupid as me, I said. Because I believed what you said, because you said it well and brought gifts like marmalade, and you believe what you see because you were told what to see.

He looked at me. And then he looked at me harder.

Then he sat back, like some of the wind had gone from his sails.

I am stupid, he said. Might as well shit and go blind. Can't see what's right in front of my nose…

You're right, I said.

You're—he began.

Yes, I said.

I'm a girl.

He blew out his cheeks and looked at his boots. Like he suddenly found it uncomfortable to look at me.

Well, he said. That's no good. Not here. Not now.

No, I said. No, it isn't.

Chapter 34

Liars lie

Why did you have to tell me that? Brand said, after he'd given his boots a long and painstaking inspection. I told you how much they want girls.

Breeders, I said.

It might have been a trick of the light, but he seemed to wince.

If they're going to make us strip, you're going to find out soon enough, I said.

Why tell me now? he said. He really looked angry for some reason.

Because I'll make you a deal, I said. You're a trader, right?

Griz, he said. These Cons, they're . . .

I know what breeding means, I said. I don't think he heard the crack in my voice. You're still thinking I'm a young kid because my beard hasn't come in. I'm older than you think, remember?

He nodded. I've never seen a face that split the way his did. Like half of it was fascinated and couldn't tear itself away, and the other half wanted to be anywhere but where it was.

So, I want to make a trade, I said.

Griz, all that you've got to trade, they're going to take anyway, he said.

Here's the deal, I said. They're going to see I'm a girl. Then they're going to wait and see if I've got *la pest*.

La what? he said.

The plague, I said, moving on fast before he started asking questions that would lead to my time with John Dark. Once I'm out of quarantine, they're going to want me as one of their breeders, right?

Right, he said. I'm sorry.

He looked so hangdog I wanted to believe him. Almost did.

So there's nothing we can do about that, I said. That's just going to happen.

Again I think he missed the shake in my voice. I cleared my throat to cover up and make sure.

The deal is this: when I'm out, and not locked up in here, you steal me and take me home.

He stared at me.

You think I'm a better man than I am, he said.

I do, I said. I think you're a better man than you think you are.

I hadn't listened to him without learning a few tricks. A little sweetness to ease things along. No harm in making him feel good about himself.

But that's not what I'm relying on, I said. What I'm relying on is you doing what's best for you. Making a better trade than they could offer you for anything.

Like what? he said

You know the other thing you don't know about me, I said, reaching inside my shirt. What else you don't know about my family?

No, he said.

No, you don't, I said, and I pulled out the key and showed him.

We're Freemen.

I showed him the symbol on the key.

Do you know what this symbol means?

He leant forward and stared at it.

Infinity, he said. And the moment he did, I realised that the eight was in fact not an eight at all, but meant to be read on its side, not standing up. It was the symbol for infinity.

How do you know? I said.

Because I've seen it before, he said. It means infinite in all directions.

Exactly, I said. And do you know what lies behind the doors this can open?

Dead electric brains, he said. Broken computers.

No, I said. Not everywhere. You save me, I'll take you to a place where medicines are stocked that still work. Where there is some old tech that still functions.

He stared at me.

Or leave me here and I'll make the same deal with them, I said. I'd rather you helped me, because you've got a boat, but I can take them the long way overland and I'm sure that'll be fine too.

Old tech that works, he said. Like what?

Screens that move, show pictures and stories. Little computers that still compute. Electric compasses, binoculars that pull the horizon into your lap and make pictures of it you can look at later. Music players.

I was running out of things to tempt him with.

You think that I would need a trade to try and help you, he said. His voice sounded a little hurt.

Yes, I said. You told me. You're a trader. This is a good trade.

You don't think I would try and help you just because these are bad people? he said.

I'd like to, I said. I'd really like to. In fact you have no idea how much I'd like to. But my experiences with you so far don't make me think that'd be a good idea. And like you said, I'm not a fool.

He stared at me.

You were at least correct about that one thing, I said.

He took a deep breath.

This is going to take some doing, he said. And we're going to have to work out how to play this before they get here.

You're right, I said.

Music players? he said.

I nodded.

He was hooked.

Chapter 35

A choice made

Until I met Brand, I didn't think I'd met anyone who told lies. As a result, I wasn't very good at knowing how to deal with them. But that was then. This is now, and here's what I know about them: when liars say they're going to tell you the truth, it's time to listen extra carefully to their stories—not because they're going to try and hide the truth inside them, but because the truth's not going to be there at all. The real truth is going to be in the things they don't mention. So if you listen to the shape of their lie, you can see the room it takes up, and then you look for the truth in the empty spaces in between.

You used the map to get here, said Brand.

Yes, I said.

And where is it now? he said.

It doesn't matter, I said. I didn't want to tell him or anyone about Jip and the horses. Not yet. Not until I had to.

You can't let them find it, he said. I'm serious.

Okay, I said. They're not going to find it. Not unless I tell them where it is.

If I told them where to go to untie Jip and see to the horses, they would find it. I couldn't imagine they wouldn't look through my bags. I just didn't see any point telling him that. He looked at me and shook his head. I suppose liars are good at spotting other lies and half-truths.

Griz, he said, if they find that map, you're dead.

That's not a very good way to start our agreement, I said. Not by threatening me.

I'm not threatening, he said. I'm warning. I'm trying to help. If they find that map in your possession, they are going to think you did something very bad. And they will punish you for it.

I thought for a bit. Trying to see the shape of what he was saying.

You mean you did something bad, I said. I took the map from you. If it's evidence that you did something bad, I'll just tell them that.

And I'll tell them you're lying, he said. I wouldn't want to, but if you told them that, I'd have to. Just a matter of survival.

Your word against mine, I said.

They know me, he said. They trust me. I bring them stuff they like. Stuff they need. They found you sneaking around. Hiding things from them.

Like being a girl, I said.

That, he said, but mostly I meant being a Freeman.

I wondered then if I'd fallen into a trap of my own digging.

Last Freeman came through here killed people they cared about, he said. So they're not going to be much disposed to like you or what you have to say. But, Griz...

He seemed like he was in mild pain as he paused and looked at me.

Griz, he said. This is a stupid conversation. We're on the same side. I'd never betray you. Unless you betrayed me first.

That's all I'm saying. And like I tried to tell you—keeping the map out of their hands is just a matter of survival.

Sometimes Jip or Jess will look at me and make their eyes big, and it usually means they want some food but can't get it, like if we're on the boat and they can't hunt their own meat. That's what his eyes looked like. Soft and warm, despite the blueness of them. I made myself remember how quickly they could turn wintry.

Who died? I said.

I could make my eyes go wintry too.

I didn't say anything else. I just waited him out. And he always hated silence. So eventually he moved closer, holding his hands open and palm up to show he meant no threat, and then he began to tell me another story, speaking quietly as if afraid someone outside might hear.

I told you they're scared of long voyages, he said. The ones they used to take, raiding for girls.

Yes, I said. You said the three men who did them sailed away and never came back, because of a storm.

I never said it was three men, he said. Interesting you think that. No, it was two men and a woman. The woman was the best sailor, and she also put people at ease when they met them as strangers. She would talk to the girls and the men, and both would like her for different reasons. She was the one made the marks on the map.

I looked at him, betraying myself a little.

You thought they were my marks, he said. Is that right?

I still do, I said. I had seen the pencil line marking his passage to our island. I didn't know why he would be lying about this but I was sure it'd become apparent if he carried on talking.

That map is theirs, he said. The three sailors. It shows where they went. If you were on the *Falki*, I would show you.

What's the *Falki*? I said.

My boat, he said. I have the other maps hidden there.

Hidden? I said.

I told you, he said, it would not be good for them to be found. But they are maps of their travels.

So they didn't drown, I said.

He moved a little closer.

No, he said. They didn't drown. They got to their destination safely enough. They just didn't leave it.

And then he told me another story.

He told me it was the real truth. I don't know if it is. The Conservators had come to the house that was his real home on the Swedish archipelago, seemingly to trade but actually to take the pale girls who were his sisters. And he and his kin had stopped them, because they were not fools.

They came, they stayed, they ate with us, they asked if we'd like to come join their settlement—and when we said no, we liked it where we were, they left friendly. And then they came back after dark, he said. Nothing friendlike in their hearts. Carrying weapons in their fists. And handcuffs. They said they just wanted one girl. They called it a "tithe". Do you know what a tithe is?

No, I said.

It's like a bribe, he said. Like they used to take taxes from people or they'd put them in prison if they refused to pay up. Except a tithe is for gods. These people are dangerous because they think they are doing this because a god wants them to do it. It means they don't have to think like humans.

So you killed them, I said.

No choice, he said. Even if we'd hidden—or fought them off—they'd have come back. They now knew where we lived. We liked where we live. Still do. We didn't want to spend our lives hiding from them, moving around, living in fear of the next time they tried, of what would happen if they brought more people to help them. We had no idea how few of them there are here. That's why I came, the first time, to see if there was a threat. That's when I discovered they had grown afraid when the others hadn't returned. They turned from the sea.

And you killed them, I said again. The others.

We did, he said. My sisters are strong women. They did not take well to the idea of being someone else's breeder. I did not take well to the idea of someone stealing my sisters. Nor did my parents. Or our friends.

Friends. Parents. He had not said there were more than the pale girls when he first told the story. Now he seemed to come from a village. I didn't say anything, but I stored the thought away. It could have been another lie.

We knew they'd come back, because there was something extra in the men's eyes after they had met my sisters, he said. So we waited and when they slunk back, we did what we had to do. I did not like doing it, but it had to be done. It was their choice. They could have stayed away, but they came back, with weapons and handcuffs.

All that and yet you thought you could steal my dog and no one would follow you, I said.

A dog is not a sister, he said.

No, I said. But it's still family.

And then things went quiet between us for a long time, and eventually he walked off and lay down in his own cell across the way, and seemed to do nothing but stare at the ceiling.

You think I'm a bad man, he said after a while.

I didn't answer. I could see no point. I was too busy trying to figure out what to do. If I told them to go and look after Jip and the horses, they would then find the map and that would not be good, because there was no way of knowing how they would react to it. It was a sort of proof that the holder of the map might well have been involved in the death and disappearance of their loved ones. But if I didn't tell them, and I was unable to escape in time, then the horses and Jip would die, tied up and hobbled. And in this half-buried bunker with concrete walls, barred windows and a locked gate, I didn't think an escape would be a quick thing, even if it was eventually possible.

The choice was of course not a hard one. I knew what I had to do, but the tough thinking was all about the how of doing it. I was struggling. I tried to keep believing that if I was just calm and clever enough there would be a way to do this. Without it being more disastrous than it had to be. Because Brand was right. They would believe him long before they believed me. And since it looked like I was going to have to rely on him to help me escape this place once quarantine was over, it didn't make much sense to betray him or even make them distrust him a little bit more than they might already do. I had seen that one of the men who had brought the food liked him but that the other was not as friendly. There was no point in feeding the second one's misgivings.

My feelings about Brand at that point could be neatly summed up by my wanting to cross the hall and slam the door on his cell tight shut, just as we had been warned not to do, locking him away behind a door that had no key. I thought it would serve him right, and I also thought I would be spared the distraction of his company. I don't imagine many other people could have thrown themselves on a bed and stared silently at the ceiling in such an irritatingly conspicuous and noticeable way. It was almost childish, as if he—the thief—was resenting that I—the victim—had objected to the theft and had called it for what it was.

The dog jerked me from my thoughts, her excited barks immediately recognisable.

It was Jess, and she was close by and getting closer with each bark. My heart suddenly felt like it had swollen to twice its normal size and was now trying to punch its way out of my ribcage.

I scrambled up on to the ledge below the window and looked between the bars. As I said, the bunker was half sunk in the ground so that the opening was only perhaps twenty centimetres above the grass. I saw Jess and Saga and then a figure running after them, awkwardly yanking on a gas mask as they got close to the bunker. Saga was still held on a rope, but Jess was bounding across the grass towards me trailing her own long length of rope behind her. She must have caught the scent of me and pulled free of the hand holding her.

Jess! I shouted, and jammed my hand out of the window, reaching for her, my shoulder wedged between the narrow bars. Jess! Good girl!

The chasing Con managed to stamp on the end of the trailing rope and bring Jess to a sudden brutal halt. She lost her footing and yelped as she was yanked over onto the ground. The Con scrabbled for the rope and then fell and landed in a sitting position, pulling Jess towards them.

Hey, I shouted, then felt a hand on my shoulder, pulling me back.

Quarantine, said Brand, peering over my head. Can't let the dog touch you or they'd have to do something to it to stop it spreading whatever infection you might be carrying.

The Con pulled Jess back into their arms and sat there. He or she wore a sort of glove on one hand that seemed twisted in on itself, as if the leather covered an injury, though they seemed to pay it no mind. The blank glass eyes of the mask seemed to be pointed at me, not the dog.

Don't worry, shouted Brand. The dog must have smelled me.

There's no reason for them to find out you know the dog already, he said very quietly, for my ears only. That'll just raise more questions than we have comfortable answers for.

The gas mask just watched us. Jess seemed to calm down a bit, but kept trying to twist in the Con's arms and find her way to me.

Although I hated the way Jess had been yanked off her feet by the rope, what Brand said made sense. And I could see the Con actually had kind hands and was trying to calm the dog and not hurt her.

They might have shot the dog if they thought it had touched us, said Brand, as if he had heard my thoughts.

So I had to satisfy myself by staring at Jess and just being pleased and amazed that after all these miles she was, as I had hoped against hope for, at the end of my journey.

The Con stood up and stared at me. I couldn't tell whether it was a friendly or a hostile look. The mask made it impossible to read: the glass just reflected the gunmetal sky overhead and gave nothing away.

Jess whined and barked again, tugging at the rope. The Con reached down and calmed her with hands that were, again, kind and tuned to the way a dog likes to be touched. And then abruptly turned away.

It was in the turn that I made my decision. Looking back on it now, I know I made it for some of the right reasons, and all the wrong ones. The first was the way the Con had handled Jess after the initial violence of bringing her up short. They had not been the actions of someone who was cruel to animals. They were the opposite, and Jess had responded, as if she too trusted the Con in some way.

The second reason was that as the Con turned, a thick braided pigtail swung behind her head in a way that reminded me immediately of Bar.

I figured, wrongly, that a woman would be kinder and more understanding.

The third reason was that if there were wolves out there, as the Cons believed, then Jip and the horses would not have much of a chance against them, tied and hobbled as they were, even for one night.

All sorts of bad things flowed from that decision, but I still think it was the right one to make, given what I knew at the time.

Hey, I shouted. Hey you!

The Con stopped but didn't turn.

I have a dog too, I shouted. And horses. They're out there, tied up. Waiting for me to come and get them.

Griz, said Brand, his voice deepening to a warning growl.

If I tell you where to get them, can you fetch them? I said, shrugging off the hand that had gripped my arm. They're not far. But they're not safe alone.

Griz, hissed Brand. Don't—

They're tied, I said. They can't run or fight if anything comes for them. And the dog will starve or die of thirst if it's left.

If they find the map, said Brand.

They will, I said, turning to hide my mouth, as if the gas mask could read my lips even if I spoke low, which I did. But I can't help that. I told you. What goes for Jess goes for Jip. They're family. And even if they weren't, what kind of person leaves an animal defenceless and without food?

A person who wants to stay alive, he said, his face grim. These Cons do not have a sense of humour. And the god they like seems to be the unforgiving kind.

The Con turned and cocked her head at me.

Please, I said.

That's Tertia, said Brand.

Tertia, I said. I'm Griz. I can see you like dogs. I can see you have the way of them. Please save my dog, and you can have the horses.

Tertia stared at me some more.

You think she's going to be all friendly just because she's not a man, said Brand quietly. Again, irritatingly it was like he knew what I was thinking. Bad mistake.

Jess whined and tugged the rope, straining towards me.

The woman Tertia stood there like a statue. I couldn't tell what she was deciding. She was so still that I couldn't even be sure she was thinking about what I had said at all.

I once asked why she wasn't kept with the breeders, said Brand. They said she was too hard. Like a cold and rocky cliff that life can't cling to was what they actually said. She's tough enough, that's for sure, but she does have a thing about Saga. And now I guess she's taken to the other dog as well.

And he turned away from the window and sat on the ledge, looking back into the room.

The one you stole, I said. Her name is Jess.

You're going to get us killed, he said.

My dog, I said. My responsibility.

My neck though, he said. Fair warning. I like it as it is, uncut and unbroken. I'll do whatever it takes to keep it that way.

All's fair in love and war, I said.

What? he said.

Something I read, I said. Means you do what you must. I just did what I had to.

And then I turned back to Tertia, and told her where I had left Jip and the horses, describing the lonely pine and its fallen brothers and sisters.

I still didn't know if she was going to do anything about it, but she listened and then abruptly turned away, pulling the two dogs behind her, and dropped out of sight over the edge of the low slope towards the settlement.

None of what you just did changes anything, said Brand. They're still going to wait the quarantine out, and by then they'll have figured you're a girl, and then they'll make you a breeder. You changed nothing and all you did was put us in danger.

I saved my dog, I said. And—

I cut myself off before I said John Dark's horses. John Dark had been a good thing and I had no wish to share anything good with this thief. It would be like staining a clean memory the next time he talked about it.

And my horses, I said. I saved my horses.

You really think a dog's life is worth a human's? he said.

A life's a life, I said. And those lives were in my care.

You're crazy, he said.

I know what I am, I said. And I know what you are too.

And what's that? he said.

Someone who doesn't know what they are, I said. Someone who lies, even to themselves. A thief who thinks he's not a bad man.

He looked at me then, eyes flaring flat and cold as iceblink.

You think you're a hero because you did one good thing, because you saved your sisters? I said. Maybe you were then. But now? Thieving, lying, stealing people's dogs?

I found I wanted to hit him too. Instead I spat on the floor.

Heroes aren't for ever, I said. You shit on your past, you don't stay shiny.

I think I preferred you when you were a boy, he said.

No, you didn't, I said.

I looked back up at him, right in the eye.

See? You don't know the first damn thing about yourself.

Chapter 36

A reunion betrayed

All the lies came home at first light. And they didn't come home to roost like gentle doves, they came home like scavenging birds of prey, ripping and tearing and leaving nothing but the bones.

Brand and I had not spoken again as the night came on. I know he had watched me waiting at the window, straining my eyes trying to see if anyone had in fact gone to get Jip and the horses. When full black erased everything but the stars and a glimmer down in the settlement that might have been lamplight or a kitchen fire, I remained there, listening instead, ears reaching out into the dark for what I could no longer see.

But a punishing rain came on early and carried on through the night, and I heard and saw nothing other than the downpour. I used the old steel toilet in the end cell and tried not to feel self-conscious about the noises Brand must have heard, then I swilled a bucket of water down it to make it go away, went back to a cell Brand could not look into from his and slept, surprisingly deeply and dream-free.

It was the last good sleep I had. My nights nowadays are

torn and uncomfortable things, and though I do doze off at some stage towards mornings, I wake feeling more tired than I was the day before, as if I have spent the dreamtime running and running, but always ending up awake back in these four walls, with a barred slit for a window.

Maybe fate knew what was coming and gave me one last good night's sleep out of pity.

I woke to the sound of metal hitting metal in a fast and insistent rattle. I stumbled out of my cell and blinked at the figures standing behind the bars at the end of the hall. Brand emerged from the door across the way and as he did so the tallest figure stopped rattling the pistol barrel between the bars, which was the source of the noise that had woken us.

I thought they looked like judges, standing side by side, shoulder to shoulder behind the bars, their faces hidden by masks that—this close up—I could see were all different and patched with tape or stitched leather. Their voices were muffled but easily understandable. There were four of them—three tall ones—and the shorter figure of Tertia.

The next shortest figure was in the middle of the other two men, but he was clearly in charge. Despite the mask there was a kind of energy coming off him like the buzz in the beehives back in the ruined stadium a lifetime ago.

He held out the map.

Even as I saw it and tried to ready myself for what might be coming, I felt a strong sense of release, because if they had the map that meant Jip had been rescued.

You, said the man with the map, pointing at me.

My name's Griz, I said, trying to ignore the black metal gun now hanging from his hand, pointing at the floor.

Don't mess with him, said Brand from behind me, speaking low, for my ears only. That's Ellis. He's the father.

Ellis shook the map at me.

Where did you get this? he said.

I found it, I said.

Where? he said. Where did you find it?

His voice sounded like he was talking to a child who was either being stupid or impolite on purpose. Like him it was short and taut, like it might snap into something much louder and nastier at any moment.

On a boat, I said. He actually shuddered visibly with impatience.

Where? he said.

One of the figures beside him spoke. Despite being taller than him, the voice surprised me by being female.

Who was on the boat? said the woman. Who was on the boat and what did you do to them?

There was no one on the boat, I said.

And as I said it, I made a very strong effort not to look at Brand, whose eyes I could feel burning holes in the side of my face. His silence seemed to me to be as loud as any shout. I hoped they couldn't hear it too, or begin to wonder why the normally voluble pirate was saying nothing.

It was deserted, I said. This much was true. I had after all found the map on a deserted boat. That made the lie easier to tell. I wasn't having to make a story out of nothing. I had a truth to build on.

There was no one aboard, I said.

Liar, spat the woman, taking a step towards me as if the sudden rage that fuelled her might let her walk right through the metal bars that separated us in order to grab me and shake me.

Let him speak, said Ellis. Let him say what else he wants to tell us.

The calmness in his voice was small and hateful.

I found I had nothing to say.

They stared at me.

He's not a boy. He's a girl.

The silence broken by a familiar voice.

But it wasn't Brand's.

It was the girl. It was Tertia.

She lifted her mask off her face with her twisted glove-hand and glared at me.

My world split in two.

I had never seen this woman before. And I had known her all my life.

I had never seen the woman she was, but the girl she had once been was as much a part of me as my heart. In fact she was the deepest crack in that heart—the best-beloved broken bit we all lived with.

I had expected to be betrayed by Brand.

I never expected to be betrayed by my own dead sister.

And the hatred in her eyes widened that crack in my heart and tore me in two, dropping me to my knees so unexpectedly and so brutally that it was only Brand catching me that stopped me falling further.

Tertia! snapped Ellis. Put your mask on *now*!

Joy just stood and glared at me, the hostility and fury in her eyes somehow locking us together in an endless unbreakable moment. I couldn't breathe. I don't think she could either.

But how—? was all I could say.

They sold me, she said.

I didn't know what she meant. Who she meant. I stumbled to my feet and stepped towards her, standing there on the other side of the bars.

They sold me to have a quiet life, she said. For the rest of you.

Who? I said.

She hit me then. Like the question I had asked was too big

to answer. Her gloved fist a tight knot of bone and skin that came through the gap in the bars and split my lip and left the taste of blood in my mouth. The taste surprised me more than the impact knocked me backwards. A blow is a blow, but blood makes it personal.

Why didn't you come earlier? she said, hard eyes shiny with tears like wet steel. You were my sister. You were a part of me. But you all let me go and be brought to this flat land...

Tertia! shouted Ellis. Your mask! Or by God I will—

The man between Ellis and Joy grabbed the mask and jammed it back over her face. We never heard what Ellis was going to do by his god or anything else. He just snapped his fingers and spluttered at her instead, like he was choking on a fury all of his own.

Take off that glove and burn it! he snarled. If you weren't wearing it, I'd lock you in quarantine too, you stupid little bitch! Now get out before I maim your other damned hand.

I am sure it was the prospect of being made to be any closer to me that made her peel off her glove and stumble away up the stairs, as much as the vicious threat.

It got bad then.

I don't remember the right order of things, because I was sleepwalking in shock. But this is the patchwork I do recall. They made me strip. They wanted to check that I was not a boy. It wasn't the undressing or the way they were demonstrating their power over me, making me take my clothes down so they could see me that I minded—I have swum naked with my whole family and the Lewismen too without giving it much of a thought. They're just bodies after all. It was the fact that the men turned away while the woman checked me that made it horrible. As if my body was a dirty thing they should not be made to see. I don't know if Brand stole a look, because he was behind me, but being a thief I expect he did.

Then they made me sit on a chair and face them through the bars and tell them about the map and how I'd found it. I told the story again and again, the words coming haltingly over my split and puffy lip, and the more they asked the more real it became in my head, perhaps because I was building my lie on the truth of stealing from Brand's boat, the *Falki*. I just added two things to the story. I told them I had found the boat washed up next to a pier like the one I had moored the *Sweethope* to in Blackpool. I told them I thought something must have happened at sea, because the sails were torn but still raised, and the anchors had not been dropped.

And when they asked me what had happened to the three people who they said had crewed the boat, I told them I did not know but that if they had made it ashore it might be that the wolves had got them, since that stretch of coast was teeming with them. I told them this because at that point I was still under the illusion that I might somehow escape and that it would be good if they were as afraid of the mainland behind them as they were of the sea in front of them. Then I did not know I was going to be where I am now, writing this. Trapped. Hopeless. And never going home again.

And after that they abruptly put me where I am now. In the end cell. And they closed the door until it locked itself shut.

I didn't know they were going to close the door until they did. I shouted when I saw it about to happen, and I heard Brand's voice drown mine as he too tried to stop them.

But the tiny click of the lock closing me in drowned us both. Maybe it was so loud because we knew it had no key to open it again.

I remember a jumble of voices after that, muffled by the heavy steel door. The gist was that they had to keep us quarantined, but they couldn't have Brand and I locked in together in case we fucked.

They didn't use that word. They said "bred". Somehow the way they said it stained the day much darker than an honest swear word would have done.

Brand's protests that the door was without a key were met with assurances that once the quarantine was up they would find a way to get me out, even if it meant knocking a hole in the wall.

Don't worry, Ellis said. We've not got so many that we're going to let her rot in there. She'll be fed and watered as good as you. We're not bad people. She'll come to see that. We'll treat her well.

By "not so many" he meant breeders.

I don't remember much more of that day because I spent most of it dazed by seeing Joy alive, and then seeing her full of hate for me. I was torn apart. Like the lightning tree I had found on the ridge, the source of the light I'd seen from the tower. I was split in two—my heartwood blasted and burned out. I was dead on my feet. I couldn't get the taste of blood out of my mouth. It, and the thought that it came with, made me sick. Literally. I lay on the bed ledge, my mind stumbling around the horror of it, trying to catch up with itself, deaf to whatever Brand kept saying through the slit in the door, and then I felt my body convulse as if rising in rebellion against the facts of the day. I only just made it to the bowl before I threw up the contents of my stomach in what seemed like an endless chain of convulsions. It felt like I was trying to vomit myself inside out, and when it did finally stop I was left shaking and weak but too tired to be able to find any relief in sleep. I lay there, convinced I would never sleep again. The horror of Joy pushed everything out of my head. I don't think I thought of Jip or Jess or anything other than the nightmare I had woken into.

Somewhere in that blurred-out day, they brought me food

and they brought me water—water to drink and water to flush the steel toilet. They set up a length of old steel pole poked through my window and poured from a distance as I mechanically filled a jug and the buckets. And then they asked if I wanted anything else and I did have enough sense to ask for my backpack and they brought it and took anything like a tool or a knife from it, as well as medicines, but that's at least how I got this notebook I'm writing in.

Welcome to the now.

Chapter 37

The now

I suppose everything becomes a routine that you can get used to if you do it all the time—even sadness and horror and loneliness. I miss Jip and Jess, though I do sometimes catch a glimpse of them being walked on a rope in the distance through the trees. I find I miss them even more than my home, which is strange. Maybe it's because they are close enough to see and almost near enough to touch.

I have been stuck in this concrete box, on my own and writing all this for twenty-three days. It feels like I am never going to be allowed to leave.

I have quarter of a pencil left. I will have to ask for more.

They feed us well enough and they keep the water coming and they often ask if I want things. I say I want to get out and it's so routine that they think it's a joke when I say it and laugh like they're sharing something pleasant and fun with me. They've explained being walled up in this cement box is all for my own good. It's for my protection (from Brand) and theirs (from the imaginary germs I might be carrying to blight them). They probably believe it. They say that when I am allowed to leave here they will make it up to me and I will like them and their home and want it to be mine. I try and smile and say maybe, but I don't smile well when I would rather shout. I smile to help them relax about me.

They do not know what I do at night.

They come and sit on an old stool outside my window at any hour of the day and ask all sorts of other questions. About my family, how I got here without being eaten by wolves, would I like to know about their god because he's really good at helping you understand why the world has trials and tribulations and how it's all a way for him to show his love, and much other stuff like that. They keep their masks on because they believe in germs too.

I tell them my family is dead, because I don't want them knowing where they are, and I tell them that I was safe deeper in the mainland because Jip is great at keeping wolves away. I want them to feed him and treat him and Jess like something of value. I also tell them I'd like to know why—since they seem to think breeding is such an important thing—that their god is a father and not a mother. I told them I did like the sound the bells on their church make though.

And that's true. I like hearing them at the end of every day when they all go in to have a big pray-up together, because that means there's one less day until they come and knock down the wall and get me out of here, and then all I have to do is grit my teeth and trust that Brand will be good on his word and help me escape before it gets too grim or repetitive. Though since Brand and I aren't talking at the moment I write this, maybe I do also hate the church bells because they might just be marking off the time until he betrays me again.

Ellis told me that my liking the bells was a start and that I should likely come to love his god because his god loved everyone. I didn't argue. Everyone in my family likes the lobsters we pull out of the deep clear water. I don't think the lobsters like us much. Nor do I think they're obliged to do so.

Ellis asked me if I'd ever been with a man. His manner was equal parts swagger and furtive.

I didn't answer.

He dared to come closer, as if shy about being overheard.

He told me I should like it. He told me in a soft voice that made my flesh creep. That he would make me very happy. That it was not a painful but a wonderful world of sensations he would introduce me to. He told me not to worry about disappointing him, that he would show me how to give him pleasure too.

I think he stumbled as he left because the glass on his gas mask had steamed up a bit. I saw him wipe it as he took it off and walked away.

When Brand and I were still talking, I asked him about Joy's hand. Why it was twisted. Why she wore a glove.

What he told me hit as hard as that knotted fist coming through the bars.

I only know what they told me, he said. I don't know how much is true.

Just tell me, I said.

He was looking at me through the Judas hole in the door.

Ellis gave her a child, he said.

Do you mean he gave her someone else's child, or that he made her pregnant? I asked.

He made her pregnant, he said.

There's a word for that, I said.

I know, he said.

But I had no words. Just sadness. And a sudden need to find Joy and hold her and say I understood why she was so hard and angry. I was still a fool. Soft. I didn't know anything.

She carried the baby but it was delivered dead, he said. Maybe once upon a time doctors could have saved it.

Joy. Breaking my heart again and again. I sank to the bed and stared at the floor.

She was too young, said Brand. That's what the woman said.

What woman? I said.

The tall one who was beside Ellis, said Brand. Mary. She's called Mary like the mother of their god. She said Tertia was too young, so the baby died and then she was useless as no life could cling to her womb any more.

Her hand, I said.

Ellis wanted to try again is what she told me. Years later. Maybe he said it was for breeding, but I expect it was just for the doing of it, said Brand. He has hot little eyes, Ellis. He tried to force her and frighten her with a hot poker from the fire. That's how her hand got burn-scarred into a claw like that.

He burned her hand, I choked.

No, said Brand. She said no. And she said that she wasn't frightened of him. He said he'd see about that, and he put the red poker in front of her face and asked if she was still so brave and...

His voice trailed off.

And? I said. And what?

And she was, said Brand. She just grabbed the hot end and pushed it right back into his face. So her hand is puckered and pulled out of shape by the burn scar, and he nearly lost an eye, and carries her mark across his cheek beneath that mask.

Good for her, I said.

Yes, he said. Good for her. Tough little nugget. No doubt she's your sister. Looks like you too.

That's why I first cut my hair short at the back and sides,

like a boy. Because even when Mum was at her worst she'd see me and get distressed, thinking I was Joy come back. I thought Dad would be angry with me for hacking off my pigtails, but he wasn't. He said it looked good and even tidied it up for me. Now I think maybe he also wanted me to look like a boy in case they came back, looking for more young girls to steal. I don't know. I just like my hair like this. Out of the way, no fuss when you're in the wind, working.

I do know that's why he introduced me as a boy to Brand. For my own protection. It was a warning, even then. Do not trust this stranger. Any strangers, really. That's why I went along with the lie with John Dark. Dad's always been overprotective about me, but somehow in his eyes Bar's always been big enough to look after herself. He's not used to the fact I grew up and am just as tough as her now.

Was it always safer being a boy than a girl, even when you were alive?

I thought about what else Joy had said.

Do you think they sold her? I said. My parents?

His eyes went away from the Judas hole. I heard his body slide down the door into a sitting position, leaning back against the metal.

Do you? he said.

Not for a minute, I said. Not for a minute.

For a tithe, he said. Would they have paid her as a tithe?

You mean because of what she said? I said. So they'd leave the rest of us alone?

Yes, he said. Would your father have done it?

I didn't have to think.

No, I said.

Because you're so sure he's a good man? he said.

No, I said. Because he's not soft.

No, he said after a bit. No. He didn't seem to be.

He isn't, I said. Any more than I am.

Or I, said Brand.

We're not the same, I said. You're not the same as us.

Maybe, he said. But we're all from the north. Things are harder there. And soft doesn't get much done.

He was like that, Brand. He always said one thing too much. He liked the sound of his voice I think. So he would overspeak and get braggarty—and then you trusted him less than if he hadn't gone on.

"We're all from the north" was the sort of thing that sounded good until you tapped it and realised it was hollow as an empty bucket.

I'm sorry she hates you, he said.

And then he was like this too—he could say just the right thing, the words that swung in under your guard and got right to the core of you.

Me too, I said. But I don't know what to do about it.

I've been thinking about it, he said.

She's not your sister, I said. You don't have to.

No, he said. But I can't help thinking that she could have been. And what it must feel like.

He could get so close with his words that you had to hate him to keep yourself protected from him.

They poisoned her mind, he said. They must have done it to try and make her accept what had happened. To stop her trying to escape, because if you all had given her up, then where was she going to try and run to?

She was so young, I said.

This world? he said. It's so far past old, nobody's young any more. We're all living on borrowed time.

That doesn't mean anything, I said after I'd thought about it, giving his words another good tap in my mind.

I'm just trying to say we're all on the edge, he said. You know what extinct means?

Sort of, I said. Yes.

Well, that's us, he said. Humans. Sort of extinct.

That's when we were talking. Now we're not. It's all because of the Leatherman and what I do at night. Which is lie under my bed and scratch away at the wall. I started doing it to mark the days, using the sharp screwdriver bit to mark a day in the paint. Except the paint cracked and flaked off and revealed the powdery plaster underneath. When I scraped some more I found the plaster was just a thin skin on top of those knobbly blocks you used to build with—bigger than bricks and with hollow spaces in between them. I went under the bed and did some more scraping, and very quickly had the plaster off a block and decided if I could move the block I could crawl into the next cell, and if I could do that I could maybe do it to the half-wall at the end under the bars where Joy had hit me.

Brand told me I was crazy.

Then he told me they would hear me.

Then he told me I would get us both in big trouble. And then he said he'd have to tell them if I carried on because even if they didn't hear me at first, when they eventually found out I was trying to dig my way out they would know he had kept quiet.

I told him he had to do what he had to do. And I had to do what I was doing.

He didn't tell them.

But he did stop talking to me.

I told you a book saved me. All the time I was lying on my side, scraping the cement out of the gap between the blocks I thought of *The Count of Monte Cristo*, an adventure of mistaken identities and a man who doesn't give up as he tries to escape the impossible Chateau d'If.

My if was equally impossible. If I got through one wall, why did I think I could get through the next? But you can't let ifs and buts stop you. So I kept eating and sleeping and writing in this notebook and scraping when I wasn't and was sure the Cons weren't around to hear. I became a sort of dazed character in my own adventure, unsure of the outcome, only knowing I could not stop, wherever I was going.

And however much I strained my eye to look for her, I never saw Joy again. Though some nights I would wake up and look at the window, sure that she had been watching me as I slept.

It was a stronger sense than a dream, almost tangible, like a scent of her in the mind, but whenever I jumped to the window to see her, the night was always empty and only peopled by my unfulfilled hopes drifting away in the dark.

Hope eventually became just like half the things that had stalked me on my journey across the mainland: not really there at all, just something prowling around me in my mind, distracting me from the darker truth of my situation.

There is one other reason Brand and I have stopped talking, and maybe I'm not writing about it because I've caught my story up to the now and every day is so much like the other that I've started to ration things.

Because when I have written it all down I won't have you to talk to, and will truly be on my own.

Book I was writing my story in was stolen last night. So writing last words on back of this photo. Not much space. Was writing till night fell on window ledge to use last light to get saddest part over so it would not stain today too. Left book on ledge. Tried to sleep. Now book taken. Again my heart breaks. Not even my story remains. Not big but its mine.

I came here for my dog. I found my dead sister. She hates me. I am lost.

If you find book, please put these words with it. Whoever you are. My imaginary friend. All my friends are imaginary. Even the one in this photo: the boy and his dog at the end of the world. Wish I could have spoken to him—known him somewhere other than between the lines of story I wrote for him but now have lost. But there are no happy endings. My name was Griz. Bye. x

Chapter 38

The then

I am the one who took that photograph with that last bit of writing on the back and put it between the leaves you hold in your hand as you're reading this. First I reread all the words that came before—the story in the book—some of them now hard to make out, the lines jammed in close to make the most use of the paper, sometimes so thinly scrawled I had to guess at what they were. And having got to the end, I thought that I should slide the photograph between the pages and explain how my story and that photograph came together and ended up so very far from the place my book was stolen. There are only a few of them, but I think there are enough empty pages left to do so.

My name is Isabel. My mother used to tell me it was a pretty name. She said it was her mother's name. And yes, Isabel turned to Grizabel in my father's mouth when I was too small to walk even, and then it got shortened to Griz—and now you know my fancier name, the one that doesn't fit me at all.

What I didn't know, although I suspected it, was that it was Joy who had stolen my book.

I told you stories saved me. This one did. Because she read it. And like a magic spell or a prayer—all the right words in the right order—that changed everything. Or maybe it was a curse. Maybe a curse is sometimes just a desperate prayer seen from the wrong end.

There was—after all—a death to come.

But first there was a noise outside my window. Two days after the book had gone, I had put all my energy and despair into scraping away at the mortar around the block in the wall beneath my bed.

I had scraped and scraped and gouged and hacked and swore until my hands hurt and my back felt like it was never going to unbend and be straight again. And then as I was hunched on my side in the tight space beneath the bed, my ears caught a noise and I stopped.

I heard nothing else, but the nothing that it was sounded dangerously like someone else being very still and listening right back. For me. So I rolled quietly out from under the bed and lay on my back in the middle of the floor and looked up through the darkness at the moonlight slanting in through the barred window.

Are you sick? a voice said.

Joy's voice—but very different to the last time I heard it spitting at me.

I stopped breathing, not consciously, but as if my body had just forgotten it was necessary. I was trying to work out what it was that had changed in her tone.

Yes, I said. Sick of being in here. But no. I haven't got a disease.

Good, she said. Because I'm not wearing their bloody mask.

An arm reached out and then her hand—the scarred one—hooked one of the bars and then her face swung into the window, cutting out half the moonlight. And there she was. Looking down at me.

To me, in that moment, she was a wonder. She looked like I did, I realised. And she looked like Mum. And she wore her hair like Bar's. I don't know if it was because I was starved of them or just starved of any people to look at, but I stared at her for a long time just drinking in both the strangeness and the familiarity of her.

Joy, I said, sitting up.

Mum's not dead, she said.

No, I said carefully. No—she's not. She doesn't talk though. But she still smiles and her hand is still her hand and she likes us to sit and hold it with her.

I was slowly getting to my feet—moving deliberately carefully so as not to spook her into leaving.

She won't like my hand, she said, a catch in her voice. It's just an ugly claw now.

I reached up and put my own hand on it. She flinched and tried to pull it away. I didn't let her. I gripped it. There were scar ridges but it just felt warm and normal. Like a hand should.

Brand told me how it happened, I said. I'm so sorry. And I'm so happy that—

I know, she said. I read your story.

And then there was nothing to say, because there was suddenly too much to say so we just stood looking at each other. After a bit, she relaxed and stopped trying to pull her hand free. She looked away from me, up at the moon. Her voice was raw but steady. Only the pale moonlight betrayed the wetness streaking down her cheek.

She took a deep breath.

They told me she was dead, she said. They told me and I saw her lying on the ground. And then I fainted or they did something to me because the next thing I remember is that it was night, or maybe two or three nights, and when it was day I didn't recognise any of the land we were passing. They told me I had been traded and that Dad had done the deal, that Mum had had second thoughts and chased after me and fell and they hadn't hurt her, not like I thought they had.

And you believed them, I said.

Not at first, she said. But when Dad and Ferg and Bar didn't come after me, the only reason I could think of was that they were telling the truth.

I'm sorry you lost your baby, I said.

Yes, she said. Yes, I am too, though I didn't want him to start with. And then when he was born the way he was, a poor little blue shred of a thing, I thought he looked like a doll no one could have loved except me and I was sadder than you could ever imagine.

He was a boy, I said.

Ellis told me it was not as big a loss as if it had been a girl, she said. They want more breeders. Not more boys. That's why Ellis is so excited that you're here.

Ellis, I said. He's . . .

Yes, she said. All the bad things you're thinking? He's them and more. And the way he looks at me it's like he knows.

Knows what? I said

That I'm going to kill him, she said. I've always meant to. Now I have to.

I'd spent most of my life—ever since that worst day—thinking of her as a little girl. That difference in her voice? She sounded like Bar. Or like Bar would have sounded if she'd ever felt the need to be dangerous and protective. That was my big sister talking.

You don't, I said. Can you get me out of here?

No, she said. I mean I can open the barred gate at the end

of the hall, but there are no keys to your door. Ellis is going to take a sledgehammer and knock a hole in the wall when it's time to get you out.

But I've nearly done it, I said. The excitement made my voice catch. Joy, I said. I've nearly done it. I've scraped out a big block under the bed. I just need a couple of hits with a hammer to get it moving back out of the way and I can crawl through.

They'll hear a sledgehammer, she said. Sound carries. But I know what you can do.

Her voice had caught my excitement.

Whatever I can do, it's "we", I said. Or I'm not doing it.

What do you mean? she said.

I mean I'm not doing anything, I said. I'm not doing anything on my own. Maybe never again. But definitely not this. We're doing it. Us.

What? she said.

You know what, I said.

We're going home.

Her idea was better than a sledgehammer. It was a jack. The kind you would have put under heavy things like cars to lift them by cranking a handle. She went away for a bit and came back with one that she handed through the bars. She passed in another length of pipe like the one they used to bring the water to me.

Here's what you do, she said.

I got it, I said. Good plan. Brilliant really.

She smiled.

Hard to believe, she said. But you're really nearly as old as me, aren't you?

Yes, I said.

Right, she said. Ellis has forbidden me to come near this place. But if the jack works, call for the dogs when I walk past in the morning. I'll whistle for them so you'll know to look. If it doesn't work? Don't call out for them and we'll have to think of something else.

What are we going to do if we do get me out? I said.

Well, she said. For a long time I thought about locking them in their church one day and burning it down. But that seems a little too much. They're not even really bad people. Not without Ellis. They're just easily led. They like the god stuff. It makes them feel special, and it makes them feel less lonely about having been left behind at the end of things, the way we have been. I think Ellis knows the god stuff is not real. Or not real for him. But it was a good way to tell a story they could all agree to, that put him at the top of the pile. That made breeders seem like a good idea. Like it was god's work, so if it felt a little not quite human, that was the reason.

We're not burning them alive in their church, I said.

No, she said. And her eyes went away for a moment, like she didn't want me to see what she was thinking. No. We won't do that. But we'll have to stop them following us.

We can take Brand's boat, I said quietly. She shook her head and leant in to explain why we couldn't.

I don't think he was listening anyway. But it was a wise thing to do.

He heard me later, when I jammed the metal pole across the room and used the jack against the other wall to push it against the block. The grating noise as it moved woke him and he came to see what was going on.

It worked well. As the jack opened, the block pushed back,

and though it jammed a few times, all I had to do was slack it off and reposition the pole and before long I had opened my trapdoor to freedom.

Brand was sitting on the bed in the next cell as I crawled through.

You're going to get us killed, is all he said.

I asked him if he had a better plan.

Yes, he said. The one we agreed on. Where I save you once we're out of quarantine.

You see the two reasons why mine is a better plan? I said. I mean, quite apart from not having to end up underneath Ellis before you get me out?

Well yes, he said. Well, one at least. You don't have to trust me to save you.

That's a big one, I said. And the other is bigger. I save myself.

Well, I know you can trust me, he said. But I can't persuade you of that. And I certainly can't argue with the Ellis point.

I just don't see how this helps, he said, pointing at the hole I had come in through and then at the locked barred gate at the end of the hall.

I'm okay with that, I said. Good night.

And I crawled back and pulled the block back in place and rolled the jack and the pole lengthways under my bed ledge so the Cons would not see it if they looked in in the morning. And then I tried to pretend to myself that I wasn't too excited to sleep.

I heard Joy whistling for the dogs in the middle of the morning and when I looked out of the window I saw she was appearing to innocently walk them past my window at a suitable distance. Jip was moving in a lopsided way.

Jip, I shouted, Jess! Good dogs!

She let Jip loose, seeming to accidentally drop the rope and chase after her. He lolloped towards me, his happiness making him ignore whatever was making him limp. One of the other Cons was visible in the distance.

Jip ran up to my window and barked happily at me.

Good boy! I said. Good good boy.

It hurt us both not to reach out and touch him, but I didn't want to have the Cons think he was infectious, not when we might be so close to being free.

Come here! Joy shouted angrily as she grabbed Jip and made a show of pulling him away from the window.

Tonight then, she whispered, and winked.

Why is he limping? I said.

Ellis stamped on him, she said. Then kicked him hard.

Why? I said.

Because I like him, she said.

Then she stood up and waved at the distant Con who had turned and was walking towards her.

It's all right, she shouted. Got him before she touched him.

The Con nodded and waved and turned away again.

That was a long day. And then night fell after they brought us food and refilled my water through the pipe. And then infuriatingly nothing at all happened as the darkness deepened. And I must have fallen asleep.

I woke with her tapping the bars.

Now, she said. We go now.

My heart began thumping with adrenaline as I jumped off the bed and scooted beneath, pushing the breeze-block aside and worming head first into the next-door cell.

Joy was moving fast, because she was at the barred gate and trying to open it when I emerged into the hallway. She was trying a series of keys from a big ring held in one hand.

Don't worry, she said. It's one of them. I'll get it in a second.

Jip and Jess were boiling around her legs and trying to get to me through the bars. I buried my face in their neck fur and hoped there was no one close by to hear their happy whines.

The horses are outside, she said. It won't be long and we'll be gone.

What about me?

Brand's words came slipping sideways through the darkness behind me.

You can come too, said Joy after a beat.

Thank you, he said, though not like he meant it. He stepped out into the moonlight. He wasn't quite threatening, but he did change the atmosphere in the room. But if I did, then I could never come back here and maybe there are not so many places with people in them who want to trade that I want to lose one.

Then we can leave you here, I said. Better that way.

And if they send you after us, and you do it, said Joy. I will kill you.

Joy, I said. This doesn't have to end in blood.

Maybe it does, maybe it doesn't, she said. But that's my choice. They've taken everything from me, but they have left me that one thing. Ellis deserves...

But we can escape without killing Ellis, I said.

No, she said. Voice low and suddenly flat. No, Griz. Killing Ellis is done. That's why we have to go now.

I felt a cold pit open in my stomach. I stared at her. She shrugged. She didn't look different. But because of what she had done, she was. She had to be. I didn't care much about Ellis. I was worried that her having killed would hurt and change her, but she looked calmer than I'd seen her. Released even.

It's done, she said. It was mine to do.

What? said Brand. His voice raw, filling the silence that seemed to have somehow imploded the room, turning it into a tiny, claustrophobic place.

He ate something he shouldn't have, she said, carrying on trying the keys. Seemed a fitting end. He was always greedy about taking things that weren't his to take.

Bar had been teaching Joy about herbs before she was taken. It was one of the things Joy was in a hurry to learn, always pestering her.

The moon caught the side of her face as she moved a little, steadying herself against the bars on the gate as she tried yet another key. I saw she was looking right at me. Watching to see how much this had changed things between us.

He was looking forward to taking something else he shouldn't have too, she said.

Joy, I said.

I couldn't allow that, she said. You know that, Griz. The others are all a little sick too. But they didn't have enough to do any permanent harm. He had the special portion. They think it was the salted mutton.

But won't they know it's you? I said.

No, she said. They don't know I know what I do. If they did, they'd stop wondering why I never had another baby. But it doesn't matter. They'll figure I've just gone to find my own private bush to be sick behind.

And then the right key clicked the lock open and she pulled it wide. I went through it fast and filled my arms with Jess, who I never thought I'd really see again, and who now bucked and curved around me, tail thrumming as she tried to lick my face and simultaneously nudge Jip out of the way as he tried to do the same thing. Even though we weren't yet free and away, it felt and sounded and smelled like home.

Are you coming? said Joy.

I looked up to see she was looking at Brand.

I suppose I'll have to, he said, otherwise you'll steal the *Falki*.

Is that the only reason? she said.

Yes, he said. Well—

I closed the gate. He stared at me as I locked it.

Too late to steal your boat, said Joy. I'd seen to it before I knew Griz and I would be leaving.

What have you done? he said, bounding forward and grabbing the bars.

I haven't burned your boat. Not like you burned the *Sweethope*, she said. Though when I read what you did I wanted to. But then I had a better idea.

Open the gate, he said. Let's—

And I've left you your dog, she said. So there is no reason for you to follow us.

Griz, he said. What has she done?

I cut all the ropes from your boat. And the rudder-lines. Not as permanent as burning. So you can thank me for that, said Joy. I threw them in the water. And the anchors. You've a lot of work to do before the thing's seaworthy again.

But she didn't burn it, I said. And if you work hard, the *Falki* can take you home again.

His eyes burned into me.

I know where you live, he said.

And I know where your home is too, I said.

You believed that story, did you? he said.

Yes, I said. Now you're trying to make me doubt it like that, yes, I do.

He looked at me, long and hard. Then his beard split and revealed that infuriating flash of white that came when he smiled.

If I come after you, he said, what of that?

If you bring these people, it'll go badly for you, I said. I expect then there will be blood at the end of that story.

And if I come alone, he said. Griz?

Don't, I said. It's not that kind of story either.

Joy looked at us.

You heard, she said. Don't come with them. And don't come alone.

He just stared at me. I don't know what he was thinking. And I hadn't seen that thing in his eyes before.

Maybe it was doubt.

Don't come alone, she said. Bring your sisters.

Joy, I said, my head whipping round to look at her. She shrugged.

Ferg might like to meet them, she said. And no one knows the end of their own story, not except the very end, where they die. Not even you, Griz. Now we have to go.

Chapter 39

True north

Leaving happened in a fast, furtive dash through the darkness towards the stable and what must have been the paddocks around them, the dogs running beside us, Jip's limp improving with every step, staying silent as if they instinctively knew we should not draw any attention to ourselves. Joy had my bow and arrows strapped to the saddle, and our horses ready to go. We turned loose the Cons' other horses so they couldn't follow us, but we kept the two best ones to carry any useful things we might vike on the journey ahead, and then we rode hard into the night, taking them and my horses north, back the way I had come, following the happily reunited dogs all the way.

Until we lost sight of the settlement over the first low rise of land, I had my shoulders hunched and hardly breathed, as if expecting a bullet out of the dark with every hoofbeat. Once out of view and lost in the night, I relaxed. No one came after us, the next day or any other.

The journey that followed is a whole other story and there is no room in the pages remaining here to tell it properly. But we made two stops that belong in this one:

First, we stopped at the Homely House to bury John Dark.

Maybe because we were nearing somewhere I already knew was a place of death, my thoughts turned a little blue as we got closer to it. I think Joy found the same thing happening to her, so perhaps it was just the comedown after the relief of our escape.

Should we have freed the other women? I said as we carefully crossed the expanse of giant hogweed near the house.

They were free, she said. Most of them. Two of them held me down when Ellis tried to scare me with the poker.

We rode on a bit more.

It will be easier on the softer ones now Ellis is gone

she said.

And as we started up the slope to the house she sighed.

I don't know, Griz, she said. Maybe we should have tried to persuade them, but then maybe we wouldn't have got away. Maybe I was too scared to do all the right things.

Maybe doing most things right is good enough, I said.

Maybe, she said.

And then, after a pause:

Perhaps one day we should sail back and see if I'm right.

We weren't able to bury John Dark as I'd planned to. Mainly because John Dark thought it was a bad idea, as she hadn't quite managed to die. Instead she'd gained a limp, which she didn't like, but which didn't seem to slow her down. So she came north with us too, and she is sitting beside my mother and Joy and Bar in front of the fire as I write these last words. She is scratching Jess behind the ears.

Jess seems to have become Joy's dog now. And I couldn't be happier about it. It feels right. It's a good sight, and if I had the knack I would sketch it and leave it as the last image of this story. The once dead daughter who never died but was gone returned to the mother, and the grieving mother whose girls have gone but who finds herself with a new family. There is a mismatched symmetry in there somehow, a patched-together happiness. Maybe that's what we have to make do with now, here at the end of the world. Or maybe that's just what people have always had to do since time began.

The second stop was Glasgow, where we camped in the library where Mum and Dad once slept in a fortress of books. The roof was still on, and there I found the Freeman's book. It was the other reason we stopped there. Other than looking for a boat to vike and repair and sail home. I have the book on my lap now, under the thin last pages as I write. It's a wonderful book, about science—which we've lost—and hope—which we haven't. There is stuff in it I don't understand, but what I do makes me happy and sad in equal measure. It's about spirit as much as science, and about life, not just humanity—how it's strange and tenacious and good at adapting to almost any circumstance. Like us, really, when we're at our best. It's called *Infinite in all Directions* and that first Freeman's other name was Dyson. I can see why he inspired the Freemen to try and put life in computers before we all died out. Even though I believe they failed, I think trying made them human. And I think I'd have liked him.

Life on the islands is the same and different. There is more laughter but more carefulness too. Having been in the ruins of your world, I feel the fragility of life like I never did before, but also the glory of it. I want to see more. Jip and I will make more voyages, I think. But maybe not on our own. Perhaps Joy will come too, and Jess.

I do not think the Cons will come here. But I still watch the horizons for sails more than I once did. Jip and I find time to sit on the top of the island most days, and from there on a clear one you still feel like you can see for ever.

Joy says if I'm looking for red sails they will likely come from the north, and I tell her to go boil her head.

She also told me no one knows the end of their story, other than at the very end we all die. But I have half a page to fill and then this book is full.

I never really told you why Brand and I stopped talking, before the book was stolen by Joy, and now there is no room. That's fine. It was maybe not such an important reason as I thought at the time. As either of us thought. I don't know.

But on this last empty page, here's what I do know.

I know I'm tough. And I know I'm stupid. I'm clever too. I'm scared of things. I try to be brave. Mostly I succeed. Sometimes I spend so much time thinking that I don't actually do anything. Sometimes I work so hard I forget to eat. Sometimes I don't plan ahead. I just jump in and do things impulsively, without working out what happens next. I talk too much. I don't always say what I mean. I don't always mean what I say either. I kill things. I make things. I break things. I grow things. I lose myself in stories. I find myself there too. I read them because I like getting lost. And I wrote this one because I thought I was lost, for real and for ever. And maybe because I had no hope and no power and was entirely alone, I made up a friend and talked to them in a world I made out of nothing but words.

And then a book saved me. Because Joy read this and found the truth. So here I am, writing much more than I knew I was going to be able to, right to the end of the last page.

That makes it look neat, but it didn't work out like I planned. Nothing's perfect. Especially not me. I'm just like you were. Human. Hanging on. Holding out for a happy ending. But knowing it ends badly.

And then being surprised by joy.

Acknowledgments

The Outer Hebrides have a special place in my heart: I owe a huge thank you to Lucy Rickards who first introduced me to them, and made me fall in love on the spot. Thanks also to Mary Miers whose unstinting generosity in later years made it possible to share the beauty of the islands with my children, whose world is that much bigger and wilder because of it

Very many thanks to all at Orbit—especially Jenni Hill and Joanna Kramer in the UK and Priyanka Krishnan in the US (especially Jenni for her patience, understanding and restraint…). I'm grateful to Lauren Panepinto for the cover (and to Jack Fletcher (@kid_woof) for the assist in drawing precisely the right kind of dog for it…). Thanks to my family for being so good-natured about the grumpy writer in their midst, and D, thank you for being first listener. As ever, this one's for you.

extras

meet the author

Photo Credit: Nazia Khatun

C. A. Fletcher has children and dogs. He lives in Scotland and writes for a living.

On dogs and stories...

A note from the author

Dogs and stories are wound tightly through my life. And though they did not exactly save it, they have made it infinitely richer, and—I think—made me a better person than I would have been without them.

The dog who was the model for the fictional Jip in this book was called Archie. And much like Jip, he wove himself through the childhood of our son and our daughter like a golden thread—through their childhood, from one end of their adolescence to the other, and on into their young adulthood. Or perhaps more of a gold and black thread, since like Griz's Jip, Archie was a rough-coated black-and-tan terrier, long-legged and fearless. He was somewhere between an Airedale and a Patterdale, a "fell terrier" if anyone asked, which they often did. He was an eye-catcher. My wife—who is an artist and dog maker of some repute—has a pile of books about dogs that she often uses for reference and inspiration, and browsing through an antiquated encyclopedia of dogs published in the early part of the last century, I found a reference to an extinct breed called the Old English terrier. The description fit Archie perfectly, so—since make-believe is after all my stock-in-trade—I used to imagine that this was what he was—a noble remnant, the canine equivalent of the last of the Mohicans. He was really just a scrappy mongrel, and all the better for his mixed blood. And then, as I was finishing the last chapters of this book, he died. It made me think about the dog that ran through my own childhood and remember what my father wrote to me when that dog had to be put to sleep.

As an only child, I grew up without siblings, but I never felt lonely. Partly this is because neighboring families had boys of my age, so I was part of a ready-made gang of five; partly it's because I began to read early and always had a story to lose myself in when alone. (I would climb a tree and wedge myself in a fork in the trunk and read hidden in among what felt—in a light breeze—like a slowly moving sea of leaves. But that's a whole other story. . . .) The main reason I never felt alone was because of a dog. And that dog was the best present an only child was ever given. On the morning of my fifth birthday, I walked into the kitchen and was pointed to a cardboard box in the corner. I can still feel the lurch of pure joy in my heart as I realized it was a puppy, a golden retriever, and he was for me.

First thing he did was run into the larder and steal an onion. So I called him Robber, and the name stuck. And he wasn't a pet or a possession, because that's not really how kids and dogs work: he was just family, and he ran alongside me through *my* childhood as playmate and companion, and was a touchstone of security and loyalty. When I was small, he lay beside my bed, his fur under my hand as my parents read me stories at night, and though he was expressly forbidden to ever get on the bed, the moment they left, I would pat the mattress and he would wake from feigned sleep and jump up. My parents were very good at turning a blind eye. Maybe they knew I really thought of him as a brother.

He lasted until I was away at university and died when I was twenty-two. When my parents called to tell me, I walked to the end of a lonely pier jutting into the eye of a narratively convenient storm coming in off the North Sea and hid my tears in the wind and the rain. My dad was not of a generation of men who spoke easily about emotions, but I still have the letter he wrote to me at the time. In unexpectedly moving language, he said that if you were lucky, you got several great dogs in a lifetime, but you were guaranteed at least two great ones: the one you grew up with, and the one you watch your child or children grow up with. Because of Robber and Archie, I now know that to be true. I also know he was trying to tell me that the end of something wasn't always a permanent end but could eventually be the start of something new and different. But the real point of the letter was not the truth of what my father was saying, but the fact he was saying it at all; it was the first time I looked up and realized that there was a whole unexpected emotional story going on beneath my father's habitually gruff and somewhat stormy exterior, which I had, until then, been blind to.

And maybe because I was studying literature and was for the first time acknowledging to myself that I wanted to be a writer and so was thinking about stories as something I wanted to make rather than just consume, I now think that letter made me realize two important things: firstly that character reveals itself as much by what is not said as by what is, and secondly that character reveals a lot about itself by the timing of that moment when what has not been said is finally voiced. That unexpectedness, those contradictions between light and shade, all the inner conflicts at odds with the outer appearance are what make characters really sing and stick in our minds. That's why I've always loved Robert Louis Stevenson's Long John Silver and Alan Breck Stewart; the one an unrepentant, silver-tongued pirate but an honest one in his way, the other a gallant hero but also—possibly—a murderer.

Maybe the real work of stories is actually done in the bits between the words, where there is space for the reader to get in and come to their own conclusions about the truth.

PS. Turns out my dad was right about something else. I'm lucky. I got more than just the two guaranteed great dogs. So far, the count is four: not only do we have Bobby—Archie's "wife," whom my wife rescued off the streets—but the week I sent the manuscript of this book to my editor, we got a new dog. He's a terrier too—shorter legs, but so far, all the indications are that he has just as fearless a heart.

And, because of course we had to, we call him Jip. And so the story continues...

reading group guide

1. Why do you think the author selected the title *A Boy and His Dog at the End of the World*? Did the title impact the way you perceived Griz throughout the story or cause you to make any assumptions? If so, what did you think about the final reveal regarding Griz's identity? How did it make you feel about yourself as a reader and Griz as a character?
2. Do you think Griz is a reliable narrator? Does that harm or help the storytelling?
3. The power of stories is an important theme throughout the novel. Discuss the roles stories and storytelling play in shaping the characters of both Griz and Brand.
4. Griz's decision to go after Brand and Jess is an impetuous one. Do you feel you would have made the same choice?
5. How does the relationship between Griz and Brand evolve over the course of the novel? What are the major turning points? How did you feel about where the author left things between them?
6. The novel is rich with descriptions of the wild landscape of Griz's home and the wider world as it falls into ruin. Is there a particular passage or scene that stood out to you? If so, why?
7. On the journey, all that Griz encounters triggers questions about what it must have been like to live in a more crowded and technologically advanced world. Did this make you

think differently about the things we take for granted in our present?

8. In some ways, the book is a letter to the present written to us from someone in the future. If you could write a message for a "Griz" to find in the emptier future of this book, what would it be?
9. The Freemen tried to find a way to save human consciousness by "downloading" it onto computers. What do you think is more important—survival of humanity, or survival of life on the planet? Do you think the two things are mutually achievable, or are they in conflict? Whichever way you answer—how could that change?
10. If you had been one of the 0.0001% of people who still could have children after the Gelding and had decided, like Griz's forebears, to go and live quietly away from the gaze of the Lastborn generation, where would you choose to go? If you realized you or your kids or grandkids were part of the Lastborn generation, what would you do?
11. If you could leave one old record for Griz and John Dark to find and play on the wind-up gramophone, what would it be? And why?
12. If the story continued, what do you think would happen next?

if you enjoyed
A BOY AND HIS DOG AT THE END OF THE WORLD
look out for
OUR WAR
by
Craig DiLouie

A prescient and gripping novel of a second American civil war, and the children caught in the conflict, forced to fight.

Our children are our soldiers.

After his impeachment, the president of the United States refuses to leave office, and the country erupts into a fractured and violent war. Orphaned by the fighting and looking for a home, ten-year-old Hannah Miller joins a citizen militia in a besieged Indianapolis.

In the Free Women militia, Hannah finds a makeshift family. They'll teach her how to survive. They'll give her hope. And they'll show her how to use a gun.

Hannah's older brother, Alex, is a soldier too. But he's loyal to the other side and has found his place in a militant group of fighters who see themselves as the last bastion of their America. By following their orders, Alex will soon make the ultimate decision behind the trigger.

On the battlefields of America, Hannah and Alex will risk everything for their country, but in the end, they'll fight for the only cause that truly matters—each other.

ONE

Every week, Hannah asked when the war would end.

Soon, Mom always said, which her child's mind translated as, *Longer than you want.*

The war had taken her home, friends, and family. If it didn't end soon, it might take everything.

Ten months ago, Hannah and her mother arrived at the refugee camp set up at the Indiana Convention Center. They'd settled in Hall D, a vast space sectioned off by metal pipe and dark blue drapes into rooms ten feet square. Rough living, the days suspended between tension and tedium, but it was safer than outside.

Now Mom sat on her cot and inventoried their weekly aid package. Spam, rice, cheese, beans, sugar, powdered milk, soap, cooking oil. The bland basics of survival.

Before the war, she'd been an accountant. Now she added up calories, while Hannah counted the hours to their next meager meal.

Mom licked her finger and dipped it in the sugar. "Taste test?"

They used to bake together in their kitchen back in Sterling. Cookies and cupcakes and scones. Hannah helped out, knowing she'd be the official taste tester.

She licked the sweetness. It only made her hungrier, but she didn't ask for more. She already received more than her fair share of the food. Once a plump woman, her mother had wasted away to gauntness.

"We have enough to get us to Friday," Mom said. "Except water."

"Okay." Hannah looped a belt through three plastic gallon jugs.

"Why don't you stay here and play with your friends?"

Mom always said this before they went outside. The streets were dangerous now with muggers, bombs, and rebel snipers who'd infiltrated the city.

"I want to go with you," Hannah said.

She'd already lost Dad and Alex. If Mom went without her, she'd go out of her mind waiting. She hated being alone.

Mom understood all this. "All right, honey."

They left their tiny room and closed the drape behind them. People traded rations and gossip in the aisle. A couple was having a loud argument. The air smelled like pee and frying Spam. Smoke from cooking fires hazed around the dead ceiling lights high over their heads.

Mrs. Bevis yanked her drape aside. "Did I hear you're going out for water?"

Mom pursed her lips. "You did."

"Because my back is still killing me." She was already holding out her jug.

Hannah took it. "We can fill this up for you, Mrs. Bevis."

"My waste bucket is getting full too."

"Some other time," Mom said before Hannah could say anything.

The old woman shot a look down the aisle. "Listen to them. Arguing again. They go at it all day and then again all night."

Mom said, "Well, we should get going."

Mrs. Bevis regarded her with a judgmental frown. "Don't let me hold you up."

They walked down Aisle 1500. War news droned on a portable radio. A swarm of kids ran laughing through laundry hung on lines spanning the aisle. Hannah sometimes joined in the fun but more often stayed close to Mom, an oasis of warmth and love in a world that had otherwise turned against her.

"Mrs. Bevis told me the war will be over by Christmas," she said.

"It's more like a hope than a prediction," Mom told her.

More code that grown-ups used. "Okay."

"It can't go on forever, honey. It'll stop one day, and then we can go home. We'll all be together again."

Mom always talked about Hannah's dad as if he were still alive and as if her older brother, who'd disappeared, had made it back to their house in Sterling.

"I can't wait," Hannah played along.

"Until then, we're doing okay. All we have to do is keep going."

Outside, bright sunlight washed the cold street. Dirty snow covered the ground. Bicycles zipped around dead cars. Gunfire crackled at the front line a few miles away. A band of militia walked past, hard men and women wearing ratty uniforms and carrying rifles.

The water tanker was three blocks east. They waited in line until they could fill their jugs. Hannah shuffled her feet to stay warm and read political graffiti covering the wall of a nearby building. FREE INDY, THIS GUN KILLS FASCISTS, RESIST.

At last, it was their turn to fill their jugs from the spigots, and they started home.

Mom gave her a sly smile. "If Christmas is coming, you know what that means."

"Hooray for me," Hannah sulked.

"You only turn eleven once. I'm going to make you a cake."

Hannah understood grown-ups told white lies to protect their kids, but this was going too far. "We don't have any flour or butter. We barely have any sugar."

"Then I'll have to make something out of nothing."

She shot Mom a warning look. They'd once had an imaginary dinner, where they'd pretended to eat a sumptuous feast. "Okay."

"It's a real thing, honey. I got a recipe from another mom."

Hannah believed now. The women at the refugee center were like mad scientists when it came to making new meals from the monotonous aid packages. They knew how to turn rice, vinegar, water, and powdered milk into cheese.

"What's in it?" she said.

"It's best if you don't know."

Hannah laughed. "Like a hot dog."

"It'll be yummy," her mother assured her.

"I can't wait." She was still smiling. "It's gonna be awesome."

"When the world goes back to normal, we can have a proper birthday party."

The grown-ups always talked like that, how nothing was normal, as if the war was an embarrassing mistake. But this, talking about a birthday cake. This felt normal, even after everything she'd lost. Something out of nothing.

"I love you, Mom—"

Blood sprayed across her cheek.

Bikes crashed in the roar of the rolling gunshot. The street emptied.

Mom shuddered on the blacktop.

Hannah blinked in shock. "Mommy?"

"Sniper!" a woman shrieked.

A large man scooped Hannah like a football as he charged past. She screamed and clawed at the air as Mom dwindled with each step.

The man set her down behind a burned-out bus but kept a tight hold of her arm to prevent her from bolting. Other people had sought safety here in a gasping huddle.

Crying, Hannah watched her mother struggle to rise.

"Stay down," the man hissed. "Don't move."

Mom freed herself from the belt and its heavy water jugs. She heaved onto her elbows. She started to drag her body off the road.

Hannah was wailing. "Mommy."

Their eyes locked. A smile flickered across Mom's face.

The second shot rammed her back down. The crowd screamed.

Hannah howled with them. *"MOMMY!"*

Nothing out of everything.

if you enjoyed
A BOY AND HIS DOG AT THE END OF THE WORLD

look out for

THE SHIP

by

Antonia Honeywell

In this thought-provoking and lyrical debut novel, a young woman's only hope for survival in the dystopian future is a ship, a Noah's Ark, that can rescue five hundred people.

London burned for three weeks. And then it got worse....

Young, sheltered, and naive Lalla has grown up in near isolation in her parents' apartment, sheltered from the chaos of their collapsed civilization. But things are getting more dangerous outside. People are killing one another for husks of bread, and the police are detaining anyone without an identification card. On her sixteenth birthday, Lalla's father decides it's time to use their escape route—a ship he's built that is only big enough to save five hundred people.

But the utopia her father has created isn't everything it appears. There's more food than anyone can eat, but nothing grows; more clothes than anyone can wear, but no way to mend them; and no-one can tell her where they are going.

ONE

A trip to the British Museum ❁ *the manifest is full* ❁ *we leave*

Right up until the day we boarded, I wondered whether the ship was just a myth. There were so many myths in my life then. The display cases in the British Museum were full of them, and the street prophets crowding the pavements outside ranted new ones at my mother and me every time we walked past. From time to time, there was a government raid and, for a few days, the streets would be empty, except for the one prophet who always survived. He sat on the corner of Bedford Square and Gower Street, filthy in worn denim, holding up a board that said, "God has forgotten us." I don't know why the troops left him. Perhaps they agreed with him; in any case, he must have had a card. He was still there when we left, sailing past the car window as though he were the one on water. It was my sixteenth birthday.

I was born at the end of the world, although I did not know it at the time. While I fretted at my mother's breast, demanding more milk than she was able to give me, great cargo ships sailed out of countries far, far away, carrying people from lands that were sinking, or burning, or whose natural bounty had been exhausted. While I took my first stumbling steps, cities across the world that had once housed great industries crumbled into dust, and pleasure islands that had been raised from the oceans melted back into them as though they had never existed. And as I began to talk, the people in the surviving corners of civilisation fell silent, and plugged their ears and their hearts while the earth was plundered for its last scrapings of energy, of fertility. Of life.

I was seven when the collapse hit Britain. Banks crashed, the power failed, flood defences gave way, and my father paced the flat, strangely elated in the face of my mother's fear. I was right, he said, over and over again. Wasn't I right? Weren't we lucky that we owed nothing to anyone? That we relied on no one beyond our little trio? That we had stores, and bottled water? Oh, the government would regret not listening to him now. The government would be out on the streets with the rest of the population. Weren't we lucky, he wanted us to say, weren't we lucky that we had him? He ranted, and we bolted our doors; my mother tightened her arms around me, and for months we did not leave the flat.

Across the country, people lost their homes, the supermarkets emptied and the population stood, stunned and helpless, in the streets. My father watched the riots and the looting, the disasters and the forced evictions on every possible channel; he had the computer, his phone and his tablet and juggled them constantly, prowling about the flat and never seeming to sleep. The government resigned, and then came the tanks, and the troops with their terrible guns. My father vanished. Oxford Street burned for three weeks, and I watched the orange skies from the circle of my mother's arms, weeping for him. Hush, my mother whispered to me, hush. But I was only a child; I had not learned to be silent, and when he returned, tired and triumphant, I cried just as loudly and buried myself in him. But he was no longer the man who had walked away. The military government had listened; they had bought the Dove from him. He was a rich man now, and a powerful one, and he had more important things to do than cuddle me.

Within weeks of my father's return, the Nazareth Act came into force. I remember the queues, the identity checks, the biometric registrations, and surrounding it all, my father's jubilation at his success. Opponents called the Dove a violation of human rights, but as my father said, it worked. Your screen was registered, you were issued with an identity card, and from then on you were identified by your screen address, no matter where the social and financial earthquakes had left your land one. The satellites were still operational, so the authorities always knew where you were. What food there was could be distributed fairly. New laws could be communicated quickly and card-carrying citizens got the information they needed to survive. Food drops, medical assistance, re-registration requirements, work opportunities. New acts came in thick and fast: to the Exodus Act and the Optimum Resourcing Act were added the Land Allocation Act, the Prisoner Release Act, the Possession of Property Act—each heralded by a triumphant fanfare on the news bulletin, which was now the only source of information. The Dove was the ultimate firewall; anything it did not approve went onto the raven routes and over time, the raven routes became more and more dangerous. A screen open to raven routes burnt out in seconds; whether the virus that did so was a government initiative or a legacy from the days of unrestricted access, no one could say. And so, with cards and screens and the Dove, order was created from chaos. Regular biometric re-registration meant that stolen cards, and the cards of the dead, were only ever valid for a limited time. By the time I was ten, a valid card was the most valuable thing in the world, and my mother and I, duly registered, were able to go out for a walk.

"Where's your card?" my mother demanded the first time we went to unbolt the door. "Show me."

We'd practised so many times. I unzipped the inside of my pocket, felt through the hole, opened the card compartment of my belt and held it out to her. "Seven seconds," she said. "It's not fast enough."

"You do it then," I said, but my mother was holding her card up before I'd even started the timer.

"The troops will shoot me if you don't show your card," she said, "and it'll be stolen if it can be seen." And so I tried harder, but she wasn't satisfied, and took my card away to look after it herself. We went to Regent's Park, to look at the tents people had set up as temporary accommodation, although she wouldn't let me speak to anyone. We went to the new banks of the Thames, too, to see Big Ben and the London Eye peering mournfully out of the water, but even with the security of the troop patrols, London had become desolate and dangerous, and soon our outings became confined to the British Museum, just around the corner. We went there every day; it became my schoolroom, my playground, my almost home.

"Things will get better," my mother said, holding my hand, and I believed her. The bulletins said the same.

And yet—and yet. Time went by, and still people starved. Still they slept in floating death-traps, or in the campsites that had been created in London's parks, now surrounded by razor wire. I saw these things through the bubble of safety and relative plenty in which I lived; I saw them so often that I became immune. My father saw them too. I think he was a little bewildered that his great triumph, the Dove, had not saved the world, and so he set about saving his own world—my mother and I—another way. He always did like to be in control.

The paper ran out, so my mother tore labels from tins and taught me to write on the back of them; when there were no pencils left, we burned splinters of wood and made our letters with scratches of black. And after a year or two, a new word began to creep through the wall that divided my parents' room from mine, whispered at night in hopeful voices. *A ship. What about a ship?* I scraped the word laboriously with my burned sticks. Ship. Ship. I grew quieter as I grew older, and listened as hard as I could to my mother and father's intense, whispered conversations. I was spelling out the titles on the spines of my mother's old books when I first heard the word spoken out loud.

"A ship," he said to her. "Shall we do it?"

And my mother said, "But Lalage's future?" and my father said, "There's no future here. We'll make one for her," and from that time on he was barely ever home. It was years before I learned that Anna Karenina was the title of the novel and not the name of the author.

The ship. The word floated through my childhood, a thought with nothing to tether itself to. *There'll be paper on the ship*, my mother told me, when I complained about the labels. *There'll be rice on the ship,* my father said, when we ate the last of the rice in our stores. *The ship,* my father said when the public executions went from weekly to daily. When the marketeer riots spread from Oxford Street to Bloomsbury and the bodies stayed outside our flat for three days; when the screen crashed, or the rats got inside our building; when the water gave out, or a food drop failed, he always said, *Just you wait, Lalla. Wait until we sail.*

The only actual ships I'd ever seen were the stinking hulks that drifted up the bloated river every now and again, relics of the great evacuations, and I knew they weren't what my parents meant. Mostly they were empty; anyone left alive on them was shot as they swam to the bank, if they didn't drown first. The rusting carcasses lined the river from London to the sea, lowering into the water until they keeled over, complete with the homeless who'd taken refuge on them. My mother would go pale and clench her fists as we watched the bulletins on our screens. I hated seeing my mother so unhappy, but to me she seemed naive. After all, no one had forced those people to sleep on the Sinkers, any more than they were forced to live in London's public buildings. My parents and I lived in a proper flat, with food and clothes and locks on the door, and because we had these things, it seemed to me that they were available, and anyone who lived without them was making a choice. My father was very big on choice.

"Turn it off," my mother always said, but she never meant it. She would no more have missed a bulletin than she'd have let me go out into the streets alone.

Food became scarcer; on my twelfth birthday, for the first time since the Dove, there was no cake.

"There's no power spare for the oven," she told us.

"Why can't you just melt chocolate over the fire and stir in biscuits, like last year?" I asked, but my father told me to hush, and my birthday was ruined.

My mother got thinner, and when my father came home the two of them pored over papers and screens while I read and played approved screen games and tried to remember the things my mother had taught me during the day. Daytime London gradually emptied, drained by the curfews and the Land Allocation Act, and the terrible penalties of being discovered by the troops without a card. My father's appearances were gala days; the rest were about survival. Food drops. Hiding the car, which my father claimed we'd need one day. The fingerprinting and flashing lights of the biometric re-registrations, which became ever more frequent. And the ship, the ship, the ship, held out like a promised land between them, hung on words like equality, kindness, safety and plenty. "Wouldn't it be nice if the good people had a chance?" my mother would say, but in post-collapse London, my father and mother were the only people I knew, and in any case, she never seemed to expect an answer.

Who were the good people, anyway? The street people, or the prophets or petrolheads, who avoided me as instinctively as I did them? Were the strangers who came to the flat when my father was at home good people? I had no way of knowing; I didn't talk to them, and in any case they never came twice. You'll have friends on the ship, my parents told me. By the time I was fifteen, my parents were still all I knew, and their stories of the ship had become as fascinating and impossible as fairy tales. I didn't know that the people who came to the flat were being interviewed for berths, or that the hours my mother spent on the screen were spent exploring the forbidden raven routes, looking for stories of people who deserved to be saved. I didn't know that my father's frequent absences were spent tracking down supplies and vaccinations; I didn't know that he finally bought the ship itself from a Greek magnate who'd decided to tie himself to the land. I knew nothing. Except that I was lucky, and that was only because my parents kept telling me so. We walked to the British Museum almost every day, and the dwindling of the collections was the only marker of time I had.

The evening before my sixteenth birthday, I sat watching the news bulletin with my mother. At least, she watched the bulletin; I didn't bother. I couldn't understand how she could waste precious power when the bulletins were always the same. I never watched them; what I watched was my mother watching. She sat on the edge of the sofa, twitching and shifting as she sifted the presenter's words, her hand resting automatically over the pocket where she kept our identity cards, right up until the bulletin finished, as it always did, with the recording of the commander's original promise to the people. I could recite it word for word. "Keep your card. It is your life. This Emergency Government has but one task—to ensure fair distribution of limited resources. I, Marius, Commander of the Emergency Government, promise that no card-carrying, screen-registered, law-abiding man or woman in this country will go hungry, or homeless, or watch their children walk without shoes. But with that promise comes a warning. Do not let your registration lapse. Carry your card and keep it safe. My citizens are my priority. I cannot feed those who are not mine. And without your card, I cannot know that you are mine."

"Your card, Lalage," she said suddenly. She had handed it over to me just before the bulletin.

I felt in my pocket. "It's fine," I said. Her face tensed. "What?" I demanded. "I've got my card. It's here, all right?"

"No. It's not all right."

"Why not?"

"Because you'll be sixteen tomorrow. You'll be responsible for your own card. They will shoot you if you can't produce it. Not me. You. Your card, do you hear me, Lalage?"

"Happy birthday to me," I muttered. But I listened. I always listened to her, although I rarely let her know it, and on the day of my sixteenth birthday, as we walked to the museum, I was so conscious of the little plastic rectangle nestled inside the pocket my mother had made for it that I forgot to complain that my father was away for my birthday. I was an adult; the card in my pocket said so, and I looked around at the museum dwellers with judgemental eyes, asking myself how they could have been so careless as to lose their cards and end up homeless. While my mother spoke with them in undertones, and handed over the food we always brought, I wandered the display cases.

So many objects had disappeared over the years. The Mildenhall Treasure. The Portland Font. My favourite exhibit, a little gold chariot pulled by golden horses, had vanished just after my fourteenth birthday. Instead, the cases were filled with little cards—*Object removed for cleaning, Object removed during display rearrangement.* Lindow Man was still there, though, huddled, leathern, against whatever had killed him two thousand years before. I stared at him, and through the glass at the sleeping bags beyond, inside which living bodies huddled against what London had become. My mother made sure we kept up our registrations, and she took me to the British Museum and talked at me, and we read her old books and waited for my father, and scratched letters with burnt sticks, and that was my life. A closed circle shot through with irritations, soothed by the promise of a ship that never seemed to come any closer.

"If the ship is real," I asked my mother as we walked back to the flat, "why don't we just get on it?"

"It's not that simple." She tapped in our entry code and began to fit the separate keys into their various locks.

"Why not?" I asked. It was my job to keep watch while she did the door, but nothing ever happened. My mother liked things to be done properly, that was all. Even the milk, which came in cardboard bricks when it came at all, had to be poured into a jug before she'd let me or my father have any. When the outside door was safely bolted behind us, she began the long process of unlocking the front door of our flat. We went in, and the door clunked solidly behind us. As I began to fasten the bolts, she went to the pantry, took down one of the few tins on the shelf and stood staring at it. It didn't have a label. She held out the tin to me, smiling. "It's your birthday," she said. "You decide. What do you think? Shall we risk it?" I refused to look and went into the drawing room. We had always eaten roast chicken on my birthday, and I'd never forgotten it, even though the last one had been five years ago.

There was a bang at the door, then a pattern of knocks. Before it was finished, my mother and I were both there, our almost-quarrel forgotten, racing to see who could get the bolts and locks undone first. "It's my birthday," I protested, but she still got to him first, and clung to him, and left me to close the door and start on the bolts again.

"I've got something for you, birthday girl," my father said, leaning over my mother and kissing the top of my head. I wondered, wildly, whether he'd managed to find a chicken. But the box he produced as he grinned at my mother was smaller than the palm of his hand. "We haven't seen one of these for a very long time," he said, and I felt my mother trembling beside me, crowding in closely as he put the box into my shaking hands. I opened the box and her face fell. She began to cry and he moved away from me in consternation.

"I thought you had found a flower," she said. And he held her, and while she sobbed against him and he said sorry, sorry, sorry into her hair, I shook a pool of white fire onto the palm of my hand. I remembered him bringing home diamonds years ago, when the banks were teetering and there was still roast chicken, but I'd never even been allowed to hold them, and before long the diamonds had given way to rifles and grenades, piled up throughout the flat. My mother's face had become pale and lined, and my father went away, and then the rifles gave way to stacks and stacks of screens, pristine in their boxes. Then the Art Trials began, and my father was gone again. And so it went on, but now I had a diamond of my own. I stared at it, gleaming in my hand, and could not imagine how any flower could be more beautiful.

It was good to have him back on diamonds. I think my mother thought so too, because she looked at the diamond in my hand and said, "Another rivet in the ship," just as she had done all those years ago, and once again I imagined a boat studded with sparkling rainbows, like something from a dream.

"How was the trip?" she asked, drying her eyes and settling onto the sofa with her sewing.

"Fine. And I visited the holding centre. Roger told me that the people don't believe in Lalla because I never take her with me." He laughed, but my mother didn't even smile. He started to say more, then stopped and looked at me. "Kitten, is there any water? Could you fetch me some?"

I went to the kitchen. The boiled water in the stone jug was mine; my mother knew I hated the taste of the water sterilising tablets we were given at every re-registration. But it was hard to boil water when power was so scarce; my father and mother always used the tablets. I looked about for them, but the tone of my father's voice stopped me. "Anna, listen," he said quietly as soon as I was out of sight. "The troops are going to bomb St James's Park. They've put the razor wire round it, and moved out the people who've got cards. It's Regent's Park all over again. We need to leave."

Regent's Park. It had been one of the first places opened up for people who had nowhere to go. I was thirteen when the government bombed it. Hundreds, thousands of people eliminated in a series of explosions that had made the windows of the flat vibrate. "Be glad I didn't let you meet them," my mother had said, taking away my screen so I couldn't see anything more. "Then it would really hurt." My parents had shut themselves away for hours after that; I heard them through their bedroom door, talking about the ship, then and for weeks afterwards. The ship, the ship, the ship, but nothing happened. There had been more food available at the food drops after the bombing, and my mother said it was because things were turning a corner, as she'd always said they would. But it hadn't lasted, and now my birthday dinner was coming out of a single tin. I stood in the kitchen doorway, holding my diamond in my hand, and watched as my father knelt in front of my mother and took the sewing from her limp hands.

"You brought home a diamond," she said. "You haven't done that for ages. Surely that means things are getting better?"

"No. It means people have given up. I got that diamond for a tin of peaches."

"A tin of peaches?" she said. I opened my hand and noticed for the first time how hard the diamond was, how cold. My stomach rumbled, and I wondered what would be inside the tin my mother had lighted on.

"It was a kind of joke," my father said. "I was negotiating for the contents of a warehouse in Sussex. The guy said that diamonds were for those who believed in the future more than they cared about survival. I thought Lalla would like it, that's all."

"What did he take, if he didn't want diamonds?"

"Munitions. He traded one warehouse for the means to protect the other, and pistols for his family. There is nothing left,

Anna. Nothing. We have to leave. You won't dissuade me this time."

My mother fastened her length of thread, shook out the material—it was a red velvet curtain that she was making into a skirt for me—and pointed the needle at my father.

"You created this situation," she said. She unspooled a length of thread and bit it off, looking up at him sharply.

"Me?" He stared at her. "Me? The Dove saved this country. Saved it."

It hadn't. You only had to look outside our window to see that. But my father no longer looked outside our window. His mind was made up, and his eyes were on places far beyond our London square. My mother picked a black button from her sewing box and said, "What about the people in the British Museum?"

"They're squatting," my father said quietly, sitting on the back of the sofa and stroking her hair. "It's all very cooperative, but how can they build an alternative society when there's nothing left to build it on? All the government can do—all it can do—is reduce the population in the hope of feeding what's left. Bit by bit. The museum dwellers are idiots, corralling themselves so they can be eliminated. It's time for us to leave." He frowned and jabbed at his screen. "It's been time for a long time."

She bent her head over the button, and when she spoke her voice was so quiet I could barely hear her. "I'm not ready, Michael. However dreadful the process is, soon the population will be manageable, and all this will improve. The ship will be the last thing we do."

"The last thing?" My father laughed, putting his screen down, swinging his legs over the back of the sofa and landing beside my mother with a bounce. "No, my darling, the ship is the start. Why do you cling to the end, when the beginning is waiting?"

"I want to grow things."

He stopped bouncing and turned away. "Still?" he said. "The Land Allocation Act's a failure. People are coming back from the countryside as fast as they left. And if they don't come back, it's because they're dead. I've seen it."

My mother put her sewing down. "What about the Lakes?" she said. "They didn't do industrial farming there. Or fracking. The soil might still be good."

"And you'd take that risk, even though we've never heard anything from any of the families who left? Remember the Freemans? The Kings? The Holloways? Think of the security we'd need just to get there. And the loneliness."

Freemans, Kings, Holloways—names from a time I could barely remember. A time of restaurants, a time when Regent's Park was a place to take a picnic, a time when people smiled at each other and sometimes stopped to talk. A time when there were still a few private cars in the street; when electricity was constant. Nothing but myths now, lost in time. But at sixteen, I knew about loneliness. I was lonely, so lonely that my stomach clenched with it at night.

"A life for Lalla," my father said. "Isn't that worth everything we have? A place to be a family, among friends, where we can learn and share without fear? A place for Lalla to grow in safety? Isn't that what we set out to create?"

"A place without money," my mother said softly, putting her arms around him. "No gold or guns. Just everyone working hard and sharing in the plenty we've provided."

"No homelessness," he replied, "and no hunger." He turned in the circle of her arms and stroked the hair back from her face. "Tell me when, Anna. Please tell me when."

"It was an insurance policy. Just that. Insurance. And now you're making it a life plan. I don't want to spend my life clinging to a lifeboat."

"How much worse do you want things to get?"

"If you loved me, you'd stop pushing."

"If you loved me, we'd have gone already."

"I love you, Michael. I just don't think you're right."

I stood in the doorway, forgetting I wasn't meant to be listening. I clenched my fist and felt the diamond cutting into my palm. "I want to go," I said. "If the ship is real, I want to go on it."

They looked at me in surprise. My father looked for his glass of water and realised that I wasn't holding one. My mother said, "You don't know what you're talking about," and took back her sewing, tucking her legs under her. "We're going to Mughal India tomorrow." But I had spoken out at last, and I couldn't stop now.

"I've seen Mughal India," I said. "I've seen Ancient Egypt and the Aztecs and Babylon and Abyssinia and Mesopotamia. I've seen them all day, every day, for years and years and years."

"But you've learned nothing," she said, standing up and marching past me into the tiny kitchen. I heard the drawer open and shut and the rattle of the utensils in it. I heard the tin opener puncturing the lid, and the ratcheting as she turned the handle. "Seriously, Lalage," she called over the rattle of the spoon as she scraped out the contents of the tin. "What have you actually learned from the British Museum? From me? From your father?" I drew breath, ready to tell her about hieroglyphics and lunar calendars, about crucifixes and fertility symbols and currency, about kings being buried with gold and sandwiches to see them safely to the underworld, but my father spoke before I could begin.

"I don't care what she's still got to learn," he called into the kitchen. "I want her safe. I want both of you safe."

"I want to go on the ship," I said again, and it was as though someone else had taken over my body, someone who carried their own card and owned a diamond and said what they thought.

"Lalla wants to go on the ship," my father said, and his eyes shone, and I felt the hairs on my arms prickle with electricity, because even though my mother had come back in the room, it was me he was looking at, my words that had brought that light to his eyes. I thought about the ship, and the promise of friends, and suddenly I needed to know, more than anything else in my limited, safe, grey world, that the ship was more than a theoretical hereafter for the hopeless, that it was not just one more of the many heavens I'd seen in the display cases at the British Museum.

My father stood up. "Lalla is sixteen now," he said. "Maybe that will persuade you better than I can." He held out a hand to me, and I stood beside him, his arm around my shoulder. My mother looked at us and, for a fraction of a second, her eyes widened. "It's over, Anna. You know it. That's why we bought the ship in the first place." He lifted his arm and I slipped out from under it, dismissed. He went to my mother, the two of them framed by the kitchen doorway, and stroked her cheek with the back of his hand. "Darling," he began.

I went to the window. It was quite dark now, and street people were gathering by the railings in the square opposite. One looked up at us, face stark white against his clothes. What did sixteen mean, when nothing ever changed?

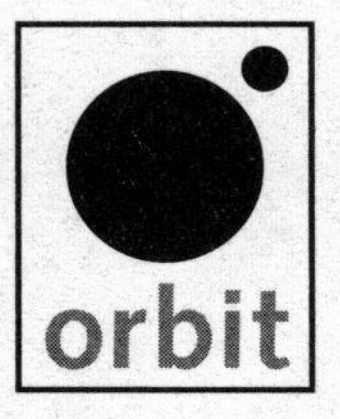
orbit